LORDS & LADIES
COLLECTION

Two Glittering Regency
Love Affairs

The Rebellious Bride
by Francesca Shaw

&

The Duke's Mistress
by Ann Elizabeth Cree

The *Regency*

LORDS & LADIES
COLLECTION

The Regency

LORDS & LADIES
COLLECTION

*Francesca Shaw &
Ann Elizabeth Cree*

*M&B™ and M&B™ with the Rose Device
are trademarks of the publisher.
Harlequin Mills & Boon Limited, Eton House,
18-24 Paradise Road, Richmond, Surrey TW9 1SR*

First published in Great Britain in 2002

THE REGENCY LORDS & LADIES COLLECTION
© Harlequin Books S.A. 2008

The publisher acknowledges the copyright holders of the
individual works as follows:

The Rebellious Bride © Francesca Shaw 2002
The Duke's Mistress © Annemarie Hasnain 2002

ISBN: 978 0 263 86652 0

052-0508

*Printed and bound in Spain
by Litografia Rosés S.A., Barcelona*

The Rebellious Bride
by
Francesca Shaw

Francesca Shaw is not one, but two authors, working together under the same name. Both are librarians by profession, working in Hertfordshire. They first began writing ten years ago under a tree in a Burgundian vineyard, but although they have published other romances, they have only recently come to historical novels. Their shared interests include travel, good food, reading and, of course, writing.

Chapter One

Love at first sight was not something in which Miss Sophia Haydon believed—not, that is, until nine-thirty in the evening of the thirtieth of March. The sensation hit her with the force of a blow, and she could only be thankful for her discreet veil. The fine net which shielded her blushing cheeks from the rest of the audience also, thankfully, hid her from the gaze of the gentleman whose appearance had had such an unexpected effect upon her well-schooled emotions.

There were quite forty members of the Quality seated in varying degrees of comfort on the gilt chairs arranged in the salon of Lady Newnham's modish town house in Mayfair. That audience, far from paying attention to Sophia as she sat in confusion in one corner, was responding to the speaker in one of two ways. Either they were listening with rapt attention to Dr Theophilus Eustace's dry account of the flora and fauna of lower Brazil, or they were attempting to mask their boredom with expressions of polite interest. Brazil was quite a novelty but not, unfortunately, as described by Dr Eustace.

It was always a lottery attending her ladyship's

monthly Philosophical Symposia, as she liked to call them. Lady Newnham was quite capable of producing the latest dashing and dangerous poet for a reading, but equally one might encounter a donnish exposition on the archaeological remains of Lower Thrace or the habits of the European bison.

The object of Sophia's sudden passion appeared to her surprise to be listening intently, his dark eyes on the map at which Dr Eustace was gesticulating. It was not the man's good looks which had first attracted Miss Haydon, although they were undeniable. His broad shoulders sat easily within the fashionable cut of his dark blue evening coat, there was scarcely room to accommodate the length of his legs between the rows of chairs and his profile showed a classical perfection that must constantly set hearts aflutter.

Sophia was no more immune to good looks than the next young lady—indeed, four years ago that had been her downfall—but it had been more the recognition of a kindred spirit that had so attracted her. The man was behaving outwardly with perfect decorum, occasionally bending his head to catch a whispered comment from his male companion, otherwise sitting with his eyes upon the speaker. Yet somehow she could tell he was sharing her amusement at the absurdity of this modish audience, perched uncomfortably on their spindly salon chairs, listening to a badly delivered talk of quite astounding mediocrity, instead of dining and dancing at Almack's or taking a hand of whist at the card tables in the clubs.

The attractive laughter lines at the corner of the man's eyes and mouth crinkled now and again and his shoulders shook with suppressed laughter at the good doctor's more pompous pronouncements. As she watched, he folded his arms across his chest as if the act would contain his amusement. Tearing her eyes away, Sophia forced herself to listen to the speaker at the front of the salon rather than imagine what it would be like to be enfolded in those arms.

'And I am sure I am right in saying that no one could er...fail to share...yes, share, my excitement at my discovery that not only is the Lactarius family of fungi flourishing in this area—lying as it does between the highlands and the southernmost plains—but that a particular favourite of mine, *Lactarius volemus,* is common, nay, widespread, at the edges of deciduous woodland. As you will all be aware, this species may be distinguished by a faint smell of herring.' Dr Eustace whipped off his eyeglasses and beamed in triumph at his bemused audience, one or two of whom broke into half-hearted applause as the wretched man appeared to expect some acknowledgement.

This was too much both for Sophia and for the object of her desires. She choked as quietly as she could into her lace handkerchief, but the tall man was unable to suppress a snort of laughter which, at a look of reproach from his companion, he hastily converted into a fairly convincing cough.

Oh, it would be such fun, she thought wistfully, to share that ridiculous moment with such a man. Of course, she chided herself, what she was feeling was not *love,* goodness knows she had learned long since just how empty that emotion was! No, it was the recognition of intelligence, the recognition of the ridiculous, a sense of fun. People with a sense of humour, let alone a sense of fun, were in very short supply in Sophia's life and had been for some time.

Dr Eustace, blissfully unaware of his effect on the

majority of his audience, had finally wound his tedious way to his conclusion and was offering to answer questions. Sophia sighed; there would be no escape for at least another half-hour, for a small number of Lady Newnham's intellectual circle showed every sign of having found the night's entertainment fascinating and were already plying him with queries.

Sophia dabbed the tears of laughter from her eyes while skillfully keeping the veil in place. The male contingent in the audience, had they known what that veil concealed, would have deplored the discretion which prompted her to wear it. For Miss Haydon's green eyes, long dark lashes and tumble of russet curls had always turned heads in the days when she was newly out in Society, and the four years of enforced retirement imposed upon her since she was seventeen had done nothing to dim either her beauty, or her spirit.

As the good doctor droned on she sighed, perhaps more loudly than was polite. There was no way the soft sound could have reached the attractive man's ears as he sat two rows in front and to her left, yet he turned his head slowly and scanned the audience as if looking for the perpetrator. His eyes could not possibly penetrate the thick lace yet Sophia felt as though he looked directly into her face, so intense was the sensation of recognition. He turned back almost immediately, but her heart was pounding and her cheeks burned anew.

Sophia clenched her gloved hands together tightly in the lap of her drab conker-brown walking dress and fought to regain her composure. What was it about this man that discommoded her so? She scolded herself: it was ridiculous, a fairy tale—she would never see him again, all she was doing was storing up discontent for herself. Over the last six months since she had returned to London she had schooled herself to expect little happiness, to be glad of the limited opportunities for entertainment that were open to her. Now it was as if she had opened Pandora's box, releasing dreams and unattainable desires.

Even the staid atmosphere of Lady Newnham's monthly afternoon reading circle for ladies, which had led to this evening's invitation, was something to be eagerly anticipated in her constrained life. Her elder brother George's suspicious mind could find nothing dangerous in her attendance at such activities—during the hours of daylight, of course—although virtually everything else was forbidden. For George, once alerted to what he saw as the moral instability of his younger half-sister, took his role as guardian very seriously indeed.

Daytime gatherings in attendance on his wife were one thing, but for his sister to be out in the evening was absolutely forbidden. However, it had not taken Miss Haydon long to discover that once she had retired to her room after dinner no one paid any further thought to her. Sir George and Lady Haydon, should they be spending a rare evening at their own hearthside, saw no reason to include her in their domestic activities, supposing Sophia to be occupied blamelessly with her sewing or a book of worthy sermons.

But Sophia's bedchamber overlooked the garden and, with careful timing and the secret acquisition of keys, it was perfectly possible to whisk down the back stairs, out of the kitchen door, through the garden gate and within seconds be in Berkeley Square. Cabbies might look askance at unaccompanied young ladies at that time of night, but whatever they thought her purpose might be, they were quite willing to take her money.

Once or twice a week, after scanning the newspaper and George's journals for notices of public talks, she would slip out, enjoying her freedom, although the most excitement she could hope for was a lecture at the Royal Society.

Sophia's train of thought was interrupted by the scraping of chair legs on the polished boards. The handsome man was getting to his feet. With a perfectly legitimate reason for staring Sophia took full advantage of it. The gentleman must be more than six feet tall, and built on athletic lines. His clothes were a credit to the best tailor in London, and no valet could hope for a better figure to dress, but there was something about him which suggested that this was no dandy and the way that he looked was, in fact, of indifference to him. Perhaps it was his hair—dark, crisp, slightly wavy and overlong, or perhaps it was simply the way he held himself with an easy, negligent grace.

His voice, as he began to speak, was no disappointment to Sophia. It was strong, deep and well modulated and with a hint of irony that she suspected was habitual. 'Dr Eustace, may I begin by saying that rarely, nay, never, have I spent an evening such as this.' At his side his companion groaned softly while the good doctor preened at the supposed compliment.

'The reference to the fungus—*Lactarius volemus*, was it not?—smelling of herring? I am anxious to know, in case I should ever come across it, is that the smell of fresh herring, or the kippered variety?'

His companion sank his head in his hands, but the

tall man's profile displayed nothing but intent interest as he sat down again and the doctor began to reply.

'My dear sir, what a fascinating question! It shows indeed the depth of your interest. I had never analysed this in sufficient detail, that is obvious, but if I am forced to pass an opinion, I would hazard that there is a slight hint of smokiness.'

Sophia, fighting a losing battle against hysteria, closed her teeth on her handkerchief and slipped from the room, thanking providence that she had arrived late and was therefore sitting close to the doors.

The hall, although populated by a host of scantily clad classical statues, was mercifully free of footmen. Sophia giving way to her emotions, threw back her veil and stood sobbing with laughter into her much-abused handkerchief. 'Kippered herring,' she repeated weakly. 'Kippered…'

Behind her a door opened and closed and she hastily shrank behind a statue of Aphrodite keeping her back turned in the hope that she would escape attention. A voice—a voice she had heard only a moment before—said with concern, 'Madam, are you unwell? May I be of assistance?'

It was he, the tall man. Sophia spun round, found herself standing almost on his toes, looked up into those dark blue eyes and gasped, 'Herring!'

He grinned back broadly, his face alight with laughter. 'I know, I should never have done it, but it was too much to resist. Sydney has made me come out; he says he will never forgive me or speak to me again.' There was a sudden increase in the sound of voices behind and scraping of chairs. 'Oh lord, they will be coming out for supper in a moment, quick, come with me.'

The stranger took Sophia's arm and with great assurance opened a door in the panelling, walked down a short corridor and emerged into the orangery. Across the glassed courtyard which sheltered them Sophia could glimpse the supper room. Faintly behind them she could hear Lady Newnham thanking the speaker amidst a smattering of applause for his fascinating insight into the natural history of Brazil, and inviting her guests to partake of the light supper laid out in the adjoining room.

The orangery, converted and maintained at great cost, was warm and fragrant with the smell of warm loam and growing things. Sophia found that the gentleman had let go of her arm and she stepped back instinctively. He was very big, very close and suddenly the intimacy they had shared with their laughter unsettled her.

He seemed to sense it, for he stepped back too and gestured to a white iron bench next to an orange tree in a tub. 'Please, will you not sit down for a moment, Miss...?'

'Haydon. Sophia Haydon.' Sophia sank down thankfully and dabbed at her eyes again, but to little avail. The handkerchief was beyond redemption.

'Here, please take this, my valet always sends me out with at least two.' He proffered an immaculately pressed square of linen, then, with a glance at her tear-streaked cheeks, dipped a corner in the basin of the small fountain and gently dabbed away the tear-tracks. He noticed that the linen came away quite clean without a trace of powder or rouge. It seemed Miss Haydon owed none of her fresh-faced beauty to the paint box.

'I realise this is extremely unconventional, but under the circumstances I hardly feel that waiting to be introduced by Lady Newnham is sensible.' He bowed, 'Hal Wyatt, at your service, Miss Haydon.'

'Lord Wyatt!' Sophia tried, and failed, to keep the recognition out of her voice, and a slight touch of colour came to her cheeks.

'I see you have heard of me,' his lordship remarked dryly. 'May I sit down? I can assure you, you have no need to scream.'

Sophia straightened her shoulders and replied, somewhat crisply, 'I have no intention of screaming, my lord. According to my sister-in-law you are a notorious rake with whom no woman is safe: however, I doubt if even you would attempt to seduce a young lady in Lady Newnham's conservatory. Do, please, sit down.'

Hal met her direct stare and his eyebrows rose. Well, well, well, Miss Haydon was as spirited and as unconventional as she was beautiful. Her clear green gaze was defiant, almost as if it concealed a secret.

What it concealed were Sophia's thoughts, which were running somewhat incoherently and regretfully along the lines that it was a pity she was already ruined, as being compromised by Lord Wyatt was a scandalously attractive prospect.

Sophia eyed the rangy figure beside her, his long legs thrust out in front of him on the flagstones. Hal was idly swinging his quizzing glass at the end of its ribbon. The silence stretched on, then he said, almost teasingly, 'Am I acquainted with your sister-in-law?'

'Lady Haydon? I think not, my lord. I cannot imagine you would move in the same circles.'

'Good God, not George Haydon's wife? Miss Haydon, I can assure you that your sister-in-law's knowledge of my character is not based on any personal experience.'

Sophia knew she should protest, but the thought of Lavinia having any sort of illicit relationship, as upright and prim as she was, was too preposterous to defend. Besides, Lady Haydon would never have spared the time for an *affaire,* devoted as she was to perfecting the art of social climbing, advancing her two cowed daughters into Society and repressing her irredeemable young sister-in-law.

'I never thought so for a minute,' she managed, rather failing to suppress the giggle that the thought of Lavinia in the toils of love evoked. 'I imagine Lavinia bases her opinion of your character on the gossip of her friends.'

'As I would not wish you to feel any anxiety at being alone with me, I think I should also assure you, Miss Haydon, that although I once was a rake, I am no longer practising as one.' The tone and the wicked glint in his blue eyes were exactly those she had seen when he was teasing Dr Eustace.

This was a staggeringly improper conversation, but Sophia was once again feeling so comfortable in his presence that she threw caution to the wind and asked the question on the tip of her tongue. 'Are you then a reformed rake?' she enquired innocently. 'And is attendance at lectures on the flora of Brazil part of your reformation?'

In the subdued light of the branches of candles which were placed in niches around the walls, Sophia could see the white gleam of his teeth. 'Minx!' he said appreciatively. This really was a most unusual young lady. She was not flirting with him, she was teasing him, giving as good as she got in a way that was strangely innocent. 'No, attendance at such lectures is *not* part of a process of penitence or reform! I was lured along by my very good friend Lord Sydney— who, believe me, is going to pay dearly for this. Or, at least, for the earlier part of the evening. I find it is improving greatly.' He stood up and offered her his arm. 'Shall we go in to supper?'

For the first time he saw Sophia look alarmed. 'Oh, no, no indeed, my lord, I had not intended to stay. I am not dressed for a supper party, and my face…'

Hal Wyatt looked at the undeniably sober walking dress, the simple cut of which did nothing to disguise a very trim figure. 'If we just get rid of this bonnet…' Before she knew it his fingers had tweaked the ribbons under her chin and the bonnet was discarded on the chair, revealing the full impact of her head of russet curls. 'You should not hide such glory,' he murmured, freeing one wayward tendril which had insinuated itself around her pearl ear-drop.

Sophia gasped and stepped back, coming up against the edge of the bench. Hal threw up both hands in rueful apology. 'I am sorry, that was most improper of me. But really, Miss Haydon, who do you think is going to even glance at your dress when you look like that?'

Sophia, glowing with pleasure at the unfamiliar compliment, gave him a severe look. 'Please do not talk nonsense, my lord!' Then she relented. 'I suppose a very little supper would do no harm, but I cannot stay long.'

'Then may I take you in?' He again offered her his arm and this time Sophia rested her fingers lightly on the dark blue superfine cloth of his sleeve and allowed herself to be conducted across the orangery and into the supper room. She was so aware of his physical presence beside her that it was almost a shock to find herself at the entrance of a crowded room.

Hal scanned the room. 'May I fetch you a drink, Miss Haydon? Ratafia, perhaps, or orgeat?'

Sophia, feeling increasingly nervous, murmured, 'Orgeat, thank you, my lord.' As Hal moved away she stood uncertainly, feeling horridly exposed despite the crowd. What if she saw someone she knew…someone who would tell Lavinia? Even as she thought it she spotted Lady Cussons, Lavinia's bosom friend and confidante and doubtless the source of the gossip about the scandalous Lord Wyatt. Dressed in the latest mode in a dress of white crepe striped with rose pink, her unbelievably blonde curls crowned with an Austrian cap of pink satin and lace, one could scarcely miss her. On an eighteen-year-old beauty the ensemble would have been eye-catching, on a matron of five and forty summers it evoked perfectly the phrase 'mutton dressed as lamb'.

Fortunately Lady Cussons was deep in conversation with the good Dr Eustace, but Sophia knew that it would only be a matter of moments before she would have become bored with him and turned in search of lighter company. It would be fatal for Lady Cussons to see her, for she was a regular recipient of Lavinia's complaints about her sister-in-law and was sure to know her entire, shocking, history. She would have not the slightest hesitation in betraying Sophia's escapade to Lady Haydon, and then even this small chance of freedom would be snatched away from her.

It seemed a heavy price to pay for having yielded to temptation and flirted with a stranger.

Chapter Two

By a miracle Lady Cussons had not seen her and Hal Wyatt's back was still turned: she could escape without him noticing and drawing the attention of Lavinia's friend to her. Stealthily Sophia edged backwards towards the door and slipped through back into the safe gloom of the orangery.

Her hat was where Lord Wyatt had cast it down: she scooped it up and tied it on her head as she hurried through the passage to the front hall. She checked before emerging to make sure the veil once again obscured her features, then stepped out on to the chequerboard floor of the hall.

A footman immediately came forward. 'May I be of assistance, madam?'

'My pelisse, if you please.'

He helped her into it, then looked round. 'Shall I call your maid, madam?'

'Er…no. She is outside waiting for me. In my carriage,' she added confidently. Not for the first time the ready falsehood tripped off her tongue and the footman went to open the door for her.

There was a row of waiting vehicles at the kerbside

and the man would have descended the steps to assist her. 'No, no, please do not trouble. My own man is there, see, at the end.' Sophia gestured airily at the last carriage in the line and the footman bowed and returned inside.

Once safely around the corner Sophia scanned Grosvenor Square for a hansom cab, but could see none. It was an awkward time in the evening: many of the cabbies would be making their way to the theatres and opera to get a good position for the end of the performance and would not be interested in picking up solitary women. Besides, Grosvenor Square was the sort of highly fashionable address where residents kept their own carriages and passing trade was thin on the ground.

The lanterns outside the ranks of fashionable houses guttered in the breeze, a wind sharp enough to threaten a late frost but prevent it settling on the pavements. Sophia snuggled into her pelisse and set off towards Brook Street, watching her footing in the dark areas between the pools of light shed by the newly installed gas lamps. She walked, resigned to the chill, her mind warmed by thoughts of Lord Wyatt...

Unconsciously her steps slowed as she walked, her memory full of him: the crinkle of laughter lines at his eyes, the sense of controlled power in his tall frame despite the correct evening dress, the awareness of a sharp intelligence behind the deep blue gaze. If she never saw him again, at least her memories of him would be clear enough to while away the lonely hours.

By the time she reached the corner with New Bond Street, Sophia had come almost to a halt in her bittersweet reverie. The sound of hooves on the cobbles penetrated her thoughts and she stopped, half-turning in the hope it was a cab. But it was only another private carriage, its greatcoated coachman on the box, two chilly footmen in livery standing up behind gripping the straps. One of them gave her an impertinent stare as he was carried past, which had the effect of reminding her just how unsuitably late it was to be walking the streets alone.

Sophia quickened her pace, realising as she did so just how cold she was. She should have put on more sensible shoes: the stones struck cold through the thin leather soles as she hurried along.

Her breath was coming in short pants, visible in the chilly air, by the time she gained Bruton Mews. The laughter of grooms drinking over a game of cards above one of the stables was the only sound beside the stamp and snort of horses as she slipped down the side entry which gave access to the rear gate of her brother's town house. The catch was stiff with cold and for a dreadful moment Sophia thought it had been bolted on the inside, then it gave and she was through and into the tiny garden, her heart beating loud in her chest.

Fanny, her maid, was waiting patiently in the kitchen, knitting by the range. Cook, as always at this hour, was safely snoring in her rocking chair, helped by a generous measure of her master's gin.

'There you are, miss, I thought you said you were going to be back by ten, and it is near eleven now!' Fanny scolded in a whisper, flapping her hands in front of her to urge her young mistress towards the stairs. 'Oh, look how cold you are, come along upstairs, I've put a warm brick in the bed an hour since. Do you want a cup of nice hot milk, miss?'

'Oh, yes please, Fanny, and some bread and butter—and a slice of cold meat if there is one. I declare I am famished.'

'Well, if you will go out without your dinner, miss, I don't know what else you expect. Cook made a nice apple pie this evening too, and there's most of it left. I'll cut you a slice of that.'

In her chamber the fire blazed invitingly. Sophia kicked off her shoes, pulled up her skirts and rested her chilled feet on the fender feeling the warmth penetrate her numbed toes. Her fingers and toes tingled with returning heat, and she suspected that the tip of her nose was pink, but the rest of her glowed warm with the memory of the night's encounter. 'Hal Wyatt...' She let the name run off her tongue, then jumped as Fanny bustled in with a tray.

'Sorry, miss, what did you say? Oh, miss, get your feet off that fender and put your slippers on. You'll get chilblains for certain! Now I'll just put these down on this table beside you and you eat up.'

Sophia smiled as she watched the small plump figure of Fanny Meadows moving around purposefully checking the warmth of the bed, shaking out Sophia's nightgown and hanging it over a chair back to warm near the fire.

Despite behaving as though she was at least forty-five, and fussing over her mistress like a mother hen at every turn, Fanny was no older than Sophia. They had been together for the last four years, ever since Sophia had been sent home to her brother's country estate in Hertfordshire in disgrace. To become a lady's maid, even to a young debutante under a cloud, was beyond the wildest dreams of a country girl from Tewin. She modelled herself on every lady's maid who had ever snubbed her when she had been a tweeny and they had come to the house with their mistresses in the old baronet's day.

Full of apple pie and warm milk, Sophia sat with her hands cupped around the glass and gazed unfocused into the fire, which was gradually burning down into embers. But instead of the scents of wood smoke, cinnamon and apple she smelled loam, orange blossom and just the hint of a spicy male cologne. Hal Wyatt's blue eyes, full of laughter filled her thoughts and the memory of his voice, earnestly asking Dr Eustace about the fungus, echoed again in her ears and she giggled.

'Miss?'

'Oh, I'm sorry, Fanny, I was miles away. Yes, I am going to come to bed now.'

'You look happy, miss,' Fanny observed as she dropped the nightgown over Sophia's head. 'Was it a nice talk?' She had not the slightest idea what it was that Sophia went off in the evening to listen to, but she was pleased that her mistress was getting some fun at last. Not that she hadn't had fun in the country at Bright's Hill, but it wasn't the sort of thing that a young lady of quality should be doing. Riding by herself—and riding astride at that—learning to fish from Mr Gold the estate manager and even persuading the gamekeeper to teach her to shoot.

No wonder she had turned into a tomboy. Why, Sir George and that Lady Haydon never came near the place! Cook would have it that that was because her ladyship was bored in the country and there were no smart parties for her to puff herself off at. But Fanny knew better. She was one of the few household servants who had known about the scandalous escapade which had ended with Miss Sophia being banished to

Bright's Hill. Of course, ladies of Quality had to be careful of their reputations, but it wasn't as though Sir George hadn't arrived in time...

Six months ago Sir George had summoned his half-sister back to London and it seemed that Sophia's disgrace had finally been forgiven and forgotten. Fanny dreamed that her young mistress would be taking her place in Society again, resuming her come-out alongside her brother's two daughters. But a mere day in the company of Lady Haydon had swiftly disabused both Sophia and her maid. Miss Haydon, her sister-in-law made it very plain, was in London under sufferance. She was most fortunate to be allowed back, Lady Haydon had announced, and she could show her gratitude for this indulgence by putting herself at the disposal of her sister-in-law.

Despite the passage of half a year, neither of them was happy with the result. Sophia was constantly in trouble for behaving in an unladylike manner, saying what she thought, leading her nieces into scrapes by encouraging them to think for themselves. And Sophia chafed under the constant surveillance, the endless reminders of just how unsatisfactory and unworthy she was.

She was not allowed out by herself, even with Fanny as escort: always she found herself in attendance on her sister-in-law or with Miss Charlotte or Miss Grace Haydon and whoever was chaperoning them. One day she had flared, 'Am I never to be allowed any freedom? What do you think I am going to do if you allow me to go to the circulating library with a footman in attendance? Run off with him?'

'Well, you did so before,' her sister-in-law had retorted. 'Although at least it was not with a servant—

you showed that much discretion at least!' She had shuddered theatrically at the memory of the Great Disgrace, as she always referred to it to her husband. In front of their daughters it was never referred to at all, they were aware only that their young aunt had committed one of the numerous sins that their mother was always warning them would be the downfall of their hopes.

'The talk?' Sophia returned to the present and Fanny's question with an effort. 'No, it was quite awful!' She very nearly added, 'But I met a rake in the orangery', and, warmed by that thought, she went to bed and slept like a log.

Next morning at breakfast Lady Haydon eyed her sister-in-law over the tea urn with dislike and envy. How could she look so…so…luminous? Lady Haydon strove to instil modesty, decorum and a sense of humility in Miss Haydon in many ways, one of which was by ensuring that her garments were plain, untrimmed and befitting her role as unpaid companion. In that shade of dull green she should look colourless and dowdy: Charlotte and Grace most certainly would. But no, Miss Sophia was positively sparkling this morning. Her chestnut curls gleamed red in the spring sunshine that streamed through the breakfast-room windows, her eyes were bright and alive and her complexion glowed.

Lady Haydon sought for some criticism she could legitimately level, failed, and instead snapped at her younger daughter.

'Sit up straight, Grace, your posture is quite slovenly and I declare you have butter on your sleeve. Do not think yourself too old to spend an hour in the nursery with the backboard!'

'Sorry, Mama,' Grace murmured meekly, dabbing at the stain with her napkin. 'What are we doing to-day?'

'You are attending your deportment class, your sister is going to her music lesson and Sophia will be accompanying me this morning. I wish to visit Dickens and Smith to match those silk patterns for the drawing-room curtains. Then this afternoon Sophia may come with me to Lady Cussons's At Home.'

'Oh, Mama,' complained Charlotte, who had an unfortunate tendency to whine. 'Why cannot we go shopping with you too? I promise I will practise my sonata this afternoon instead.'

'Please, Mama,' Grace joined in. 'You did say that we might have new gloves and stockings for Lady Cussons's dress-party on Friday.'

'Indeed, Lavinia, I could take them to buy their gloves and stockings while you are choosing the silks,' Sophia offered, earning glowing glances of gratitude from both girls, which transformed their plain little faces.

Lady Haydon put down her coffee cup with some emphasis. 'Certainly not. I have no intention of upsetting my plans and I require *you,* Sophia, to assist me with my purchases at the silk warehouse. Monsieur LeBoeuf is engaged for eleven this morning and a lady does not change arrangements at a whim. Now Charlotte, Grace, go and get ready.'

'Yes, Mama,' they chorused docilely, to Sophia's despair, and, with a curtsy to their mother, filed out of the room.

'As I have so frequently to remind you, Sophia,'

Lady Haydon snapped, 'it is not your place to teach my daughters to question their parents' authority. I have often had occasion to remark to Sir George that your own upbringing must have been scandalously indulgent. Nothing else can explain your subsequent behaviour.'

The memory of her own mother and her laughing, loving approach to bringing up her little daughter flashed into Sophia's mind and she almost snapped back at her sister-in-law. But Lavinia's sallow cheeks were stained by two spots of high colour and long experience had taught Sophia the consequences of not holding her tongue. Sometimes she disregarded them, but today she felt too restless to risk being left at home.

'I am sorry, Lavinia,' she replied, keeping her eyes cast down so that her sister-in-law did not see the spark of rebellion in them. 'What time do you wish me to attend on you?'

'Eleven o'clock, and do not forget to bring those silk samples.'

Sophia stopped in the drawing room to pick up the strips of shimmering fabric that were draped over the newly upholstered chairs. One of them was a deep cobalt blue, just the colour of Hal Wyatt's eyes: Sophia stood for a moment running her finger over it and remembering the warmth of his gaze, then with a little shake she picked them up and hurried back into the hall. Dreams were all very well, but reality was quite another thing and the best that reality held today was Lady Cussons's At Home.

When they arrived that afternoon, the salon in which Lady Cussons's guests were assembled was filled with a flock of fashionably dressed ladies sipping refreshments and exchanging tittle-tattle with each other.

Sophia, ignored at her sister-in-law's side as ever, had plenty of leisure to observe that Lavinia had finally penetrated a set that reflected her social ambitions to a nicety. For a granddaughter of a wealthy Hertfordshire merchant to have married a baronet was a major triumph, but Lavinia had soon discovered that it required more than her married respectability—and the not inconsiderable wealth she had brought to the union—to be received in the very best circles.

Sophia sighed faintly, but it was loud enough to reach Lavinia's ears and she shot her a sharp glance of reproof. Sophia got to her feet, drifting across the room to a quiet window seat drenched in sunlight.

From one of the sofas set around the Chinese rug Venetia Lovell set down her tea cup and gazed around the over-decorated drawing room, wincing imperceptibly at the sound of Lady Cussons holding forth on the trials endured securing what she had wanted from the various craftsmen involved. The result was strongly French but with the addition of Egyptian features and, Venetia Lovell reflected, they did not sit happily together. However, Lady Cussons had the money, if not the taste, for such schemes, and Venetia supposed spending it in this way gave her pleasure.

She was not the only one of the ladies present who was not giving their hostess her due attention she realised. Venetia's gaze rested again on the badly dressed young woman sitting alone on the window seat and gazing out on to Mount Street below. How did she manage to appear elegant despite that quite dreadful gown? And what an interesting face, Venetia mused.

She was attracted by the unusual and unconventional and this girl had both qualities as well as uncommonly fine looks. Not a conventional beauty, Mrs Lovell decided: that unfashionably chestnut hair seemed to threaten escape at any moment, and the young woman's skin had the faintest hint of tan. And she certainly seemed to be far too independent and intelligent to be the paid companion she appeared.

'Such an original and striking scheme, dear Lady Cussons,' that thin woman was saying. What was her name? Venetia racked her memory and came up with Haydon. 'Only someone of your taste and knowledge of fashion could have achieved it.' Toady, Venetia thought, then glimpsed the echo of her thought on the face of the girl at the window. The expression of distaste was fleeting and rapidly replaced by a carefully controlled neutrality. Perhaps she *was* Lady Haydon's companion. Intrigued, Venetia got to her feet.

Sophia looked up as the young matron, whose dashing chip straw hat she had been admiring earlier, came to her side. 'May I join you? I do not believe we have met before. I am Venetia Lovell.'

'Please sit down,' Sophia said warmly, her face lighting up. She moved her skirts aside to allow Venetia to sit beside her in the window. 'The sunshine is very pleasant, is it not? Oh, I am sorry, I should have said, I am Sophia Haydon.'

'Thank you, Miss Haydon. Indeed, the warmth is very welcome, one feels the spring has finally arrived. Please excuse my ignorance, but are you Lady Haydon's daughter?'

There was a slight incredulity in her tone which Sophia picked up and her eyes were dancing with mischief as she replied, 'No, indeed not! She is my sister-in-law—my half-brother's wife. She has two daughters, both somewhat younger than myself: the elder is making her come-out this year.'

Venetia gestured to a footman who brought them both more tea. They sipped companionably until she asked, 'How is it that we have not met before? You must have been out for a year or two, surely, Miss Haydon?'

She was unprepared for the sudden colour which stained Miss Haydon's cheeks. She looked away abruptly and said in a stilted voice, 'I came out three Seasons ago but I did not take. I have been living in the country on my brother's estate until a few months ago. Now I am my sister-in-law's companion.'

Mrs Lovell kept her thoughts to herself but she found it hard to believe that what she was hearing was all of the story. *Did not take!* How could this girl fail to be a success? She had looks, character, breeding…possibly not a great deal of wealth, but the Haydons were obviously comfortably off at least. Surely she was more than eligible? How very intriguing: there was a mystery here and if there was anything that Venetia Lovell adored, it was a mystery, as her doting husband frequently complained.

'How do you amuse yourself in town?' she asked. This girl was obviously not well used by her family and she determined to do something about it. As Mr Lovell could have warned Sophia, rescuing strays was another of Venetia's hobbies.

'Oh, I accompany Lavinia, of course, and shop for her. And she and my brother permit me to join Lady Newnham's reading circle. And sometimes I attend lectures…'

Venetia noticed the slight edge to the word *permit*.

Yes, indeed, there was a mystery here. 'Well, do you think they would have any objection to you coming to my Literary Group? We meet every Thursday evening at my house.'

Miss Haydon's green eyes lit up. 'Oh, how delightful, yes, I would like to very much, if Lavinia will allow.'

'Let us go and ask her now,' Venetia declared firmly, springing to her feet and offering Sophia a hand. 'Come along!' She lowered her voice to a whisper. 'See, she is enjoying herself, and nothing makes dragons more amenable than a little pleasure.'

Sophia was still choking on the giggle that this provoked as they arrived beside Lavinia and Lady Cussons. Lady Haydon began to frown at Sophia's intrusion, then saw who she was with and immediately rearranged her expression into one of amiability. She might not move in the same circles as Mrs Lovell, but she read her *Peerage* and was well aware that she was in the presence of an earl's granddaughter.

'Lady Haydon, I have been trying to persuade Miss Haydon to join my Literary Group, but she is reluctant to agree without your blessing. Now, do, please say yes, or I will be bereft! It is, I need hardly say, solely for ladies and I am most careful about what is selected for study.'

In the face of Venetia's confidential manner Lady Haydon felt all her defences crumbling. Why, Mrs Lovell was speaking to her quite as if she was one of her own exclusive set!

Positively simpering, she turned to Sophia and said with mock severity, 'Why, silly girl, of course I could not deny you such a treat. So condescending of Mrs Lovell, so kind! How could I possibly refuse?'

At this point the clock struck the hour and, as if summoned by the chimes, the butler appeared at the door. 'Lord Wyatt, milady,' he announced, to Sophia's complete horror.

Chapter Three

There was no mistake: the butler withdrew, leaving the new arrival in the doorway, the focus of every pair of feminine eyes in the room. Unaware of Sophia stiffening with shock Venetia's face lit up with pleasure and she fluttered across the room to meet the newcomer's long-legged stride halfway. 'Hal, dearest,' she exclaimed, holding out her hand. 'Only half an hour late, my love, positively saintly by your standards!'

Lord Wyatt bent his dark head to kiss Venetia on the cheek and Sophia thought, with an inexplicable ache in her midriff, that they made a very handsome couple.

They turned so that Hal could greet his hostess and Venetia remained at his side, her hand resting lightly on the sleeve of his deep blue coat. She had claimed him like that before, Sophia observed with something like envy, racking her brains to remember whether Mrs Lovell was a widow or not. But, not having her sister-in-law's encyclopaedic knowledge of the *Peerage,* she failed to place her.

Sophia took a side-step behind Lavinia as if the action would hide her from Hal. Why on earth was she feeling so discommoded? For discommoded she was—her heart beat uncomfortably in her chest and she knew her colour had risen. In broad daylight Hal Wyatt was even more attractive than she had thought last night in the shadows of the conservatory.

As he bent his head to speak to Lady Cussons she noticed the curl of crisp black hair at his nape and the broad set of his shoulders and her heart beat even faster. This was ridiculous! Sophia gave herself a little shake: her life must be circumscribed indeed if one brief encounter with a personable man reduced her to this state. I must get out and about more, she resolved grimly, remembering again that giddy moment when she had first set eyes on Hal Wyatt and believed herself to have fallen in love.

Mrs Lovell was bidding her hostess goodbye. 'Thank you so much, Lady Cussons, for a delightful afternoon. I really should have left half an hour ago, so I can only be grateful that Lord Wyatt's lack of punctuality has allowed me more time in your company.'

Hal turned from Lady Cussons's chair and Sophia realised with sudden panic that he must certainly see her—and just as certainly he would greet her, doubtless referring to the evening before. And then Lavinia would know not only that she had been out last night, but that she could escape at will and without her brother's knowledge.

The smile started in Hal's eyes as he saw her and Sophia did the only thing she could think of.

Hal Wyatt had never been on the receiving end of quite such a comprehensive cut in his life before! Miss Haydon's expression of frozen hauteur and half-turned shoulder were as telling as if she had slapped his face.

The smile died in his eyes and he turned abruptly, ushering Mrs Lovell briskly out of the salon and down the sweep of stairs to the hall.

'Hal!' Venetia protested once he had handed her into his curricle. 'Why did you not simply throw me over your shoulder and stride out instead of towing me down the stairs like that? I can quite understand anyone wanting to get out of that room, but really! My feet hardly touched the ground!'

Hal gathered the reins up and guided the pair of matched Welsh bays out into the traffic of Mount Street before answering her. 'Have you any idea why Miss Haydon should cut me quite so comprehensively?' he enquired.

'Did she? I did not notice.' Venetia studied his profile from under her lashes as Hal caught the point of his whip neatly in one hand, steadying the bays as he took the sharp left and right turn into Berkeley Square. She was almost home—and she wanted to get to the bottom of this intriguing mystery before she did so and Hal could escape her interrogation. 'I was not aware you knew Miss Haydon? I find her charming— fresh and somewhat unusual.'

Hal knew her far too well to be fooled by her disingenuous tone. His grin was broad and white as he said, 'Stop fishing, Venetia. Ask me in when we get to Albemarle Street and I will tell you all about Miss Haydon and my adventure last night.'

Venetia clapped her gloved hands together, her eyes gleaming. 'Oh good, an intrigue. Hal, what have you been up to? I thought last night you had attended a blameless cultural event at Lady Newnham's with Sydney? Are you telling me now that this is not so?'

'Wait until we get inside,' he replied firmly. 'Now,

I need some advice about Elizabeth: she is driving me quite distracted.'

'Well, she is seventeen now,' Venetia remarked. 'She is out of the schoolroom and you cannot continue to be the strict big brother for ever: you should let me bring her out as she has no mama to do it.'

'She is far too wild,' Hal said with a sigh. 'I thought bringing her up to the villa I rented in Chelsea would answer for a month or two, but her governess cannot control her and I am certain she is up to something.'

'Well if you take my advice, Hal, you'll let her come and stay with me at the town house and I will take her shopping and introduce her to some other girls of her own age. Only let her get into the right circle and find her feet and she will soon settle down. Incarcerating her in Chelsea is not going to help, she is close enough to London to yearn to enjoy it, but far enough away not to be under your eye.'

Hal agreed, somewhat doubtfully, with Venetia's plans for his wild little sister, but refused to be drawn on the subject of Miss Haydon.

Not until they were safely ensconced in Venetia's own sitting room, a brandy and water at his elbow, did Hal satisfy his companion's curiosity. He told her of meeting a heavily veiled young woman at Lady Newnham's who, in the security and intimacy of the conservatory, had confessed herself to be Miss Sophia Haydon.

'We were getting along famously when she took flight without so much as a by your leave,' Hal said. 'We had just gone into the supper room, I went to fetch her a drink and when I returned she had vanished—and not so much as a glass slipper left behind her.'

Venetia snapped her fingers at the little King Charles spaniel which was sitting on Lord Wyatt's highly polished Hessians and regarded her companion with some suspicion. 'Hal…what did you do to upset Miss Haydon? What could you have done to deserve such a cut? Have you been flirting?' She raised an admonitory finger. 'And do not seek to look both injured and innocent, I know you only too well!'

Freed of the weight of the dog on his feet, Hal stuck out his legs in front of him and managed to look both so injured and so innocent that Venetia could not suppress her laughter. 'Hal, stop it! We have known each other since we were in small clothes and I am not going to be gulled by you.'

'Very well, cousin.' Hal leaned back, hands behind his head and stretched like a big cat. 'I admit to being in a conservatory alone with Miss Haydon, I admit to tucking one very charming curl behind one equally charming ear, and, no, I did not kiss her. And, yes, I wish I had.' Venetia tutted at him and he added, 'No, our conversation consisted mainly of such topics as Brazil, herring and fungi.'

'*Herring?*' Venetia wrinkled her nose. 'Hal, you must be losing your touch if you can spend time in a conservatory with a charming young lady and talk about *herring!*'

A short silence ensued and then Lord Wyatt said ruminatively, 'Yes, she is charming. And also very mysterious—there is a secret there.'

'Just what I thought!' Venetia crowed with delight, clapping her hands. 'Now I know I am right! And she needs rescuing from that ghastly dragon of a sister-in-law—'

Any other observations that Mrs Lovell might have

been about to make on the subject of Lady Haydon
were interrupted at this point by the door opening and
a tall blond gentleman strolling in. 'I thought I heard
you, my dear. Afternoon, Wyatt, keeping my wife out
of mischief, I hope?'

Venetia leapt to her feet, spilling an indignant lap-
dog on to the carpet, and threw her arms around as
much of her husband as she could. 'Charles, darling!
How lovely you are home—I thought you were sitting
on that dreary Bill in the House tonight. Hal and I
have found a mystery, in fact, a mysterious young
woman, and I have quite resolved to rescue her.'

Charles Lovell handed his wife back to her chair
and went to stand with one arm along the mantleshelf
and his foot on the fender. He gazed with fond indulgence at the petite figure of his wife, her pretty face
alive with a mixture of joy at seeing him and the mischief of whatever she was up to with her cousin. In
five years of marriage Charles had been seduced, entertained, charmed and totally wound around the finger of his young wife and he found the experience
infinitely pleasurable.

'Are you quite sure this young person wishes to be
rescued, my dear?' he enquired mildly.

'Charles, do not be stuffy! She *needs* rescuing
whether she knows it or not. And Hal wants to rescue
her too,' she added as if this clinched the matter.

Charles regarded Hal, who was looking too innocent to be true. 'Oh, yes, indeed. And exactly what
does Wyatt want to rescue her for?'

Hal spread his hands in mock protest, 'Don't look
at me like that, old boy, she knows perfectly well that
I'm a rake—in fact she told me she knew I was and

that she felt quite safe because she doubted that even
a rake would attempt seduction in a conservatory.'

Charles Lovell snorted. 'Obviously the girl is a
complete innocent if she thought that the scant cover
of a few potted palms would save her virtue from
you!'

'Charles, really!' Venetia scolded, obviously more
put out by the slur on her cousin than the impropriety
of her husband's remark. 'Now, listen, both of you,
you know my Literary Evenings…'

'You mean your Thursday evening gossip sessions
with your bosom friends?' her husband interjected.

'Charles, you are being tiresome, you know we discuss books!'

'Yes, the latest scandalous novel and the latest crim.
cons.,' he grinned.

'As if I would gossip about other people's marital
misdemeanors!'

'Everyone else does,' Hal drawled, swinging his
eyeglass idly to and fro.

'You are getting off the point,' Venetia said severely. 'I have invited Miss Haydon to this Thursday's
gathering and her ghastly sister-in-law has agreed she
may come. And then I will discover her secret and we
can rescue her! Now, that is settled, we have done all
we can until Thursday—Hal, are you staying for dinner?'

The object of these schemes was sitting alongside
her sister-in-law as Sir George's carriage pulled up
outside the house in Bruton Street. She had just endured a long harangue from Lavinia about how favoured and fortunate she was that Mrs Lovell, grand-

daughter of an earl, had condescended to notice her, much less invite her to her home.

'I just hope that you do not let yourself or, more importantly, your brother down,' Lady Haydon opined as she swept into the drawing room. 'I can only assume that Mrs Lovell has not heard anything about your…circumstances. You must be very, very careful to behave in such a way that no memory of the scandal is stirred in anyone.' Almost to herself she added, 'I wonder after all if I was wise to allow it…but it could open up such a useful connection for Grace and Charlotte.'

So that was it, Sophia thought bitterly as she went upstairs to remove her bonnet. She has not given me permission for myself, but in the hope that my acquaintance with Mrs Lovell will open up avenues for my nieces.

Now that she had escaped Lavinia's stream of conversation she could think about Hal Wyatt and how she had snubbed him. It was an awful thing to have done—so rude!—and quite the opposite of what she wanted to do when she saw him. And now, even if she did see him again, he would never speak to her. How could he after such a comprehensive insult on top of her running away without a word the night before?

She plumped herself down in front of the dressing-table mirror and gazed gloomily at her appearance. Not that any gentleman with a choice in the matter would look twice at her in a gown such as this. Mrs Lovell, who had been so kind, had looked quite stunning in jonquil twill with pretty slippers and gloves in amber kid. No wonder Hal Wyatt had been so pleased to see her, and had kissed her so charmingly.

What was the relationship between them? That sort of speculation was ill bred, showed signs of jealousy and an improper interest in Lord Wyatt, she chided herself. But none of that made any difference at all! Sophia peeped out of the door, saw the landing was empty and tiptoed into Lavinia's chamber. As she expected, the *Peerage* was on the night stand.

Sophia flicked through the pages swiftly, her heart beating slightly fast and found first Hal Wyatt, grandson of the Earl of Kidderminster. She read his entry with close attention, then found Mrs Lovell—also a grandchild of the Earl. She was his cousin! Well, that was all right then, they had probably been friends since childhood. Sophia felt quite unreasonably cheered and ran downstairs in an almost sunny mood.

From the back sitting room came the sounds of Charlotte struggling her way through Mozart. With a grimace at the effect, Sophia pushed open the door and dutifully went in to turn the pages for her.

The anticipation of Thursday evening made the dreary routine of the intervening days seem endless. Mrs Lovell had said that the group was for ladies only, which meant that Sophia had no hope of meeting Hal again—but that was a very good thing she told herself stoutly. Rigorous self-examination had convinced Sophia that the only reason that Hal Wyatt filled her thoughts by day and her dreams at night was because she led such a dull and restricted existence and knew no other gentlemen.

And leaving that aside, what place in her life could an acknowledged rake have? His protestations that he was 'reformed' amused, but did not convince her. He was doubtless surrounded by charming young ladies and sophisticated and willing married women. She was just a boring, dowdy country mouse from Hertfordshire who was under a cloud.

By Thursday morning anticipation had given way to apprehension. Firstly Mrs Lovell had forgotten to tell Sophia what the group was going to be discussing so she had had no opportunity to read the book beforehand. Secondly, her set was bound to be as well dressed and fashionable as she and not one of Sophia's gowns could be regarded as even tolerable. Gazing at them in the clothes press, Sophia was trying to make a choice between hair-brown silk, which made her look washed out, or dove-grey twill, which looked like the second stage of mourning, when the door opened and Lavinia swept in, neglecting to knock as usual.

An almond-green silk gown was draped over her arm and she thrust it at Sophia. 'Try this on. It was the one I ordered for Charlotte, which arrived yesterday. But it will not do: with her being so blonde, it leaches away all her colour.' That was a more polite description than Charlotte's papa had employed when he saw his daughter gowned. 'Good gad, woman, she looks like a bilious sheep in that colour!' he had declared in ringing tones, reducing his unfortunate child to tears.

Sophia could not believe her good fortune. She ran a finger reverentially over the soft silk, seeing the colour shimmer as the light fell upon it. 'Oh, Lavinia, it is beautiful, thank you so much.'

'You should indeed be grateful. This is an important connection for Grace and Charlotte and I would not have you make a poor impression on Mrs Lovell and her friends.'

Of course Lavinia's motives in giving her this gown were not benevolent, how could she have thought otherwise? But for once Sophia did not care; she had a ravishingly pretty gown that would suit her and she was going out, all by herself, in the carriage, to a real social event as the guest of someone she liked. Unfailingly honest, Sophia admitted to herself that she was once again thinking more warmly of Venetia Lovell because she knew she was not Hal Wyatt's mistress.

The almond-green silk was a great success, a perfect foil for her chestnut hair, which Fanny dressed with a charming simplicity to which even Lavinia could not object. Her mama's pearl drops and single-string pearl necklace were unexceptionable for an unmarried lady of one and twenty and on her feet she was wearing her evening pumps, which fortunately went well with the new gown.

All in all, the short carriage journey from Bruton Street to Albemarle Street felt like those few evenings before the Great Disgrace when she had driven off to parties and dances at her come-out.

Mr Lovell's butler opened the door on a young lady whose cheeks were charmingly stained with colour and whose green eyes sparkled with anticipation. He took her wrap and ushered her through to a salon blazing with lights where Mrs Lovell was surrounded by a chattering group of perhaps nine ladies.

'Miss Haydon, ma'am.'

'Miss Haydon!' For a moment even Venetia's famed poise slipped as she took in the slender figure robed in the palest almond silk, which seemed to sheath her high-bosomed body like leaves around a flower stem. Could this be the same girl as the miserable figure clad in dull serge of earlier in the week? Venetia pulled herself together and came to welcome her guest. 'Good evening, Miss Haydon. How very charming you look! Now, do let me make you known to the rest of our group, they are all eager to make your acquaintance.'

Chapter Four

Stepping into the room took all Sophia's courage, but she need not have feared: Venetia Lovell's friends did indeed make her welcome. They were an unusual, even oddly assorted group, but Sophia soon realised that they were all united by spirit and a strong sense of independence.

First there was a pair of veritable bluestockings who were describing their plans to set up house together in the village of Twickenham, 'Away from the tyranny of men, my dear Miss Haydon! We shall write poetry, cultivate our garden, and possibly keep goats.'

Then there was a dashing young widow who had been left a considerable fortune by her elderly husband and who had only herself to consider. She was making plans to visit Italy just as soon as the continent was considered calmer and was filling her time acquiring classical art and admiring young men. Sophia hoped to find a moment to talk to her about Italy, for it was her secret ambition to make just such a trip herself.

But Venetia whisked her away and introduced her to three married ladies of Venetia's age, two unmarried girls of about her own years and a middle-aged woman with inky fingers who was a best selling novelist, but only under a male pseudonym.

The 'literary discussion' she had been expecting proved to be an exchange of somewhat racy novels hot off the presses, news of Lord Byron's latest work *The Siege of Corinth* and a breathless account of the charms of a new poet, even more beautiful than George Byron himself by all accounts, who had been seen giving a reading by one of the married ladies.

The clocks were striking ten and Sophia was beginning to feel a little awkward at not knowing how the evening was expected to end. The ladies had put down their books and the conversation had become very general, yet no one showed any inclination to leave. She had been too nervous to eat before she came out and was now feeling decidedly peckish and hoping that her tummy would not rumble.

The double doors swung open and to her relief the butler announced, 'Supper is served in the Chinese room, ma'am.'

'Thank you, Spratte. Has anyone else arrived?'

'Yes, ma'am, several of the usual gentlemen are here already and I believe I heard another caller at the door as I came in.'

Gentlemen? Sophia had a momentary qualm about what Lavinia would say, then decided that if she was not told she would never know. Even so, it was a long time since she had been at a social event with gentlemen who were not of George and Lavinia's circle— and on those occasions she was most definitely not expected to put herself forward and join in the conversation.

Venetia saw the sudden look of alarm on her new

acquaintance's pretty face and came over to reassure her. 'Please do not be concerned that Lady Haydon is not here to chaperon you, Miss Haydon—I am more than happy to take that role.' She took Sophia's arm and guided her towards the door, chatting as she went. 'I hold open house on Thursday evenings—quite informal, you know. Some of Charles's political friends like to drop in after business at the House, and some other friends call on their way to or from clubs or the theatre.' She paused at the doors which Spratte was holding open and added, 'One never knows who will be here, but I am sure there will be no one that Lady Haydon could possibly take exception to.'

Indeed, Lavinia would be in a seventh heaven if she saw the gentlemen who now turned from their conversation to bow to their hostess and her friends. The majority of them were prominent in government circles—friends and colleagues of Charles Lovell—but there were also several well-known men about town, including one earl and the tall figure of Lord Alvanley, as always the most striking member of the Dandy set.

A rapid scan of the room revealed no sight of Lord Wyatt, which was, of course, a great relief. Her natural reluctance to see him again must explain the sinking feeling in her stomach, she told herself firmly, but Sophia was far too honest to truly believe that.

'Let me introduce you to my husband.' Venetia swept her forward towards a tall, very distinguished man in early middle age. 'Mr Lovell, may I make known to you Miss Haydon, who has just joined my group.' Sophia would not have noticed, but Charles recognised the slight steely undertone in Venetia's voice and realised that this charming young woman must be his wife's latest protégée. Although looking at her he could not imagine why she needed 'rescuing'—she seemed well dressed, poised and altogether charming.

'I am delighted to meet you, Miss Haydon, I do hope this is but the first of many visits to our house.' He bowed over her hand. 'Now, to whom may I introduce you?' Venetia watched with some satisfaction as her husband bore Sophia off. Very soon she was surrounded by a group of admiring young men, all vying to fetch her a glass of ratafia or a lobster patty.

Charles reappeared at her side. 'There, my dear, is that what you wanted?' He nodded towards Sophia, who was laughing at a remark made by the Earl of Illchester.

'You have done very well, dear, her sister-in-law would be *livid*,' Venetia praised him, taking his arm and giving it a squeeze. 'But *where* is Hal, the wretch?'

Sophia was having a quite lovely time. Everybody was being so kind, so attentive, interested in what she was saying—and she could not help but notice and be flattered by the admiring glances she was receiving. She felt transformed in the new dress, and when she caught a glimpse of her reflection in one of the long pier glasses she could scarcely believe she was looking at herself. The woman who looked back at her had sparkling eyes, burnished hair and the light was dancing on the soft fabric of her gown. After the dullness, the repression, the constant disapproval of life in Bruton Street, this was like a happy dream.

She was giving herself a surreptitious pinch when there was a flurry around the doors, evidently a late arrival as she could hear Venetia's voice over the hum of conversation. 'There you are, you wretch! You promised me you would be here an hour since!'

Sophia was standing with her back to the door, but as she glanced up she could see it clearly reflected in the long glass opposite. Framed by the doorway Hal Wyatt stood, his glance flicking swiftly over the room as if seeking something—or someone. She saw his eyes pass over her, then his gaze focussed on the mirror and she saw the sudden recognition and dawning pleasure in his eyes as he recognised her.

Sophia felt her mouth go dry and she could not turn, instead standing staring into the glass as he made his way across the room towards her. It seemed to take forever for him to reach her side: he stopped to exchange greetings with several gentlemen, kissed the hands of the two bluestockings who had told her about their plans to retire to Twickenham and left them fluttering, and relieved a passing footman of two glasses from his tray.

Frozen to the spot, Sophia did not even turn when he arrived behind her, so close that she could feel his breath stirring the fine hairs at the nape of her neck. 'Miss Haydon?' he said, very softly and she turned to find herself staring fixedly at his cravat. For a long moment she stared at it until he said lightly, 'I am gratified that you admire my cravat, Miss Haydon. It is called the Waterfall style and is excessively difficult to achieve.'

It broke the spell and with a little gasp of laughter Sophia looked up into his face, into his warm blue gaze. 'Good evening, my lord.'

'Good evening, Miss Haydon,' he echoed, handing her one of the glasses he held. 'May I say that you are looking quite ravishing this evening?'

Sophia felt her blush deepen. 'Please do not, my lord,' she stammered. 'I do not know how to...flirt.' Her hand trembled and a little droplet of liquid splashed on to her gloved fingers.

Instantly Hal's hand caught hers, steadying it and gently tipping the glass back to the vertical before releasing her. 'Is that why you ran away from me at Lady Newnham's—and why you cut me dead last time we met?'

Sophia coloured and cast down her gaze: how was she going to explain herself? She had never felt so confused and gauche in her life.

But Hal Wyatt did not wait for an answer or appear to notice her confusion. 'I can assure you, Miss Haydon, that I am not flirting, merely telling you the truth. You look beautiful.'

Sophia shook her head, her pearl earrings dancing with the movement. 'Oh, no, my lord,' she said with an attempt at lightness, 'it is merely my new dress.' Hastily she took a deep sip from her glass and discovered it was not ratafia but champagne. The bubbles fizzed up her nose and tickled the back of her throat and, suddenly defiant, she took another good sip. Goodness! That felt better—strange, but better!

Hal raised one eyebrow, clicked his fingers for the footman and took another glass from him, exchanging it for Sophia's virtually empty one. His cousin Venetia was quite right, there was a mystery here. Miss Haydon was not so young that she could not have encountered outright admiration, let alone flirtation before, yet the naïveté of her remark about her new gown was almost that of a debutante just out. And his remark about her evasive behaviour at their previous meetings had obviously hit a raw nerve.

He could not let it lie. 'Come, come, Miss Haydon. I refuse to believe that you are not skilled in the gentle art of flirtation: you could not be so cruel as to deny my sex this harmless dalliance!' It was said lightly but Lord Wyatt was taken aback by his companion's response. Her face paled and he could have sworn there was the glint of tears at the back of her green eyes.

Sophia had herself under control almost immediately and said somewhat stiffly, 'Please do not tease me, my lord. I do not normally go out into Society much: I do not understand the rules that you gentlemen play by.' The hint of hurt he had noticed in her early remarks was more overt now.

Hal lowered his voice and said, 'Is there something wrong, Miss Haydon? Please believe I do not seek to tease or to annoy you, but if I may offer you my services in any way…?'

'No, no, I thank you, but please do not question me further, my lord.' Sophia turned away in relief to see Venetia at her side.

'I am sorry to lose you so early in the evening, Miss Haydon, but your carriage is at the door and I understand from the footman that you are expected at home.'

Venetia returned five minutes later from seeing Sophia out and immediately sought out her cousin, cutting with ruthless charm into his conversation. 'Hal, I need a word with you. Excuse me, gentlemen.' She seized him firmly by the sleeve and steered him into Charles's study, closing the door with some emphasis.

'Hal, what are you about? I could see from across the room that you were upsetting Miss Haydon, yet I could have sworn that she was pleased to see you! What have you discovered?'

Hal dropped his long frame into one of Charles's comfortable wing chairs and stared thoughtfully into the embers of the fire while Venetia paced up and down, her long skirts swishing on the rug. Finally he said, 'What I have discovered, my dear cousin, is that somebody has hurt that young woman very deeply indeed and I am determined to find out who, and in what way.'

The next day Lavinia Haydon drove Sophia almost distracted with the barrage of questions she fired at her over the breakfast table.

'Do concentrate and tell me everyone who was there last night! Really, Sophia, I would have expected you to have paid more attention to the company: they could be of the greatest importance to Charlotte and Grace. Tell me again,' Lady Haydon demanded, her fingers busy in the pages of the *Peerage* as she assessed each guest at the Literary group for their connections, pedigree and possible usefulness to her daughters in their come-out. She pulled a face at the mention of the two bluestockings despite their impeccable breeding. 'They are of no use,' she snapped. 'Were there no matrons there? No one with daughters making a come-out to whom you could introduce Charlotte and Grace?'

'I have only just met them, Lavinia, it would have seemed very forward to have been angling for invitations,' Sophia protested, but her mind was not on the female members of the Literary Circle at all. No, she kept returning over and over again to that endless moment when her eyes had met Hal's in the looking glass, when he had seemed to look into her heart and her mind. She had hardly slept, tossing restlessly in bed as she remembered his breath on the nape of her neck, imagined herself in his arms, held tight against that broad chest…

'There is no necessity to be quite so snappish,' Lavinia rebuked her. 'We must call this morning, leave cards. I would not have Mrs Lovell think I have neglected the least observance after her condescension in inviting you. Now, wake up and pay attention, Sophia! You look quite washed out.'

Any further reproaches were mercifully cut short by the arrival at the breakfast table of the master of the house. Sir George Haydon, a man whose main concern was to have an easy life, was rarely seen at home unless his wife demanded his attendance at some function or summoned him to rebuke his unsatisfactory sister. He belonged to a number of the rather less fashionable clubs, enjoying heavy eating, drinking and card play. This morning, following an unfortunate combination of lobster and a rather poor port, his normally florid complexion was positively choleric.

Lavinia, who was always most attentive to her husband, instantly switched her attention from Sophia to her spouse. 'Good morning, Sir George, shall I ring for fresh coffee?'

George had overheard Lavinia's raised voice and immediately assumed Sophia had been causing problems again. He glared at her, grunted at his wife and dropped heavily into his chair at the head of the breakfast table, grimacing as the shock jarred his hangover. 'Coffee? Nonsense! William! Fetch me a jug of porter and a good beefsteak.'

Sophia winced as Lavinia began to chatter, quite ignoring signs of rising ire from Sir George. 'Sophia has finally made a quite excellent connection, my dear. It will be of such utility to your daughters in their come-out.'

'What? What? Sophia out and about? Is this sensible? Is this wise, Lady Haydon? What if her Disgrace were to be remembered? What of Charlotte and Grace's chances then?' He took a deep draught of porter and glowered at his half-sister over the rim of the tankard.

'Of course, that must be at the forefront of my mind,' Lavinia soothed. 'But she is aware of her responsibilities to her nieces in this matter. Are you not, Sophia?'

'Yes, Lavinia,' Sophia responded meekly, failing to notice the suspicious look this elicited from her brother. 'Shall I go and make sure the carriage is ready for you, Lavinia?'

Without waiting for her sister-in-law's curt nod, Sophia slipped out, her pleasant daydreams of Hal now overlaid by anxiety about what might happen if Lavinia met either Venetia or Mr Lovell. What if the politician remarked upon her presence at supper with male guests the evening before? No matter how dazzling the connection, such a comment would be enough to cause Lavinia to break it. And what if their visit coincided with a visit to his cousin by Hal Wyatt? She could hardly cut him dead a second time and Lavinia would be sure to notice if he spoke to her that they had met before. How long was Lord Wyatt in London for?

Her brain was still buzzing with questions and worries as the barouche made its way to Albemarle Street. To her enormous relief the Lovells were not at home and Lavinia left cards, carefully turning over the requisite corners to show that she and Miss Haydon had called. With the insecurity of one not born to her present station, Lavinia had learned the books of etiquette by heart and followed them scrupulously.

On their return Lady Haydon was instantly swept upstairs by the girls' governess with the news that Miss Charlotte was in hysterics, having just heard that her dearest friend and rival, Miss Portman, had received and accepted a most flattering proposal of marriage and that before she was even officially out. Charlotte's wails of chagrin were faintly audible, even in the hallway.

Sophia stood alone on the chequerboard marble, idly unbuttoning her pelisse, relishing the sudden withdrawal of Lavinia's attention. Then a discreet cough behind her made her turn to find William the footman proffering a salver with a folded note upon it. 'This came whilst you were out, Miss Haydon.'

Sophia's heart was thudding as she looked at the direction on the cover. It was in an unfamiliar hand. Hastily she went to her room and shut the door. Could it be from Hal?

In fact, as she spread the stiff page with trembling fingers, it proved to be a hasty note from Venetia. She was so sorry, she explained, but her dear sister had been brought to bed of twins and needed her help with the other children. She doubted that she would be back in town for a fortnight and would therefore have to cancel the Literary evenings until further notice.

Sophia sat down on the bed and thought, 'How kind of her to let me know.' Then a large tear rolled down her cheek and fell on to the letter in her lap. She had been so sure it had been from Hal...

But why would he be writing to her? It would be

highly improper and, besides, he had given her not the slightest reason to believe his sentiments were engaged in any way. She blew her nose briskly, got up and went to the mirror to take off her bonnet and tidy her hair. No, rakes—even reformed rakes—flirted as a matter of course. It was her own lack of experience and sheltered life that led her to refine too much upon a slight acquaintance and some gallantry on his part. She must not be deceived into reading the slightest partiality for her into his attentions either at Lady Newnham's or last night.

She stopped suddenly, her lower lip caught between her teeth as she recalled their conversation last night. He had seemed very intrigued by her reticence, had hinted that he guessed there was some mystery about her. What if he made it his business to enquire about her and learned of the reason for her retirement from Polite Society four years before, so soon after her come-out? If he knew she was ruined, would he assume she was an easy conquest? She could not bear the thought that he might think less of her—or, even worse—that he might treat her differently if he knew of her history.

Chapter Five

Fortunately for Sophia's tranquillity Lavinia was too absorbed with calming Charlotte and launching her at her first big party to recall that she had not spoken to Mrs Lovell in person and therefore decide to make a further visit.

The next Thursday night, Lavinia and the girls took the barouche and departed for a dance, leaving Sophia, as usual, on her own in the house. Without Venetia's Literary Circle to look forward to, Sophia settled by the fire with a book and tried to concentrate, but she was interrupted by the butler with a note only moments after the partygoers had left.

It proved to be from Mrs Ashdowne, another member of Venetia's reading group, offering her a very late invitation to her house in Montague Square. She was hosting Venetia's Literary group in her absence, she wrote, and apologised for overlooking its latest member. She would therefore be delighted to see dear Miss Haydon should she be able to come at such late notice.

Rushing upstairs to change into her dove-grey silk, within the quarter-hour Sophia found herself heading in a hansom cab to Mrs Ashdowne's residence in Montague Square. In her haste it did not occur to her that this was far from being one of her secret expeditions. On this occasion Lavinia would have no objection to the outing and therefore she could take her maid with her, but the habits of secrecy were so entrenched that she was well on her way before she realised that she could have spared Fanny another evening sewing by the kitchen fire.

The evening went well, although the supper afterwards was a quiet affair, with only the ladies present. However, it was extremely congenial, conversation flowed and Sophia began to feel she was getting to know the other members of the circle and to make friends. Unfortunately it proved too congenial—with alarm she heard the clock strike eleven, nearly an hour later than she had intended to leave from this distant part of Mayfair. With a smile she gulled the Ashdownes' servants with her usual skill and slipped out into the night before they realised she had no carriage waiting.

It was a raw evening now, not frosty, but with a penetrating drizzle that soon dampened the hem of her gown. Sophia bit her lip in frustration at her foolishness in not taking her maid and asking the footman to secure her a carriage. Now there was not a cab to be seen and worse, as she hurried down Gloucester Street towards Portman Square, she could hear the sound of loud male voices and raucous laughter approaching. She remembered that the Life Guards' stables were situated only a block away off Dorset Street and it sounded as if a group of men were returning there after an evening's entertainment. A lone female on the street would be the target of vulgar cat calls, at the very least.

Alarm lent wings to her feet as Sophia ran down the deserted street and around the corner into the respectable, well-lit surroundings of Portman Square. She paused there to catch her breath, wondering if the resident night watchman might be bribed to find her a cab. The drizzle increased in intensity as the wind rose, tossing the shrubs in the central garden, but she could see the flicker of light from the lantern hanging outside his little shelter on the far side of the Square. Sophia pulled her cloak and hood more closely round her, shrinking into the warm wool as she began to walk briskly again towards the Charley's cabin, chastising herself for her silliness in finding herself out alone at this time of night.

The silence of the Square was broken by the sound of carriage wheels on the cobbles. Sophia stepped back and waited at the kerb in case the conveyance turned left across her path, but instead it stopped abruptly beside her and before she knew it a heavily muffled man had jumped down from the box, seized her and bundled her into the carriage. She could not even catch her breath to scream before the door slammed shut.

With a lurch that sent her tumbling on to the cushioned seat the carriage sprang forward and, turning sharply, sped off. Too surprised at first to be afraid, Sophia fumbled for the door handle, but on both sides the catches were locked fast. Nor could she see where they were headed, for the blinds were firmly drawn down and secured in some way. With her clenched fists she pounded on the panelling above the front seats until her gloves split, but although the noise must have been audible on the box, the coachman paid no heed to it, instead seeming to whip the horses up.

Now she was indeed becoming frightened. Sophia forced herself to sit down, hold on to one of the straps and collect her thoughts. She might be living in a sheltered environment, but she knew about the existence of houses of ill repute and the stories of how young women were entrapped into working in them. True, these tales usually concerned innocent country girls newly arrived in the capital, but perhaps such girls were also snatched from the streets—and, loitering alone on a dark street, she must have appeared an easy target.

Sophia wrenched off a shoe and began hammering on the window with it, shouting 'Help!' at the top of her voice. But the thick blinds protected the glass and the heavy upholstery muffled her cries. Defeated, she sat down again and pulled off her gloves, breaking a nail as she tried futilely to unpick whatever fastened the blind.

Gradually, despite the near darkness that enveloped her, a sense of the luxury in which she was trapped penetrated her panicked thoughts. She pulled off her hood, careless of the damage she was inflicting on her hat, but she could see virtually nothing. Her fingers kneaded the heavy silk of the upholstery; where she could feel wood it was polished to a fine lacquer, and underfoot was a thick, warm carpet. Hardly the sort of conveyance a brothel would employ, surely?

On reflection the thought was no comfort. A brothel keeper, confronted by a lady of quality would soon realise his mistake and the danger of detaining her and would speedily release her. But what if she had been kidnapped by some dissolute madman? She could be kept a prisoner and no one would know.

Fighting her panic, Sophia pulled on her shoe again and began to search her reticule for a weapon. The best she could find was a nail file. Determinedly she clutched it and tensed herself to react the moment the door was opened.

After what she judged was about three miles the sound of the road surface changed, potholes became more frequent and she realised they were out in the country. The pace quickened, then slowed as the carriage swung round a corner and on to a gravel drive. It came to a halt amid a crunching of stones and she took a deep breath, poised to spring.

The door opened slowly on a dark figure which began to climb in, blocking her escape. 'Now, miss…' the man began as Sophia launched herself at him, nail file raised to strike. She collided with a broad chest and found herself enveloped by a pair of ruthlessly strong arms. She was bundled unceremoniously back against the cushions with a force that knocked the breath from her lungs.

'Miss! Miss! Be still! Oh, I tell you, the master will be powerful angry with you if we keep him waiting. Now, come along and put that thing down. Don't make it any worse than it already is…'

Taken aback, Sophia was literally disarmed, the weapon falling unheeded from her fingers to the floor of the carriage. Who…? What…? Her thoughts raced. Who was 'the master', and why was this bear of a man convinced he was waiting for her?

'Come along, miss, you climb down and get on into the warm. Look where you're putting your feet now, it's a little slippery underfoot.' The man tucked her hand firmly under his arm and began to walk her towards the house, grumbling away in his deep voice as if she were a naughty child. 'Putting everyone to all this trouble, carrying on this way.'

Sophia stared up at him from under the brim of her hat, but he was so tall and intent on the path ahead, that he could not see her face. A more unlikely kidnapper she could not imagine: his tone was that of a trusted old retainer, used to being indulged when he chose to scold his employer.

Her head in a whirl she allowed herself to be helped up a short flight of steps. As they reached the top, the front door swung open to reveal the silhouette of a man standing there, arms crossed implacably. Dazzled, she could not make out his features, but the light from the hallway flooded across the porch, lighting up her face plainly.

'What the devil are you doing here?' a familiar voice demanded angrily, but she hardly heard the words, for he stepped forward as he spoke and she saw his face.

'Lord Wyatt!' Sophia gasped out. She felt dazed and breathless. What on earth was Hal Wyatt doing here—wherever they were?

'Miss Haydon!' Hal sounded as surprised as she did, but surely that must be a pretence in front of the servants. He was the master here: no one was going to kidnap young women off the street without his knowledge! With a frown he stood aside to allow the coachman to usher her inside.

Stumbling over the threshold into the warmth and light, the reality of the situation Sophia found herself in hit her like a blow. After all the warnings delivered by George and Lavinia, which she had disregarded

and scorned, it turned out that they had been right all
along. She had been ruined, that ruin was known—
and here was a man who, on discovering it, was prepared to treat her as a loose woman.

'Why am I here?' Sophia asked in a hoarse voice,
hoping against hope that she was wronging him. 'And
why,' she added angrily, as her fright and chagrin
were replaced by indignation at his presumptuous actions, 'have you abducted me, sir?'

'*What?* You had better come inside, Miss Haydon,
I have no wish to stand here in the draught exchanging
words with you for the edification of the servants.' He
must have read Sophia's apprehension on her face, for
he added, in a slightly softer tone, 'It is quite safe,
you know, my housekeeper will chaperon you.'

Sophia, still in a daze, stepped on to the black-and-
white hall tiles, blinking in the blaze of light from the
branches of candles on every surface. As she did so,
a small figure in black bustled down the stairs, scolding as she went. 'Bad, bad girl and foolish too. You
never listen to a sensible word that is said to you—
and see what happens as a result! I shudder to think
what might have become of you. You are fortunate
indeed to have such a resourceful and forgiving
brother.' The woman's tirade stopped abruptly and her
eyes widened in astonishment as she caught sight of
Sophia. 'But you are not Miss Elizabeth!'

Sophia's indignation was hardening into real anger.
If someone did not explain to her what was going on,
and do it *now,* she would stamp her foot!

'No, I am not Miss Elizabeth, whoever she may be!'
She drew herself to her full, unfashionable, five foot
six inches. 'I do not know who you are, ma'am, but
I am Miss Sophia Haydon—as this gentleman very

well knows.' She turned furious green eyes on Hal's taut features and demanded, 'I insist that you tell me what this is about, Lord Wyatt. Why have you seen fit to snatch me from the street, bundle me into a carriage and jolt me for miles without so much as a by-your-leave? Or are my suspicions of your ungentlemanly behaviour and dubious reputation correct?'

Anger, the remains of her fear, and a strange excitement at being in the presence of this man gave Sophia an attractive flush and added a sparkle to her furious eyes. Copper curls were escaping from her disarrayed bonnet, glinting redly in the candlelight and her bosom rose and fell with emotion within the tight bodice of her grey gown.

She thought, but she could not be sure, that there was a gleam of appreciation in Hal Wyatt's eyes, and his lips were certainly curving in that smile which had first attracted her to him. But these emotions only overlaid an expression of anger and concern which confused her still further.

'You are obviously labouring under a misapprehension. It would certainly appear that you are owed both an explanation and an apology, Miss Haydon. But you are chilled and naturally alarmed. Please come into the salon, there is a fire there and I will explain everything. Mrs Wood, fetch our guest some tea and cake.'

There seemed to be little choice but to accede to his suggestion and Sophia allowed herself to be settled in front of a briskly burning fire. She removed her bonnet, patting vaguely at her tumbled curls, and shrugged off her heavy cloak. The housekeeper bustled in, set down a tray and looked at her anxiously.

'Are you all right, miss? Is there anything else I can get you?'

'No, thank you, Mrs Wood.' Sophia ignored the tea tray and sat silently until Hal closed the door behind the housekeeper. She was no longer frightened—whatever Hal Wyatt's intentions, he could hardly intend rape or seduction with such an eminently respectable upper servant in attendance. But it was only now that the enormity of what had been done to her was dawning on her. She had been abducted, stolen from the streets of London, and now found herself, goodness knows where, in the power of a man.

Hal came and sat in the chair opposite her, his long legs stretched out. He steepled his fingers and gazed at her over them. His brow was furrowed and his lips were tight: once again she had the clear impression that her arrival on the scene was a complication to another story altogether, something which had been absorbing all his attention and concern until he was forced to deal with her. The realisation that she did not even have his full attention was the last straw.

'I had better be frank with you, Miss Haydon—'

'Frank!' she stormed at him, jumping to her feet. 'You have the effrontery to talk of frankness, sir? You are an abductor and a rake and a criminal and my brother will set the law on you!' She subsided into the chair again, her cheeks burning and her heart thumping and found, absurdly, that she was pouring herself a cup of tea with a shaking hand.

Hal held up a hand as though imploring her silence. 'Miss Haydon, I know you must have been very frightened, but what has happened is really the most outrageous coincidence…' Sophia put down her cup with a clatter and glared at him, but he persisted. 'You will probably feel you owe me nothing but reproaches after what has befallen you, but I beg your discretion for my sister's sake.'

'Your sister?'

'Elizabeth, my younger sister. I know I have no right to ask it, but I can only ask you to keep secret what I am about to tell you now.' His voice was grave and there was no laughter, nor anger either, in his eyes.

Suddenly what the housekeeper had said, how she had addressed her, made sense. Sophia guessed they were dealing with an elopement. She shivered slightly—this was too close for comfort. 'Please, rest assured, sir, whatever my feelings about this incident and what has befallen me, I would not dream of doing anything which might harm your sister.'

'Thank you.' Hal Wyatt broke off, obviously weighing what he could tell her, how much he could rely upon her. He seemed suddenly to come to a conclusion, his face changed and relaxed. 'Miss Haydon, I feel I can trust you, although you have no reason to show me any consideration or favour after this mischance. I am placing my sister's honour entirely in your hands. You were mistaken for Elizabeth. John, my coachman, knew where she would be and acted on my instructions in snatching her—you—from the street. But obviously, in the dark, he mistook you for her.

'I cannot blame him for his error. In the dark, one young lady in a cloak must look very like any other, and,' he added apologetically, 'you must admit it is unorthodox for a young woman of your class to be abroad at night on foot and unchaperoned.'

'Oh, forgive me, my lord,' Sophia remarked caustically, her anger resurfacing. 'Naturally I would not have set foot in Portman Square if I had realised it would interfere with your plans.' She broke off, seeing the look in his eyes. 'I am sorry, that was ungenerous of me—this incident has shaken me more than I realised. Please go on.'

Lord Wyatt ran his hands through his somewhat overlong dark hair and met her eyes with a rueful smile. 'I will speak plainly: the little minx fancies herself in love and, thanks to her maid confiding in another servant with more sense, I discovered that she is plotting to elope with the object of her desire. The young man, I need hardly tell you, could not be less suitable.'

Sophia's heart jolted. This tale could be her own history, for she too had made a fool of herself over an unsuitable man and had run away with him.

'My cousin Venetia Lovell suggested to me that instead of leaving her here in the country it would be better to bring her up to London where Mrs Lovell could take her to a few young person's parties—give her mind another direction, divert her from this unfortunate attachment. It seemed sensible: Elizabeth was certainly doing nothing but making wild plans out of sheer boredom. But Venetia has been called away to her sister's home. I had not realised just how serious this flirtation of Elizabeth's had become, and I am sure my cousin had not either.'

Hal must have misread Sophia's horrified expression as disapproval of his sister, for he flushed slightly as he continued. 'Her maid—who came to her senses, thank goodness, realising that this would ruin her mistress—sent me word that an elopement was planned for tonight. I thought a sharp scare and a dose of reality might make Elizabeth realise that this sort of thing is not romantic. I also hoped to scare off the young man. But, as you see, with John's mistake it has all gone terribly wrong.'

He held out his hand to hers, concern etched on his face. 'How can you forgive me for embroiling you in this? Of course, you must stay here with Mrs Wood while I go after Elizabeth, you will be quite safe. But first let me have your direction. If you write a note to your family, I will send a groom with it. They must be beside themselves with anxiety.'

Hal got up and fetched inkwell and paper, setting them beside her on a small table. Sophia looked up at him as he stood, head bent, mending the point of a quill for her with a small penknife. He handed it to her, but she made no move to take it, meeting his gaze with a steady regard. It was her turn to be frank. She took a deep breath and prepared to put her honour in his hands, just as he had trusted her with Elizabeth's.

Chapter Six

Sophia let her gaze drop, knowing what she was about to confess was shocking and she did not want to see Hal's expression change if he thought the worse of her for hearing it. 'Thank you, my lord, but I will not write to my family, there is no need. My situation is such that they have no idea I am not in my chamber.'

There was silence and she risked a glance, seeing that his eyebrows had shot up. He asked with incredulity, 'But how can that be? When your maid reached home without you, surely they would set up a hue and cry? Why, I would not be surprised if they have not called upon the Bow Street Runners.'

'My lord, I can assure you that will not be the case. No one knows I am not at home except for my maid, who is waiting to let me in.' Sophia got to her feet, smoothing down her dress, finding it suddenly difficult to meet Hal's eyes. 'But we are wasting time in needless conversation. We cannot delay while your sister is embarking on such an escapade: she will undoubtedly be ruined if you cannot stop her. Come, let us go! There is not a moment to be lost! I am feeling quite myself again, and Miss Elizabeth's parlous situation must be our only concern.'

But Hal was not to be persuaded, taking Sophia's hand and trying to urge her to resume her seat by the fire. 'No, Miss Haydon, you must stay here. My silly sister has at least brought this on herself; you, however, are an innocent passer-by. Please, let me send a message to your family before I go, for I cannot delay any longer!'

But Sophia was not deterred. 'My lord, you must take me with you!' She saw the stubborn look in his eyes and added cunningly, 'You can take me home, for I presume you will go first into town?'

'Yes, for I must see if any news of her has been found. But you cannot travel that distance with me in a closed carriage at night! Miss Haydon, think of it, it would be social ruin! I cannot risk compromising you further.'

'Oh, that is quite by the way, my lord,' Sophia assured him, taking a deep breath. If Hal Wyatt could trust her with his sister's reputation, then she could trust him with hers—or what remained of it. She raised her eyes to his and faced him squarely. 'You see, I am already ruined—in theory, you understand,' she added hastily, seeing his growing astonishment. 'I have no reputation to maintain. Whereas Miss Elizabeth still has everything to lose.'

Hal crossed the room and stood looking down into her face. After a long moment he took her hand in his. She made no move to free it: his grasp was warm and strong as he continued to look at her, apparently weighing up the evils of the situation. 'So be it. Come, then, if you are certain.'

In the hallway he called for a footman and shrugged

into the heavy coat the man brought. 'A lap rug for the lady, and tell John to bring round the carriage with fresh horses.'

'He has already done so, sir, presuming you would wish to return to town immediately.'

'Good. Come, Miss Haydon, if you are determined on this, let us not delay a minute longer.' Slamming the carriage door, he shouted, 'Drive on, John, to Bruton Street!' As the vehicle gathered speed he added, 'I cannot thank you enough for your understanding and your generosity in overlooking what has happened to you. I would not have had this happen for the world, Miss Haydon.' It was so dark in the carriage she could not see his expression, but his voice was warm.

'Can you not open those blinds, my lord?' Sophia's heart was thudding in her chest so hard she could scarcely speak. Now she was alone with him her composure was deserting her. That night her world had turned upside down: one moment in Mrs Ashdowne's drawing room, now scandalously closeted with the man who was beginning to fill her thoughts to the exclusion of everything else.

Hal touched a catch and the blinds flew up, flooding the carriage with moonlight. The rain clouds, chased by the stiffening wind, had quite dispersed, leaving the night cold but clear. 'Is that better? Now, I am sorry to press you, but I must have your exact direction if I am to return you home.'

'The house is at the eastern end of Bruton Street, but we must go around to the mews so that I can enter through the back gate. But, please, cannot we go first to your house? I will not be able to sleep if I do not find out what has happened to your sister—perhaps she has thought better of her foolishness and returned home.'

'Very well.' He dropped the window and leaned out, shouting instructions to the coachman on the box to go first to Portman Square. When he sat down again he remarked, 'I suppose twenty minutes is hardly going to make any difference to your reputation if you truly have been ruined, will it?'

Sophia felt that she was beginning to read Hal's mood more clearly: now they were moving he seemed to relax a little and the spark of humour was back in his voice. His teeth shone fleetingly white in the semi-darkness. 'I really feel you are going to have to explain exactly how one can be ruined ''in theory'', Miss Haydon.'

Encouraged by the fact that he seemed neither shocked nor prurient, but simply intrigued, Sophia took a deep breath and began the tale that in four years she had told to no one outside the family. It was surprisingly easy to tell him in the shadows where he could not see her expression or the blush rising to her cheeks. It had always seemed such a shocking thing to have happened, but now, as she spoke, she found she was more embarrassed at her own youthful foolishness than at the impropriety of it all.

'I was seventeen and I fell head over heels in love—well, I believed I had—with a young man, a neighbour of ours. My brother, who is—oh dear, how best can I describe George to you so you will understand…?'

'A pompous ass who is more concerned with his own comfort and respectability than with your happiness, if I am any judge,' Hal supplied, grinning again. 'I have met your brother, you see.'

'Yes, that is exactly right, poor George. I am sure he means well but he has very little imagination, and he does so hate having to exert himself with anything unpleasant.' Before Lord Wyatt could reply to that, Sophia added impetuously, 'Unlike you, my lord, George has never aspired to be a rake, or even the slightest bit unconventional or dashing, so it must have been very difficult to apply his imagination to my feelings. It seems to me that only a rake could think up such a shocking, but practical, solution to his sister's impending ruin as to kidnap her.'

Moonlight was flickering through the trees and she thought Hal's eyes twinkled. 'My maiden aunts certainly tell me that I am a rake, and I have always admitted to being one when charged with it, but I was not aware it made one particularly inventive! But we were talking about you, Miss Haydon, pray do not change the subject. I am waiting to hear how you came to be ruined.'

Hal leaned back against the silk squabs of the carriage and folded his arms, his enjoyment in his companion and her tale evident even in the gloom. 'Well, Miss Haydon? Do not seek to deflect me, I am waiting for you to continue your intriguing tale of scandal and high romance.'

Sophia took a deep breath, emboldened to confide in him by the semi-darkness and the strange feeling of trust and intimacy he inspired in her. His teasing air diminished neither feeling; in fact, as this strange journey continued, she was beginning to feel as though she had known Hal Wyatt all her life.

'Well, you see, my brother George did not approve of Henry—that was the name of the young man I believed I was in love with—and forbade me his company. George would not even receive him, never mind hear his proposal of marriage. So, of course, being so much in love, Henry and I resolved to run away together to Gretna Green and be married.' She bit her underlip as she paused, then added with disarming honesty, 'Well, I thought I was in love, but I have wondered since if Henry was not motivated by my fortune. It is quite considerable, although I know I should not say so.'

She met Hal's amused eyes and laughed despite herself. 'Oh dear, it proved to be such a fiasco and not at all like the books of romance one reads! In fact, I believe that girls should be prevented from reading such tales, for they give a very false impression of reality. Or perhaps it was simply that Henry was a bad choice. You know, my lord, I have since come to the conclusion that if one is to elope it should only be with a man of decision and resource—and one with a sense of humour.' Like you, she thought wistfully, but did not voice the thought aloud.

'Am I to deduce that the unfortunate Henry had none of these desirable attributes?' Hal enquired with mock seriousness. He crossed his legs and settled back more comfortably in the corner of the carriage.

'No, not a single one.' Sophia sighed regretfully at the memory of her disastrous suitor. 'And it transpired that he could afford only a coach and two—and of course we were making for the Scottish border. It would have taken *days*.'

'How very ill judged of him,' Hal remarked dryly. 'Quite the last place to choose if eloping on a strict budget. Personally, I never embark on elopements which take me more than ten miles out of town. Leaving aside the question of cost, the nervous strain upon the lady is considerable, rendering the entire enterprise far too fatiguing.'

Sophia flashed him a dubious glance, then realised he was teasing her again and suppressed a giggle. 'Well, by the time the first pair of horses—which were poor beasts to begin with—were tired and we reached a posting house, Henry had discovered that he had left his roll of banknotes behind and had only enough money for one more change of horses. So we decided that the best plan was to stay the night at that inn and for him to return to town the next morning to secure additional funds for us to continue our journey.'

As she paused for breath, Hal thought darkly that the true story probably was that the roll of notes had never existed and the young man had intended all along to compromise Sophia as quickly as possible so that her brother's hand would be forced.

'But the landlord became suspicious that we were runaways,' Sophia continued, 'and he was very insolent, placing us in the smokiest little chamber you could imagine. That was when I discovered that Henry was capable neither of mastering the situation nor of seeing its ridiculous side and making the best of it. My eyes were quite opened—it was a salutary experience,' she added solemnly.

Lord Wyatt's shoulders shook, but he controlled the laughter in his voice enough to ask, 'It must have been. And then I suppose the young fool decided that that was the ideal moment to make love to you?'

'How did you guess?' Really, Lord Wyatt was showing almost supernatural powers of understanding. 'Naturally I had expected to occupy a separate bedchamber until we were married, so I was very shocked when he became so…er…amorous. But Henry said we could not afford two rooms, and that my scruples were too nice. He pointed out that I was already ruined, and that I might as well be hanged for a sheep as a lamb.' Suddenly shy, Sophia looked out of the window, unable to meet Hal's eyes. 'Henry became very pressing.'

After a moment she rallied and added with a small smile, 'Can you imagine an atmosphere less conducive to romance? Surely, my lord, not even the most hardened rake would attempt to seduce a young lady who was cold, tired and not a little apprehensive, in a smoky chamber with an ill-aired bed, and before she had had any supper?'

'I can assure you, Miss Haydon, the more hardened the rake, the less likely he is to expose a young lady to discomfort. It is hardly the way to a lady's affections nor, I imagine, to a successful seduction. But pray continue, what did you do?'

'Why, boxed his ears, of course! What else could I do? Even if I were still in love with him I would not behave in such an abandoned manner as to yield to his advances.' Sophia sat up, quivering with remembered indignation, her green eyes sparking fire. 'You should have heard him howl and rant! I do believe by then he was ready to box my ears in return, for nothing was turning out as he expected. And, of course, everybody in the place heard him and came running.

'When George arrived the whole place was in turmoil. Oh, my brother tried to cover it up, but his manner made everyone even more suspicious and then old Lady Westmoreland stopped in her travelling carriage to change horses and George was convinced she had seen us. After that, of course, I was quite ruined. George sent me off into the country in disgrace, and there I stayed until six months ago when Lavinia decided I could make myself useful to her. I rarely go out; George insists that I attend only the most respectable, quiet gatherings with the family. He says if I attempt to go into Society my Disgrace will be remembered and I will bring dishonour upon the family name and ruin my nieces' chances.'

'The man's a fool,' Hal said contemptuously. 'All he has done is to shut you away needlessly. And as a rake…' his voice softened '…I should know that young ladies as beautiful and intelligent as you are in short enough supply in Society as it is.'

'But the scandal, my lord!' Sophia tried to ignore the warm glow his words had given her.

'What scandal?' Hal shrugged his shoulders dismissively. 'There was none and there is none. Lady Westmoreland is an eccentric old trout, to put it mildly, and cares for nothing but her food and her smelly lap dogs. She would not notice if your seducer was making love to you on the steps of her carriage, and would care even less. I have to tell you, Miss Haydon, reluctant though I am to criticise your brother, that he has handled this very badly. The man's a fool.'

Sophia knew she should protest at the insult to George, but instead she found herself agreeing with her companion. 'Oh, I know he is.' She looked at Hal levelly. 'I think Miss Elizabeth is fortunate to have a brother who is a rake, it makes you far more understanding about…things.'

Hal grimaced. 'She may not find me very understanding when I catch up with her, the little minx. I have spoiled her, I know, but she is such an innocent under all her high spirits and mischief.' The amusement was gone from his voice and his face looked bleak. 'I just hope she has not done something irretrievable and finds herself tied to a man who has neither prospects nor character.' He glanced out of the window. 'We are nearly at Portman Square. But before we arrive, there is one thing I must know.' Sophia's heart gave a strange little jolt, then subsided as he added, 'What happened to Henry? Surely Sir George did not call him out?'

'My brother? Duelling? Certainly not, he considers it barbaric and irrational. No, Henry made good his escape while George was blustering at the landlord; the last thing I heard of him, he had become a curate in Wales.'

Hal could no longer contain his laughter and let out a shout of amusement. 'What an escape for both of you! Can you imagine yourself as a curate's wife? And what a waste.' The flambeaux outside each town house they passed and the glow of street lighting was enough to show her his eyes, warm and appreciative on her face.

There was a long silence while Sophia fought with her blushes and her beating heart. If she had foolishly thought she had fallen in love with Hal at first sight, now she was discovering how much she liked him too. His humour, his ready sympathy, the interest he took in her shocking tale all attracted her and made her feel she had known him for years. But, of course, it was probably an illusion and he was only flirting with her. That was what rakes did, no doubt. It was a good thing that she was learning to get her foolish fancies under control; she had been right in believing that her sheltered life caused her to refine too much on his easy manner.

'Now,' Hal was saying briskly, 'you must let me take you home.'

'No.' Sophia leaned over and boldly took his hand in both hers. 'Please, my lord, let me be of use to your sister! When we find her I can pretend I have been with her the whole time. It may seem odd as we are not known to be friends, but, if I am seen to return to London with her, no one will be able to say she was alone and unchaperoned. And if she is unwilling to break the connection with the young man I can tell her of my history, which may persuade her of her foolishness. Please, will you not trust me in this?' she implored, seeing the doubt on his face. 'Besides,' she added prosaically, 'I can hardly be in any worse of a scrape than I am now—it must be past midnight.'

'That is a brave and generous offer and I cannot pretend I would not be glad of your company, but I cannot ask such a thing—' He broke off as the carriage slowed. 'Here we are, turning into Portman Square now.' He pulled down the blinds to shield her in case anyone passed by, and climbed out. 'Please wait here and I will see if there is any news.'

Hal returned minutes later, a look of grim amusement on his face, a crumpled note in his hand. 'She has left a note—really, in some things my little sister is very conventional. They are on their way to Gretna Green: I do believe she thinks they can get there within the space of a few hours.'

'How long will it take you to overtake them my lord?' Sophia enquired anxiously, leaning from the carriage window.

'With these horses? By the early hours of the morning I would hope.'

'Very well, then, what are we waiting for?'

'Nothing whatsoever, I will be away as soon as I have dropped you at the Bruton Street mews.' He opened the door and jumped in. 'Bruton Mews, John.'

'No, my lord, this is not sensible! We are wasting time: if you find her tonight, and you have another lady with you to chaperon her, then we can bring her off safe. But to waste precious minutes by taking me back home is such a risk! Let me scribble a note to my maid to let her know what I am about and not to expect me until the morning.'

Sophia held her breath while Hal swiftly weighed up the possibilities. Then she breathed out in relief as he ran back up the steps to return in a few moments with pen and paper. He took her hasty note, folded it and called down a footman to listen to her careful instructions.

'The mews entrance,' she emphasised. 'The kitchen door will be on the latch and Fanny will be waiting. Take care not to wake anyone.'

Hal did not wait for the footman to cram on his hat and hurry off before climbing back into the carriage. 'John, change of plan, head for the St Albans road!'

The team surged forward at the urging of the coachman, who understood only too well the urgency of finding his young mistress. It seemed only seconds before the carriage swung out into the Edgware Road and headed north.

Chapter Seven

Silence fell inside the carriage as it bowled up the highway. Soon they were in the dark of open countryside, the only illumination a fitful moon and the occasional light from a farm or hamlet. Hal said nothing, his face turned towards the window, but Sophia sensed that he was not seeing the darkened countryside, but was looking inwards, thinking of his sister, planning and reviewing their course of action.

Sophia shifted on her seat and his head turned towards her. 'Are you warm enough? Here, take this lap robe.' Sophia thankfully tucked it around her knees, suddenly realising how chilly she had become, partly because of the damp weather, but also in sheer reaction to the night's events. 'Go to sleep,' Hal suggested and she could hear the smile in his voice.

Against all the odds she found herself dozing, her half-dreams full of a strange and disturbing mixture of this adventure, her own unhappy elopement and the discussion at the Literary Circle. Who would have thought that, when she had set off for a respectable, if illicit, visit to a ladies' reading group, she would find herself alone with a man in a speeding carriage…?

Her dream had reached the point where Mrs Ashdowne was recommending a fascinating new book of poetry to Hal Wyatt, but he was complaining that he could not read it because the air in the inn room was too smoky and, besides, the eloping couple in the next room were arguing too loudly for him to concentrate, when the carriage slowed and turned sharply.

'The Pea Hen, my lord,' John's voice announced from the box.

'Wait in the carriage,' Hal ordered as she woke with a start and rubbed her eyes. 'I doubt if they have stopped here, it is the most expensive inn in St Albans, and besides, the landlord might recognise Elizabeth—but I must check them all.'

He was back within a minute, calling, 'Try the Lamb and Flag next, John.' They drew a blank there again, but at the third inn, the White Hart, they struck lucky.

'Whip them up, John,' Hal called, as he leapt back into the carriage. He subsided against the squabs and in the light from the inn yard Sophia could see his face clearly. The relief was obvious as he said, 'Thank God, they were here. We are an hour behind them and he has only a pair harnessed up. We should overtake them shortly after Dunstable.'

Sophia clutched the strap tightly as John took his master at his word and whipped up the team. 'They seem good horses, my lord,' she ventured.

'The best, I won them off Lord Falmouth at piquet last year and he hasn't forgiven me yet! I don't like to push them like this, but needs must and they will take us as far as Redbourn without coming to harm. I can get a reliable change at the White Horse there.'

They made the change as planned, and even had the encouragement of the sleepy ostler remarking that a light carriage with a rather inferior pair had passed through less than an hour before without stopping. Dunstable was reached without incident and at the first inn they discovered that the fugitives had stopped to snatch a bite to eat and rest their horses and were now only twenty minutes ahead.

'We will have them before Fenny Stratford,' Hal said grimly, his eyes once more fixed out of the window.

Sophia felt a thrill of fear trickle down her spine. Hal Wyatt was not a man to be trifled with: he was large, fit, furiously angry—although he did his best to hide it from her—and deeply concerned for his sister. What would he do when he got his hands on her would-be seducer?

'What are you going to do with the young man when you catch up with them?' she asked apprehensively. The words dropped into the silence and it was some seconds before he answered.

'Horse whipping is tempting, if somewhat melodramatic. Beyond that, and a strong desire to beat the living daylights out of him, I had not thought.'

Sophia's heart beat uncomfortably in her chest. 'You will not call him out, then?' Besides being dangerous, duelling was illegal and she had no wish to see Hal Wyatt having to flee to the Continent to escape justice. Even without seeing the young man concerned she had no doubt that, whatever the weapon, Hal would not be the loser.

'Rest assured, Miss Haydon, I have no wish to compound the scandal by killing, or even wounding, the young fool.' The carriage swayed wildly and he gripped the strap tightly. 'This road leaves something to be desired.'

'Who is he? He is well known to you?' Sophia pressed, too intrigued to be alarmed by the speed at which they were now travelling.

'Oh, yes, I know who he is all right. Justin Fanshaw, the younger son of a neighbour of ours in the country. His father cut him off after his gambling debts became too much for even a doting parent to tolerate. He started his career by being sent down from Oxford for associating with loose women, fell into the hands of card sharps and now badly needs something to restore his fortunes. I have tried to explain this to Elizabeth, but she will not listen.'

'But how could Miss Elizabeth be taken in by such a man?'

'He is quite the most good-looking young man you will ever set eyes on, a veritable Adonis. He has golden curls, a fine figure and considerable charm. She sees him as romantically persecuted by his father for mere youthful indiscretions. Miss Haydon…'

'Please,' Sophia said impulsively, 'will you not call me Sophia? After all, we are in the middle of a quite extraordinary adventure together—it seems strange to be so very formal.'

She thought Hal's stern expression softened. 'Sophia…' he said, as if trying out the name on his tongue. 'Such a very *stately* name for one with your vivacity. Does no one call you Sophy?'

'No, they never have but, do you know, I rather like it.' At least, she rather liked it on Hal's lips.

'Then I will call you—' But he never finished the

sentence. The carriage gave a wild lurch, she heard John the coachman shouting at the horses and then with a grinding crash the whole vehicle toppled on to its side.

Sophia was aware of tumbling through the air, of Hal's hands reaching for her, a searing pain in her head and then darkness swallowed her.

She was swimming in the old mill pond behind the Home Farm at Bright's Hill. The water was very black, very deep—deeper and blacker than she remembered, and no matter how hard she tried, she could not get back to the surface. She was struggling, kicking her legs hard, pushing upwards with her shoulders, but the surface above remained unattainable, unbroken. Fanny had told her so many times not to swim there, that she would surely drown, sucked down to the muddy depths…

Someone was calling her…but not calling her proper name… 'Sophy? Sophy! Wake up, can you hear me?'

Somebody wanted her, she must try and reach the surface again, but it was so dark and the cold was numbing her limbs. The voice began again, calling her. It was a nice voice, deep and strong, but still she wished it would stop: it wanted her to keep trying and she was far too tired. It was easier just to drown. It all went black again…

She must be out of the water, for somebody had raised her shoulders gently, supporting her, and someone's fingers were stroking gently, probing the mass of tumbled hair. 'Sophy, Sophy, wake up!' She thought she heard the voice add, 'Hell, she has a lump the size of a duck's egg on the back of her head,

John!' Then the probing fingers touched something that sent a wave of pain coursing from her scalp to her toes and the water closed over her head again.

It was the sunlight streaming through the casement that finally woke her. It hurt: jagged needles of pain forced her eyes closed again, but still the lights danced on the inside of her lids. Sophia lay still, a feeling of panic growing inside her that she fought hard to quell. This was not her chamber, not her bed. Try and remember! she told herself, try!

With another lurch of panic she recalled strong hands snatching her from the pavement in Portman Square and bundling her into a locked carriage. She had been kidnapped and this must be where she had been taken! Cautiously she opened her eyes again, keeping them narrowed into slits against the light. This time she saw that she was lying in a bed covered with a homely patchwork quilt. The sheets were rough but very clean and the uneven walls of the room were freshly whitewashed. A door at the foot of the bed stood ajar. If this was the haunt of some abductor, it was a very strange one.

A breeze puffed out the curtains at the window and Sophia realised she was not alone. In the window seat that filled the embrasure Hal Wyatt was sitting, fast asleep. He had propped his back against one wall, one foot was on the seat, wedged against the opposite wall and one had slipped off. His booted foot rested on the floor. Of course! The memory flooded back of their pursuit of Elizabeth Wyatt and the awful moment when the coach had tipped.

Gingerly Sophia pulled herself up against the bolster and looked at Hal. He had discarded his jacket and she was sure the shirt he was wearing was not his own for the fabric was homespun and stretched taut over his shoulders and biceps. His breeches were mud-stained, although someone had made a not very successful attempt to brush them.

His head had fallen forward on to his chest and she saw with alarm that a bruise marked the side of his face from eyebrow to jaw, with a trickle of dried blood at the temple. Forgetting how much her head hurt, Sophia pushed back the bedclothes and swung her feet out on to the rag rug by the bed. The nightdress she was wearing belonged to a much larger woman, for it pooled at her feet and she had to gather up the fullness as she tiptoed across the boards, wincing as the movement jarred her bruised body.

Cautiously she stopped a pace away from the sleeping man. Even in his dishevelled state he made her heart beat faster and her mouth feel dry. She scanned swiftly up and down his sleeping form, then breathed out a sigh of relief: there was no sign of bandages or other damage beside the purpling bruise on his face. Impetuously Sophia reached out, to brush the heavy lock of hair that had fallen across his eyes, tangling with the long lashes. Hal muttered something in his sleep and she snatched back her hand, but the sharpness of the movement unbalanced her and sent the pain lancing through her temples.

The room pitched and swayed and, unable to stop herself, she fell forwards. The next thing she was aware of was being held very firmly in Hal's arms. 'Good God,' he said huskily, 'I must still be dreaming. Oh, to hell with it,' and kissed her, hard, full on the mouth.

Sophia gave a little muffled squeak of surprise, then

kissed him back with more enthusiasm than skill. No man had ever kissed her like this before. Henry had tried, but she had always ducked away, tolerating only a peck on the cheek. But this was the real thing, and it was *wonderful!*

Hal's lips were hard yet gentle and she wondered at how that could be. Stubble from his unshaven chin grazed her skin, but that was strangely pleasurable too. And he was so warm. Sophia snuggled closer into his body, feeling his warmth through his shirt and her thin nightgown. She opened her eyes cautiously, but his were closed and his face intent. She felt her mouth yielding, opening under the pressure of his, which was very exciting until the tip of his tongue met hers. The *frisson* of pleasure was quite shocking and she recoiled with a little murmur of alarm.

The next thing she was aware of was Hal's horrified blue eyes staring into hers. 'Sophy! Oh, my God, I am sorry! I had no idea…I thought I was dreaming.' He released her abruptly, then caught her again as she swayed on his knee. 'What happened? What are you doing out of bed?'

'I got up…and I lost my balance and fell over…I am sorry, I did not mean…' But she could not say what she meant and cast her eyes down to where her bare toes just peeped from the hem of the borrowed nightgown. Still clasped in his arms she was aware of the blush that seemed to start at her toenails and reach to the crown of her aching head.

Hal got to his feet with an inarticulate oath, sweeping her up easily as he did so and deposited her back in the bed in one stride. Sophia found the covers pulled up to her chin and tucked in tight before she could breathe. Well, he could not have made it plainer if he had written it in letters two feet high! He had half-woken from a dream to find his arms full of a woman and had reacted instinctively as any man—or at least, as any rake—would. But as soon as he realised who he was kissing he could not wait to tuck her up safely in bed again like a small child!

It was humiliating, and made even worse by the fact it was entirely her own fault. Hal looked furious as he stalked towards the open door, his fingers raking angrily through his unruly black hair. Pulling the door wide he roared, 'Mrs Warren! Come up here, please!'

Sophia winced as the pain shot through her temples with the volume. 'There is no need to shout,' she protested as he began to pace irritably up and down the small room.

'I'm sorry. Is your head very bad?' He stopped at the foot of the bed and looked at her with concern on his face, but made no effort to come any closer.

Sophia was exploring the back of her head with tentative fingers. 'Ouch! Well, it hurts no more than yours would if you had a bump this size on it and someone was shouting!'

'Yes, I know it's a large lump, I felt it when you were knocked out.'

Any more explanation was cut short by the arrival of a plump, harassed woman, wiping her hands on her apron. 'Yes, my lord? Oh, you're awake, miss, how about a nice cup of tea?'

'Thank you, Mrs Warren,' Hal said swiftly before Sophia could reply for herself. 'I am sure my sister would find that very acceptable, would you not, my dear?'

'Er...yes, lovely,' Sophia replied feebly. Yes, of course, he was quite right to remind her of the impropriety of all this and to offer her the veil of respectability by pretending she was his sister.

As soon as the inn keeper's wife was out of the door Sophia demanded, 'Where are we? What has happened to Elizabeth?'

Hal settled himself once more in the window seat, unconsciously tracing the bruise on his cheek with one finger. 'We are in an ale house just outside the village of Hockcliffe. The carriage is in a ditch, unless John has managed to get it towed out by now—and I have no idea where Elizabeth is.' His face was bleak and Sophia wanted nothing more than to hold him in her arms and offer him the reassurance she knew she could not give. They had been so close to rescuing the runaway: now it seemed as if nothing could stop Elizabeth's elopement and the certain ruination of her life.

'How long have I…have we been here?'

'About seven, eight hours. Long enough to ensure they will get away.' He raised angry eyes to hers. 'He will have to marry her, but that is not irrevocable.'

'Divorce?' Sophia's eyes widened at the thought of such a scandalous option. 'But, surely, that takes an Act of Parliament?'

'Divorce?' He laughed shortly. 'Divorce was not what I had in mind.'

Sophia swallowed hard. She did not doubt that Hal would kill Justin Fanshaw now, if—when—he got his hands on him. She could not let that happen. 'But you are still not too late—go after them at once!'

'The carriage is wrecked.'

'You do not need a carriage—you will travel faster on horseback.'

Hal started to reply, but was interrupted by the reappearance of Mrs Warren with the tea tray and the news that the doctor to see Miss Wyatt was expected at any minute.

As soon as the woman had departed and the door was safely closed again, Sophia pressed, 'Well, surely there is a horse to be hired? You must go, you are losing precious time. I can guess how Elizabeth is feeling—frightened, worried and horribly sure she has done the wrong thing. She needs you!'

Hal looked at the figure in the bed, the chalk-white face and pleading eyes. 'You need me,' he said flatly.

'But I asked to come, it is not your responsibility... *I* am not your responsibility!'

Hal thrust out his booted legs and pushed his hands into his breeches' pockets. 'Of course you are my responsibility. I was damn fool to bring you, and now I have to look after you.'

Sophia took a gulp of cooling tea. It did not do much to improve the way she felt. This was all going horribly wrong. She tried again. 'Mrs Warren seems a respectable woman, I am sure this is a perfectly safe place to leave me. When I am feeling better I can hire a maid from the village and a carriage to take us to London.'

'And your brother?'

'George?' It was the first time she had given George a thought since this mad adventure began. 'What can he do? Send me back to Bright's Hill in disgrace again? I can assure you, that would be a great improvement on my life in London.'

Hal looked at her and realised that she had simply not comprehended the true situation she was in. How was he going to tell her? Now was not the time, especially with the bustle downstairs that heralded the arrival of the doctor.

Dr Leys appeared, ushered in with much ceremony by Mrs Warren. 'Now then, young lady, what is all this I hear about a carriage accident?' he asked kindly, peering at her over the top of his eyeglasses. 'Come, my lord, out you go while I talk to your sister. Get some fresh air and I'll clean up that cut on your temple before I go. Mrs Warren, please remain...'

Half an hour later Dr Leys called Hal back upstairs. 'Well, your sister is a lucky young woman, my lord. The bump on her head is large, but she has no fracture, and no sign of a brain fever. Another day in bed, quiet, some fortifying broth—go and kill a chicken, Mrs Warren, and start boiling it—and she will be as right as rain. Now, my lord, downstairs to the parlour and I will take a look at you. Good day to you, Miss Wyatt, and remember what I told you.'

'Yes, doctor. Thank you.' It was a relief to lie back and not to have to remember who she was supposed to be. Sophia dozed, soothed by a cordial Dr Leys had given her for the headache until she was woken by the sound of carriage wheels in the yard below. Crossing to the window, she saw John leading a pair of farm horses harnessed to their carriage. Other than some scars on the woodwork, it seemed intact.

Hal came out to talk to the coachman and Sophia pushed open the window, leaned out over the sill and prepared to eavesdrop shamelessly.

'The blacksmith's done a good job, my lord, that axle's as good as new and I've checked over all the traces and couplings. The horses, though, are no use to us, they're both lame. I'll have to go into Dunstable and hire a new team, then come back and pick you and the young lady up, my lord.'

Hal shook his head. 'Yes, you will need to do that, but not today. We can go nowhere while Miss Haydon…' he glanced around to make sure they were not overheard '…is confined to bed.'

Sophia stiffened. Stubborn man, he had not listened to a word she had said! Well, she was not going to live with Elizabeth Wyatt's fate on her conscience for the sake of an aching head. Moving carefully, she lifted her clothes off the chair and began to dress. She had to rest once or twice while putting her stockings on, but at last she was ready to tackle the stairs. She held tightly to the banister rail but got down safely and found Hal sitting brooding in the parlour, a pile of notepaper, a quill and standish and a flagon of ale on the table in front of him.

'What the…!' He leapt to his feet as Sophia appeared.

'We are going after Elizabeth,' she said more firmly than she felt. 'We have wasted enough time already.'

'But the carriage is not ready.'

'Hal, I was listening at the window and I know all we need is for John to go for the horses. If he goes now, we can have dinner and set out when he returns.'

'No, it is out of the question. And you are going back to bed, if I have to throw you over my shoulder and take you there.' He advanced towards her purposefully as if ready to carry out the threat.

'If you do, Hal,' Sophia said, her jaw defiantly set, 'I shall scream and when Mrs Warren arrives I shall tell her that I am not your sister and that you have abducted me and are a wicked seducer and she should send for the constable immediately!'

Her legs suddenly unsteady, Sophia flopped down on the settle and looked at him as if daring him to challenge her.

A short silence followed, then surprisingly Hal grinned. 'You know, Sophy, I am becoming increasingly resigned to my fate.'

Suspiciously she asked, 'What do you mean?'

Hal grinned again and shook his head. 'Never mind.' He turned to the door. 'John! Mrs Warren!'

Chapter Eight

Hal insisted that Sophia write a letter to her brother before they set out, which she did, but only after a spirited argument which he won by pointing out that it was unfair to leave Fanny to break the news. This had not occurred to her, so after much chewing of the end of the quill, Sophia produced a brisk note, informing her brother that in order to accompany her new friend Miss Wyatt on a trip to relatives in the north she had deceived poor Fanny. She blithely informed him that he need not worry about her and she would no doubt write again at a later date.

Once he was satisfied that at least they would not have the Bow Street Runners on their trail, Hall handed Sophia carefully into the carriage and settled the rug around her knees before taking his own place opposite her. The team that John had brought from Dunstable was fresh and he was having trouble holding them steady. The carriage wheels rolled back and forth on the uneven cobbles of Mrs Warren's yard as they backed and fidgeted in the traces.

'Whoa!' the coachman shouted, then, 'Shall I let them go, my lord?'

Sophia, who had not felt nervous until that moment, felt a little thrill of fear as she remembered the accident and unknowingly both her face and her fingers betrayed her apprehension.

'Yes, John, give them their heads,' Hal called, but his attention was not solely on the coachman. He could see the tension in Sophia's features, saw how she clutched the edge of the rug as if for comfort. God, he was a fool! Why had he lost his head like that and kissed her? He remembered again the softness of her lips, her evident innocence and trust in his arms. Despite her bold statements, Sophy was no ruined woman—not that he needed to kiss her to confirm that.

'Sophy, there is no need to be afraid,' he began, realising he needed to reassure her that he was not going to take advantage of their situation and make love to her again.

'I cannot help it, I just keep remembering. It was awful.' She could not conceal the shiver that convulsed her suddenly.

Hal was both taken aback and piqued. She had not seemed *that* repulsed when she was in his embrace! In fact, he seemed to recollect, with some pleasure, that she had responded with enthusiasm to his kisses. 'Oh? It did not seem so bad to me at the time,' he replied. 'In fact, I quite enjoyed it.'

Sophy regarded him as though he had lost his wits. '*Enjoyed it?* Have you lost your memory? It was I who had the bump on the head, was it not? How could I be expected to enjoy being thrown head over heels into a muddy ditch and knocked out cold?'

Hal laughed out loud. 'Ah, we are at cross-purposes. All you are worried about, then, is the fear of another accident?'

Sophia was still looking at him as though he had lost his wits. 'Of course! What else would I be worried about?' Her green eyes were puzzled and innocent as she asked the question.

Hal decided that there was no point in beating about the bush. He took off his hat, tossed it onto the seat beside him and ran his long fingers through his hair. It was a gesture Sophia was beginning to associate with his need to concentrate his thoughts.

'Well, to be frank, I thought you might be concerned about being alone with me in a closed carriage after what happened this morning.'

'Oh, no, Hal!' she exclaimed without thinking. 'How could you believe I would not trust you? Why, I trust you more than any man I know—with my life if necessary,' she added, becoming melodramatic in her need to convince him.

'You have certainly trusted me with your honour,' he responded dryly, his eyes on her pretty, intent, face. She suddenly looked much younger than the twenty-one years he knew her to be.

'I have not got any honour to lose,' she said firmly. 'I keep trying to explain to you.'

Hal leaned over and took both her hands in his. They were warm and soft and fitted comfortably inside his curled fingers. He restrained himself with an effort from stroking the tender flesh swelling at the base of her thumb. She really had no idea just how alluring she was…

'Sophy, I despair of getting this through to you! You are *not* ruined, merely in disgrace with your family for a silly escapade some years ago. If your brother had had even half his wits about him, it would all have been smoothed over without anyone being any the wiser. When I kissed you, it was quite evident that you are a vi—' Hastily he stopped himself and chose his words with more care. 'I mean, it was obvious to me that you are inexperienced in the ways of love.'

'Oh,' she said flatly, her face falling. Damn, Hal thought, I have really shocked her now. 'Oh,' she repeated, 'was the kiss so unpleasant? I suppose, now I think about it, it must be the sort of thing which needs practice.'

Hal released her hands and sat back abruptly against the squabs. He shut his eyes and thought determinedly about suppers at Almack's, the tedium of his estate accounts, of shooting pigeons on a cold wet autumn day—anything unerotic he could call to mind. This mixture of innocence, intelligence and piquant beauty was testing his resolve to the limit.

A short silence ensued. Sophia wondered if she had overstepped the mark with this man. The trouble was, not only was she very attracted to him, but she felt he was a friend, someone to whom she could say whatever came into her head. 'I am sorry, Hal, perhaps I should not have spoken so frankly.'

Hal opened his blue eyes and regarded her with a twinkle. 'You may say whatever you like to me, Sophy, you are hardly likely to shock me. But just remember, it is not a good idea to wake up sleeping gentlemen quite so abruptly and in that style.'

Sophia blushed and dropped her eyes. Hal noticed how her lashes fanned her cheekbones and thought what a pleasure it would be to make those eyes close in ecstasy. 'So you only kissed me because you were three-quarters asleep?' she asked, disappointment tingeing her tone.

Hal sat upright in, had Sophy known it, a very passable imitation of his late father in magisterial mood. 'Of course, Sophy! Surely you did not think I would presume to make advances to you?'

'I thought rakes always did that sort of thing. I thought that is what made them rakes in the first place.'

'And as I told you, I am a reformed rake.' He cast round for something to change the subject. 'Ah, look, a fingerpost. Two miles to Fenny Stratford, if I read it aright.'

Sophia watched the first straggle of cottages come into sight. It was reassuring, of course, to know that Hal was so reliable, but inside her she felt a little pang of disappointment, which she was careful not to examine more deeply. They passed a pompous looking red-faced man driving a dog cart and she was suddenly, forcibly, reminded of George. How could she have forgotten him again!

She gave a small snort of laughter, attracting Hal's attention. 'What is wrong?'

'George! I keep forgetting all about him and what must be happening at home,' she explained. 'I wonder if they will have received the note yet! Even George and Lavinia will have noticed I am not in my room by now—why, it must be quite three o'clock!'

'I would have thought they would have noticed from about breakfast time,' Hal said.

'Not necessarily. Fanny would have done her best to cover up for me, and anyway George would not notice a troop of the Household Cavalry passing through the breakfast room provided his steak was cooked to his liking. Lavinia and the girls went to a party last night so they probably had breakfast in their rooms.'

'But surely they would have wanted to tell you about the party? Would not your nieces have wanted to tell you about their evening and ask about yours? And would you not discuss your plans for the day with your sister-in-law at some point during the morning?'

Sophia struggled, but could not keep the bitterness out of her voice as she said, 'Lavinia cares nothing for me. She would only wonder where I was when she wanted some errand or task doing. Otherwise she has no interest in me, my life or my hopes for the future.'

Hal was appalled and it showed on his face. 'I had no idea things were so bad for you, my little Sophy. I am sorry.'

It was in that moment Sophia, looking into his deep blue eyes, fell irretrievably in love with him.

'What are those hopes you hold?' he asked gently.

'I know I can never marry because of...you know all about that. My mother left me a substantial inheritance, but it is in trust for me until I marry, or reach the age of twenty-five. On my twenty-first birthday I asked George if he would not release the capital to me so that I could employ a lady companion and set up my own establishment. A cottage in Chelsea, perhaps; the air is so clean and the countryside so beautiful and unspoiled. I also want to travel abroad—to Italy—not that I would confess that to George, of course.'

'What did he say?' Hal asked, but he could guess.

'He said that I had shown such moral instability that I could not be trusted not to bring yet more disgrace upon the family and that he had the gravest misgivings

about what would happen if I was not under Lavinia's
scrutiny. He threatened that if I did not become more
conformable he would consult the family solicitors
about extending the time during which he had control
of my affairs—perhaps until I was thirty. Still,' she
added with a worried frown, 'perhaps he will not consider me running off for a holiday with a respectable
young lady as a companion quite so bad. Although he
can hardly consider it conformable behaviour.'

'Does your brother George ever box at Jackson's or
one of the other saloons?' Hal enquired.

'George? Box? Of course not!'

'Pity,' Hal drawled with a wealth of expression in
the one deep word. 'I have an overwhelming ambition
to encounter him there and punch him firmly on the
chin.'

Sophia giggled. 'Oh, yes! I know I should not say
it but I would love to see you do so! Do you box
then?'

'At Jackson's saloon in Bond Street. I have even
had the honour of the occasional sparring session with
the great man himself.'

Sophia cast a covert glance at Hal's broad shoulders
and remembered the muscles straining at the seams of
the borrowed shirt. That disturbing scrutiny was cut
short by their arrival at the Woolpack. This time Sophia jumped down after Hal and followed him into
the inn parlour as he questioned the landlord.

'Let me see, sir,' the man rubbed a gnarled hand
over his chin. 'Small hours of this morning, young
couple in a carriage and hired pair? Yes, I remember,
sir. The young lady bespoke a chamber for an hour,
but the young gentleman would not stop for longer,

kept saying they had to press on.' There was a knowing gleam in his eye as he recounted his story to Hal.

'Yes, indeed, they would have been in a hurry,' Hal replied smoothly, refusing to be drawn.

Sophia, coming through the parlour door behind him, felt this was somewhat bald if he hoped to suppress speculation. She slipped her hand through Hal's arm and gushed, 'Our poor cousins! So anxious to reach their dear mama in Northampton—the doctor despairs of her, you know—why, they would not even wait for my husband's return but insisted on setting out at once, with quite inadequate resources for a change of horses...'

Hal responded only by placing his left hand over hers to hide the fact that there was no wedding ring under the tight glove. Sophia prattled on, 'Oh dear, I do hope you were able to give them a nice change of horses...'

'Northampton, you say, ma'am?' The man took a rather grimy rag from his belt and began to polish the bar counter in a desultory sort of way. 'Can't have been the same couple then, 'cos these two reckoned they were going to Stamford.'

'Stamford? Are you sure?' Hal asked sharply.

'Well, that's what they said after they had had the row, sir. Wasn't listening too carefully, of course, sir,' he added, slyly watching Hal from the corner of his eye.

Hal sighed, 'I see. Will this help your memory?' Sophia heard the clink of coins as money changed hands, then the man stopped pretending to polish and gave them his full attention.

'The young lady went upstairs with my missus for a wash an' that, and I sent her up a cup of coffee and some bread and butter. And the young gentleman—your cousin, as you say, sir—he had a pint of porter but he wouldn't settle, walked up and down, pulling out his pocket watch and cursing her for being so long. I never knew the gentry knew such words.'

'Distraught,' said Sophia hastily. 'Poor cousin Clarence.'

'Distraught, that's as may be. Anyways, after an hour he marched up the stairs—them over there—and fair pounded on the door. She let him in and they had a right set to. Woke up Squire Thompson in the next room, I can tell you, 'cos he complained about it. The young lady—your cousin, sir,' he added slyly, 'she was stamping her foot and saying she wasn't going nowhere and she regretted the whole trip and she'd been deceived and just wait until Hal arrived.'

'That is my husband,' Sophia cut in hastily. 'I did tell them to wait for him, but they would not listen and just see, she was soon regretting it. Young people these days, you cannot advise them!'

Hal gave her fingers a squeeze which was none too gentle and she subsided. 'Thank you, landlord, you have been most helpful.'

They retreated with what dignity they could retrieve. As Hal was handing Sophia into the carriage John joined them. 'They are heading for Stamford, my lord. I had a word with the ostler and he heard young Fanshaw telling the postillion to make for there. Don't understand it, my lord, why aren't they going to Gretna?'

He swung himself up on to the box without waiting for an answer, but Hal's face when he sat down opposite her alarmed Sophia. 'What is it, Hal? Is it not a good thing that they are not going to Gretna?'

'If they are heading for the border they are not going to stop long enough for him to—' He broke off, but Sophia had no doubt of his meaning. 'He will know I am behind him and will not risk a long halt. But Mr Fanshaw senior is a keen huntsman, rides regularly and I think has a hunting box somewhere in the Stamford area. If Justin has changed his plans and is taking her there, it may be too late before I find them.'

Sophia was fast asleep when they clattered into the inn at Wellingborough. 'What…where are we?' She peered out of the window but all she could see were the lights of an inn yard and darkness surrounding it.

'Wellingborough.' Hal scooped her up in his arms and carried her straight through the front door and upstairs. Sophia sleepily snuggled into the warmth of him and in reply his grip tightened before he set her on her feet in a pleasant bedchamber. 'I will get the landlady to send you up a maid and something to eat. Then go to bed and get as much rest as you can. We will be up betimes.'

'But, Hal…should we not keep going?' Sophia protested.

'John's exhausted, you are exhausted and it has started to rain. We are not going to get anywhere crashing about in the dark trying to find a hunting lodge when we do not even have its direction. Sleep well, Sophy.' He hesitated, looking at her and Sophia caught her breath. Then he said lightly, 'You look about twelve,' bent forward and kissed the tip of her nose. Almost before she was aware of it he was gone, leaving her staring after him down the now empty landing.

* * *

Hal took a private parlour for breakfast the next morning. Coming downstairs, refreshed and without a trace of her headache Sophia found him poring over a book. The bruise on the side of his face was developing into an angry purple and she gave a little exclamation of concern, touching it gently with her fingertips.

Without looking up, Hal caught her hand and kissed her fingertips. 'Good morning, Sophy. And, yes, it does hurt.'

To cover her confusion at having both her mind read and her hand kissed, Sophia sat down hastily and poured herself a cup of coffee. 'What have you got there?'

'A route book. I think our best plan would be to go into Stamford and enquire there after Mr Fanshaw's hunting lodge.'

'Very well. More coffee? Would you like a slice of ham?'

'Yes, please,' Hal responded, his eyes still on the map. 'Thank you.' As she put the plate by his side he suddenly looked up and smiled at her. 'You are being very domestic this morning, Sophy. Practising being Lady Wyatt? Somehow I do not think you convinced the landlord yesterday.'

Suppressing the warm glow that the thought of being Lady Wyatt produced, Sophia said tartly, 'I do not think it would be good to persist with that idea—especially if you had to insist on separate bedrooms last night.'

'I told them you were my sister. Have you had enough to eat? If you will excuse me, I will go and see what sort of change of horses John has managed to secure.'

'Hal, we would do so much better if we left the carriage and rode instead, would we not?'

His dark brows rose in surprise. 'Well, of course, but how can we? You can hardly go careering around the countryside with me on horseback, and beside, side-saddle for the distances we may have to go would be too tiring.'

'That is true,' Sophia conceded meekly, but her mind was racing with a new idea. 'May I have some money, please? I need a change of linen and some toothpowder, and if I hurry I will not keep you waiting.'

'Here.' Hal fished a roll of notes from his pocket and handed it to her. 'Please will you buy me another couple of shirts and some toothpowder too?'

'What about a razor?' Sophia asked, then realised that he was clean shaven.

'I have bought one from the landlord, thank you. Now, off you go!'

Chapter Nine

'That idiot ostler at the George has got a lot to answer for,' Hal said bitterly as John pulled up outside a set of plain iron gates between two stone lodge-keeper's cottages. 'We must have wasted three hours up the highways and byways of Lincolnshire. It is probably too much to hope that, finally, this is Mr Fanshaw's hunting lodge.'

Sophia said nothing, but looked at Hal's tense, drawn face and realised that he was almost as apprehensive about what he might discover when he found Elizabeth as not finding her. She ventured gently, 'Well, Hal, you must concede, all these little lanes with stone walls look very much the same when you go down them, and our map is not very detailed. It is not surprising that John has been having so much trouble following the directions.'

Hal merely grunted, his eyes on John as he talked to the man who had emerged in response to ringing the bell that hung on the gate post. Then she saw his shoulders relax as John strode back to the horses and the man pushed back the gates to let them through.

'This is the place, my lord,' John called as he swung up on to the box again.

Sophia peered out of the window as the carriage moved up the short tree-lined drive to the front door of a modest-sized but handsome brick house. The drizzle had become heavy and the day had turned cold and gloomy, but there were no lights to be seen in the windows.

'It does not look as though there is anyone at home,' she said doubtfully.

Hal had swung open the carriage door and jumped down before the vehicle had come to a full halt. He hammered on the glossy door, unaware that behind him Sophia had also jumped down. She had every intention of sticking firmly to his side and being there when he came face to face with Justin Fanshaw. She had no doubt that Hal was in no mood to parlay.

After a long wait the door was opened by a respectable woman of middle age, dressed in a black gown and crisp white lace cap. 'Yes, sir?'

'I believe this is the house of Mr Fanshaw?'

'Indeed, yes, sir. Mr Fanshaw is not in residence, however, I believe he is still in London.' The housekeeper was regarding them steadily. It was obvious that that was as much of her master's business as she was prepared to disclose to this stranger.

Hal dug his card case from his breast pocket and offered her a card. 'I am Lord Wyatt, and this is…' the hesitation was a second long, '…this is my sister's companion, Miss Haydon. Could you tell me, ma'am, is Mr Justin Fanshaw here?'

The woman's face stiffened, then she said in clipped tones, 'Will you not come in, my lord, Miss Haydon? I am Mrs Watson, the housekeeper here.'

They were soon settled in a well-furnished sitting room beside a small fire. The housekeeper had rung for refreshments and, as soon as the door closed behind the maid, said, 'My lord, Mr Justin was here. He left just before noon. The young lady—forgive me, my lord, but am I correct in assuming she is your sister?—left with him.'

She poured tea with a hand that was not quite steady, despite her outward composure. Then she burst out, 'I am so sorry, my lord, if I could have kept her here I would have done, but she would not listen to me. And as for Mr Justin…' Both her voice and her face hardened.

Hal looked at the housekeeper and said, almost gently, 'I realise it must be difficult for you, Mrs Watson. I can assure you I attach no blame to anyone except Justin Fanshaw for what has befallen my sister. But you must understand, I need to know where they have gone.'

'I do not know, my lord. Would that I did! I have written to my master, and the groom took the letter to the receiving office just before your arrival. Mr Fanshaw will be deeply grieved, but I knew he would want to be able to warn the young lady's family—and here, like a miracle, you turn up upon the doorstep!'

'I am sure you did all you could, Mrs Watson,' Sophia soothed, leaning over to touch the sleeve of the woman's gown. 'You must not blame yourself, and I am sure your master will not blame you either. Did Miss Wyatt go with him willingly?'

'I am afraid so, Miss Haydon. Last night I hoped that in the morning she would see sense, for they were quarrelling when they arrived. She was so tired and cold—and I think rather frightened, poor lamb.' She broke off at an inarticulate sound from Hal. 'No, my lord, I do not think he had given her reason to be frightened of him. It was the realisation of what she had done.'

'Where did she sleep?' Hal asked between clenched teeth.

Mrs Watson looked shocked. 'There will be nothing improper in this establishment while I am housekeeper, my lord,' she said sternly. 'Your sister had the best bedchamber and young Rose to sleep on the truckle bed at her side. That door was locked and I had the key, be assured of that!'

Sophia, who was watching him closely, saw the look of relief pass swiftly over Hal's features. So, Elizabeth was safe thus far. She put her cup down. 'Do you know where they have gone, Mrs Watson?' But as she asked her insides were tight with apprehension: if the housekeeper knew that she would have told them by now.

'No, Miss Haydon. He refused to tell me—'

Hal broke in. 'Did they take a change of horses from your master's stables?'

'Yes, my lord, his best team: four matched Welsh bays. Mr Fanshaw had sent them up ahead to be rested for when he arrives next week. Oh, my goodness! What is he going to say about all this?'

'Are there any more carriage horses in the stables?' Hal asked urgently.

'No, my lord, there was only the bays—and Mr Fanshaw and Mr Richard's string of hunters which came up at the same time. Mr Richard is the elder son, sir,' she added. 'And a very nice young gentleman he is too.'

Sophia cast down her eyes so that Hal would not

see the gleam of triumph there. She had made her plans, and done her shopping, in Wellingborough, hoping that they would find riding horses at Mr Fanshaw's. But this was better than she could have hoped for. Now all she had to do was to put Hal into a position where he could not gainsay her plans…

Hal was still talking to the housekeeper when Sophia stopped plotting and concentrated once more on the conversation in hand.

'No, my lord,' Mrs Watson was saying. 'Mr Fanshaw has no other houses north of here, nor any relatives I know of either. I cannot imagine where Mr Justin can be intending to take your sister.'

There was a rattle of hard rain against the windows as Sophia asked, 'Lord Wyatt, where shall we go next?'

Hal stood up and walked to the window where the dark clouds made the late afternoon seem almost as dark as night. 'At this time of day, in this weather, with no change of horses and no idea where we are going, I think we must go back to the George in Stamford for the night.'

This did not suit Sophia's plans one bit, but she was saved by Mrs Watson saying, 'But, my lord, you must stay here. Mr Fanshaw would not forgive me if I did not offer you the hospitality of his house under these trying circumstances. Your man can stable the horses here and they will be rested for the morning.'

Hal looked dubious, but Sophia cut in quickly, 'Please, my lord, it does seem like an excellent scheme, and I am very tired.' She added mendaciously, 'It would be comforting to stay the night here, with Mrs Watson…'

For the first time since they had arrived Hal's face

relaxed into a smile. 'Very well, thank you, Mrs Watson. It may well be that a decent night's rest will clear our minds and give us an idea of what to do.'

'I am sorry the groom is not yet returned from the receiving office, my lord, but if you would like to speak to your man and tell him to make whatever use of the stables he wishes for your horses, I will tell Cook to prepare dinner. If you would care to come with me, Miss Haydon, I will show you to your room.'

Over dinner, which the housekeeper had set out for them in a small parlour, Sophia succeeded in diverting Hal's attention from his worries with her enthusiasm for the suite of rooms to which Mrs Watson had shown her and the wardrobe that she insisted her mistress would expect the young visitor to avail herself of.

'Are you sure?' Sophia had asked, wide-eyed as she looked into the clothes press.

'Of course. And besides, you cannot sit down to dinner in that gown you have been travelling in. You must have had a very swift departure if you were unable to pack anything.'

'Lord Wyatt had every expectation of catching the runaways within a few hours,' Sophia explained as she stepped out of the mud-fringed gown. 'But we had a carriage accident and that delayed us considerably. So here I am with nothing but the clothes I set out in.'

'I will have this brushed and sponged, ma'am. Meanwhile, please choose what you will: Mrs Fanshaw—she is the second wife, you understand, and somewhat younger than the master—is much the same size as you.'

The result, as Sophia was pleasurably aware, was

very fetching. She had chosen a gown in an embroidered lawn just a shade darker than her eyes. Made for a married lady, it was cut rather lower than Sophia had ever worn and she rather self-consciously pinned a lace fichu around her shoulders and over the swell of her breasts.

'Is this gown not lovely?' she enquired enthusiastically.

'Very nice,' Hal replied dryly, smiling at her over the rim of his wine glass. 'One of the benefits of being a married lady. I believe Mr Fanshaw is an indulgent husband.'

Sophia was not to be repressed. 'Indeed he must be! You should see her bedroom—it is in the very kick of fashion, and this is only a hunting lodge. There are two gold cherubs holding a gauzy veil over the bed and mirrors *everywhere*.'

Hal choked and set down his glass abruptly. 'Indeed! I understand this is part of a suite?'

'Yes, there is a very pretty sitting room too.'

The meal was excellent and the wine, which Sophia was unused to, was potent, warming its way right down to her toes.

She stifled a yawn and Hal got to his feet. 'Come along, bed for you, Sophy.' He held out his hand and Sophia obediently took it, her heart thudding loudly in her ears. Of course, he was just being brotherly and concerned, she told herself, but his hand was warm and strong and at that moment she would willingly have gone anywhere with him.

'Which is the door to your luxurious sitting room?' he asked lightly when they reached the landing. 'This one? I am right next door: we have obviously been allotted the master suite by the conscientious Mrs Watson.'

Sophia felt slightly giddy. 'That wine was strong! I am not used to red wine.' It sang in her veins and she turned to face him, not quite sure what she was hoping for.

Whatever it was, she was disappointed. Hal merely smiled and said, 'Sleep well, Sophy.'

She wandered through the sitting room into the bedroom where the fire was crackling, the lamps lit and the bed turned down. The housekeeper had laid out a nightgown and peignoir, probably one of Mrs Fanshaw's plainest, but even so, incredibly luxurious to someone who was expected to sleep in sensible plain cotton.

Sophia slipped it over her head and it fell to brush her bare toes. The peignoir fastened with blue ribbons and the whole ensemble felt light and diaphanous as she twirled in it. Crossing to the mirror to unpin her hair, she caught a glimpse of herself in the cheval glass and gasped at the effect of the firelight on the fine lawn. It rendered it almost see-through. Sophia hastily wrapped the peignoir tightly around her: this was a startling revelation into married life!

Well, it was not as though there was an alternative to putting it on; perhaps, if she went through to the sitting room where there were no betraying mirrors, she could unpin and brush her hair without putting herself to the blush.

She was sitting with her head bent over, brushing out the russet curls when there was a slight tap on the door. Before she could call out it opened and Hal strode in. Sophia, half-hidden by the back of the sofa, gave a little squeak of surprise.

'Oh, good, you are still up,' he remarked, walking further into the candlelit room. 'John said the parcel with my new shirts in was sent up to this room along with your shopping from this morning. Ah, is that it?' He strode across to where the brown paper parcel was resting on a low chest and Sophia could see that not only had he taken off his jacket and cravat but that his shirt was unbuttoned at the neck. He picked up the parcel and began to turn. 'You really should get changed and go to b...my God!' His deep blue eyes widened, not in shock but in amazed delight at the vision sitting on the sofa.

The fine fabric of the peignoir over the equally diaphanous nightgown revealed where it touched, clinging to Sophia's curves, doing nothing to conceal her womanliness. Then she stood up which merely made things worse...or better.

The parcel slid unheeded to the boards as with one step he caught her in his arms, burying his face in her neck, nuzzling the softness under the clouds of newly brushed hair. His lips sought her earlobe, licking and nibbling, and Sophia gave a little gasp of pleasure as the new sensation coursed through her body.

Sophia slid her hands under the open shirt and felt Hal's body, smooth, hard and very warm. She could not believe that a man's skin could feel so supple and smooth, yet be so muscled beneath. And his lips, which were doing wonderful things on the sensitive skin of her neck, were hardening, sending messages which she did not understand but her body did instinctively. Her hands moved as if of their own volition up and round to trace the line of his spine, pressing and stroking as she arched against him.

Hal groaned in response and his mouth found and

took hers with an insistence which took her breath away. It did not seem possible that he could hold her any tighter, but he pulled her closer still and she could feel the insistent warmth of him.

'Hal, I love you,' she thought, then realised she had said it aloud, murmured it against his lips as she drowned in the intoxication of his kiss. For a moment she thought he had not heard, then he drew back, gazing down into her face.

'What did you say?' he asked, and the words were sharp in that dreamy, intimate atmosphere.

'No...nothing,' Sophia lied, stumbling over the word.

'I had better go. I had not realised you were...I thought...' But what he had thought she never knew, for he was out of the door before he finished the sentence.

Sophia was left staring at the brown paper parcel of shirts. 'Oh, what have I done!' she wailed out loud. 'Embarrassed Hal, made a complete fool of myself. He will never take me with him now.' And one tear slid down her hot cheek.

The results of a restless night convinced Sophia that if she was not to be left with Mrs Watson her only hope was to ruthlessly put her plan into effect.

Thus it was, the following morning, after an interview with the housekeeper, she sought out John in the stableyard. 'There is no need to harness the carriage horses, John. His lordship has decided that we will make better progress if we ride. Mrs Watson has the authority to let us take Mr Fanshaw's hunters. I think I would like to take that grey mare—can we just have a look at saddles?'

Ten minutes later, leaving a very puzzled coachman scratching his head and eyeing the saddle horse dubiously, Sophia slipped into the kitchen and took a rapid breakfast with Mrs Watson.

'Oh, you can tell his lordship's a worried man,' the housekeeper confided. 'Almost snapped at me this morning when I asked him about breakfast.'

Sophia reflected, but did not say, that that was more than likely her fault. She thanked Mrs Watson and asked for the loan of a pair of sharp scissors.

Hal, looking for her, was told by the housekeeper that she had already gone down to the stableyard. He gritted his teeth for what he knew was going to be a difficult encounter, but when he reached the yard, instead of the carriage and four, John was leading out three hunters, all in prime condition, and all saddled up.

'John? Where is the carriage? And where is Miss Haydon?'

'She's in the back there,' John said evasively, stooping to run a hand down the fetlock of one of the horses.

Puzzled, Hal opened the door and entered the tack room casting round for Sophia. It was empty, but he could hear a rustling and the sound of her voice muttering imprecations from the loft above. Cautiously Hal ascended the ladder, stopping as his head emerged through the hatchway, too amazed to go further.

Seated on a bale of hay, clad in breeches, jacket and boots, was a slight figure. Its face was obscured by a cloud of hair which Hal had no difficulty identifying. As he watched an entire hank of red curls fell on the dusty floor and Sophia's face, flushed with exertion and annoyance, was revealed.

'What the devil are you doing, Sophy?' Any embarrassment either of them might have felt after last night's encounter disappeared in the face of this extraordinary scene.

'Oh, don't stand there gawping!' Sophia snapped. 'Come and help me, I can't get to the back. I never thought it would be so hard to cut my own hair!'

Hal shook his head in total bewilderment, but scrambled up into the loft. 'Why on earth are you mutilating your hair?' He picked up the dusty hank and looked at it.

'Well I can hardly dress like this and have long hair, now can I?' Sophia demanded, hot with her exertions and annoyance.

Hal's eyes travelled from her boots—obviously ready made—up her slender legs clad in breeches, to her long jacket which effectively skimmed over her curves, flattening them. She had tied a kerchief around her neck and a hat lay beside her on the bale.

'But why are you dressed like that anyway?' Hal demanded as she thrust the scissors into his hand.

Sophia eyed him defensively through the long strands of hair which still fell across her face. 'You were the one who said I couldn't ride side-saddle all day and *you* were the one who agreed we should take to horseback.'

Hal shook his head as if to clear it. 'Sophy, that is not what I meant and you know it!'

'Well, I've cut it now, and I can't dress as a girl looking like this—it won't stick back on—so we will have to carry on, won't we?' she declared defiantly.

Hal looked at her for one long moment. In front of him stood a scrubby youth with badly cropped jagged hair and a mulish expression. Anything further from the alluring, desirable woman he had so nearly taken last night was impossible to imagine.

'Sit down again,' he ordered. 'Goodness knows what John's going to say when he sees you.' And, taking the scissors, he began to cut.

Chapter Ten

John stood waiting, half-expecting an explosion of wrath from the harness room. Goodness knows what the master would say when he realised the wild scheme Miss Sophia had come up with. But then this whole tangle was getting out of hand in John's opinion. Why didn't the master just pack Miss Sophia back to London—or leave her here with Mrs Watson—and let the two of them get on with finding Miss Elizabeth? He dragged one boot heel through the dust and straw covering the cobbles; it was awful quiet in there…

'John!' The master strode out alone, looking as near flustered as John had ever seen him in all the years he had served him. 'Wait here.' He vanished into the kitchen, only to re-emerge five minutes later with something in his hand. 'I want you to go back to London. Take this letter to Mr Fanshaw. He will be a very worried man and I want to reassure him, and thank him for the loan of his horses. I was reluctant to take them, but, talking to Mrs Watson, I feel she is such a trusted family servant that we can accept her authority to borrow the horses.'

'But, my lord!' The look on John's face would have been almost comical in other circumstances. 'My lord…Miss Sophia…she won't be chaperoned at all— not that I'm much of one, but I'm something!'

'Oh, take that sanctimonious look off your face, John, and leave me to worry about Miss Haydon's reputation,' Hal said, not unkindly. 'That young lady, I am beginning to discover, is more than capable of looking after herself.'

As he spoke a slim youth appeared at the door of the harness room, hat in hand. John shot a harassed glance at the stranger, then his jaw dropped as he recognised the russet hair, or what remained of it.

'What the…? Miss Sophia, what will your mother say?' he demanded, horrified.

'Never mind that, John. Here, take this.' Hal handed him the letter and a roll of banknotes. 'Now, off you go and wait for my orders at the London house.'

Hal turned from watching John, back rigid with disapproval, ride out of the yard to find Sophia competently checking the length of the stirrups before leading the grey mare to the mounting block and swinging up into the saddle. She looked up from tightening the girth to find Hal's eyes on her, eyebrows raised.

'This is not, I assume, the first time you have ridden astride?' he remarked as he mounted in turn.

'No,' Sophia responded, her chin coming up. She was a competent, confident rider and she knew it. 'When I was living on the estate in Hertfordshire I asked the head groom to teach me and I used to ride daily.'

'And I suppose no considerations of propriety, or the protestations of your brother's servants, made a ha'porth of difference,' Hal commented drily as he gathered up the reins and urged his horse out of the yard.

'George told me I should fill my time profitably, so I did. I learned many very useful things.' Sophia kicked her heels and trotted up alongside him. 'Where are we going?'

'To the nearest turnpike. And when we get to the gate, stay back and be quiet!'

'Yes, my lord, whatever you say, my lord,' Sophia mocked in her best Hertfordshire accent, touching the brim of her hat.

Hal shot her a dark look and cantered off without a backward glance.

The keeper at the first pike gate on the road north looked a sensible, observant fellow. Hal leaned down to hand him a coin somewhat larger than the toll demanded and remarked casually, 'Fine country around here. Must be good hunting.'

'It is that, sir, thank you, sir.' The man knuckled his forehead, slipping the coin into his pocket.

'I was hoping to see young Mr Justin Fanshaw while I was in this vicinity, but I understand he's away from home. Just wish I'd thought to ask his new direction.'

'Young Mr Fanshaw is it, sir?' The man rubbed his weathered chin. 'Haven't seen him for a month or two. Mind you, I wasn't on the gate all day yesterday. Clem!'

A younger version of the gatekeeper emerged from the toll booth wiping his mouth on the back of his hand. 'Yes, Dad?'

'You see young Mr Justin Fanshaw yesterday?'

'Yes, Dad, quite a surprise that was, didn't know there was anyone up at the Lodge. Come by just after noon: I recall it because I'd that minute cut a hunk off the bacon hock for my dinner and when I got back the danged cat had had it. In a fine carriage Mr Justin was, with a team of four harnessed up, and a postillion. Very fine,' he added slyly, 'but not as fine as the beautiful young lady I saw looking out the coach window.'

'Mind your tongue, boy,' his father remonstrated, seeing Hal's face harden. 'Which way did they go?'

'Well, north, Dad, of course, or they wouldn't have needed to pass this gate,' said Clem in an injured tone. 'And he took a ticket for the next three gates, so I reckon they were heading for Newark for the night.'

Hal spun a coin to Clem, which the lad caught deftly one-handed, then spurred on to the pike road at a canter. The two gatekeepers watched the retreating riders in silence for a while, then Clem said, 'Something going on there, Dad.'

'Elopement, I reckon. Wild piece that younger Fanshaw boy, like his mother by all accounts. Come on, let's go and sort out those chickens.'

Hal and Sophia cantered on in silence for several miles. She kept shooting glances at his set face and her spirits sunk lower and lower. At first she had been buoyed up by the success of her audacious scheme, now she was not so sure it was a good idea. She was miles from home without any protection other than this man of whom she knew very little. She might like him, she was very attracted to him, might even believe herself to be in love with him, but she did not know him—nor anyone else for a hundred miles around.

Eventually Hal reined back and let the horses walk.

After a few minutes of uncomfortable silence she asked, 'Are you still angry with me?'

He looked at her for a long minute, then shook his head. 'No, not angry with you, I am angry with myself. Hell!' He snatched off his hat and raked his hand through his hair. 'What am I doing, dragging you through the countryside like this? It was madness even to bring you as far as St Albans, but at least I expected to catch them there. But this! Look at yourself! What was I thinking of?'

'Your sister,' Sophia said tartly. 'And I asked to come, it was my idea.'

'The more I come to know you, the more reason I have for mistrusting your ideas,' he retorted, then relented at the hurt expression on her face. 'Oh, hell, Sophy, I am sorry.'

'But it is not as though I am any young lady. I am probably the only one in London whose circumstances mean that I cannot be compromised any further by being in your company alone. I mean, in the absence of a married lady I am the safest...'

Her voice trailed away at the expression on Hal's face. His eyebrows rose and his lips curved wickedly and she knew he was thinking about what had happened the night before. The blush rose up her throat, staining the pale skin above the neckerchief and suddenly she could not meet his eyes.

'Twice ruined being no worse than once, Sophy?' he asked, his tone mocking himself as much as her.

'Absolutely,' she retorted, nettled that he could make her feel like this. 'I am enjoying my adventure before I have to go back home to George and Lavinia.'

'And respectable spinsterhood in Chelsea, as you told me?' Hal teased, thinking that she was still damnably, temptingly attractive, even with her hair hacked off and wearing youth's clothing. Then Sophy pulled a face at him and was suddenly the picture of the scrubby boy she was pretending to be.

The long ride up the Great North Road passed uneventfully with news of the fugitives at several of the toll bars along the way. But it was the furthest that Sophia had ever ridden and she was sore and bone-weary by the time they walked the tired horses off the market place and into the yard of the Clinton Arms.

Sophia threw her leg over the saddle and swung down to find her legs giving way as her feet met the solid ground. Only her grip on the saddle kept her on her feet. Stiffly she limped after Hal, finding him in conversation with the landlord. 'Only one chamber free, sir, it's late now, of course—if you'd been here two hours ago, then you could have had your pick. But the lad can bed down with the ostlers, can't he?'

Sophia gave a muted squeak of alarm, but Hal intervened smoothly. 'I prefer him to sleep in my room, not be sitting up drinking ale, or worse, with the ostlers. I want him sober in the morning or I'll never get any work out of him.'

'Very well, sir. I'll have a truckle bed set up for him.'

'And hot water and a bath,' Hal added. 'Send that up at once and I will dine afterwards.'

The room they were shown to was spacious with old beams and a view over the market square. The main bed was a four poster with heavy curtains and the servants set up a low truckle bed at its foot. Two sweating potboys staggered upstairs with a hip bath and several buckets of steaming water, setting them down with a thud on the wooden boards.

Sophia, fidgeting by the window, pretended to be admiring the view of the famous towering spire of the church: anything to avoid looking at that big bed, or the bath, or Hal.

When he spoke it was so sudden that she started in alarm. 'I am going downstairs for a drink and to order our dinner. You get in the bath while I am gone. Don't be long in it—I'd rather find some hot water left when it's my turn!'

The door shut briskly behind him, leaving Sophia staring at the bath. The men had set it down before the fire with a pile of rough but clean linen towels beside it. Giving herself a shake she poured in the water, dragged a battered leather screen from the corner of the room around the tub and began to drag off her clothes. Her weary limbs protested at the effort, but that pain was as nothing to the shock of hot water on her blistered heels and sore bottom.

'Ooh!' Sophia complained to the empty chamber, 'that hurts!' Bu the hot water soon soothed both the soreness and the aches and before she realised what was happening her head had fallen forward and she had nodded off to sleep.

Entering the darkened room twenty minutes later after he had received no answer to his tap, Hal looked around and could see no sign of Sophia. 'Drat the girl,' he muttered under his breath, taking up the one taper in the sconce by the door and touching it to the branch of candles which stood on the dresser. 'Still, I suppose she cannot come to much harm in the middle of Newark at this hour.'

Wearily he began to shuck off his clothes, stretching his stiff shoulders before crossing to the screen, one of the remaining jugs of now cooling water in his hand. He must have knocked against the screen as he rounded the corner, for it fell with a thud on to the boards, revealing Sophia, as naked as the day she was born, blinking wildly at the sudden awakening.

'Bloody hell!' Hal backed away, the pitcher strategically placed to preserve what decency he could.

Sophia gave a shriek and grabbed a square of linen to cover herself. There was a moment's appalled silence as they stared at each other, then Hal's shoulders began to shake. With a shout of laughter he collapsed on to the bed with his back to her.

'It is no laughing matter!' Sophia stormed at him, scrambling out of the bath with cooling water slopping everywhere. She seized more towels, but strangely nothing seemed to help, she still felt as naked as she had when she had awoken to find him there.

'I am sorry,' Hal finally managed to say from behind the bed curtain that he had dragged across. 'But your face…'

'I might have looked funny, but it was nothing compared to you trying to conceal your…your…body…with that jug!'

Further sounds of mirth from behind the curtain did nothing to cool her temper. Sophia stamped her foot in fury, splashing her feet in the puddle of bath water which was gathering on the boards.

'May I come out now?' Hal ventured cautiously.

'No! You are sitting on my clothes!'

'Well, pull a sheet off the truckle bed,' he suggested.

With a snort of fury Sophia jerked off the sheet and swathed herself in it. It was at least both ample and clean, if slightly rough. 'Now you may come out,' she said with as much dignity as she could muster.

There was the sound of bare feet on the boards and Hal emerged, clad only in breeches, shrugging on his shirt. The subdued light of the candles flickered over his face and the hard-muscled plane of his chest revealed by the unbuttoned shirt. Sophia swallowed hard, realised that she was staring and dropped her eyes to the floor. It was a mistake: the sight of his bare feet was just as unsettling.

There was a moment's telling silence, then with a deliberate step Hal walked around the foot of the four-poster bed, tugging the remaining curtains across it. 'You had better get dressed,' he said in a neutral tone. 'You will catch your death of cold wrapped only in that sheet.'

Sophia wrapped the linen even more tightly around her form and scuttled with more haste than dignity behind the curtains. She did not notice the effect the tightened sheet on her damp body had had on Hal.

He cleared his throat and said tightly, 'If you do not mind staying there for five minutes I will take my bath before this water gets completely cold.' As he removed his clothing he reflected that the temperature of the water might be a useful antidote to the sight of Sophy's body moulded by the damp linen, no curve untouched…

Sophia huddled on the bed, shivering slightly as she dragged the boy's clothing over her still damp, unco-operative limbs. She tried not to listen to the soft sounds of Hal's clothes falling to the floor, tried not to recollect that glimpse of hard muscle, tried not to imagine his body glistening wetly in the firelight. These disturbing thoughts were abruptly shattered by the sound of an oath as Hal lowered himself into the now cold water.

The atmosphere was somewhat constrained as the two of them descended into the inn's dining room. It was thronged with market-goers and farmers and other travellers and the landlord found them two seats at the end of the communal board. Hal pushed Sophia firmly into the corner, shielding her somewhat from the rest of the company ranged down both sides of the long oak table.

'Remember you are not at a London dinner party and try and eat like a boy,' Hal hissed out of the corner of his mouth as a plentiful and homely dinner was placed before them. After a glance at the table manners of a youth sitting across the table from them, Sophia reached out and took a hunk of bread from the trencher and waited expectantly while Hal heaped slices of roast meat and steaming vegetables on to her pewter plate. Once she began to eat she realised that she was absolutely starving and needed no acting to attack her food with gusto.

The jug of ale which appeared before them was quite another matter. Sophia took a cautious sip from her tankard, spluttered and nearly spat it out in disgust.

Hal muttered, 'Drink it, you will soon get used to it and I can hardly order ratafia for you.'

'I don't want ratafia, just some water! This is revolting, so bitter to the taste.'

'But a lot safer than the water,' Hal responded unsympathetically. 'Go on, don't sip at it, just swallow it down.'

Although they had been speaking in undertones, the interchange had caught the attention of a showily dressed middle-aged woman opposite. Her red lips curved in a smile and, naturally friendly, Sophia smiled back, thinking that she was wearing rather more face paint than was acceptable in polite society.

Obviously encouraged by the smile the woman closed her left eye slowly in a lascivious wink and Sophia realised with a shock that she was being flirted with. She stifled a gasp of laughter just as Hal realised what was going on and spoke sharply. 'Ned! Behave yourself, boy.' He turned an outwardly charming smile on the flirtatious lady. 'I do apologise for the manners of my lad, ma'am. He is naïve in the ways of the world and has not yet learned discretion.' It was said with an edge, unmissable by both Sophia and the woman, whose expression showed a mixture of anger at being taken up in that way and a certain *frisson* at being rebuked by such an attractive man.

The feeling the exchange evoked in Sophia was a shock. It was the first time she had really noticed the effect Hal had on other women. This one, attraction overcoming pique, ran her tongue round her lips and leaned forward to address him. Her low-cut gown scarcely contained an ample bosom and the effect was both startling and, Sophia realised, quite deliberate.

With her own more modest curves firmly restrained by her tight waistcoat, she realised she was glowering at the flirtatious diner. If that thread lace gave way the woman's charms would be totally on display, doubtless giving pleasure to every man in the room! She took a swig of the ale without tasting it, resentfully watching Hal, who, however much he might disapprove of the lady's style, was responding quite predictably.

How could anyone pass a platter of bread with so much *meaning?* she stormed inwardly as Hal offered the woman the trencher, then watched as she delicately nibbled at the crust, dwelling rather too long on it in Sophia's opinion.

Irritably she kicked Hal under the table, connecting with his booted ankle with a satisfying thump. He looked at her, startled, and she hissed, 'Stop it, your tongue is positively hanging out!'

Hal's brows drew together sharply. 'That is a highly improper remark from a well brought-up young girl,' he hissed back.

'Well, I'm not a well brought-up young girl, am I? I'm Ned, aren't I?' she retorted, eyes flashing, her fingers crumbling bread savagely.

'In that case, *Ned,* it's time you were in bed. You are obviously overtired and unable to mind your manners,' Hal muttered *sotto voce.* Then aloud added, 'Off to bed with you, lad, and don't hang about talking to the grooms on your way.'

Thus dismissed, Sophia got to her feet and stalked, stiff-legged, out of the dining room. She would have liked to flounce, but servant lads couldn't flounce. She paused in the doorway to look back and saw, to her dismay, that the woman had slipped round and taken her place beside Hal. Already she was leaning in closer, her long beringed fingers caressing the sleeve of his coat.

Sophia spent the next two hours lying rigid in the truckle bed, fuming with anger, jealousy and humiliation that she should feel like this. What was he doing? Oh, do not be such an innocent, she chided herself. Of course you know what he's doing, what any red-blooded man would be doing, given that much encouragement!

When he finally came to bed the church clock was

striking midnight. Sophia lay still, trying to make her breathing deep and regular, listening to the muffled sounds of Hal dragging off his boots and clothes. When he got into bed she could tell from his breathing that he had fallen into a deep sleep almost immediately.

'Grr,' Sophia snarled into the pillow. No wonder he was finding it so easy to sleep after two hours' drinking—and whatever other entertainment—with that, that *harlot!* She must have eventually fallen asleep, for the next morning she had no recollection of hearing the church clock strike one.

Chapter Eleven

The sound of whistling cut across Sophia's dreams and woke her up. The sunshine was streaming across the boards and Hal was standing in front of the dresser, dragging a cut-throat razor through the foam covering his cheeks. Sophia watched him between half-closed lids, wondering how he managed to shave and whistle at the same time. At that moment he broke off to carefully shave his upper lip and she gave a little snort of laughter at the expression of concentration on his face.

He did not turn, but remarked, 'Ah, you are awake at last, are you? Sleep well?'

It was on the tip of her tongue to say something cutting about the previous evening, but she swallowed the comment and merely replied, 'Yes, thank you.'

Hal threw down the towel with which he was wiping his face and pulled on his coat. 'I'll see you downstairs in the parlour in a few minutes then. I want to have a word with the ostlers, see if they had any sight of our quarry yesterday.' With that he was gone.

Sophia scrambled out of bed, poured Hal's shaving water into the slop bucket and refilled the bowl from the ewer. It was her turn for the tepid water so she washed and dressed hastily, reflecting that one of the less obvious advantages of men's clothing was the ease with which one could get dressed.

After last night Sophia expected there to be some constraint between them, but Hal seemed quite relaxed when he joined her at the breakfast table. They arrived together, coinciding with the waiter bringing their coffee and rolls.

'And some cold meat and a tankard of ale, if you please,' Hal asked the man. He turned to Sophia approvingly. 'That was quick work.'

'Short hair and no petticoats,' she responded, provoking a grin from Hal. 'Have you found anything out about Elizabeth?' She poured herself some coffee and broke open a warm roll.

'Yes, some firm news at last.' Hal waited for the waiter to put down the meat and depart, then continued. 'They are still about half a day ahead of us. They did change horses here, the ostlers remember them. And what is more, from what one of the postillions said, they are heading for York.'

'*York?* Why on earth would Justin Fanshaw be taking your sister to York?'

Hal shrugged. 'I have no idea. I suppose he might have had some idea of getting a special licence from the Archbishop—but then, he could get one of those from any bishop, providing he could persuade him that Elizabeth was of age. No, I have no idea what young Mr Fanshaw might be about, other than getting his hands on Elizabeth's fortune, of course.'

A rather grim silence followed, then Sophia ventured, 'Surely it is encouraging that they are keeping on the move? He can hardly be…er…' She couldn't say the words, but Hal knew her meaning exactly.

'Oh, yes, he could,' he said darkly. 'And when I get my hands on him I am going to kill him.'

Sophia looked at his set, hard face and realised with a shiver that this was no idle threat. 'But Elizabeth's reputation…'

'All right, she can marry him first and then I'll kill him.'

'Hal, you cannot do that! Think of the scandal! And, there is always the chance that she still loves him.' Thinking back on her own experience that seemed highly unlikely, but she did not like to say so.

'Humph,' was all Hal replied in what Sophia thought was a typically male response. But, watching him from between her lashes as he did justice to the cold meat, she reflected that he was far from typical.

It seemed as though she had known him for ever, instead of a matter of days. In that time she had seen so many facets of his character: Hal happy, Hal angry, concerned, Hal aroused to both humour and passion…

And all that anger directed at Justin Fanshaw sprang purely from his deep affection for, and worry about, his sister. Would that George had cared as much for her! No, all he cared about was propriety and that was one word she had never heard Hal use about Elizabeth's predicament.

And despite the madness of being here with him, of chasing the length and breadth of the country she was loving it, loving being with Hal. Loving Hal… A deep sigh escaped her parted lips and he looked up at her over the rim of her tankard.

'What's the matter, Sophy? Are you tired? This

must be very exhausting for you; I keep forgetting you are a girl.'

Sophy put down her mug with some emphasis and glared at him. Hal returned the affronted look with a wicked grin, completely unabashed. 'Well, I have to admit there have been moments on this journey when I have been forcibly reminded of your femininity, but on the whole you make a very passable boy.'

Half an hour later they were ready to leave. Sophy stood with her saddlebags over her arm, waiting for the stableboy to lead out her mare when there was a stir at the doorway of the inn and Hal's *friend* of the evening before emerged. She minced slowly across the cobbled yard, lifting her skirts the better to reveal neat little feet shod in blue kid and rather too much silk-clad ankle for Sophia's liking.

She shot a look at Hal standing beside her and muttered, 'Your mouth's open.'

'No, it's not,' he countered automatically, then shot her a look between narrowed eyes. 'Don't be so waspish.'

The lady glanced round, artistically appeared to catch sight of Hal for the first time, and trilled, 'My lord! A very good morning, is it not? I trust you slept well.'

'Very well, I thank you, ma'am,' Hal returned with such a straight face that Sophia was left still speculating whether or not he had passed part of it with the lady in question or not.

Getting into the carriage proved a lengthy performance, involving showing even more ankle, drawing on a pair of exquisitely tight gloves and finally blowing Hal a kiss as the carriage bowled out of the yard.

By this time Sophia was positively grinding her teeth in fury at this blatant display. 'Trollop!' she declared, only to have the judgement fall on deaf ears as Hal had already mounted and was checking the buckles on his saddlebag.

They cantered in silence for several miles, stirrup by stirrup. As the morning wore on the weather improved and with it Sophia's mood. The countryside on either side of the turnpike was lush and green. Here and there the hedges were splashed with white blossom and the wildflowers covered the verge and banks.

The amount of traffic on the highway surprised Sophia. There were farm carts, a slow-moving dung cart that made its presence felt for some distance, several gigs and traps with one or two occupants, but the most thrilling sight was the Mail at full stretch with a fresh team in the traces, heading for London. Hal reined on to the verge as that went past, sending their horses curvetting and sidling at the upset.

Making good progress, they lunched at the inn in Sibthorpe. Hal left Sophia sitting outside on a bench under a spreading oak tree and emerged five minutes later followed by a waiter laden with a tray of bread, butter, cheese, ham and two tankards of ale.

Sophia, who had worked up a fine thirst, found she could swallow the ale without so much as wincing now, earning an amused glance from Hal who offered helpfully, 'Now, Ned would wipe the foam off his mouth with the back of one hand.'

Obediently Sophia did as she was bid, then spread butter on a hunk of cottage loaf and proceeded to demolish it in a most Ned-like manner.

Fifteen minutes later, and replete, she closed her eyes and lay back against the tree trunk, wondering if she could snatch ten minutes to doze in the sunshine. Hal, however, was wide awake. He dumped the tray on the ground, swept the crumbs off the table for the waiting sparrows and spread out the route map he was carrying in his pocket.

'Come on, Ned, wake up and pay attention! We need to decide on our route.'

Reluctantly Sophia sat up and peered sleepily at the map. 'Must we—don't we just keep going up there?' She pointed vaguely at the line of the turnpike as it headed towards Retford and Doncaster.

'We could do, but the stretch of road south of Doncaster is notoriously bad in the spring and could hold us up. Willougby was telling me he had a nightmare journey south only two weeks ago—got stuck in the mire and had to be pulled out by farm horses.'

'Yes, but we could ride round, couldn't we?' Sophia leant both elbows on the table in a manner which would have produced a severe rebuke from her sister-in-law, and began to take an interest.

'We could do, but I wondered if, as we are mounted, we couldn't strike across country from Retford. See, here,' Hal said, leaning forward and pointing.

As she bent over the map Sophia felt his hair touch her temple. It tickled, but she made no move to pull away. 'Yes?' she encouraged, controlling her breathing with an effort.

Hal seemed to notice nothing untoward. 'If we ride due north we should strike Blaxton, then Thorne and spend the night there. We could reach York by tomorrow evening at that rate.'

The road to Retford was good, if winding, and they made steady progress without unduly tiring the horses. After that, heading north, they had a long, easy canter across country for about ten miles. The day had fulfilled its promise and was now really warm, without a cloud in the sky. At one point, when they reined in to walk the horses, Hal shrugged off his coat and, twisting round in the saddle, strapped it on to the saddlebags.

'Why don't you do the same thing?' he asked. Sophia hesitated, then unbuttoned the coat, sighing with relief as the cool air fanned through the coarse linen of her shirt.

She had just secured the coat when two farm workers rounded the bend in the lane they were following, hoes over their shoulders. Both tipped their hats at the sight of a gentleman and his servant and muttered, 'Afternoon, sir.'

Hal reined in. 'Good afternoon. Are we on the right track for Mattersey?'

'Yus, sir,' the older replied. 'Less than a mile up ahead.'

Hal tossed them a coin with a word of thanks and rode on. After they crossed the Gainsborough road they found themselves in far less inhabited country. The land rolled gently away without a village in sight, crossed here and there by quickset hedges, fields of sheep and the occasional meandering line of trees marking the course of a stream.

The hotter it got the worse the clouds of gnats became. When they cantered the wind took them away, but when they walked the horses the insects swarmed, irritating both riders and mounts. Sophia rode with her hat off, swatting them away from her face and wishing they could canter again.

But just as Hal gathered up the reins she realised that the grey mare was limping. 'Hal, stop, I think she's picked up a stone.'

Hal threw a leg over the pommel, slid down and rummaged in his saddlebags until he produced a hoof pick. 'Which foot?'

'Off fore.' Sophia shifted her weight as Hal ran his hand down the horse's foreleg and it obediently lifted its hoof.

'Yes, nasty great flint.' Hal levered carefully, then held up a jagged stone for Sophia to see before tossing it away. 'See how she goes on now.'

The mare was still not happy, pecking at each step and when Sophia reined her in, cocking the hoof up.

Hal walked up from where he had been watching the animal's gait. 'Hmm…must have bruised the frog of the foot, it was jammed right up into the middle. We'll only do her a permanent damage if we make her walk far tonight, but if it's soaked she ought to be better in the morning.'

Sophia stood up in the stirrups and shaded her eyes. 'I think there's a river ahead—look, can you see the willows?' She dismounted and began to lead the reluctant mare down the gentle grass incline.

When they got to the river bank they found a delightful grove of willows, an area of flat, dry grass and a shallow river that bubbled clear over a pebble bed. 'Well,' Hal said, looking round, 'if we have to spend the night in the open, I doubt we could find a better spot.'

'Spend the night?' Sophia echoed, then pulled herself together. 'Yes, of course we must.' After all, it was no different from spending the night with him in the inn; in fact, one could argue that this was more proper, being roomier...

Hal found a dip in the bank where the mare, snorting at the cold, let herself be led in to stand, fetlock-deep, in the soothing water. 'You hold her head, Sophy, and I'll find some firewood.'

'You can light a fire?' Sophia queried.

Hal grinned, 'I come very well equipped. A tin of Lucifers, a twist of salt, the heel off our breakfast bread, and a flask of brandy. The water looks and smells clean. We'll not be very well fed, but we can always find a farm for breakfast in the morning.'

Sophia stood idly watching the swirl and twist of weed in the current until a sudden flash of shimmering silver caught her eye. Gently she leaned forward, scarcely daring to breathe and there it was again—a trout. In fact, as she watched, she realised that there was the flash of sunlight on scales down the length of the little river as far as she could see.

When Hal returned, his arms full of dry twigs and some broken branches, she dropped the mare's reins on the bank, placed a stone on them and said, 'If you light the fire—and stay here quietly—I'll fetch us some dinner.'

'Dinner? And why have I got to stay here?'

'Because you have big feet,' Sophia observed enigmatically, ducking under the willows and vanishing upstream.

After ten minutes Hal had made and lit the fire. Sophy still had not reappeared so he led the mare out of the water and tethered her with his gelding on a lush piece of shaded turf. She seemed comfortable enough, dropping her head to graze.

What had happened to the girl? Despite her instructions, he was not going to sit around and wait for her to reappear. Moving quietly, Hal ducked under the willows and followed the bank around the next bend.

At first he did not see her. Then he stumbled over her waistcoat, boots and stockings lying abandoned on the bank. She was lying full length on the very edge of the bank ahead of him, bare legs in the air, her feet waving gently as she concentrated on the water only inches below her nose. Hal was puzzled for a moment, then he saw that her right shirt sleeve was rolled up to the shoulder and her arm was in the water. He began to advance stealthily, but she must have heard him for she gesticulated irritably with her left hand.

He then saw that in amongst the grass on the far side of her lay a fish. Hal froze, realizing that she must be tickling for trout and his footsteps were sending vibrations through the bank and scaring them. Big feet, indeed! He cautiously eased off his riding boots and stockings and tiptoed up beside her. He dropped to his knees and lay full length, holding his breath as he watched her skilled fingers moving gently under the water, tempting the fish to investigate this strange intrusion into their world.

One slim brown trout nosed up, hesitated, swam a little further forward right over the palm of Sophia's hand and she struck, closing her fingers and lifting her hand. But she had not reckoned on Hal being so close and her fast rising hand hit his shoulder. The trout flew into the air and landed behind them in the grass, Sophia, her body rolling with the throw, hit him sideways and together, with nothing but each other to hold on to, they fell with a resounding splash into the shallows.

Hal landed underneath, the cold water almost knocking the breath out of him. Sophia, landing on top, gave a shriek as his efforts to get up threw her into the deeper, colder water beyond the shelving edge.

Hal lurched to his feet, shook the water from his eyes and yelled, 'Hang on, Sophy, I'm coming, don't panic.'

With as much dignity as she could muster Sophia rose to her feet, waist deep, water weed streaming from her drenched body. 'I hardly need rescuing, Hal. It can't be more than three foot deep, and in any case, I can swim.'

Hal reached out. 'I begin to think there is no limit to your talents, Miss Haydon. Presumably, if you had had enough time, you would have built us a boat...'

Anything else he had to say was cut off as Sophia gave his proffered hand a sharp tug, hard enough to pull him into the deep water alongside her.

Hal emerged, dark hair sleek to his head like an otter's pelt, the linen shirt plastered to his torso with anatomical exactitude. 'You witch,' he observed pleasantly with an evil grin, then, before Sophia could splash out of the way, grabbed her and fell back.

He had not intended to kiss her, only to pay her back for his ducking, but when he felt her in his arms, felt her slender, curved body through the soaking cloth, and then as they surfaced chest to chest, felt the peaks of her nipples hardening against his own, he could not fight it.

'Sophy darling,' he murmured, before his mouth fastened on hers in a kiss so deep that she was only hazily aware of where they were, only of the urgent demand of his lips and the answering surge of heat from her own body.

She wrapped her arms around his neck, cleaving to him, feeling the strange mixture of body heat and cool cloth against her own excited skin. Hal shifted his grip and his mouth left hers, leaving her protesting, 'No...Hal, don't stop!'

'Oh, I've just started, sweetheart,' he assured her, his voice husky. His eyes meeting hers were dark with promise, but before she could think, speak, do anything, he had swept her up in his arms and was laying her gently back on the short-cropped turf of the bank.

The sun was beginning to set, slanting shafts of light through the willow fronds, sparkling on the disturbed surface of the brook. It reflected on the wet planes of Hal's naked chest as he pulled off the clinging shirt and tossed it aside, and as he bent over her again she could see the droplets like diamonds on his brows and lashes.

She reached up her arms to pull him down again, feel his lips on hers again. She felt as though she was in a dream: the dappling light, the quiet sounds of the evening countryside. The two of them were in another world, one in which reality did not exist, time had been suspended and they were the only people. All she knew was that she wanted Hal to carry on kissing her for ever.

'Kiss me again,' she implored.

'Don't be impatient,' he chided softly, 'we have all the time in the world.'

Sophia felt his fingers on her shirt buttons, then the sodden fabric was being eased from her body. Suddenly shy, yet trusting him absolutely, she closed her eyes, feeling only his sure fingers trailing tantalisingly down the curve of her shoulder until they cupped the warm, yielding curves of her flesh.

His fingers were mapping the route his lips were about to take and seconds later Sophia felt him nibbling, tasting, the damp, satiny skin of her shoulder, and then down to tease the aroused nipple below.

With a gasp of shocked pleasure Sophia pulled his head down, arching against the source of this pleasure. She had had no idea that kissing could be like this, no idea that Hal's lips could send such wonderful messages to her body. Messages that she could scarcely comprehend, but which her betraying body seemed to understand by instinct.

She became hazily aware of his fingers on the waistband of her breeches, then, acutely aware of the sensation of his fingertips brushing the sensitive skin of her stomach. Then, as the questing fingers moved downwards, will reasserted itself over instinct and her hand seized his wrist, 'No, Hal, no. You must not— we must not.'

Hal's fingers stopped moving, and he slowly moved his hand away from her body. He looked deep into her eyes, his own dark with his need for her. 'Yes, of course. Sophy, I am sorry…'

Before he could complete his sentence Sophia twisted away, gasping with indignation and shock as the realisation of what had happened hit her. 'How dare you! How dare you assume…presume…that I would…that because I'm ruined I will give myself to you?'

Hal got to one knee and reached for her, trying to still her tirade. 'Darling Sophy, you do not understand…'

'Oh, yes, I do!' she stormed. 'Only too well!' Tears

prickled the back of her eyes. She loved Hal, she had trusted him, and now it seemed that he was like all the others, only after one thing, even if he did stop when she told him to. She threw the nastiest accusation she could think of at him. 'Are your appetites so insatiable sir, that you are not satisfied unless you have a woman a night? Was that painted hussy last night not sufficient?'

Hal's face was rigid, but he reached for her again and, suddenly panicking, Sophia hit him hard on the side of the head.

Chapter Twelve

The sound of the blow seemed very loud in the still evening air. Sophia crouched on the bank, a wave of shame and dismay washing through her. She could not believe she could have struck Hal like that.

He got slowly to his feet, his face bleak, the marks of her fingers red on the skin just below the temple. He stood looking at her for a long moment, then bent, tossed her shirt to her, picked up his own clothes and walked away without another word.

Sophia watched him stride away, her eyes, although they were misty with tears, fixed on the rivulet of water tracing the line from his nape down the length of his spine. She put her hands over her breasts, suddenly unbearably aware of her nakedness, then, incapable of further action, sat huddled in the warm evening sun.

At last—and she had no idea how long she had sat there—some sort of composure returned, and with it common sense. She reached for her shirt, wrung out the remaining water and put it on with a grimace. Her shoes at least were dry, and she thrust her bare feet into them.

Where was Hal, and how would he greet her when

she found him? She realised she had no idea. No idea how this man would behave, despite the days and nights she had spent in his company. Well, wherever he was, and whatever his mood, they had to eat. She collected up the trout, wrapped each in a large dock leaf, and trudged back to where they had left the horses.

Both the horses were grazing peacefully in the shade and the fire was burning well. But there was no sign of Hal. Sophia took refuge in practical tasks; the saddlebags were under a tree and she quickly found a clasp knife which was sharp enough to gut the trout. As old Cobbett, the gamekeeper in Hertfordshire, had shown her, she cut small forked stems to make a support over the fire, skewered the fish on straight sticks and set them to cook. She spread a clean kerchief on a flat stone for a table, added the salt and the heel of the loaf and dipped the flask in the stream to fill it with cool water.

Her hands moved mechanically on these practical tasks, but her mind was running like a dog in a turnspit round and round the events of the past hour. No, she should not have hit Hal. And, yes, she had learned a lot, especially what happened when a man got aroused. And she had also learned how susceptible she was to Hal's lovemaking. How could it be otherwise, when she loved him?

But he should not have tried to take advantage of her like that! She had trusted him with her story, and now it seemed he had taken it as a *carte blanche* to seduce her.

'But I *love* him,' she said to the fish as they smoked gently over the fire. How could she still love him when she was so disillusioned? But then, he *had* stopped when she had told him to. But…

A snapping twig made her turn her head sharply, cutting into her tangled thoughts. Hal was stooping under the willow fronds as he walked into the clearing. Sophia looked at him cautiously. He was wearing a dry shirt, but his hair was still damp and tousled, which only served to make him look more attractive than ever, Sophia mused wistfully.

'That smells good,' he said by way of greeting, nodding towards the trout.

'Yes,' Sophia agreed. 'They are almost ready to eat.'

They both fell silent, this small interchange seeming to exhaust the conversation. After several minutes of wary silence while Sophia collected a handful of dock leaves for plates and Hal sat down on the far side of the fire, she asked, 'Shall we eat now?'

'I'm starving,' Hal admitted, his face relaxing slightly as he tore the bread into pieces.

Sophia, observing this, thought tartly that he was probably relieved she hadn't thrown the fish at his head. She lifted the spitted fish gingerly and managed to push them off on to the leaves without burning her fingers.

Just as she was raising a portion to her lips Hal said abruptly, 'Sophia, what happened just now…I think you may have misunderstood my meaning.'

She put the fish down again and stared at him, taken aback. She had expected him either to apologise, or to be angry with her. Not to start discussing it. She reacted rather more sharply than she intended. 'On the contrary, sir, I understood your meaning only too well. I may be innocent—despite your continued efforts to the contrary—but I do understand quite well what you were trying…'

'For heaven's sake, Sophy, stop calling me *sir* in that tone. All I was trying to say was that as we both seem to have a strong attraction for each other, and as—'

'That is no reason for you to try and seduce me!' Sophia protested, her eyes sparking. From the look on Hal's face she was only too aware that he could truthfully claim that she had not needed much seducing.

'If you will let me finish, what I was trying to say was, that as we are going to have to get married anyway, why not anticipate the pleasures beforehand? It won't change anything,' he added as if it were the most reasonable thing in the world. 'But of course, if you do not wish it, I would not dream of forcing you in any way.'

Sophia realised she was sitting with her mouth open and hastily closed it. *'Married?'* she croaked.

'Yes, married. It was inevitable from the moment that wheel came off the carriage and I could not get you home that night. Admit it, Sophy, you must know it is inevitable.'

Now it was his turn to be amazed as he took in the stunned disbelief on her face. She had not drawn the same conclusion as he, she still believed that her earlier misdemeanor somehow protected her from any further scandal.

He shook his head and for the first time his lips relaxed into a smile. 'Sophy, surely you must know that there is all the difference in the world between a youthful escapade from which you were rescued within a matter of hours by your brother, and with no-one else, whatever he says, aware of the facts and this.

You and me here. You and me, alone for days and nights. You dressed as a boy in my company. You sharing a chamber with me in Newark, dining with me in public.'

'But no-one *knows*. It doesn't matter.'

Hal raked his hands through his hair. 'You know. George knows. At least, he knows you are away without his permission and with goodness knows who. And I am honour-bound to marry you.'

Oh. So that was it: he was honour-bound to marry her. It was not that he liked her, cared for her—it was too much to hope that he might love her—no, he was honour-bound to marry her.

Sophia suddenly felt very miserable indeed. This was not how it should be, this was not how it had happened in the daydreams she had let herself indulge in these last few days. She was sitting in front of a rapidly cooling trout, in damp and uncomfortable clothes, with a blister on each heel and probably pond weed in her hair. And she was being told by the man she loved that she had to marry him because of *his* honour!

'Nonsense!' she said robustly. 'I do not believe a word of it. All we have to do when we get to York is for me to speak to your sister-in-law. She can provide perfectly acceptable chaperonage. When I return to London it might be thought strange I had left so abruptly, but no one will think twice about me visiting such a respectable family. After all, Hal, I cannot be twice ruined, can I?'

Hal sank his head in his hands. 'I thought I had just explained that you can,' he said wearily. 'Never mind, we'll discuss this when we arrive in York. Eat your trout, it's getting cold.'

Darkness seemed to come suddenly in the little valley and Sophia realised how tired she was, how exhausting the day had been. Hal observed her yawns and shook out the heavy cloak from behind her saddle. He laid his own a respectable distance away and they settled down to sleep.

Sophia awoke chilled, stiff and with a strange sensation of a breeze on her nape. Then she realised that the heavy weight on her waist was Hal's arm thrown across her protectively and it was his warm breath on her neck that she could feel. She lay there for a few precious moments, enjoying the feel of his long body curved against hers, then she slid carefully from his embrace and tiptoed round the bend in the river to wash.

When the two tired horses finally clattered across the cobbles under Bootham Bar, Sophia thought she had never been so glad to see anything in her life as the great mass of the Minster rising majestically before them.

The grey mare's head was down and she was beginning to peck again as her bruised hoof met the hard surface of the Minster Yard. Sophia thought she must have gone beyond being tired, hungry and thirsty about ten miles back when Hal had reined in the horses and decided they must walk them the rest of the way.

He was riding ahead of her as they circled the Minster and she saw how dusty his jacket was and how stiffly he stretched in the saddle to ease his shoulders. The neat houses of the clerics of the cathedral clustered closer, each with its carefully tended front garden facing onto the scythed grass of the lawns. There was little sign of activity, but as they passed the great doors Sophia could hear the swelling notes of the organ and voices raised in a hymn.

Hal twisted in the saddle and said, 'Evensong. I had not realised it was so late.'

Sophia smiled back wryly. 'I had no idea it was that early!'

Hal's concern showed in his face. 'I know how tired you must be, but we are nearly at my brother's house now—see, the house with the black front door.'

Hal swung down from the saddle and came to help her dismount. It was a good thing he did, for once out of the saddle her legs gave way and she found herself supported by his strong arms. 'Poor little Sophy,' he said gently. 'Can you walk, or shall I carry you?'

For one long moment the thought of being held close in Hal's arms was irresistible, then common sense reasserted itself. 'Hal,' she chided, 'what would your sister-in-law say if you were seen on her doorstep carrying a stable lad?'

His eyes twinkled, but he let go of her, steadying her against the horse until he was sure her legs would carry her. 'The opportunity to scandalise dear Emma is tempting, but poor John would be mortified. Come along.'

He raised the shining door knocker in the shape of a porpoise and let it fall against the heavy plate. The door swung open to reveal a bland-faced upper servant whose countenance broke into a smile as soon as he saw who was on the threshold. 'My lord! This is a pleasure we had not looked for!' He glanced past Hal's shoulder and saw the horses standing at the gate. 'No carriage, my lord? Well, Jones is in the mews, so if your lad takes the horses round now...'

'No, Grayling,' Hal interrupted. 'The lad stays with me. Can you send one of the footmen round to fetch Jones, please. And tell him to check the mare's feet— she's got a bruised frog which will need a fomentation.'

There was the merest pause as the butler eyed Sophia from head to foot, from battered hat to dust-caked boots, then his eyebrows rose fractionally before he added, 'Of course, my lord. The Reverend and Mrs Wyatt are at evensong, but we expect their return immediately afterwards. If you and the young…person would care to step into the drawing room, I will have refreshments sent in at once.'

As soon as the door closed behind the butler, leaving them standing in a small, but elegantly appointed room, Sophia hissed, 'He knows! He knows I'm not a boy!'

'I cannot imagine how, under all that dirt,' Hal teased, running his finger down her cheekbone and holding it up for her to see. 'Look at this dust, you look like a road sweeper.'

Sophia swallowed, her heart beating faster in her breast at his touch. It was only because she was so tired and hungry that she felt so dizzy, she told herself firmly. But in her heart she knew it was nothing to do with that at all. *I really must pull myself together before Hal's brother arrives,* she thought desperately.

A footman arrived carrying a tray of tea things which he placed on a table at Sophia's elbow. 'The decanters are here, my lord. What will you take, my lord?'

'A large brandy,' Hal replied with feeling, thrusting his booted legs out and settling himself more comfortably in the wing chair.

Wordlessly, the footman handed him the glass and poured tea for Sophia. She could sense the effort it was costing him avoiding looking at her and wondered what on earth he made of the sight of a travel-stained youth sitting on his mistress's best upholstery.

The tea was hot and sweet and the best thing she had ever tasted as it slid down her dry throat. Sophia was pouring her third cup and feeling revived enough to eye the plate of little macaroons when there were voices in the hall and she realised that their hosts had returned.

Hal shot her a reassuring glance as he got to his feet, then a man in his mid-twenties, so like Hal that there could be no doubt he was his brother, strode into the room and clasped his hand. 'Hal, my dear fellow. We had not looked to see you! Did you write? Nothing has reached us. Grayling says you came on horseback, and I can tell that by the look of you! How is Elizabeth?'

There was a slight cough from the doorway and John stood aside, saying, 'Emma, my dear, forgive me. I am talking so much you cannot greet Hal yourself.' He stood aside as a tall, high-bosomed, handsome young woman swept into the room.

'My lord,' she said in cool, but not unfriendly tones, offering her cheek to be kissed. 'This is a pleasure. I collect that dear Elizabeth is not with you? I do trust she is well.'

Hal did not reply directly, merely saluting the proffered cheek and saying, 'No, she is not with me. I must apologise for this unannounced visit.'

'Not at all, my lord,' she replied calmly. 'You know our house is yours whenever you wish to visit us.' She turned as she spoke and caught sight of Sophia for the first time. It gave Sophia, huddled apprehensively in her chair, a twinge of unworthy satisfaction to see the cool, well-bred poise shaken for a moment.

'Grayling, dinner at seven thirty, please. That will be all,' Mrs Wyatt said, then, as the door closed, she turned back to Hal and raised one arched brow questioningly.

'Emma, I know I may trust to your absolute discretion in introducing to you Miss Haydon, who finds herself in difficulties entirely due to her efforts to assist my sister. Sophia, may I introduce my sister-in-law, Mrs Wyatt, and my brother, the Reverend Wyatt.'

Sophia got to her feet and held out her grubby hand. 'I am so sorry to impose on you in this way, Mrs Wyatt.'

Emma Wyatt touched Sophia's fingertips with her own. '*Miss* Haydon,' and it was a question, not a greeting.

Her husband was less reserved. 'Good evening, Miss Haydon. Has Elizabeth involved you in one of her scrapes? But even if she has, why has Hal dragged you across the countryside in boy's…er…such attire—?' He broke off as the impropriety of the whole situation dawned on him.

'I am sure Miss Haydon would be glad to retire before dinner,' Mrs Wyatt remarked. 'Will you not come with me?' She ushered Sophia out and upstairs. 'I believe Grayling has had the Blue Bedchamber made ready.' On the threshold she broke off. 'Oh. Your luggage is not here yet.'

'I have none, ma'am.' Sophia tried not to sound defensive.

'But your own clothes? Surely, your gowns…' Emma Wyatt gestured her into the room and shut the door behind them. 'How long have you been dressed as a boy?'

'Three days.' Sophia did not know how far to explain: it was for Hal to tell his family what had happened to Elizabeth, and how they came to be in York. 'We had to make all speed, and there was no time to pack.'

There was a long pause while Mrs Wyatt absorbed this information. 'So you have been in my brother-in-law's company, unchaperoned, for *three days*?'

'Er…no, ma'am, it is nearer to a week now, but at first I was dressed in my own clothes, and we had the carriage.'

Mrs Wyatt closed her eyes momentarily, then showing the sang-froid that came from early upbringing, as not only the daughter of a bishop, but the granddaughter of an earl, said, 'If you will step into the dressing room, you will find a bath has been prepared. I will send my maid to you with some clothes. Fortunately my sister, who is much your size, leaves a small wardrobe here on account of her frequent visits.' She turned at the doorway. 'Do not hesitate to ask Hetty if there is anything you require. I look forward to seeing you at dinner, Miss Haydon.'

Sophia plumped down on the bed with a huge sigh. Mrs Wyatt's cool hospitality was decidedly unnerving. Still, the Reverend John Wyatt seemed enough like Hal for her to feel slightly more comfortable in his company.

Soaping her tired legs in the bath, Sophia mused that if her appearance had stirred the well-regulated household of the Reverend Wyatt, it was as nothing compared to the revelations to come.

Mrs Wyatt was as good as her word; when Sophia

re-entered her chamber a rather pretty dress of jonquil lawn was laid out on the bed, along with petticoats, chemise, stockings and slippers of pale yellow kid. A pleasant-faced maid was setting out hairbrushes and rosewater on the dressing table and turned to bob a curtsy as Sophia emerged, draped in a towel.

'There you are, ma'am,' she said, her flat Yorkshire vowels a novelty to Sophia's ears. 'Shall I help you get dressed? And then we can see to your hair.' She bustled round, tying laces and tightening bows. 'There, now! Might have been made for thee. Now, let's see what we can do with this.' She ran a brush through Sophia's rapidly drying hair, clucking her tongue. 'How did your hair get like this, ma'am? Looks like someone's taken the sheep shears to it!'

'That's not far from the truth,' Sophia confessed, warming to the young woman and her earthy approach. 'I had to disguise myself as a boy, you see.'

'Never! Well, that's a new one on me—lady like you!' The maid's eyes were wide with excitement. 'And you've been riding wi' his lordship, dressed as a lad?'

'Er, yes.' She didn't feel she could add anything else, as she watched the young woman's fingers deftly tease curls out of the crop and snip the worst of the rough edges off with nail scissors. 'Oh, thank you, that does look better,' she said with relief as Hetty threaded a length of ribbon through the coiffure.

In fact, she thought, twirling in front of the cheval glass, the crop suited her. Now it was properly dressed it looked modishly dashing, made her neck look long and cheekbones high. And the dress was charmingly frivolous: obviously Mrs Wyatt's sister had good taste and the allowance to indulge it. Suddenly Sophia did not feel quite so tired.

She felt even better as she entered the drawing room and saw the expression on Hal's face when he saw her. Even his brother was openly admiring—until, that was, he caught his wife's eye.

Hal came forward to meet her, took her hands and raised them to his lips. 'Sophy, you look ravishing,' he said so only she could hear. He took her hand and led her to the sofa beside Mrs Wyatt. 'A glass of ratafia?'

John had obviously been asking about his sister, and once Sophia was settled, persisted in questioning Hal. 'So if she is not in Chelsea, Hal, where is she?'

'I have no idea,' Hal said. 'I only know she is with Justin Fanshaw, and has been this week past.'

John sat up abruptly, spilling his wine. '*Justin Fanshaw!* You mean she's…'

In a breathless voice his wife completed the sentence '…ruined!'

Chapter Thirteen

With a soft sigh Mrs Wyatt flopped back against the sofa cushions, insensible. John leaped to his feet and bent over her, chafing her hands and murmuring, 'Emma, dearest.'

Hal poured a strong measure of brandy and passed it to John, who pressed it gently to her lips. She sipped, coughed, then opened her eyes and repeated, 'Ruined! Ruined! What will become of us? What will the Archbishop say?'

Sophia, who had been about to ask if she should ring for Mrs Wyatt's maid, sat down again with a grimace of distaste. So, Mrs Wyatt's first thoughts were for the effect her young sister-in-law's predicament would have on her husband's chance of preferment! It had horribly familiar echoes of George and Lavinia's reaction to her own elopement.

The Reverend Mr Wyatt looked extremely perturbed at his wife's question, then, earning himself Sophia's admiration, said robustly, 'We will worry about that when we have found our sister. Our first thought must be to find Elizabeth.' He looked at Hal, who was silently pouring brandies for everyone.

'What do we know of this Justin Fanshaw? I cannot recall him. The family is respectable enough, is it not?'

'Perfectly respectable family: excellent connections,' Hal said drily, noting his sister-in-law's colour returning at this news. 'Unfortunately, Justin is the younger son, with few expectations and no scruples about marrying to improve his prospects. After all, he has no talents, no application and no ambition. He needs to marry money and, in Elizabeth, he thinks he has found it.'

John set down his glass with a thump and joined his brother on the hearthrug where he began to pace up and down. 'This is dreadful! Have you any idea where they are headed?'

Hal ran one hand through his hair in exasperation and glared at his brother. 'For pity's sake, man, stop pacing, it does not help! They were last seen heading for York. Why else do you think we are here?'

'For a family conference, naturally,' John said repressively.

'The mails are quite adequate for communication these days,' Hal remarked. 'If they were heading in any other direction you may be sure I would have followed them there and saved myself a long, tedious and uncomfortable journey up the Great North Road!'

Sophia repressed a snort. Well, so that was how he chose to characterise their time together! It had certainly been long and uncomfortable, but tedious was hardly how it had seemed to her. In fact, the more she thought about it, the crosser she became. Thank heavens she had said nothing about her growing feelings for him—that would been too humiliating!

Mrs Wyatt, meanwhile, having finished her glass of

brandy, had rallied and was sitting with furrowed brow, muttering, 'Fanshaw, Fanshaw...now where have I heard that name?' Suddenly she sat up and said, 'Mr Wyatt! Be so kind as to pull the bell.'

When the butler arrived she said, 'Grayling, fetch me *Pigot's Directory* from the Reverend's study.'

With the book in her hands she looked up triumphantly. 'I thought so! See, here in Heslington under "Nobility, Gentry and Clergy", a Miss Henrietta Fanshaw. I thought I had met someone of that name.' She fell into thought again. 'I recall now, it was at a Missionary Society tea about a year ago. But she was a very old lady then, and quite frail. Surely the last person a dissolute young man would choose to promote his wickedness.'

'I can think of no other reason for him to make this journey,' Hal said slowly. 'And if they are there, he has played right into our hands. For no one in Town knows of her disappearance so, provided we can extract her from Miss Fanshaw's house, when she and I are seen here together the very reasonable assumption will be that we have arrived together.'

'But she has been in his company for the best part of a week!' Mrs Wyatt wailed. 'What if she...?' Her voice trailed off.

'We will decide what it is best to do once we have her safe.' Hal was grim. 'Whatever the outcome, it is better that no one knows it was the result of an elopement.'

They seemed to have forgotten Sophia's presence. The two men sat down again, John with the *Directory* in his hand, both of them focussed on Mrs Wyatt.

'I know the curate of Heslington,' John said. 'In fact, I think he may be spending the night at the Archdeacon's—he is his uncle, you know. I shall just step round and enquire of him what he knows of Miss Fanshaw.'

'On what pretext?' Hal enquired. 'I thought we were trying to keep this quiet.'

'On the perfectly true grounds that my brother, who has unexpectedly arrived to visit me, believes an acquaintance of his is staying with Miss Fanshaw.'

Mrs Wyatt, looking positively animated, added, 'And having heard that Miss Fanshaw is of advanced years, is reluctant to call in case it should discommode her.'

John shook his head reprovingly. 'Now, now my love, that is embroidering the truth, and I hardly feel I can do that.' He strode to the door, calling, 'Grayling, my hat!'

In the silence that followed the sound of the front door closing Mrs Wyatt looked round the room and seemed to see Sophia for the first time. It was a measure of just how discommoded she was that she said, 'And, Miss Haydon, what of your position? If our dear sister Elizabeth finds herself ruined, as she surely will do, you are quite as much compromised.' Taken aback by her own boldness and the look her brother-in-law flashed her, she flushed. 'Well, we have to think of it,' she said defensively.

'I am thinking of it.'

This was not enough to satisfy Mrs Wyatt and she persisted. 'But what of Miss Haydon's parents?'

Sophia decided it was time she stepped in. She was finding it more than a little irritating to be discussed as though she were not in the room. 'My parents are dead,' she said coolly.

Mrs Wyatt was not to be deflected. 'Then your guardian—'

'I am of age, although I live with my brother and sister-in-law.' Sophia struggled to keep her tone civil. After all, Mrs Wyatt had taken her in despite her apparently shocking situation. She was entitled to understand the circumstances. 'I found myself in a position where I felt I could offer assistance to Miss Elizabeth. Unfortunately a carriage accident threw Lord Wyatt and I into each other's company...' Her voice petered out, she could hardly add, 'And into his arms.'

She could not help noticing both her hostess's expression and the way in which her eyes swivelled to Lord Wyatt. Hal was sitting at ease by the fireside, one leg crossed negligently, his foot swinging. He caught his sister-in-law's gaze and raised one eyebrow.

Mrs Wyatt obviously felt she had to fill the silence. 'Well? And what are you going to do about this, my lord?' she enquired tartly.

'This evening, my dear Emma? Have my dinner as soon as John returns. Tomorrow? Pay a call upon Miss Fanshaw of Heslington. As to anything else, why, Miss Haydon and I have fully discussed the matter.' He smiled blandly at the baffled face of Mrs Wyatt and ignored Sophia's mutinous mutter of,

'No, we haven't.'

'And I would be very much obliged, my dear sister-in-law, if you would write to Miss Haydon's brother and beg the indulgence of her company for a prolonged stay. Doubtless he is a little anxious.'

At that moment the sound of John's return stopped further discussion. He strode in looking triumphant and stripping off his gloves with the air of a man who has much to impart.

'My dear, it would appear that your excellent memory has paid dividends! There is indeed a Miss Fanshaw of Heslington: a very ancient lady who never leaves her room and receives only her physician, her lawyer and the vicar. You can imagine, therefore, what excitement and gossip there was amongst the villagers when a smart closed carriage—much travel-stained—arrived last night. It is the general opinion that Miss Fanshaw's neglectful relatives have finally decided to pay her some attention. No doubt in anticipation of her demise—and the content of her will.'

'Thank heavens!' Mrs Wyatt exclaimed piously. 'Elizabeth is in a respectable household under the chaperonage of a lady.'

'An ancient lady in her dotage, apparently confined to her bed,' Hal added acidly. 'Forgive me, my dear Emma, but it does not fill me with much confidence.'

Further discussion was forestalled by the entrance of Grayling, announcing that dinner was served and the company, its collective appetite heightened by the crisis, said little for the next hour.

In the drawing room afterwards, however, discussion resumed.

'Hal and I will call early,' John suggested, but he was interrupted by his wife.

'Only think, Mr Wyatt, of the practicalities. Miss Fanshaw is very likely to be confined to her bed. It would be injudicious to call too early. And in any case, surely we would wish to present the appearance of an ordinary morning call, so as not to cause speculation in the village. We will take the carriage and I will accompany you.'

Hal and John looked dubious, their relationship suddenly unmistakable in their identical expressions. Sophia decided she was tired of being ignored, other than to be disapproved of. 'I think Mrs Wyatt's scheme is an excellent one. We shall both accompany you, preferably in an open carriage. The expedition will then have a quite innocent appearance—which is more than can be said for the arrival of two angry men on horseback!'

'Then we will set off from York at ten thirty with the ladies in the barouche and Hal and I riding,' John agreed.

By the time the tea tray arrived Sophia realised she could hardly keep her eyes open. The room seemed to swim before her and her aching limbs began to protest anew. 'If you will excuse me, Mrs Wyatt, I think I will retire.'

She had just reached the head of the stairs when she heard the drawing-room door open again and Hal's voice say, 'I will not be a moment, but I have left my handkerchief in my room.'

He took the stairs two at a time and arrived beside her as her hand was on the knob of her bedroom door. 'Sophy!'

She turned, her heart thumping, 'Yes?'

'Are you all right? You have been very quiet.'

All her insecurity welled up. She was so tired that she was all too aware of how frightened she was of the situation she found herself in. Alone with Hal it had been possible to forget the real world. Now the respectable surroundings of the Minster Close and Mrs Wyatt with her politely veiled disapproval *were* the real world. Tears threatened, but she was determined not to shed them.

'No, I am *not* all right! I am tired out, I am stiff from head to toe, I have been patronised by your sister-in-law, disapproved of—in a very Christian manner!—by your brother—and ignored by you. Now that my company, *tedious* as it was, is no longer of any possible use, I would be obliged if you would arrange my passage on the Mail back to London as soon as possible.'

'Such indignation, my little Sophy,' Hal said, sounding maddeningly amused. He had tipped up her chin and kissed her full on the lips. Before she could react he released her. 'Goodnight, Sophy, sweet dreams. And you can forget about the Mail—we have matters to arrange, as you well know.'

Sophia whisked through the door and shut it firmly behind her. Her heart was pounding, her lips tingling from the fleeting touch of his and all thoughts of sleep had fled.

Matters to arrange! So he had not thought better of that threat to marry her! Well, she would not agree. She was not going to marry a man on sufferance, just because he felt he was honour-bound to offer. He found her attractive enough, that was plain: but by his own admission he was a rake, and rakes did not go through life being choosy about the young ladies they kissed. She had no intention of marrying a man who, however attractive, would be faithful for just as long as it took for her to provide him with an heir, and possibly a 'spare', and then revert to his former ways. And as she pulled the nightgown over her head the memory of Mrs Wyatt's expression came back to her—Hal's family was not going to receive with complacency her imposition as Lady Wyatt when Hal could hope for a far more brilliant alliance.

The best thing she could do for Hal, for the man she loved, was to remove herself as quickly as possible. She would go back to London and force George with threats of scandal to allow her enough money to live independently and retire to the countryside. And with this miserable resolution she fell into the black hole of sleep.

The next morning dawned fine. Sophia left the house by the kitchen door, hurried round to the mews and sat on the floor of the barouche while it was driven round to the front door. Emma got in, attempting to look as though she was not arranging her skirts over a young lady huddled on the floor. Once they were safely clear of the city the driver pulled in at the side of the road while Sophia got up, shook out her skirts and took her seat next to Emma. Thus the party that continued through the countryside to the village of Heslington appeared both respectable and ordinary with the roof of the barouche down and the two gentlemen riding in escort to the well-dressed ladies within.

The scene belied the tension which gripped the four. Mrs Wyatt said very little, but Sophia noticed her fingers gripping her reticule tightly. The brothers looked serious and there was no conversation between them. Sophia adjusted the veil of the bonnet that Mrs Wyatt had loaned her. The veiling had seemed somewhat excessive for a morning call, but then, Mrs Wyatt presumably did not wish her presence advertised in the neighbourhood until she returned, apparently accompanying Elizabeth. And Sophia, even though she was quite ready to resent Mrs Wyatt's every suggestion, was too sensible to disagree.

The house in Heslington was a charming small house of the previous century, although the grounds had a faint air of neglect. The bell was answered at length by a very old retainer in an old-fashioned livery, who blinked his amazement at being asked if his mistress was At Home.

'I am sorry, my lord,' he said, glancing at the card in his hand, 'but Miss Fanshaw no longer receives visitors.'

'In that case,' Hal asked casually, 'I assume Mr Justin Fanshaw is receiving?'

If the butler was surprised that this stranger knew that Justin Fanshaw was in the house, he did not show it. 'Mr Justin is in the bookroom, my lord,' he quavered, turning unsteadily to let them in. 'If you and your party would care to wait in the drawing room, I will just—'

'No need,' Hal said breezily, striding past him into the musty gloom of the hall. 'Mr Fanshaw and I do not stand on ceremony. Through here, is it?'

Only Sophia caught the hint of steel in Hal's voice. Oh my God, she thought, hurrying after him, he really is going to harm Justin!

Hal made his way down the hall, glancing in rooms as he passed until he reached a closed panelled door at the back of the house. Without knocking he threw it open and stood on the threshold. Sophia, hot on his heels, almost crashed into him, and stood, hopping from one foot to another with impatience, unable to see around his broad shoulders.

There was a long silence: a silence one could have cut with a knife, then Hal drawled, 'Writing letters, Fanshaw?'

There was a choking gasp and the sound of a chair

overturning on the boards as Hal strolled into the room, his brother and the two ladies at his heels.

Sophia saw a slender young man whose rather pretty good looks held the promise of a double chin in middle age. He was regarding Hal with his mouth hanging open. He looked wildly at the piece of paper on the table in front of him, then back at the intruder. 'Lord Wyatt! I was just...I mean, I was—'

'Writing to inform me that you were about to become my brother-in-law?' Hal suggested, strolling across to twitch the paper up between long fingers. Only the direction had been written at the top. 'Not getting very far, are you?' he mocked, casting a glance at the overflowing wastepaper basket beside the table. 'Rather a tricky social problem, is it not? Let us see, how would it go? *I am writing to inform you that I have deceived your young sister into believing me a man of good character and honest intention and have induced her to flee with me in circumstances that can only lead to her ruin in the eyes of polite Society. I will, of course, make an honest woman of her, at my own convenience. Please arrange for her inheritance to be paid to my account at Coutts Bank.*'

Justin backed hastily around the table to put its width between him and Hal. 'You misunderstand me, my lord, my intentions...'

'It is you who misunderstand, you bloody little rat!' Hal snarled. The next minute he had vaulted the desk and had Justin by the collar and was shaking him like a hound with a rodent.

'Put him down, Hal,' John commanded, striding round the table. The two ladies breathed a joint sigh of relief and to her amazement Sophia realized that she was clutching Emma's hands in both of hers.

It took them both by surprise when Hal obediently relinquished his hold and stood back. But, instead of the words of reconciliation and calm that Sophia expected the Reverend Wyatt to deliver, he folded a workmanlike fist and hit Justin Fanshaw squarely on the jaw, sending the young man crashing to the floor.

'Damn good style,' Hal remarked, clapping his brother on the shoulder.

John massaged his knuckles, and said, somewhat smugly, 'You forget I had my Blue for boxing at Oxford.'

Emma, to all their surprise, clapped her hands together and exclaimed excitedly, 'Oh John darling! Well done!' then fell silent, blushing vividly.

Hal looked down at Justin, crumpled and insensible on the floor. 'He'll live,' he said indifferently.

The butler appeared in the doorway. 'My lord?' he quavered. 'Is anything amiss? I heard a crash.'

'Mr Fanshaw has had an accident,' said John. 'While my brother looks after him, perhaps my wife and I could have a word with the young lady who is staying here.'

'*John! Hal!*' There was the sound of running feet and a small figure hurtled down the hall, through the doorway and threw herself on to John's chest, bursting into noisy sobs.

The scene deteriorated into utter chaos. Elizabeth, for it was she, still sobbing wildly, clutched at both her brothers. Emma flapped around the three of them crying, 'Give her air, fetch sal volatile,' and was totally ignored. The aged butler showed every sign of having a seizure, turning an alarming shade of red and clutching at his chest.

Sophia took the old man by the arm and led him

into the hall. 'There, there, sit down, I will find the housekeeper.' She pushed him firmly into the hooded porter's chair by the front door and hastened through the green baize door which led into the servants' wing.

In the kitchen the cook was in the act of dispatching a maid to answer her mistress's bedchamber bell, which was jangling fit to fall off the wall. She stared in amazement at the sight of a well-bred young stranger demanding her attendance on the butler and ordering the remaining maid to fetch refreshments to the bookroom immediately. 'Oh yes, and some arnica, a bandage and some sal volatile. And at least three or four handkerchiefs,' Sophia added before hastening out again.

An anxious glance at the butler reassured her that he was recovering from his shock. In the bookroom Elizabeth was sobbing quietly on to John's shoulder on the sofa. Emma was patting her shoulder ineffectually and Justin was groaning and attempting to sit up.

Hal leaned down and, seizing him by the collar, hauled him into a chair. 'Sit there, don't move and keep your mouth shut.'

The young man nodded mutely.

There was a tap at the door and Sophia opened it just far enough to take the tray from the maid's hands. 'Thank you, that will be all for the moment,' she said briskly, closing the door on the girl's startled face.

Hal had joined John on the sofa. Sophia handed the smelling salts and handkerchiefs to Mrs Wyatt and turned to regard Justin Fanshaw. Far from looking like a dangerous seducer, he looked like a frightened boy. His bottom lip was cut and his chin was already beginning to bruise and swell.

She tipped some of the arnica on to a handkerchief and passed it to him. 'Here,' she said, not unkindly, 'it will sting, but it will take the bruising down.'

He took the pad with ill grace, causing her to regret her kindly impulse, then winced as the stinging lotion met his cuts.

John was bending over his sister, whispering something into her ear. She became very agitated and shook her head vehemently. 'No, no, of course not, I would never permit...'

Hal met John's eyes across their sister's dark head and the two exchanged a nod of agreement. 'Do you wish to marry him?' John asked. 'Because, after what you have just told me, you do not have to if you do not wish to. Your absence from home is not known and we can find some story to account for your unexpected arrival in York.'

Elizabeth looked up at that, her tear-streaked face made unattractive by anger. 'Marry *him?* I would not marry him if he were the last man on earth! I would sooner marry a toad!'

Hal got to his feet and went over to stand over the cowering figure of Justin Fanshaw. 'And as for you, you will stay in this house until you have my leave to go. And do not think to run home to your father, for he knows all about your stupid wickedness.' Young Fanshaw went pale and buried his bruised face in the handkerchief. 'I will call later this week and we will...discuss...what is to be done with you.'

Justin Fanshaw was still quivering in the chair when Hal handed Elizabeth up into the barouche and the reunited party departed for York.

Chapter Fourteen

The following day Sophia opened the door of the front parlour and found Emma and Elizabeth presiding over the tea cups and a group of ladies who, although of a variety of ages, all shared an air of well-bred gentility. Without quite knowing why, Sophia was certain that each had some connection with the clergy of the Minster.

She was taken aback to find them there, and also not a little nettled by their immediate and scarcely veiled curiosity directed at herself.

Emma, although looking a little strained, made the introductions with her usual calm *sang-froid*. Sophia gathered that she was in the presence of the Archbishop's granddaughter, the wives of the Dean, the Archdeacon and two vicars serving the Minster, and the widow of the late Dean. The names became hopelessly jumbled in her mind, however, for all her attention was focussed on how Emma was going to account for her presence.

The Dean's widow, obviously the most senior there, regarded Sophia through her lorgnette, and remarked, 'Mrs Wyatt, you are indeed blessed with young visitors! I do not recollect you saying that Miss Elizabeth had been accompanied by a friend.'

'Oh, did I not, Mrs Cheriton? Well, of course, with poor Elizabeth feeling so low after her ague, and the natural concern of her brother, it seemed sensible to ask Miss Haydon—such a dear, reliable friend to Elizabeth—to accompany her on the long journey from London. And fortunately for us, Miss Haydon's family were able to spare her.'

Sophia managed to smile modestly at this tribute, masking her astonishment at the ease with which the fabrication tripped off Mrs Wyatt's tongue, and also that she appeared not to mind the impertinent questioning of the older lady.

Now she knew what the story was that she must abide by, Sophia relaxed slightly and parried a flood of questions about the rigours of the journey, the weather, her family, whether or not she was related to the Devon Haydons and—only slightly more delicately—whether she was betrothed to be married. The latter question she was able to turn, managing to suppress her embarrassment at being asked.

Finally released when the collective curiosity turned to Elizabeth again, Sophia sipped her tea and suppressed a smile. Never had she had a more thorough grilling: the ladies would have done credit to the Spanish Inquisition! Now, she was certain, they were mentally searching through *Debrett* to place her lineage and deciding whether she was a threat to their unmarried daughters, a possibility for their unattached sons, or merely a fresh face to invite to social functions.

Her eyes met Elizabeth's and she saw the humour in them, so like her brother's. Against her two strapping brothers, both of whom were over six foot tall, Elizabeth was like a delicate china doll, but there was no mistaking the relationship. Her hair was very dark with the curl which showed at the nape of Hal's neck. Her eyes, as intensely blue as his, were shaded by long, dark lashes but, unlike the men, she was very pale.

The strains of the last week had added a pallor to Elizabeth's cheeks which gave credence to the story of an illness and there were faint, dark circles under the pretty eyes.

The animated chit-chat was broken by Mrs Wyatt saying firmly, 'Now, Elizabeth, my dear, I know how much you are enjoying yourself, but it is time for your rest. Recall what Sir William Knighton told you!'

The ladies were obviously impressed by mention of the most eminent physician in London, and no one demurred when Elizabeth rose to take her leave. Sophia took the opportunity to escape too, with a murmur of, 'Please excuse me, I must make sure she is settled. So nice to have met you all.'

They were scarcely out of the door before first Elizabeth, then Sophia, burst into a fit of giggles. 'My dear! What a crew!' Elizabeth spluttered as they tumbled into her bedroom and shut the door. 'Did you ever come across such a lot of old tabbies?'

'I have to admit, they are even worse than my sister-in-law's friends,' Sophia admitted.

'It is because of the Minster,' Elizabeth explained as she plumped down on the bed without a thought for creases in her muslin skirts. 'They all want preferment for their husbands, sons or brothers, so they are constantly on the look-out for scandal in each other's establishments.'

'Poor Emma, between the two of us we must be posing her a real headache.'

Elizabeth snorted in a most unladylike manner. 'Poor Emma nothing! She is the most ambitious of them all. John will find himself an Archbishop by the time he is fifty if she has anything to do with it. All that is missing from her campaign is a large and promising family—and the start of that, I understand, is already under way.'

Sophia was taken aback at this reference to her hostess's condition. 'Elizabeth, if Mrs Wyatt is in the family way, I am not at all sure you should be discussing it.'

'Oh, pooh! Do not be so stuffy, Sophia.' She curled up on the bed, kicking off her kid slippers. 'What shall we do when those old biddies have gone? Shall we go shopping?'

Just one day in Elizabeth's company had convinced Sophia that Hal was right: his young sister was a handful! 'We are not to go *anywhere* until your brothers have returned from Miss Fanshaw's.' The two men had left after breakfast with a groom leading Mr Fanshaw's hunters. Their intention was to make it quite clear to Justin that one word of his escapade with their sister would have consequences which he would deeply regret. And, as Hal had remarked to John on the way there, the older Mr Fanshaw would no doubt punish his errant son far more effectively than they could, and without risk of scandal.

'Do you think they will horsewhip him?' Elizabeth speculated with gleaming eyes. 'Or Hal could call him out—John cannot, of course, being a man of the cloth.'

Sophia was feeling positively middle-aged in the

face of Elizabeth's girlish enthusiasm, although there
was a scant four years between them. The girl was
certainly pale, but her spirits seemed to be fully restored. It appeared never to have occurred to her that
one of her wonderful brothers would not have rescued
her eventually, or that she had been in real danger of
scandal—or worse.

'Of course they cannot call him out, or horsewhip
him either,' Sophia said rather impatiently. 'Your family is jumping through hoops to keep this whole business quiet and that would be the very thing to set
tongues wagging. You do not wish to find yourself
married to Justin Fanshaw, do you?'

'Certainly not!' Elizabeth responded with a shudder. 'Anyway, why should I? Nothing happened.'

'You were alone in his company for a week,' Sophia pointed out tartly. 'Most people would consider
that ample reason, even if you spent the entire week
reading sermons together.'

Elizabeth subsided, but not for long. She regarded
Sophia speculatively from those disconcertingly alert
blue eyes. 'It had not occurred to me, for everyone
was making such a fuss about my situation—but, Sophia, how exactly *did* you come to be here with Hal?'

Try as she might Sophia could not suppress the
blush which rose to her cheeks. Like a kitten who has
seen a twist of paper, Elizabeth pounced. 'I knew it!
There is a secret! Tell me at once, or I shall ask Hal.'

To hesitate would be to fuel the fire. Sophia said,
as calmly as she could, 'I happened to be at hand
when Hal, that is, Lord Wyatt, discovered your disappearance. As I happened to be unengaged at the
time, I offered to accompany him to provide you with
chaperonage.'

'Oh.' This sounded depressingly respectable, then Elizabeth thought it through. 'But…you are not married, so who was chaperoning *you*?'

Sophia's blush deepened. 'Er…no one. But we did not think it would be long before we caught you, so no one would be any the wiser and you and I would be safely in our beds by morning.'

Elizabeth was thinking hard now. 'But *why* did you not catch up with us? Hal has such wonderful horses. And there is no carriage in the stables here, other than Emma's barouche: I know because I went round this morning to see her new mare. So you did not arrive by coach.'

'There was a carriage accident, which is why we did not catch you. And the repairs would have taken too long, so we had to ride.'

'All that way? Side-saddle?' Her excited gaze alighted on Sophia's head. 'Oh, how daring! I thought you had a very fashionable crop, but it isn't that, is it? You cut off your hair and pretended to be a boy!' Sophia had obviously risen greatly in her estimation. 'What an adventure, far more exciting than mine!' Another short silence ensued, then she added, 'Hal is going to have to marry you, isn't he? Oh, good! I would much prefer you as a sister than Hariette Miller.'

Sophia blinked at Elizabeth: she felt as though she were on a runaway horse and had lost the reins. 'No, he has *not* got to marry me! And who is Hariette Miller? Does Hal want to marry her?' She was conscious of a stab of jealousy.

'You must know Lady Hariette, she is terribly eligible, and she's been throwing her cap at Hal these last six months. I'm not sure if he wants to marry her or not. She is rather beautiful, of course,' Elizabeth added, and Sophia felt another stab in her heart.

'But if you have travelled with Hal all the way from London to York,' she continued, 'then I believe that you are as ruined as Emma fears I would be if my story had got out.'

Sophia was beginning to feel distinctly beleaguered. 'But my story has not got out, any more than yours has. So we are both free to remain as we are.'

'Oh,' Elizabeth said flatly, her voice full of disappointment. 'But why do you not want to marry Hal? I am sure most ladies would, he is extremely eligible and, even though he is my brother, I can see he is very handsome. And just think, you would save him money as well.'

'Money?' Sophia asked, perplexed.

'Well, if he was married he would not have to maintain his expensive opera dancer. Or is it an actress at the moment? I cannot recall, and, of course, I am not supposed to know anyway. Hal is a rake, you know,' she added naïvely. 'Justin would like to be one, but he was no good at it.'

She sounded disappointed, and suppressing all painful thoughts of opera dancers and actresses, Sophia asked, 'Did you want him to be? Why did you want to elope with a rake?'

'Well, it sounds romantic and exciting, do you not think so? And I was so bored in Chelsea and Hal was so stuffy about letting me come up to town and do the Season. Only once we were running away Justin was just silly and clumsy and not at all dashing.'

Sophia shook her head at the girl's innocence. Was *she* ever that innocent? She supposed she must have been, or she would never have eloped with Henry Winstanley!

There was a clatter of hooves on the cobbles beneath Elizabeth's window. She tumbled off the bed and ran to look out. 'It is Hal and John returned from Heslington! Let us go and hear what they have to say!'

When the two young ladies reached the foot of the stairs Grayling was just stooping to hit the gong. 'Ah, Miss Elizabeth, Miss Haydon. Luncheon is served.'

Elizabeth sat, quivering with suppressed excitement as the rest of the party took their places. With a glance at her face Mrs Wyatt said, 'Thank you, Grayling, that will be all. We will serve ourselves.'

The butler was scarcely out of the door when Elizabeth, unable to contain herself, burst out, 'What happened? Did John punch Justin again?'

'No, I did not,' her brother said in a tone of mild disapproval. 'Hal and I explained to Justin the consequences of speaking of this unfortunate matter in any way. I think he has taken the point,' he added, spearing a slice of cold beef in a meaningful manner.

'And Hal did not call him out?' Elizabeth persisted, despite Emma's warning frown.

'I would have done,' he assured her with a straight face. He looked up and smiled at Sophia, whose heart did a sudden somersault. 'I had every intention of calling him out, but I heeded Sophy's advice that it would be an unwise thing to do.' He ignored the sudden shocked silence around the table at the use of the affectionate pet name and added, 'She felt it could cause scandal.'

'As indeed it would,' Emma said sanctimoniously. 'It is vital that we keep your reputation intact, my dear. And we cannot allow our guard to slip, now we seem to be over the immediate danger. One careless word and not only would you find yourself quite ineligible, but John's career would suffer badly. He would never be a bishop with such a scandal in the family!'

Elizabeth's pretty face was livid with anger. She jumped to her feet, her napkin dropping to the floor and shouted, 'Oh, so that's what all this is about! You don't care about me at all, all you are worried about is John's reputation and how he won't be Archbishop of Canterbury or whatever he wants to be because of some silly little scandal surrounding me!'

Hal said coldly, 'Sit down, Elizabeth, and stop throwing tantrums to be interesting, you are not in the nursery now. We have put your brother and his wife in a very difficult position, but we are all trying to do our best for you.'

Sophia shivered. He was quite right to be angry, but she had never heard him sound so cold. But Elizabeth was not to be cowed.

'Oh, do not seek to lecture me, brother *dear*! What about the scandal you have risked, being alone with Sophia night and day! You are in no position to criticise me, for we have heard nothing of your wedding plans, even though you have compromised poor Sophia.'

Emma gasped and got to her feet. 'Elizabeth, you forget yourself! You should not speak so to your brother, and of…such matters too! You should go to your room until you are calmer and can apologise to Miss Haydon and your brothers.'

Elizabeth tossed her dark head and flounced out, leaving a hideous silence behind her. Sophia wondered if she could just slide beneath the heavy ma-

hogany table and hide there until her hectic colour had
ebbed. She fixed her gaze on her plate, as if by not
meeting anyone's eyes she could become invisible.
For the first time the enormity of the situation she
found herself in threatened to overwhelm her.

While she and Hal had been on the road, in pursuit
of Elizabeth and her lover, the consequences had
seemed far away. Now, in this respectable house, in
this respectable city, and with the crisis over Elizabeth
all but settled, there was nothing between her and the
consequences of her headstrong behaviour. George
and Lavinia were right, she thought miserably, I am
not fit to be out in Society, my judgement is so poor.

Gradually her concentration returned and she was
aware of the conversation which the other three were
engaged in, albeit with an air of desperation.

'Is it not today that the Dean of Exeter is expected
to arrive at the Palace?' Emma was saying brightly to
her husband. 'The Archbishop's Palace is at Easing-
wold,' she added for the others' benefit. 'We are hoping that his Grace's wife will have a reception for the
Dean and his party—they are always such interesting
events.'

'Most interesting,' Hal agreed smoothly. Despite
keeping her head down, Sophia could feel his gaze
almost burning her, willing her to look up. Stubbornly
she resisted.

'Some fruit, Miss Haydon?' John enquired kindly.
She did look up then, to accept the bowl with a small
smile. John's face was so like his brother's, but so
unlike it too. It was strange that Hal could stir her so
when the same looks in John roused nothing in her
breast.

She picked up an apple and was just about to put

it on her plate when Hal's warm fingers took it from her hand. 'Let me peel that for you.'

'Thank you,' she whispered and then sat watching his hands as the peel curled up from the silver fruit knife, spiralling unbroken to the plate. She could not take her gaze from those long brown fingers, remembering them caressing her face, her neck, her untutored body. Almost against her will she looked up and met his eyes, seeing the desire there. The scalding blush started at her toes, rose inexorably up her bosom and neck and suffused her face.

Hal's fingers paused for a fraction of a second, then continued steadily to peel, quarter and core the apple. When he passed her his plate, their fingertips brushed and it was as though a bolt of lightning had passed through her. It was a shock to realise that she was still sitting demurely at the table with the Reverend Mr Wyatt discussing parish matters with his wife, apparently unaware of the sensual tension between his brother and herself.

As they rose after the meal Hal touched Sophia's arm. 'Sophy, I would like a word with you. Will you step out into the garden with me? We should not be disturbed out there.'

Before she could say anything he had opened the doors leading out into the walled garden behind the house. The sunshine was on the old stone walls, warming the spring flowers, sending the bees drowsy with their scent.

Hal took her arm and guided her firmly down the flagged path to where a little rose arbour had been created, the tangled growth an effective screen from the house. Sophia instinctively moved to sit on the ornate iron bench, but Hal's arm restrained her and she found herself standing very close, staring at his cravat.

She felt his hands cupping her shoulders, warm through the fine wool of her borrowed gown. 'Sophy, look at me.'

She shook her head, her short curls bouncing with the vehemence of the gesture.

'Look at me, Sophy,' he insisted gently, and this time she obeyed, meeting his dark blue gaze, hoping against hope that all the love and longing she felt for him was not written on her own face. 'I must apologise for my little sister,' he began, but Sophia caught up his words and rushed in.

'Oh, please, no, my lord, there is no need. She is very young, and the strain she has been under this week has obviously affected her nerves. I take no account of what she says—'

'But I do,' Hal interjected. 'For once, what she was saying, however tactlessly, is right, just as I told you on the riverbank. I must marry you.'

'Must you?' Sophia asked slowly, all her resolution to simply say 'No!' vanishing as his mouth came down on hers.

It was a very long, very gentle kiss and Sophia's knees buckled under the intensity of it so that when she came to herself she was sitting on his knee in the arbour, her head resting on his chest. It felt very right, very safe and she wanted this feeling to go on for ever. She snuggled closer, hearing his heart thudding under her ear, pressed against the smooth cloth of his coat.

After a long, long silence Hal spoke, his words rumbling in his chest as she stayed close against him. 'Sophy, my dear, you must agree to marry me.'

At that moment she wanted nothing more than to

be in his arms, to be his wife, and he sounded so gentle, so loving, she thought suddenly that he must love her too.

'Oh, yes, please, Hal,' she whispered, 'yes, I will be your wife.'

Chapter Fifteen

Hal sealed her acceptance with a long, tender kiss which took away what breath Sophia had left, along with every rational thought in her head. She would have been happy to spend the rest of the day, entwined with him in the arbour, but Hal soon set her on her feet.

'I could sit here all day with you,' he said, echoing her thoughts, 'but we have much to plan and do. I must speak to John about getting a licence. Would you like John to marry us in the Minster?'

'Oh, yes!' Sophia agreed happily. 'I would like that very much, if he will be willing.'

'I am sure he will be,' Hal reassured her. 'Now, I think I will find him in his study.'

He parted from her in the hall with a brief, intense kiss, which sent her thoughts flying from thoughts of the glories of a Minster wedding to those of what would follow. The effect was so disturbing that Sophia took herself severely to task. A walk in the Minster precincts would calm her turbulent emotions and cool her pink cheeks. She ran up the stairs, her mind whirling. The Sophia who looked back at her from the mirror as she tied on her bonnet was a woman transformed: her green eyes shone with happiness, her complexion glowed and her lips were full and pink from kissing.

The very undutiful thought crossed her mind that even George and Lavinia would be silenced by the overwhelming kudos of a wedding in the Minster, and to such an eligible bridegroom! She flew down the stairs again, suppressing the knowledge that she should take one of the maids with her on her walk. Surely the Minster precincts were safe enough for an unaccompanied young lady.

The bonnet strings, tied with more haste than care, slipped as she reached the bottom of the stairs. There was a long glass at one end of the hall and Sophia stopped in front of it. The bow had slipped but the knot remained and she had to pull off her gloves before she could unpick it.

She was struggling with the slippery satin when the door of the study creaked and swung partly open in the draught, releasing the sound of a conversation within. So intent was she on the knot that it took Sophia a moment to realise that she was the object of discussion. She should have moved away, she knew, but she was so full of happiness that she wanted to hear Emma and John's first reaction to Hal's news.

'But *must* you marry the girl? Surely things are not at such a pass? Her family will not be able to insist, given the very respectable situation she now finds herself in. And although I suppose the connection is well enough, it is hardly brilliant and not at all an enhancement to your situation—or your brother's, for that matter.' Emma sounded positively querulous.

'She is a very nice young woman,' her husband

reproved gently. 'And while she might not be a brilliant match, as you say, my dear, she is not ineligible by any means.'

'She might be a nice young woman,' Emma retorted tartly, 'but that did not stop her setting out like a veritable hoyden on a madcap venture with a man she hardly knew.'

'But it shows the goodness of her heart, my dear,' John interjected.

Emma snorted. 'It shows a distinct lack of judgement, if my opinion on the matter is of any interest.'

'Of course we care for your opinion, my dear, and I say again, Miss Haydon would not be my choice for Hal, if you press me. After all, there is always the danger that this impetuous behaviour may evince itself in other ways, once they are married,' he added thoughtfully.

'Ha!' Emma responded. 'Lady Caroline Lamb all over again!'

Sophia stopped all attempts to untie her bonnet strings and was listening with every nerve. She felt hurt and hot with embarrassment, but worse was to come.

'One would trust that Miss Haydon is not going to disgrace the family by plunging into an affair with a leading Romantic poet, as Lady Caroline did,' John said repressively. 'However, there may be some underlying moral instability.'

'Surely you would rather marry Lady Hariette Miller?' Emma said and for the first time Sophia realised that Hal must be in the room with them. Why was he not speaking out and defending her? She stood there, her hands twisting the bonnet ribbons, her ears straining for the sound of Hal's voice.

'Lady Hariette is now out of the question,' he said, his voice sounding cool to her distressed mind. 'It must be obvious to you that, as a gentleman, it is my duty to marry Miss Haydon.'

'You have not felt it Mr Fanshaw's duty to marry Elizabeth!' Emma riposted.

'Justin Fanshaw is eminently unsuitable for Elizabeth. I cannot feel that I would be considered an ineligible husband for Miss Haydon.'

'No, indeed, she might consider herself a very lucky young woman at such a catch,' John remarked. 'I am sure her brother will think so!'

Sophia waited, quivering, for Hal to defend her, to say that he wanted to marry her for herself, that he loved her.

'My mind is quite made up on the matter, John. It is my duty to marry Miss Haydon: she was compromised in helping this family and I was wrong to have let her embark on the enterprise in the first place. I am honour-bound to make things right—and as Elizabeth is your sister, John, and you are equally in Miss Haydon's debt therefore, I expect you to support me in this. Now, what is the best way to go about getting the necessary licence? I have no desire to cause local gossip by having banns read.'

It was enough. Sophia could not bear to hear any more. She had been right the other evening on the banks of the stream when they had so nearly made love and he had told her she must marry him. It was for *his* honour, for *his* sense of duty. If he loved her, surely he would have defended her to John and Emma, told them that he *wanted* to marry her.

Sophia found herself walking along the street outside the house, the majestic bulk of the Minster on her left. There were tears on her cheeks, her bonnet ribbons hung like string, and strolling towards her were two of the ladies she had met that morning in Emma's sitting room.

Hastily she turned on to the greensward surrounding the Minster and walked away, under the sheltering boughs of the trees whose branches, clad with young foliage, were already hanging low. Some benefactor had provided a drinking fountain in a clearing and she splashed her cheeks, patted them dry with her handkerchief, retied the ribbons on her bonnet and found a bench, tucked well out of sight.

What could she do? The thought of life as the wife of a man she loved, but who regarded the marriage as a duty, repelled her. If she wrote to George, he would do everything in his power to make sure the marriage went ahead: her only hope was to travel down to the estate in Hertfordshire. Once she was there, perhaps Hal would realise that she meant what she had said at first and that he did not need to marry her.

Could she confide in Emma and ask for her help to take the Mail coach south? Would Mrs Wyatt's ambition for her husband and her distaste of her brother-in-law's proposed marriage override her instinctive obedience to their wishes? Now was the time to find out, while Emma was still full of indignation at the proposed match. Biting her lip to quell the tears that were threatening, Sophia got to her feet, smoothed down her dress and stepped firmly out on to the path, straight into the arms of a slender young man dressed in clerical black.

'My dear lady! Pray forgive me!' He disengaged himself and stepped back, whipping off his hat and bowing slightly. 'Unpardonably careless of me, I do trust I have not…Sophia!'

Sophia stared back. Older, unfamiliar in black coat and clerical collar, but unmistakably the same, Henry Winstanley stood before her. Far from the frightened, indignant and blustering youth from whom George had snatched her in that smoking inn parlour, this elegant and smooth young cleric was, without doubt, the man with whom she had eloped four years before.

'My dear Miss Haydon! What a pleasant surprise, I had no idea you were in York.' He sounded quite composed and not at all as though he had just come unexpectedly upon the young woman with whom he had once so scandalously eloped.

'Indeed, it is a surprise to see you, Mr Winstanley. I have not long been here in York,' she replied in a colourless tone, trying not to let him see just how much his presence alarmed her. 'I am making a very brief visit to friends.'

'Would they be anyone I know?' he enquired, stepping forward to offer his arm. 'Allow me to escort you home. Naturally I will call upon you at the earliest moment—we have so much to talk of.' It was incredible! He showed not the slightest embarrassment, which was astonishing considering how they had parted. He was addressing her as though they were the merest acquaintances who had met at the Assembly Rooms, not as erstwhile lovers.

'Thank you, but I will not trouble you, I am merely taking the air.' Sophia took a deep, steadying breath and appeared not to notice he was offering her his arm. The thought of Henry Winstanley in Emma's drawing room, dropping goodness knows what indiscreet hints, filled her with dread. 'I regret it would not be possible for you to call, Mr Winstanley, my hostess is…indisposed and does not receive visitors at present.'

Despite her cool tone, Henry was not to be rebuffed and remained at her side. She found herself walking along the gravelled path, quite unable to think of how to shake him off. 'I see you have taken Holy Orders, Mr Winstanley. I had understood you had gone to Wales.' What *was* she going to do when they arrived back on the road? The last thing she wanted was for this man to discover where she was staying. Thank goodness it was not Sunday! The shops were open so she could pretend an errand at a linen draper's, or a milliner's, or some other feminine destination that would allow her to shake Henry off.

'You are most kind to have followed my career,' Henry replied smoothly with the air she had once mistaken for real sophistication. 'I have just been appointed to a curacy here at the Minster, a most favourable step in my progress in the church, I need hardly say.'

Sophia's heart sank. She would have to take to her bed in the time she remained in York, for nothing less would excuse her missing church services. It was a miracle that Henry had not already seen her with Mrs Wyatt.

They reached a corner in the path where several paved walks split off. 'You will excuse me,' she said firmly, 'but I must leave you here, I have promised my hostess to carry out several errands for her.'

He stepped to one side and doffed his hat. 'But you will at least furnish me with your direction, Miss Haydon?'

'Er…yes.' What could she say? Frantically she

made up an address and was about to give it to him
when a voice called, 'Oh, Miss Haydon, oh, there you
are.'

It was one of the Wyatts' maids, hurrying along the
path, her face beaming with triumph at having found
her quarry. 'Mrs Wyatt was so worried that you had
gone out without a maid, miss, she sent me right off
to find you.'

With sinking heart Sophia saw Henry's eyes narrow. 'Mrs Wyatt? Would that be the Reverend Mr
John Wyatt's wife?'

'Yes, sir, if you please, sir,' the maid agreed with
a bobbed curtsy, colouring at being addressed by this
handsome young cleric.

'I am sorry to hear she is indisposed,' Henry said
slowly, smiling at the girl, his eyes still narrowed in
speculation. 'I was sure I saw her yesterday at evensong.'

'Oh, no, sir, Mrs Wyatt is quite well, sir,' the maid
assured him earnestly, before responding to Sophia's
sharp hand gesture to take her place behind them and
out of earshot.

'My dear Sophia,' Henry said thoughtfully, standing close. 'Can it be that you do not wish me to call
upon your hostess? I wonder why? Could it be she is
ignorant of your…past? I do hope you will introduce
me, for it can only do my career good to be brought
to the notice of such a gentleman as the Reverend Mr
Wyatt.'

'And if I choose not to?' Sophia said, unable to
suppress the anger in her voice.

'Why, that would be very unwise, Miss Haydon,
for I am sure your friends would be most distressed
to find their guest was not quite what they thought

her.' He smiled, showing beautiful teeth, but his blue eyes were cold with calculation.

'Do not attempt to threaten me, Henry,' she retorted. 'The Wyatts are well acquainted with me, and while they know my history they are not aware of your part in it. I would suggest that it would not do either your reputation, or your preferment in the Church, any good if it were to become common knowledge.'

Henry Winstanley merely raised his hat, bowed slightly and, smiling, strolled off towards the east end of the Minster.

Sophia watched him go, filled with dismay at the encounter, and with a sense that she had not come off best. What *had* she seen in the man? True, he was good looking, but they were the shallow type of good looks that swiftly faded with middle age, and she could readily discern now that his character would be no compensation.

'Miss? Miss Haydon?'

The maid had obviously been addressing her for some seconds. Sophia shook off her disturbing thoughts and concentrated on a solution to this added complication in her life. Her resolve hardened: Hal had little desire to marry her, a sentiment which had all too obviously been shared by his relatives. Well, then, she must leave, but not to return to London, to the joys of life with Lavinia and George. She would keep to her original plan and go to Hertfordshire, where she could find seclusion and no questions as to these last few missing days in her life.

Sophia had no resources of her own, not a penny piece in her pocket. She had only a hazy idea how much a ticket on the Mail would cost, but she was

sure the fast coach would be far more than the slower
stage, or the plodding accommodation coaches. Very
well, then, there was no help for it, she would have
to ask Emma Wyatt for a loan, as well as for her help
in slipping away without Hal's knowledge.

As she was peeling off her gloves in the hall the
butler passed through with a tray of silverware. 'Grayling, are the gentlemen at home?'

'No, Miss Haydon, I believe they had an appointment with the Archdeacon.'

That sounded ominously like the first steps towards
securing the marriage licence. 'And Mrs Wyatt?'

'Mrs Wyatt is in the garden room arranging flowers,
miss.'

Emma was, indeed, occupied in filling a pair of
matching urns with greenery. She greeted Sophia
pleasantly enough, although with a hint of reserve and
was obviously taken aback when her guest sat down
and said, 'Mrs Wyatt…Emma…may I ask for your
assistance in a very delicate matter?'

Two spots of colour appeared on the older woman's
cheeks. 'Assistance? Is something amiss? You are
not—?' She broke off in some confusion, her hands
unconsciously resting over the slight swell in her
gown.

Sophia blushed hectically. Oh, no! Mrs Wyatt had
jumped to a conclusion that had never occurred to her.
'No, no! I assure you, Mrs Wyatt, nothing of that nature. You cannot be unaware that Lord Wyatt has
asked me to marry him?'

'I see.' Emma hastily began hacking at the stem of
a branch of laurel. 'And in the absence of your own
mama or sister-in-law you want to ask me about…er,
marriage.'

They were both now as pink as peonies. 'No, no indeed, Mrs Wyatt. I do apologise, I am not making myself plain at all. The fact of the matter is, I do not wish to marry Lord Wyatt.'

'And why not, might I ask?' Emma was immediately on the defensive. 'You could not hope for a more brilliant match. Why, half the unattached young ladies in London have their hopes pinned upon his lordship!'

Sophia, despite the situation, could see the humour in Emma's response. She kept her face very straight. 'But surely you do not wish to promote this match, given that your brother-in-law is so eligible?'

Emma was obviously embarrassed that she had let her reservations show. 'Well, it is never ideal when people are thrown together by circumstance, and not by choice.'

That was a palpable hit and Sophia winced inwardly. So it was very clear to his family that Hal felt he must marry her. 'Exactly my feelings, Mrs Wyatt,' she agreed firmly. 'Unfortunately, I cannot persuade Lord Wyatt of this. Under your chaperonage I see no reason for a forced alliance, as you obviously cannot, therefore it would be best if I return to my family estate in Hertfordshire. Lord Wyatt will then see that no further action is necessary on his part, however sensitive his honour.'

Emma was positively beaming until she recalled herself and managed an expression of thoughtful regret. 'Oh, dear. I must congratulate you on the fineness of your feelings in this matter: to turn down the prospect of a brilliant marriage to a man who is…so well set up is sacrifice indeed.' She hesitated, watching the play of emotions on the younger woman's face. 'You do not love him, then?'

Sophia's head came up and she looked directly at her questioner. This was something about which she could not bring herself to lie. 'I do love him, far too much to trap him in a marriage that is not of his free will.'

The tip of Emma's nose went quite pink and she produced a handkerchief from her reticule and dabbed her eyes. 'Oh, my dear Sophia! I wish with all my heart that Hal did love you in return. Such nobility of character! I have quite wronged you. Oh, dear!' And she turned her head away.

So, everyone knew he did not love her. Sophia bit her trembling lip, determined not to join Emma in weeping or she would never arrange her escape before the men returned.

'Mrs Wyatt, may I ask you to make me a loan of the money I need to buy my ticket on the Mail? And I am afraid I must also ask for something for food along the way and to hire a chaise when I arrive at Baldock. I am sorry to have to ask, but I do not have any money of my own on me. Naturally, as soon as I arrive home I will arrange for a bank draft to be sent to you.'

'But of course, dear Sophia.' Emma blew her nose briskly and turned to the practicalities of the escape. 'I must find you a portmanteau and a hatbox and enough clothing and toilet articles for the journey. And, let me think, what else will you need? A parcel of food for the journey—one can never trust these inns.'

'Thank you, Emma, that would be marvelous,' Sophia began, but stopped abruptly as Emma's hand flew to her mouth. 'What is it?'

'Today is Saturday!' Mrs Wyatt wailed.

'Yes?'

'I have spent all my housekeeping for this week, and Mr Wyatt always gives me the new week's sum on Monday morning. I cannot lend you anything until then.'

Another day and a half to get through—and at least two inescapable attendances at church with the risk of meeting Henry Winstanley. She would have to plead an indisposition. If she did not say what it was, the men would assume it was a feminine matter not to be discussed. The thought of having to stay in her room for the whole day to add verisimilitude to the story was not appealing, but it also meant she would not have to see, or speak to, Hal. Mrs Wyatt might think she was being noble, but it hurt, it hurt to give him up and every contact with him rubbed salt in the wound.

As she thought it, the sound of male voices echoed in the hall and John pushed open the door. 'Here you are, my dear! And Miss Haydon!' He walked in beaming, followed by Hal, who was looking staggeringly attractive in a dark formal suit with his wayward hair firmly ordered, as befitted someone who had been paying a call of ceremony on the Archdeacon. He was also looking extremely serious, in marked contrast to John's ebullience.

Mr Wyatt crossed to kiss his wife on the cheek. 'Such news, my dear Emma! The Archdeacon was most helpful about the licence, and he believes that his Grace will wish to conduct the marriage ceremony himself!'

'Such an honour!' Emma gasped. 'The Archbishop of York himself! Sophia, you are very favoured indeed.'

Then she caught Sophia's frozen look and realised what she had committed herself to. Not only was she defying her husband in helping Sophia escape, but now she would place him in an incredibly difficult position in having to explain to the Archbishop that, despite his condescension, the bride-to-be had fled.

Chapter Sixteen

Fortunately for Emma, her expression of guilt, so evident to Sophia, was lost on the men as Grayling arrived at that moment to announce that tea was served in the front parlour.

'Tea!' said Emma brightly, 'Why, I do confess, I am more than ready for a cup of tea. I feel unusually fatigued.'

John immediately was at her side, taking her arm solicitously. 'Have you done too much, dearest? Should you go and lie down? I will have the tea brought up to you.'

Sophia hung back as John and Emma led the way, Emma protesting that she was quite all right and would take tea downstairs. 'Grayling, please send to see if Miss Elizabeth will join us.'

Hal held the door for Sophia. 'I expect you have realised that my sister-in-law is in a delicate condition. With it being their first, John is very solicitous.'

Sophia averted her face as she preceded him out of the door. 'It is very natural that Mr Wyatt should feel a proper concern for his wife.'

Hal appeared not to notice her constraint. He gently

tucked a wayward curl of hair back behind her ear, letting the back of his finger trail down her hot cheek. 'Of course. And when the time comes, I am sure I shall feel the same concern for you.'

Sophia's blush deepened. Inside her, a sudden stab of pain echoed the realisation of just what she was giving up. She wanted Hal, she wanted his children— and all that was now lost to her. But she could not marry a man who did not love her—and more especially now, with Henry Winstanley in York. Sophia had no doubt he was ambitious enough to use the past scandal of their failed elopement to his advantage in furthering his career. If she married Hal and it all came out, it would reflect not only on herself and Hal, but also on John's position. Henry did not know just how resolute and tough the two brothers were: far from yielding to blackmail and helping Henry along the path to preferment as he no doubt hoped, they would drag him off to the Archdeacon. But it would still be most unpleasant and she could not risk doing that to Emma and John, who had been so kind to her despite the circumstances.

Tea was quite the most ghastly experience. Hal was demonstratively attentive to her, passing her cake and bread and butter, his fingertips touching hers in a way that sent a *frisson* of desire through her. Elizabeth had joined them, but with a very bad grace, and spent all her time feeding pieces of macaroon to Emma's little lap dog. No one had enquired if Elizabeth was feeling better, or indeed paid her any attention whatsoever, so she subsided into a deep sulk.

John was still concerned about his wife and fussed so much that Emma's agitation was even more inflamed. Sophia stole a glance at Emma and their eyes met. Each woman knew what the other was thinking, of the absolute impossibility of the situation now that the second most senior clergyman in the land was involved in the ceremony.

When the clock on the mantelshelf tinkled four, Sophia made an excuse and left to go to her room. She was followed a few moments later by Emma. Elizabeth joined them in Sophia's room without invitation, and then flounced out again when Emma said kindly, but with an edge of firmness, 'I have to speak to Sophia on a delicate matter, alone.'

They looked at each other for a long moment, then Sophia blurted out, 'I know you can no longer help me, I have placed you in an impossible position. But I must still go away. I will just have to think of some other plan.'

Emma did something quite unexpected, crossing to Sophia and putting her arms around her comfortingly. 'No, I gave you my word I would help, and help I will. After all, it would be much worse if you ran away with no resources and got into some scrape, or even danger. I will explain things to John afterwards, he will understand.' But her voice wavered on the last defiant statement and Sophia knew he was most unlikely to be sympathetic.

Having made the decision, Emma got to her feet and hurried from the room, returning moments later with a little velvet bag. 'Here, take this, I had forgotten about it earlier when we were talking about funds for your journey. And I feel much better about giving you this rather than the housekeeping, for it is my own money, not John's. My papa makes me a small allowance every year and I had put this on one side for a new evening gown.' She shook the money into Sophia's lap, a small shower of guineas which would be more than enough to see her safely to Hertfordshire by the Mail.

'It is too much,' Sophia protested, but was overborne.

'No, better to have some in hand in case of an emergency. And I have checked with Grayling, the Mail leaves the King's Head at six this evening. If we hurry and pack a portmanteau, you will easily catch it.'

Sophia caught her hand. 'Thank you, Emma, from the bottom of my heart. I know how difficult this is for you, but I am sure in the long run it is the best thing for all of us. I will return the money just as soon as I can.'

Both women started as the bedchamber door clicked shut in the draught from the window. 'My nerves are all to pieces,' Emma said with a nervous laugh. 'Now, let us find a portmanteau.'

Half an hour later, a hastily packed bag in her hand and the hood of her cloak concealing her face, Sophia slipped out of the garden-room door and through the mews towards the King's Head.

Her sense of relief at escaping was tempered by the pain of not being able to say goodbye to Hal. Which was ridiculous, she told herself firmly, she was just going to have to become accustomed to being apart from him. They had been thrown together for almost a week, now it felt as though part of her body had been cut away.

As she hurried through the crowded, cobbled streets, Sophia reflected that he would soon forget her, be glad he was not obliged to marry her. He would marry the very eligible Lady Hariette Miller and doubtless she would read of their doings in the social columns of the smartest journals.

In the bustling inn yard she realised that she should have purchased a ticket in advance, and this caused some delay while it was established that there was room—fortunately inside, for she had no desire to spend the night bouncing along on one of the exposed rooftop seats.

The groom hoisted her portmanteau on board and Sophia had one foot on the step of the coach when a hand grasped her shoulder and pulled her back. 'Oh, no, you don't!'

'Hal! Let me go! Please, let me go!'

'You all right, miss?' The coach driver rolled over, a massive figure in his many-caped greatcoat, his long whip in his fist. 'This gentleman bothering you?'

Hal turned to the man and spoke quietly to him for a moment. Sophia took the opportunity to scramble into the coach and take her seat, only to be unceremoniously hauled out again, this time with the coachman standing by, commenting to all who cared to listen that it was scandalous the way young people carried on these days, running away from home and upsetting their guardians.

'He is not my guardian!' Sophia wailed.

'Stand aside there,' the coachman called, totally ignoring her and climbing on to the box. 'Let go their heads, Joe!' Her portmanteau was tossed down, narrowly missing her foot and the mail rattled out of the yard, to the sound of a long blast on the horn.

'Hal,' she protested again, 'you must see—' but she got no further for Hal was kissing her with an intensity which left her dizzy.

Eventually he freed her mouth, but continued to

hold her close, despite the fact that they were standing in the middle of the yard of one of York's busiest hostelries, the object of a great deal of interest.

'Did he say he were her guardian?' one ostler asked another, not bothering to keep his voice down. 'Funny way for a guardian to carry on, if you ask me!'

'Hal, stop it! People are staring at us. Let me go!'

He held her even tighter. 'I do not care if the Archbishop and the full Minster choir is watching. We stay here until you tell me what you think you are doing.'

Sophia stopped struggling and looked up into his deep blue eyes. 'Hal, it is impossible! I cannot marry you, I cannot risk—'

'This morning you agreed to be my wife. What has changed, Sophy?'

'I…I realised I should not do it. I am not the wife for you and your family do not want me to marry you, I know that. And if the story of the last few days comes out, there would be such a scandal. It would affect John and Emma and Elizabeth and you…' Her voice broke. What she really wanted to say was that she loved him too much to risk all that.

To her surprise Hal smiled. 'I see what it is, you are tired and emotionally drained from all that has happened. You coped wonderfully and now the emergency is over you are overwhelmed.' He freed her from his embrace, to a collective sigh of regret from the interested audience, and just touched her lips with his fingertips. 'And perhaps there are things you are…nervous about. You should talk to Emma. Now, come along home.' He tucked her hand through his arm, stooped to pick up the portmanteau and steered her firmly out of the yard with a magnificent disregard for the onlookers.

Sophia was so taken aback that she found herself meekly walking alongside him. But inside she was boiling, all her sadness and regret swept away. How dare he patronise her like that! Tell her she had 'coped wonderfully' but now she was falling prey to feminine vapours! She had thought George was smug, but this took the biscuit! And goodness knows who had seen them...

They had reached the Minster precincts before Hal appeared to realise he was escorting a small volcano. He looked down and said, 'Is anything wrong?'

'Wrong!' Sophia erupted, then swallowed her anger quickly to exchange smiles and bows with one of Emma's acquaintances she had met the other day. 'Wrong?' she continued in more moderate tones when the woman was past them. 'You manhandle me in the middle of York, for all to see, then you patronise me and speak to me as if I was a silly girl prone to the vapours. How do you expect me to feel, Hal?'

'I know how I want you to feel,' he said slowly, with a look in his eyes which left her in no doubt to what he was referring. Damn the man, he only had to use that tone, look at her in that way, and all her willpower evaporated like mist on a summer's day. The trouble was, she reminded herself firmly, he might find her desirable, but that was no basis for a marriage.

'I...I...I really feel that this is not the right thing,' she began when they were interrupted by the sound of her name being spoken.

'Miss Haydon, good evening. We meet again, so soon!' Henry Winstanley stood in front of them, his newly doffed hat in his hands, his face showing nothing but polite pleasure at meeting an acquaintance.

Hal stood waiting to be introduced, obviously thinking this inopportune arrival was merely one of his brother's fellow clerics. Sophia racked her brains frantically, trying to remember whether she had told him the name of the man with whom she had eloped. Her mind had gone blank, but surely she would only have told him the Christian name, at most. All she had to do was to introduce Henry by his surname.

But Henry was ahead of her. 'Allow me to introduce myself, sir, Henry Winstanley, at your service. I can claim long acquaintance with Miss Haydon. Imagine my surprise and delight when we met this morning, quite by chance.' Did Sophia imagine it, or was there a touch of malice in his voice? She realised that her hand had tightened convulsively on Hal's sleeve and she relaxed it quickly, but not before he glanced down at her, a question in his eyes.

He returned Henry's bow with a slight inclination of his head. 'Hal Wyatt. Are you one of the clerics of the Minster, Mr Winstanley?'

'Yes, indeed, Lord Wyatt. Newly appointed here from a curacy in North Wales. York is delightful, is it not? I collect you must be visiting your brother, my senior colleague, Mr Wyatt.' His smile was ingratiating, his tone insinuating and Sophia's anxiety was shot through with humiliation that she could have risked all for such a man. Had she been mad? What had she seen in him, other than youthful good looks and the promise of escape from George?

She was in an agony of restlessness to escape before Henry said anything else, before Hal guessed who he was and the part he had played in her life. 'So pleasant to have encountered you again, Mr Winstanley,' she said, forcing herself to speak pleasantly. 'But we must hurry on, Mrs Wyatt is expecting us. Good evening.'

'You did not seem very pleased to see an old acquaintance,' Hal observed. 'Not that his timing was very good. Now, where were we?'

'I am not going to discuss this any more in the street,' she said firmly. 'I am not going to marry you, and that is that!'

'What about the Archbishop?' Hal enquired mildly, opening the garden gate for her.

'Oh, bother the Archbishop!' Sophia said, stamping her foot on the path, much to the shocked amazement of Grayling who had just opened the door.

'Good evening, Grayling,' Hal said, as if nothing were amiss, handing the butler the portmanteau.

'Dinner will shortly be served, my lord, Miss Haydon. May I bring some refreshment to the drawing room for you?'

'Thank you,' Sophia said hastily, 'but I must go and dress for dinner.' She began to ascend the stairs when Elizabeth came flying down, hair unpinned, a handkerchief clasped in one hand.

'Sophia! He has captured you! How can you ever forgive me!'

Grayling sighed audibly, and vanished through the green baize door to the servants' quarters.

'Elizabeth, what are you talking about?'

'I betrayed you,' the girl said dramatically, her blue eyes brimming with tears. 'I did not mean to say anything, but Hal was so unkind he made me lose my temper and I told him what I had overheard between you and Emma.'

'So it was you at the chamber door,' Sophia said, remembering how it had clicked shut. Suddenly she felt totally exhausted. 'Never mind that now, Elizabeth, please, let me pass, and we shall say no more of this.'

Elizabeth, thoroughly overwrought, burst into tears and fled upstairs, wailing, 'I knew it! You will never forgive me!'

Hal leaned his forehead wearily against the oak banister. 'Women!' he said despairingly.

Sophia's already taut nerves finally snapped. 'You might just as well say ''men''! This is all your fault— if you did not insist on marrying me I could be home in Hertfordshire and no one would be any the wiser. And if you were not so horrible to Elizabeth she would not spend all her time having the vapours.'

In the face of this patent unfairness Hal protested angrily, 'I am not ''horrible'' to her. She has been indulged all her life. If there is a fault in her upbringing, that is it. And I would be obliged if you did not meddle in my family affairs.'

'Meddle!' Sophia stepped back down the stairs until her eyes were on a level with his. 'Who involved me in your affairs in the first place? You were quite happy to let me meddle when you thought I could provide Elizabeth with respectability. And you are determined on forcing me to become her sister-in-law.'

'I am not forcing you to do anything, madam,' he snarled. 'I am merely representing to you the only way out of the situation your unconventional behaviour has landed you in.'

Sophia had never seen him so hotly angry before, but she was too enraged herself to be cautious. 'How dare you blame me? How dare you characterise my behaviour so? My ''unconventionality'' suited your purposes very well when you needed female assistance. Now you are behaving just like George!' It was the worst insult she could think of, and Hal knew it.

In the brief, heavy silence that followed the study door opened and John looked out. 'What is going on out here? I am *trying* to write a sermon. Oh...' He hastily shut the door again. Both the combatants ignored the interruption.

'And you are behaving like a fishwife,' Hal retorted his blue eyes almost black with anger. 'I am beginning to feel some sympathy for your unfortunate brother if he has to put up with such headstrong, unladylike, intemperate behaviour.'

Sophia was so taken aback by this onslaught that she was momentarily incapable of speech, then she saw that Hal had handed her a weapon. 'Well, if I am so comprehensively unsatisfactory, it is fortunate you have discovered it now, and not after the Archbishop had married us! Will you now accept that our connection is at an end?'

Hal regarded her between narrowed lids. 'After this exhibition you may take it that I am as unwilling to marry you as you are to marry me. However, I recognise my duty and I intend going through with this marriage come hell or high water. And if you continue to object, you should reflect that if you had done *your* duty and remained at home in obedience to your brother, we would not find ourselves in this coil now!'

Before Sophia could speak, or even react, he had turned on his heel and marched into the sitting room, his shoulders rigid, his back straight. He closed the door behind him with controlled emphasis and Sophia was still gazing blankly at the panelling when it reopened just enough for Emma's lap dog to be propelled firmly out of it. It looked mournfully at her out of rheumy eyes and was promptly sick on the tiles.

Sophia had no very clear recollection of going upstairs or letting herself into her room. She threw herself across her bed, beating her fists into the pillows until her fury subsided. Finally she sat up, pushing her hair off her wet face and saw her own reflection in the mirror across the room. A pink-cheeked, wet-faced, dishevelled young woman stared back aghast at her, her face reflecting the growing horror as Hal's final words sank in.

She had known he desired her, had believed that he liked her and enjoyed her company, found her spirit and independence stimulating. Now she knew his true opinion, spoken in anger with all restraint abolished. He considered her wayward, disobedient and had made it quite clear that the independence which she thought he had admired and enjoyed was a severe flaw in her character. He obviously had far more in common with his clerical brother than she had realised.

Sophia swung her legs off the bed and smoothed down her crumpled gown. There was cold water on the washstand and she splashed her hot face until the colour subsided and she felt she could face her maid. She pulled the ribbon out of her russet curls and shook them, disguising their disorder, then tugged the bell-pull.

If tea had been dreadful, it was as nothing compared to the atmosphere that prevailed over dinner. Emma, looking pale and drawn, was obviously anxious that John would find out about Sophia's escape to the mail coach and her own part in it. Elizabeth, who had taken her place at dinner on her best behaviour, was startled by a sharp reprimand from her sister-in-law for having overfed the lap dog with macaroons.

'Poor little Pippin was most unwell—and in the front hall,' Emma scolded. 'He has a very delicate constitution and it was very remiss of you, Elizabeth, to give him all those sweetmeats.'

If her intention had been to prevent the girl revealing any of the afternoon's events, she succeeded only too well. Elizabeth, pouting tremulously, spent the rest of the meal pushing her food around her plate and irritating both her brothers by producing martyred sighs every few minutes.

John, having overheard part of the quarrel between Hal and Sophia, kept launching into awkward conversation gambits to cover up the chilly silence between them. 'The Bishop of Exeter was kind enough to remark upon that article of mine I wrote on the various problems in studying the Ephesians. He went so far as to say that it would become the established work and be of great interest to future scholars.'

'How gratifying,' Hal remarked with a heavy irony lost on no one round the dinner table.

Sophia shot him a look of reproach and said kindly, 'It sounds fascinating, Mr Wyatt, I do hope you will allow me to read it.'

Hal's eyebrows rose. 'Your range of academic interests constantly amazes me, Sophia. Perhaps John could arrange for you to attend a lecture on the subject.'

'I would not dream of doing so without the permission of my hostess,' Sophia retorted sweetly. 'And, naturally, with an appropriate escort.'

If Hal thought he could discompose her with barbed references to how they had first met, he was much mistaken! But there was little pleasure in sparring with Hal. No matter what he said, what he did, she loved him. She looked across the table at his austere profile, turned towards Emma, and her heart missed a beat. More than anything she wanted to throw herself into his arms, but how could she?

If she had thought it wrong to marry him before, when at least she had believed him to like her and enjoy her company, how much worse would it be now, after the bitter words that had passed between them?

Chapter Seventeen

'Oh what a relief to have the house so peaceful,' Emma sighed, pushing the heap of cut flower stems on the table to one side and sinking into the chair. Pippin, no longer in disgrace, jumped on to her lap and settled down contentedly on her apron. She absent-mindedly fondled the dog's ears as she regarded Sophia, who had just wandered into the garden room. 'What have you been about, my dear?'

Sophia took the chair opposite her hostess, reflecting that the one good outcome of the situation she found herself in was that it had brought the two of them closer together. 'Well, I have mended the hem on that sprigged muslin you lent me which I caught on the grate the other morning, and I have finished matching those silks you found in such a tangle.'

'Thank you,' Emma responded, adding apologetically, 'it is a task Elizabeth would normally have undertaken, but the mood she is in, she would have made them worse not better.'

'Let us hope that her ride with Hal this morning will blow away her megrims. It does look a nice day.' Both women looked out of the glazed doors into the small back garden. The breeze was up, tossing the new green leaves of the lilac, but the sunshine was strong and bright. 'Shall we go for a walk this morning? Or perhaps you are expecting callers?'

She hoped not. Strangers were easier to cope with than the others in this household, but even so, after a wretched night, with those bitter words of Hal's still running over and over in her head, a quiet stroll with Emma was all she could tolerate. Yesterday, being Sunday, had been filled with church attendances and guests for luncheon, and had passed like a dream with no real contact between Hal and herself.

'It is not my usual day for morning callers,' Emma said, looking cheerful at the thought of getting out of the house. 'And with Mr Wyatt occupied at the Deacon's all morning, I am entirely at your disposal, my dear Sophia. Would you be so good as to carry these flowers through to the front parlour and I will ring for tea.'

They were soon settled with the tea tray, Pippin banished to the hearth rug. 'Now, where shall we go? I have some lace to match for my new bonnet, but after that I am quite at liberty. Would you care to go to the circulating library?'

'Why, yes, I have been missing my weekly visits to Hookham's Library, I must confess,' Sophia admitted. 'Do you enjoy poetry? I understand that Coleridge's *Kubla Khan* has finally been published, and I believe, although I have not yet seen it, that Byron's *The Siege of Corinth* is also now available.'

'Byron?' Emma looked slightly alarmed. 'I do not think that Mr Wyatt would approve of his works. And Mr Coleridge does have a somewhat strange reputation...although I suppose it *is* on a historical subject,' she added vaguely.

'Do not worry. If Lord Byron's poem is available, I promise I will read it in my room and not allow Elizabeth to borrow it.'

These literary musings were interrupted by the knocker. 'Oh dear,' Emma clucked. 'Who can that be?'

'Mr Winstanley, ma'am,' Grayling announced, offering Emma a silver salver with one calling card upon it. 'Are you at home, ma'am? I regret I forgot to enquire earlier.'

'Mr Winstanley?' Emma's brow furrowed as she studied the card, then cleared. 'Oh, yes, I collect Mr Wyatt did speak of a young curate, newly arrived from Wales. I am sure Mr Wyatt would wish us to offer hospitality. Please show him in, Grayling.'

Sophia's heart sank and she felt a stab of nausea. Henry, here! She should have known that he would not accept her cold rebuttal of him on Saturday. He was an ambitious man, and in encountering her with Hal he had suddenly seen a way up the ladder of preferment.

'Mr Winstanley, ma'am.'

Emma stepped forward to shake hands. 'Good morning, Mr Winstanley. I regret my husband is not at home to greet you. May I introduce Miss Haydon to you?'

'Good morning, Mrs Wyatt, I am most honoured that you have received me. I do hope I am not intruding? Good morning, Miss Haydon, such a pleasure to see you again so soon.' He released Emma's hand to bow over Sophia's reluctantly extended fingers.

'Mr Winstanley,' she acknowledged colourlessly,

resuming her seat. If she had not known Henry so well, she too might be regarding him with the same approval Emma now bestowed upon him. There was no denying he was a very well set-up young man. His coat was immaculately cut, his linen spotless, his boots burnished to a high sheen. His manners were exemplary and Emma was soon falling under the spell of his easy charm.

He accepted a cup of tea and a macaroon with grace and maintained an easy conversation with Emma about the parish in Wales from which he had been promoted and the many charms of York in comparison.

Sophia found it hard to sit still. So far, all Henry's conversation was innocuous—topography, his impressions of York and the beauty of its buildings—but she was on tenterhooks waiting for him to say something—anything—that might reveal the depths of their previous relationship.

Emma's curiosity had been aroused and she commented, 'It appears that you already know Miss Haydon, Mr Winstanley.'

Sophia held her breath. Henry laughed lightly, 'Oh, we were childhood sweethearts in Hertfordshire, Mrs Wyatt. Quite two hearts that beat as one, but it was not to be. Imagine my delight when I came upon Miss Haydon the other morning.'

Emma shot Sophia a curious glance. It seemed odd to her that Sophia had not mentioned meeting an old friend, particularly as she had no other acquaintances in York. Sophia read the glance correctly and searched frantically for some innocuous way to join in the conversation when Henry added, 'And then I had the pleasure of meeting Miss Haydon again later the same day with Lord Wyatt.'

Without knowing it, he had triggered alarm bells in Emma's mind—that meeting must have occurred when they were returning from Sophia's attempted escape on the Mail: no wonder it had not been mentioned. She hastily changed the subject.

'How nice for Miss Wyatt that she now has an old friend in the city.' She smiled. 'Now you must tell me, have you secured congenial lodgings, Mr Winstanley? Some of our young curates have had the most unfortunate experiences with very unsuitable landladies before they have found themselves settled.'

And from that point, with the firm hand of an experienced and ambitious clergy wife, Emma kept the conversation on local Minster matters. If Henry found this tiresome, his handsome face did not show it. But then, Sophia mused, her eyes flicking between Henry and the face of the mantel clock, he would recognise the need to be on the very best of terms with the wives behind the men of influence in the diocese. The clock hand moved to twenty past. Thank goodness, someone as careful as Henry would not exceed the polite expectation that a morning call would be confined to thirty minutes exactly.

Just then the front door opened and the hall filled with the sound of Elizabeth's animated voice. Hal and Elizabeth had returned. 'Oh, Grayling, please take my whip and gloves. We have had a lovely ride. Hal, may we do this every morning? Oh, look, a hat. Do we have morning callers, Grayling?'

'Yes, Miss Elizabeth. The gentleman is with Mrs Wyatt and Miss Haydon in the front parlour.'

'Oh, good! A gentleman!'

'Elizabeth,' Hal growled and Sophia's heart leapt uncomfortably at the sound of his voice.

His sister obviously heeded his warning, for it was a very demure young lady who tripped into the front parlour, putting back the coarse mesh of the veil on her tricorne hat with one white hand. She looked stunning, Sophia thought wistfully, conscious of her own heavy eyes and lack of spirits. Elizabeth's figure, as slender as a reed, was clad in a deep claret riding habit of dashing cut and her dark hair was piled into a net which scarcely controlled its luxuriance. Her blue eyes, sparkling from the exertions of her ride, turned on Henry and Sophia saw them widen as she took in the tall, slender, blond young man who had leapt to his feet at her entrance.

'Oh! Good morning, sir,' Elizabeth said demurely, lowering her lashes to sweep enchantingly over her rosy cheeks. Minx! Sophia thought savagely. The chit knows exactly what she is about. It appeared her last escapade had taught her nothing of discretion.

Henry, however, was reacting exactly as might be expected on being introduced to a ravishingly pretty, well-connected debutante. He bowed over her hand when introduced, holding her fingers for just a fraction longer than he should, then helped her to her seat as though she were fragile porcelain.

Hal, following his sister into the room, exchanged greetings with Henry, then, taking a cup of tea from Mrs Wyatt, went to sit opposite Sophia. She tried to read his face, but saw nothing there other than the healthy glow of a man just returned from an energetic ride. He met her gaze and smiled slightly and a hot shiver ran through her from head to toe. Hal was look-ing devilishly attractive—fit, tanned, his dark hair ruffled by tossing off his hat. Sophia wanted nothing more than to jump up and throw herself into his arms, kiss his mouth, still chilled by the breeze.

She coloured and swallowed hard, sure her thoughts were obvious to this man who knew her, her body's reactions, so well. Hal's eyes danced responsively, and his lips quirked as if he was remembering something particularly pleasurable. It seemed, this morning, that she was forgiven and that Hal once again considered her many character flaws less important than his need to flirt with her.

The clock struck half past eleven and Henry made as if to get to his feet. 'Oh, no, Mr Winstanley,' Emma protested. 'Please, do not hurry away. I was about to ring for fresh tea.'

Henry subsided, smoothing his hair back with one well-manicured hand. Sophia was surprised, then saw the look on Emma's face as she observed him and Elizabeth. Emma obviously thought that a respectable, attractive curate was exactly what her sister-in-law needed to salve her broken heart and restore her spirits. And even Hal appeared to be watching his sister's flirtation with indulgence.

John arrived home as the clock struck midday. Henry leapt to his feet and waited modestly to be noticed by his superior. After exchanging a few words he thanked Emma fulsomely for her hospitality, apologised for the length of his intrusion and left with a warm invitation for an early return ringing in his ears.

'Promising young man,' John observed, refusing a cup of tea. 'One hears nothing but good of him. He has been particularly helpful to the Dean, I believe.'

'I am pleased to hear it,' Emma responded. 'He has

the most charming social manners. Quite a useful addition to Society in York, one feels.'

'Indeed.' John settled himself in the place just vacated by Henry, enquired after Elizabeth and Hal's morning ride, then produced his pocket book and pulled what appeared to be a list from it. 'I am glad to catch you all at home. If no one has another engagement before luncheon, I think we should discuss the wedding arrangements. The Archbishop has been asking about our plans.'

Sophia's silence went unnoticed amidst Elizabeth's excited chatter about being a bridesmaid. John tugged the bellpull, ordered Madeira and ushered them all into his study to sit around the big table where he drafted his sermons. 'I have begun a list,' he said, spreading papers in front of him and dipping his quill in the standish. 'The first thing to decide is the precise date: I understand from his Grace's secretary that the tenth of next month would be convenient. Is that enough time, my dear?'

'Three weeks?' Emma looked pleased. 'That will be ample—more time than I had feared.'

John conned his list. 'Now, you can leave the arrangements about the ceremony to me, Hal. The most pressing matter is the announcement and the guests. Have you heard yet from Sir George Haydon?'

'I had a reply to my letter this morning.' Hal produced a folded letter from his pocket and tossed it onto the table. 'He is seeing to the announcements in the London papers, and I have said I will insert a notice in the Yorkshire news sheets.'

'George?' Sophia grasped the arms of her chair and stared at Hal. 'You have written to my brother? I thought Mrs Wyatt had done so to tell him I was staying.'

'Of course, but it seemed better if I added my news to her invitation,' Hal replied smoothly. 'Naturally, I had to ask his permission.'

'And what did he say?' Sophia demanded, in a voice that cracked.

'Why, he said "yes". What did you expect him to say?'

'He is happy?' Sophia stammered. 'What does he write?'

Hal picked up the letter, glanced at it and replaced it in his pocket. 'He expresses himself as delighted and says that Lady Haydon is ecstatic.'

'That I can believe,' Sophia muttered under her breath. Lavinia would regard this match as heaven sent for her ambitions for herself and her daughters Charlotte and Grace. 'But I have not heard from him,' she added out loud.

Hal looked at her, one eyebrow raised. 'Perhaps he feels that all correspondence should now be by way of your affianced husband.' Sophia glared back, her feeling of impotence growing. Whatever she said, however badly she behaved, it seemed that Hal was determined to make her his wife. And it also appeared that she was to have no say at all in her wedding arrangements!

Emma broke into her thoughts. 'Now, how are we to plan for guests? There will be Sir George and Lady Haydon and their two daughters…'

Hal produced another list. 'Sir George is ahead of you, my dear. He has sent me a list of those he will be inviting, just as soon as he receives confirmation of the date. If all of them accept, and I am sure not everyone will be able to leave London at this time, it will number around fifty.'

'And our own party,' Emma chimed in, rapidly calculating on her fingers. 'And Mr Wyatt's colleagues and their families, and your guests, Hal. My word! We may find ourselves entertaining well over one hundred people.'

Sophia felt decidedly faint. If she had thought about her wedding day at all, it had been in terms of a quiet affair with a very small group of people indeed. It seemed instead that she was being thrust into the leading role in a Society wedding. However was she going to get out of this now? It was not as though it were a secret any longer, for George would have lost no time in sending the announcements to the papers and Lavinia would have informed her entire acquaintance.

She must have become very pale, for Emma patted her hand kindly and said, 'It is natural for you to feel nervous about such a grant event, my dear, but there is no need to worry, I will look after all the practical details.' She caught Sophia's desperate look and leaned towards her to murmur, 'My dear, it is all for the best, you cannot run away now, you *must* see that.' She turned to her husband and said, 'But where are we to hold the wedding breakfast for so many?'

Hal produced another letter. 'Do not fear, Emma. I wrote to my old friend Lord Sydney to ask him to stand as my groomsman and he has not only accepted, but has offered me the use of Allerthorpe Hall, his seat. As you know, it is only four miles outside York. Not only will it accommodate the breakfast, but also Sir George and his family; any of the guests who do not wish to make their own arrangements are invited to stay there.'

Emma clapped her hands in delight. 'Allerthorpe Hall! Why, Sophia, we could not hope for anything better—it is such a beautiful estate, and we need not have the slightest qualm at inviting his Grace to the breakfast in such a setting.'

'Oh, good,' Sophia responded hollowly.

Elizabeth broke in. 'We must make arrangements for our wedding clothes as soon as possible!'

Hal passed Emma a sealed package. 'I understand from Sir George that this contains a bank draft and a request from Lady Haydon that you arrange Sophia's trousseau.'

'Excellent! What about jewellery?' Emma enquired, already making her own mental lists.

'Oh, yes, Sophia, your brother writes that he will be bringing your mother's jewels, including the diamond set,' Hal remarked blandly.

Sophia bit back the angry words which sprang to her lips. It would do no good to demand why George had not seen fit to write to her personally about such a sensitive issue but, knowing him as she did, why should she be surprised?

'Well, we *do* have much to plan and do,' Emma said excitedly. 'Before we do anything else, Sophia dear, we must make some lists. Now, I must have a word with Cook about tonight's dinner, and then shall we meet in the breakfast room and make our plans?' She got to her feet, unconsciously smoothing her gown over the slight swell of her pregnancy and, with a dazzling smile at her husband, left the room.

John beamed back: his wife was looking well and was obviously happy, his brother was making his somewhat unfortunate match without any of the attendant scandal they had feared and even his worrying little sister appeared to have attracted the attention of an unexceptional young cleric. 'Well, you must forgive me, for I must be off once again. I am having luncheon with the Minster Treasurer. Oh, Elizabeth, I forgot to tell you with all this excitement—your old schoolfriend, his daughter Jane, has requested that you accompany me. I expect you will have much to talk about. Come along or I will be late!'

Suddenly the room was very quiet. Sophia fixed her eyes on her clasped hands, aware that the fine hairs on the back of her neck were tingling. Her feelings were in turmoil and Hal's silent presence only increased that turmoil. She *loved* him! She should be the happiest person in the world for she was going to be his wife in a mere three weeks. But she had already resigned herself to the knowledge that this could never—should never—be. And now she was trapped, with all the doors closing in her face. Until the arrival of George's letter she had believed no one else knew and she could run away from Hal just as soon as she found a new escape route. Now the announcement would be in *The Times* and all of polite Society would know. How could she run away now?

It was all so difficult, so painful to think about, that she buried the dilemma and allowed her anger with him to rise in its place. Hal saw her burnished head come up and was taken aback by the anger in her green eyes.

'Sophy?'

'On Saturday you described me as—let me see if I can recall this correctly—ah, yes, "headstrong, unladylike, intemperate" in my behaviour and informed me that you were as unwilling to marry me as I was to wed you. So what has changed, Hal?' She got to her feet, leaning her clenched fists on the table. 'I have not changed in the course of one Sunday, so why are you suddenly so anxious to walk up the aisle with me in three weeks' time?'

Hal's tone was reasonable. 'You made me very anxious indeed, trying to run away like that. Goodness knows what dangers might have befallen you on such a long journey without even a companion. Relief made me express myself more vehemently than I would normally have. I can recall my mother scolding me as fiercely when I had gone missing as a child and she had feared the worst. When I turned up again, grubby but none the worse for an escapade, her anxiety turned to anger.'

If he thought he was placating her, he was mistaken. 'And you choose to tell me about your correspondence with my brother, about your plans with your friends for *my* wedding, in front of your whole family without so much as a word to me beforehand.'

Hal got to his feet with a rueful shrug. 'Well, I knew you would not be pleased, so it seemed the best way to avoid a lot of argument.'

'Oh!' Words failed Sophia and she vented her frustration by turning away and taking several agitated strides up and down the room. 'Yesterday I said you were as bad as George, but I have changed my mind: you, sir, are worse than George!' And then she did something most unSophialike and burst into noisy tears.

Seconds later she was enfolded in a warm embrace, her wet face pressed hard against Hal's shirt front, her nostrils full of the scent of clean linen, sandalwood and warm man.

Chapter Eighteen

'Stop it,' Sophia mumbled, but she did not mean it, she wanted to be in his arms for ever. 'I am making your shirt all wet.'

'I don't care,' Hal said, his voice sounding muffled as though his mouth were in her hair. She felt his warm hand come up, almost cradling the nape of her neck, and he stroked the fine skin there until her angry sobs subsided. He moved his hand and said gently, 'Look at me, Sophy.'

'No!'

'Why not?'

'My nose will be red,' she responded with a miserable hiccup. 'It always goes red when I cry. I wish I was like those beautiful women who can weep their heart out and look lovely at the same time.'

Hal gave a snort of laughter. 'I will think you lovely, Sophy, even with a red nose. Come on, look at me.'

She lifted her face to his and was almost overwhelmed by a wave of love for him. It was so much easier to stick to her resolution to escape when he was being unkind to her, but when he was like this…she felt all resistance failing her.

'You are quite right,' Hal said with a smile. 'Your nose is pink. Here, take my handkerchief.'

Sophia took the square of linen and blew her nose prosaically. Then what he had said sank in. 'Do you really think I am lovely?' she asked, watching him from under wet eyelashes.

'You know I do,' he said, his voice suddenly husky. 'You know what happens when I take you in my arms.' He kissed her lightly on the tip of her nose.

'That is nothing to do with anything,' she said, obdurately refusing to be charmed.

'Well, what about this, then?' He cupped her face with warm strong hands and kissed the corner of her mouth lightly.

'No, you cannot get round me like that. And anyway, it is not what I asked you!' But her voice was unsure.

'Very well. Then I will change my tactics.' And before she could speak, before she could think even, his warm lips captured her own and pressed down with a touch that was at first light, then, as she kissed him back, with passion. The tip of his tongue parted her lips and teased her own and she was lost, back on the riverbank in his arms, dappled by the evening light, the scent of crushed grass and herbs in her nostrils.

Hal groaned deep in his throat and shifted his grip on her body, impelling her into the embrace, leaving her in no doubt as to the strength of his arousal. His body was hard and insistent, and Sophia found she had no willpower at all to resist him. She wanted him, he so obviously wanted her—why fight any more?

Why not just give in, lose the only defence she had against this marriage? It would be so easy, she thought hazily, and as he caught her up in his arms without breaking the kiss, so pleasurable, so very pleasurable.

Hal was one stride from the *chaise-longue* when the study door opened, and as quickly closed again. It was enough to break the spell. Sophia found herself on her feet, Hal's arm steadying her as he looked at the closed door. Then it slowly opened, and, with a slight warning cough preceding him, Grayling entered.

By the time the butler was in the room Hal was flicking over the pages of a parish magazine and Sophia appeared intent upon picking deadheads off the flower arrangement on John's desk.

His face an imperturbable mask, Grayling announced, 'Mrs Wyatt has asked me to say, Miss Haydon, that she has ordered a light luncheon to be sent to the breakfast room so that you will not need to interrupt your wedding planning.'

'Thank you, Grayling,' Sophia replied with dignity, aware that her hair was distinctly ruffled and that her fichu had become twisted. 'Please tell Mrs Wyatt that I will be with her directly.'

The butler bowed and left. Sophia hastened to the mirror and looked at her flushed cheeks in dismay. 'Oh, look at me!' she exclaimed, taking in her pink cheeks and bright, excited eyes.

'I am looking,' Hal said softly, coming to stand close behind her, his arms encircling her waist.

'Stop it!' she said, batting at his hands. 'Emma is waiting for me and look at the state of my hair!'

Hal dropped a kiss on the top of her tousled, cropped head. 'I think your hair is charming; you will set a new fashion when we are back in London.'

'You are incorrigible,' she scolded, patting her fichu into place as she hastened from the room. Her heart was pounding and she tried to be grateful for Grayling's intervention. But she knew in her heart that, had Hal pressed her, she would willingly have given him everything that he wanted—because she wanted it too. And she must not, *must not*, capitulate and condemn them both to a marriage that was wrong. However much he desired her, he had never told her he loved her and she was not such a sheltered innocent to believe that he would not be equally aroused by any other presentable woman who yielded to him so willingly.

'Ah, there you are.' Emma was already seated before her little escritoire, a pile of hot-pressed paper before her, her quill freshly sharpened. She eyed Sophia's face and remarked, 'You look a little flushed, dear.'

'I have just been having...words with Hal. I am sorry I kept you waiting.'

'Oh, dear.' A frown crossed Emma's brow. 'You have not been arguing again, have you? Surely, now, you must see that this is all for the best? After all, you love him, don't you?'

'Please do not say anything about that, not even to John. I should never have told you how I felt about Hal.' Sophia was alarmed. It was one thing for Hal to recognise that she desired him, quite another for him to know that she loved him. It would be difficult enough without having to endure his pity!

With only a pause to consume cold meat, bread and butter and fruit and to drink innumerable cups of tea, the two women settled down to the intricacies of wedding planning. For minutes at a time Sophia found herself carried along in the flow of Emma's enthusiasm and undoubted skill for organisation.

They wrestled with menus and seating plans, aided by frequent recourse to the etiquette book for orders of precedence. 'Oh, dear, does the rural Dean who is the second son of an earl take precedence over the bishop of a minor diocese or not?' Emma muttered, flicking through the pages. Orders of service proved simpler—'Dear John will guide you over the hymns and readings'—and Emma brushed aside the question of carriages with, 'Hal will deal with that.'

But these details, comfortingly unreal as if they were to do with another person altogether, were eventually replaced with the question of her trousseau and wedding clothes and Sophia found herself recalled to the reality of what exactly was happening.

'We will go to Madame Levalle, of course, she is quite the best modiste in York, and her seamstresses also have a good reputation for embroidered—' here Emma coloured slightly '—er...undergarments.' She recovered herself, not noticing the deep blush on Sophia's cheeks, and pressed on to list the number of day and evening dresses, the sort of mantles and hats and the types of boots and shoes Sophia would need.

The words flowed over Sophia's head as she sat, cheeks burning, her treacherous imagination contemplating Hal's expression if he saw her in embroidered nightwear. She could remember his reaction that evening at Mr Fanshaw's hunting lodge when he had seen her in the diaphanous peignoir...

'Do you agree, Sophia?' Emma asked, obviously not for the first time.

'Oh, yes, whatever you say, Emma,' Sophia replied

hastily, not wishing to offend the other woman. 'You have so much more experience in such matters.'

'Ah, yes,' Emma said hesitantly. 'I had been meaning to have a word with you—in the absence of your own mama and with your sister-in-law perhaps not arriving until immediately before the wedding day...' She shifted slightly on the chair. 'If there was anything you wanted to ask me about...that is, anything you were anxious about...that is, on the more intimate side of marriage...'

Sophia was saved from answering by Elizabeth bursting into the room. 'There you both are, doing all the planning without me!'

Elizabeth was looking very flushed, very animated and quite outrageously pretty. You have been flirting, my girl, Sophia thought, observing the brightness of her eyes. But Emma appeared to notice nothing more than unladylike high spirits. 'Do not bounce so, Elizabeth! Ring for more tea and sit down.'

'Did you enjoy your visit to your friend Jane?' Sophia asked calmly, trying to suppress her misgivings about just who Elizabeth had been flirting with.

'Oh, yes, indeed! We had so much news to catch up on.'

Emma glanced up, alarmed. 'You have not been telling her about—'

'Oh, no, of course not.' Elizabeth pouted. 'I would not wish dear Jane to know how foolish I was to be taken in by a man as shallow as Mr Fanshaw.' She managed to look sanctimonious. 'I have resolved to seek only the company of gentlemen of a more serious, not to say spiritual, nature.'

Emma looked amazed, but Sophia had no difficulty in interpreting this pronouncement. 'I see,' she said quite sharply. 'By which, one assumes, you mean Mr Winstanley?'

Elizabeth pouted at the tone but retorted, 'Well, and what if I do? Just because he's an old beau of yours, you need not be jealous! After all, you are about to be married to Hal, so you don't want him any more, do you?'

Sophia kept her voice calm and uninterested, but her heart was contracting with anxiety. 'Mr Winstanley was hardly a beau, merely an old family friend.' It was an outright lie, but what choice did she have? 'And have you been speaking to him again this afternoon?'

'Yes, Jane and I met him when we went for a walk.' There was a pause while tea was poured and Sophia felt quite ill with foreboding. 'Jane's nose is out of joint because she has been wanting to meet him for a sen'night, and I was able to introduce her,' Elizabeth added gleefully.

Emma clucked reprovingly. 'He does indeed seem to be a pleasant young man, Elizabeth, and your brother John speaks well of him. But you should be more circumspect in your behaviour. You must not get yourself a reputation for being fast.'

Sophia grimaced. No, the 'fast' one was Henry Winstanley, able to spot an opportunity when he saw it. She knew now that was precisely what he had done with her. But he was older now, with more to lose, and he would play Elizabeth with caution like a fish on a line. A fish that could land him considerable benefits in both dowry and professional preferment.

Sophia's immediate instinct was to tell Emma all about herself and her involvement with Henry Winstanley four years ago. But she hesitated. It would cause the most awful scandal if John felt it necessary to tell the church authorities of Henry's moral weakness. And, after all, he might have reformed his ways. Just because he was obviously ambitious did not mean he would do anything unscrupulous to achieve advancement. Four years is a long time, she told herself. And he had been ordained in that time—perhaps he had learned from past errors.

And the knowledge that Henry was the man in her past would not deter Hal from his determination to marry her. But it might drive a wedge between him and John if John felt it his duty to report Henry's character, when by doing so he would taint the reputation of his new sister-in-law.

'Oh, what a coil!' she muttered to herself, loud enough to interrupt the conversation between Emma and Elizabeth. 'Just thinking aloud,' she said hastily as they looked at her in enquiry.

'One of the things we must do is introduce you to York Society,' Emma said thoughtfully. 'We may not live in London, but there is a busy social whirl here, and many people of breeding and influence reside in the City and in the countryside around.'

Ignoring Elizabeth's muttered 'And people with money!' she pressed on.

'It will make things so much more pleasant if you are well known before the marriage.'

Elizabeth broke in again. 'I know the very thing. Jane reminded me there is a gala dance at the Assembly Rooms on Thursday. We must go to that—*everyone* will be there!'

Sophia's anxiety rose again. She had hoped to spend the next three weeks in peace, plotting her escape, which now, she realised, was looking more and more difficult. 'But I have no suitable gown, or shoes, or…' Her voice trailed away as Emma patted the folded bank draft which George had sent.

'But we have already begun planning your trousseau: this is merely part of it. We must go to Madame Levalle's at once and see what she can furnish us with at short notice. Then tomorrow we will know what to match cloaks and shoes to.'

And so it was that Sophia found herself in the modiste's, perched on a spindly gilt chair, and being asked to choose from the elegant gowns being paraded before her. The late notice, Madame informed the ladies, was of no account, for Mademoiselle had such a neat and elegant figure that she would fit any of the gowns being displayed with only the merest pin tuck or two to render them a perfect fit.

Mademoiselle, Madame Levalle opined, was of such a distinguished and unusual colouring that white would not show her to best advantage. 'Now deep cream, that would show Mademoiselle's complexion to perfection. And see,' the modiste continued, 'how it enhances your deep chestnut hair. Such an unusual crop as well.'

Emma rushed in. 'My young friend has had to sacrifice her hair—a fever you understand. Fortunately, she soon recovered. We must ensure my coiffeuse calls soon, dear,' she added to Sophia.

'Oh, but these curls are charming,' Madame added quickly, fearing she had given offence to these clients who were obviously intent on spending a lot of money. 'If you are decided on this gown in figured cream silk with the twelve rows of ribbon around the hem, I can have a plaited filet of the same silk made up for Mademoiselle's hair. With a flower entwined in it, it will be *charmante.*'

Elizabeth was eyeing one of the more dashing creations with envious glances. 'Can I not have a new gown too?'

Emma was not going to be caught that easily. 'Now, Elizabeth, you know full well that you packed that new gown of white muslin with the jonquil underskirt. That will be most suitable,' she added, firmly frustrating further discussion.

Elizabeth, who had appalled Justin Fanshaw by eloping accompanied by a large trunk of her best clothes, subsided, knowing when she was beaten.

The next day, armed with a sample of the silk from the gown, the ladies ventured forth again with an exciting shopping list of shoes, stockings, gloves, reticule and evening cloak.

'And, of course, if we see anything else on the trousseau list, we shall buy that too. One never knows when one will see the right thing again,' Emma pronounced, a gleam in her eye. She was enjoying this almost as much as if she were spending the money on herself.

She was so enthusiastic and indefatigable that Sophia forgot her condition until Elizabeth, sighting a tempting array of pastries in a teashop window, enquired, 'Are you not fatigued, Emma dear? Should we not go in here and sit down and take tea? And perhaps a pastry or an ice?'

Emma turned to the footman who had been dogging their steps all morning. 'Please take those parcels home, Samuel, and come straight back here.' Then she led her companions into the stylish tearooms, bowing left and right to several acquaintances, all of whom regarded Sophia with interest.

'They will all have seen the announcement in the papers,' Emma whispered as they sat down. 'You will be the centre of attention at the ball, Sophia.'

'Especially in that gown,' Elizabeth muttered. 'While I am going to look positively *dowdy* in my old dress.' She sighed and dug into her ice with a long spoon.

Emma ignored her sister-in-law with the ease of long practice and conned her tablets while sipping a restorative cup of Bohea. 'Yes, yes, that is all done,' she murmured as she ticked her way down the list. 'Ordered that...ah, yes, shoes. Shall we go and find your shoes next, Sophia?'

'If you feel up to it, Emma,' Sophia agreed. 'What colour do you think would be best?'

Emma sucked the end of her pencil thoughtfully, but it was Elizabeth who broke in. 'Pistachio green would be the very thing with that rich cream colour.'

'Quite right, my dear,' Emma approved. 'The very thing. Let us hope Mr Pitchforth has the right colour or it will mean waiting and having them dyed, and that would be cutting it a little fine.'

Elizabeth's good humour having been restored by the praise, the ladies finished their refreshments and went out once more into the bustling street, where Samuel was waiting patiently.

Mr Pitchforth, the first choice of shoemaker to York Society, was delighted to see such a good customer as Mrs Wyatt again. He bowed over her hand, clicking his fingers at a young girl to attend the ladies.

'Pistachio green in a glacé kid for dancing...' he

mused, running a practiced eye over Sophia's slender foot. 'I have just the thing.'

Half an hour later, having cheered Elizabeth even further by the purchase of a pair of amber slippers to go with her gown, the ladies emerged and made their weary way home. Emma retreated to her chamber to put up her slightly swollen feet, Elizabeth rang for her maid to try out a new hair style she had seen in *La Belle Assemblée* and Sophia found herself alone.

She retreated into Emma's little parlour and, with Pippin on her lap, settled down to make a serious plan for escape. But all she could think about was the touch of Hal's lips on her own, the thrill of his body, the promise in his dark blue eyes when he had cupped her face in his hands yesterday. She shivered slightly. Could she spend just one night…no, no that was madness. Pippin stirred on her lap as her fingers tightened on his silky coat and Sophia wrenched her mind from this disturbing thought with an effort.

But her mind would not do as it was told. Instead she found herself wondering what Hal's home was like. After a moment or two she was strolling along the corridors of a gracious hall, deep in conversation with the housekeeper, choosing menus with the cook, deciding between one elegant silk sample and another…

All these unruly thoughts were banished by the dressing gong being sounded and she hurried upstairs to wash before dinner, consoling herself that she still had the best part of three weeks to manage her escape.

As they assembled before dinner Elizabeth did nothing but prattle of their shopping expedition. She was too feminine to give away a secret about clothes, but she could not resist teasing Hal. 'Just wait until you see Sophia's new gown, Hal! You will be hard put to secure a dance at the ball, for her card will be quite full when all the young men see her.'

One of Hal's eyebrows rose sceptically. Sophia thought she had never seen him look so handsome as he was this evening. It was not just his impeccable evening clothes, but his air of absolute assurance that made him dominate the room. 'I do not think so, Elizabeth. I have first call on my fiancée's dance card.' And the look he gave Sophia across the table said that he had first call on everything else he chose to demand as well. And somehow, after that morning's encounter, she did not think he would be willing to wait until their wedding night.

Chapter Nineteen

The ladies of the Wyatt party gathered in the retiring room at the Assembly Rooms whilst Hetty, their maid, gathered up evening cloaks and fussed around pinning up loose curls and tweaking hems straight. Mrs Wyatt looked magnificent in periwinkle blue, her condition disguised by the artful cut of her gown. She moved with a stately grace which gave her an air of authority and breeding. By contrast Elizabeth, determined to appear grown-up and poised at this, her first real ball, appeared both ridiculously young and ridiculously pretty.

But as they entered the hot, glittering, thronged room it was Sophia who drew the eyes of the assembled company, Sophia who glowed in the candlelight from the numerous chandeliers. There was a moment's hesitation before several young men started forward, all seeking an introduction, but Hal was before them.

He bent over her hand in its long white kid glove and pressed it to his lips. Sophia found herself walking into the throng with her hand firmly placed on his arm: it was as though he had hung a badge of ownership around her neck, and the hopeful young men melted away.

Sophia looked up and smilingly reproved him, 'You have scared all my partners away, Hal. Am I only going to be allowed to dance with you?'

His eyes were dark with desire and she found she could not drag her own gaze away. 'I do not want to dance with you, my darling Sophy,' he said slowly. 'I just want to take you home and—'

'My dear Miss Haydon! I had hoped to see you here after reading of your happy news in the paper.'

'Lady Cussons!' Sophia gasped, hastily fixing a social smile on her face. 'What a surprise to see you here in York, of all places.' Her sister-in-law's friend, not seen for several weeks since Sophia had been at her At Home and met Hal's cousin Venetia Lovell, was dressed in her usual flamboyant manner, resplendent in a pink gown and matching toque.

'Indeed, it is a surprise, my dear,' the elder woman replied with a touch of asperity, her glance flicking over Sophia's beautiful gown. 'And looking so well too—but that is hardly to be wondered at, given your amazing good fortune.'

Hal stepped in, seeing the mounting flush on Sophia's face. 'Lady Cussons, good evening. Are you well? But I should not ask—you are as…stunning as ever. I have frequently remarked to my cousin Venetia Lovell that Lady Cussons is always in the vanguard of fashion, wherever it may lead.' He bent over her hand, but not before Sophia saw the smile flicker at the corner of his mouth.

Sophia felt a wave of love for him, knowing that he had jumped instantly to her defence in the face of the older woman's barbs. Lady Cussons, sensing a jibe, but unable to identify quite what it was, flushed and drifted away.

'Hal! You were so rude to her!' Sophia whispered.

'She interrupted what I was saying to you.'

'And a good thing too! What you were saying was quite improper.'

'How do you know?' Hal enquired, managing to look hurt. 'I might have been wanting to read sermons with you. However, if you insist on staying, give me your card and let me see which dances I will claim you for. No doubt you will say I cannot have them all.'

'Certainly not,' Sophia reproved, conscious of the admiring glances still coming her way, and the envious looks of many débutantes. 'But I can spare you a country dance or two.'

'Oh, no,' Hal retorted, dropping his voice. 'I am not going to waste time on country dances: put me down for all the waltzes. At least that way you will be in my arms before I take you home.'

Sophia felt her breath catch in her throat. Hal really meant it—he was determined to make her his, ensure she had no further excuse to refuse the marriage. And looking at him now, his dark head bent over the frivolous scrap of decorated card, she wondered how she could resist him, loving him as she did. But resist she must.

'Stop it, Hal, you are making me blush. Two waltzes, then, and one country dance and that is all.'

'Then let us not waste any more time,' he said, one arm already around her waist as he led her on to the dance floor.

Swept into the dance, Sophia found she did not have to think about her steps, so naturally did her body follow Hal's lead. For a moment or two she was conscious of the eyes following them around the floor, then she did not care. All she wanted was here in her arms now, his hands guiding her, the warmth of his body reaching her even across the gap between them that propriety demanded.

When Hal led her off the floor his place was immediately taken by a crowd of young men, all begging introductions from Emma who was delighted to oblige. Mrs Wyatt was revelling in the impact that her protégée was making. Sophia found herself back on the floor for a quadrille with a young man she had never met before, then was whirled into a country dance by the Dean, who showed a surprising nimbleness of foot.

He led her back to John, who had secured the next dance, then she begged to sit out and recover her breath. While John fetched the ladies some ratafia they looked for Elizabeth in the crush of silks, uniforms and evening dress.

'There she is,' Emma said, pointing with her fan at the far corner of the room where several of Elizabeth's friends had made up a set for the cotillion. 'She is dancing with Mr Winstanley. They make a handsome couple, do they not?'

'Very,' Sophia agreed with a sinking heart. 'But do you not think she should perhaps be a little careful?'

Fortunately Emma put her own construction on the remark, which Sophia would have been hard put to explain away. 'I have checked her card, Sophia dear, she is only down for two dances with him. Nothing that can set tongues wagging.'

Seeing the happiness and excitement on Elizabeth's face, Sophia's heart was wrung. The girl had already suffered one disillusion with an unsatisfactory lover, and it seemed a second might shortly follow if Henry chose to toy with her affections.

Shortly afterwards Hal and John came to usher the ladies into the supper room. Elizabeth was sitting with a group of her friends and waved gaily as they passed, but showed no inclination to join them. 'She makes me feel very old,' John observed ruefully as they found seats with other acquaintances.

Emma reached up to touch his cheek fleetingly, an uncharacteristic show of affection in public. 'You are not old, my love,' she whispered. John returned her such a look of luminous affection that Sophia felt a jab of jealousy. Why could it not be like this for her and Hal—an uncomplicated, loving marriage?

'You are looking very serious, Sophy,' Hal commented under cover of passing her a plate of lobster patties. 'I will soon lift that pensive look from your face.'

'What do you mean?' she demanded.

'I have the next country dance with you, if you recall, and I assure you that my efforts will have you in fits of laughter.'

'Stop fishing for compliments.' She laughed up at him. 'You are a very good dancer as well you know, sir!'

'Only when I have you in my arms, Sophy. Otherwise I am quite lacking in…rhythm.'

Having effectively reduced her to blushing silence, they finished their supper and Hal conducted her back to the dance floor. As Hal was as accomplished in country dancing as everything else, Sophia had plenty of opportunity to admire his easy grace and the ele-

gance of his carriage. She was sorry when the dance
was over and he escorted her back to their table.

'I must go and find Elizabeth, I foolishly promised
her a dance,' he said with mock gloom.

Sophia hoped he would not find his sister in the
company of Henry Winstanley. As if thinking of him
had conjured him up, Henry appeared at her side as
soon as Hal's back vanished into the crush.

'My dear Sophia,' he murmured in his ingratiating
way. 'May I hope for a dance?'

'My card is full, sir,' she responded coolly. But her
wrist with the card hanging from its ribbon was resting
on the table and Henry leaned over and deftly flicked
the card open.

'But you are mistaken, Miss Haydon. See, there is
no name against the waltz just beginning.'

She had promised it to John, but had omitted to
enter it in her card and there was no sign of Hal's
brother coming to her rescue, however much she cast
around. Without making a scene, she did not feel able
to refuse, so Sophia allowed Henry to lead her on to
the floor. She was reluctant to show him he had the
power to alarm her, so she managed to keep a look
of pleasant attention on her face, hoping it masked the
instinctive revulsion she felt at the touch of his gloved
hand resting lightly on her waist.

As the music began she saw John, his head turning
this way and that as he looked for her, but it was too
late to walk away now and she set herself to make
polite conversation for the length of the dance.

When the music ended she felt a surge of relief, but
it was short lived. They had come to a halt on the far
side of the big dance floor, away from the table where
Emma and John were sitting. Henry kept his hand at

her waist and deftly steered her into one of the curtained alcoves which edged the room.

'What do you want?' she said bluntly, moving as far away from him as the confined space allowed.

Henry smiled with the old, remembered charm. 'I thought I should congratulate you on your brilliant match. After all, we are such old friends.'

'You could congratulate me on the dance floor, there is no need to speak of it in seclusion, here.' Her voice was steady, but she was beginning to feel apprehensive for Henry was between her and the curtained exit and she would have to push past him, risk creating a stir, if she wanted to leave.

'Well, there are other matters I thought it would be useful to discuss,' he said pleasantly, crossing his arms and leaning against a pillar. 'I hope before long that you and I may be relatives by marriage.'

Sophia stared at him. 'You cannot seriously imagine that Lord Wyatt would permit you to pay court to his sister?'

'Why not?' Henry demanded. 'You think I am not a good enough match? But Lord Wyatt is prepared to marry you himself, and you cannot be described as a brilliant match yourself, can you? Lord Wyatt cannot be very fussy if he is prepared to take another man's leavings.'

Sophia gasped at the crudity of his attack. 'Sir, you are offensive! Let me past!' She took a step towards him, but he countered by placing himself squarely in the way. 'Mr Winstanley, please!' she implored, raising both hands to push at his chest.

At that moment the curtain parted to reveal Hal, one hand on the fringed velvet, his eyes riveted on Sophia's hands as they grasped the lapels of Henry's evening coat.

'Hal!' she gasped. She had never been so glad to see him, but his face was cold.

'There you are,' he observed. 'Mrs Wyatt is feeling fatigued, I think it is time we left.' It was not a suggestion, it was a command.

Henry stepped back away from Sophia, turning to smile at Hal. 'Such a pity to drag the belle of the ball away so early, Lord Wyatt. I would be more than happy to secure a chair for Miss Haydon later and to escort her home.'

'Thank you, Mr Winstanley, but I will not trouble you. Sophia!'

Feeling like a naughty schoolgirl, Sophia stepped past Henry. Instead of the chastened expression she would have expected to see on his face, he looked as smug and self-assured as ever. As she followed Hal's broad shoulders through the crowd, her sense of foreboding grew.

The journey home was uneventful, but Sophia had to concede, looking at Emma, that she did indeed look very tired. John was fussing, and even Elizabeth realised that now was not the time to sulk about being taken home so unfashionably early. None of the three noticed the constrained silence between Hal and Sophia.

Arriving home in the Minster Close John took Emma straight up to her room and Elizabeth ran direct to hers, already chattering to her maid about how wonderful the ball had been and what a triumph she had experienced. 'My card was full within twenty minutes, and I am not even out yet! Just wait until I can go to

London parties and dance at Almack's!' Her voice was cut off by her chamber door closing behind her.

'Goodnight, Hal,' Sophia murmured, hastening upstairs before he had the chance to say anything to her about finding her closeted with Mr Winstanley. Her maid unfastened her necklace and helped her out of her gown, but she dismissed the girl after that and sat at the dressing table to take the ribbons from her hair and brush out the newly cropped curls.

As she brushed she counted the days backwards in her head, then alarmed, did it again. It still only came to seventeen before her wedding day. What was she to do? And now there was the added complication of Henry Winstanley and Elizabeth. After his insinuating behaviour at the ball all thoughts that he might be a reformed character had gone. No, he was every bit as unscrupulous as when they had eloped together four years ago. Except that now he had the façade of respectability. How did one accuse a member of the clergy of being a fortune hunter—or worse?

The door clicked open and the branch of candles on the dressing table guttered in the draught. 'It is all right, Mary,' she said without turning. 'I did mean it when I said you can go to bed now.'

But the door closed and there was the unmistakable sound of the key turning in the lock. Hal's voice said softly, 'Go to bed? Exactly what I had in mind.'

Sophia dropped her hairbrush and it clattered amongst the cut-glass bottles on the surface of the dressing table. She whirled round on the stool and stared at him. He must have gone to his room and undressed, for all he appeared to be wearing now was a heavy Chinese brocade dressing gown. Her eyes travelled, as if drawn, from the open neck to where the hem ended just above his bare feet.

'Hal?' She gulped, her heart beating very fast in her breast. 'What are you doing here? What do you want?' As soon as she said the words she wished she had not, for one dark brow rose and his mouth quirked.

'I thought while there was no one else around that we might discuss exactly what you and young Mr Winstanley are plotting. You are surely not contemplating running off with him for a second time, are you?'

'You have guessed that it was he I eloped with!' Sophia gasped.

'It was hardly difficult to work out. How many old friends do you have who are called Henry, were curates in Wales and are very good-looking young men of insinuating address?'

'Oh. I see what you mean. I had forgotten I had told you quite so much about him. But, no—I have no intention of running away with him. In fact,' Sophia added with a shudder, 'I have no idea what possessed me to elope with him in the first place!'

Hal remained silent but his eyes were resting on her scantily clad figure, at the soft swell of her breasts above the delicate pin tucks of lace of her camisole and her bare feet exposed below the frill of her petticoat. After a moment he observed huskily, 'But I can imagine his motivation only too well.'

Sophia swallowed hard and got to her feet, reaching for her wrapper and pulling it on. 'No such thing,' she said, her matter-of-fact tone belying the fact that her insides seemed to be turning to jelly. 'I have every reason to suppose that he was only after my fortune.'

'More fool him.' Hal dropped into the wing chair

by the fire and stretched out his legs. The action caused the dressing gown to part at his knees, confirming her first impression of strong bare legs. For a moment she felt dizzy, then rallied, ignoring his remark.

'And that is why I agreed to speak to him,' she hurried on. 'It is obvious to everyone that he has set his sights on Elizabeth. I was merely telling him, imploring him, to realise that I would not stand by and see him insinuate himself into her affections. But he is a very arrogant young man: he cannot understand that I would not let him do this, even if it means I had to tell you and your brother about our past.'

Hal regarded her silently from under heavy lidded eyes, a smile curving his lips.

'And I really fail to see, Hal, why we could not have had this conversation tomorrow morning!' To her alarm he got to his feet and walked over to where she was standing at the foot of the bed, one hand on the bedpost. 'It is most improper you being here in my bedchamber like this. Emma would be shocked!'

'She would be even more shocked if I did this in the drawing room,' he remarked, pulling her against him.

'No, Hal,' Sophia gasped, trying, ineffectually, to push him away, but her back was against the bedpost and there was nowhere to go. His eyes were glittering dark with desire in a look that she knew only too well, his fingers were loosening the ties of the wrapper which she had knotted only moments before. Then he was pushing it from her shoulders, exposing the soft skin there to the touch of his lips. Seconds later the narrow ribbon straps of her camisole were being nudged down the slope of her shoulder by his mouth.

First on one side then the other his tongue teased, tasted, tormented the sensitive curves.

'Hal, no. You must stop.' Goodness knows what part of her was still capable of protesting, for every nerve in her body was tingling with sensation and she wanted nothing more than to fall on to the bed in his embrace and abandon herself to pleasure.

With a shock she realised that his dressing gown had fallen open and the length of his hot body was pressed against hers. The shock of his heated skin against the exposed contours of her breasts caused her to gasp and the movement arched her against him. It was his turn to be startled by her response, but he smiled down into her face, then dropped his head to brush his tongue tip over her aroused nipples.

An impatient tug sent the fine lawn of her petticoat skimming past her hips to pool on the floor around her feet and with a sigh of satisfaction Hal stepped back, the better to run his hands down and over the planes of her body.

'Let me make you more comfortable,' he whispered, lifting her effortlessly in his arms and placing her with infinite gentleness against the heaped pillows. With an impatient shrug he was free of his dressing gown and for the first time Sophia saw the reality and power of an aroused man.

With a gasp she rolled over to the other side of the bed, away from him, away from the almost overwhelming, terrifying, temptation to lie back and succumb to the strength of him. Panting, she dragged the thin silk coverlet around her naked body, shocked by its cool touch on her aroused skin. Sitting with her knees drawn up defensively, she dropped her face to rest her hot cheeks on the cool silk, desperate to conceal from him the love and need she felt must be written on her face.

'Sophy, darling, look at me. Don't be frightened, I would never hurt you.' He was kneeling beside her, but without touching her.

'No! You should not be here, this is wrong.'

'It might be wrong,' he said harshly, 'but if the only way I can get you to stop this nonsense about not marrying me is to ruin you in reality, then so be it.'

He gently tugged at her locked fingers to reveal her stubborn face. 'You are going to marry me, Sophy, you are.'

'I am not! Leave me alone. I am not ruined, I am not marrying you,' but her voice wavered betrayingly and she hoped he could not read the love and longing in her soul.

Hal pulled her tightly curled body into his arms again, embracing and cradling her in his warm strength. 'Sophy, darling, let me show you what it can be like.' She made the mistake of raising her face to his to say 'No', but he gave her no opportunity. His lips fastened on hers and the word was smothered by the intensity of his kiss.

His tongue gently parted her lips and thrillingly the tip touched her tongue, hot and invasive, a promise her body understood even if she did not acknowledge it. A small moan escaped from her lips before she could prevent it and he rolled on to his back, pulling her in her tangle of slippery silk with him to lie along the length of his body.

The urgency of his need was evident, even to her untutored body. 'Oh, Sophy, darling…now!'

Chapter Twenty

The tangle of silk swathing Sophia's body was no defence against the urgency of Hal's need for her. His hands found their way to the curve of her buttocks, the dip of her waist, and he began to stroke the highly sensitive skin there, cupping and moulding.

Hal rolled her on to her back again and this time the silk fell away, leaving her naked under his caressing hands. 'Sophy, darling…'

She looked up into his face, intent yet curiously tender, and she knew in that moment just how desperately he wanted her. It was shocking to realise her power over this strong, arrogant man, shocking to realise that all she need do was to lie there unresisting and she would have everything she wanted except…except the one vital thing, his love.

She felt his lips moving gently up the column of her throat, felt his tongue tip trace up the line of her jaw, heard his ragged breathing and felt the full, hot weight of him above her pressing her into the yielding goose feather mattress. As his knee nudged gently against hers, Sophia took a deep breath and said, 'No, Hal, this is *wrong!*'

With an effort she could feel, Hal controlled himself, freed his lips and looked with questioning eyes down into her face. 'I will stop, Sophy, but only if you promise me that you stop all this nonsense about running away, about not marrying me. You must marry me, you know that.'

'No, I will not promise,' she persisted stubbornly, meeting his eyes with painful honesty.

'How can you tell me that you don't want this? I am not without experience, Sophy, I know when a woman desires a man.'

'I know I do,' she admitted shakily. 'We have both known it since the first time you kissed me. And that is not what this is about. It should be my choice who I marry—and I do not want to marry you, Hal!'

Hal released her then, his lips compressing into a hard line. He rolled away from her and sat up, his back half-turned and said, 'I could force you here and now.'

'I know you could,' she said very quietly. 'But I know you never would.'

There was a silence and she could hear him controlling his breathing. Then in one swift movement he got off the bed and dragged on his dressing gown. As he tied the belt with emphasis he turned and looked at her where she lay in the pool of rumpled silk. 'You *are* going to marry me, Sophia. In seventeen days' time the combined weight of your family and mine, Society's expectations and the power of the Archbishopric of York is going to get you up that aisle and you will be my wife, like it or not. I know what I have to do.' He strode to the door and unlocked it. Turning on the threshold, he said, 'Do not think you can escape me.'

*   *   *

Hollow-eyed over breakfast next morning, Sophia was grateful that Emma attributed her silence and drained looks to the fatigue and excitement of the ball the night before. A good night's sleep had obviously revived Mrs Wyatt and she presided over the coffee cups with bright-eyed enthusiasm. Hal looked as impeccably turned out as ever, but his face was set and he had dark shadows under his eyes, leaving Sophia to think that he had slept as badly as she.

Grayling entered, bearing a silver salver. 'The first post, ma'am.'

'Please give it to Mr Wyatt, Grayling.' Emma passed the bread and butter to Sophia who spread conserve on it, cut it into fingers and then discarded it, uneaten.

'Two for you, Elizabeth,' John said, passing her pastel-coloured missives. 'Your young friends no doubt full of gossip about last night's entertainment.' Elizabeth fell on her letters and John peered at the next envelope with its florid handwriting. 'One for you, my dear. One for me: the Archdeacon by the look of it. Nothing for you, Hal, but who is this for? Oh, yes, Miss Haydon, the last one is for you.'

Sophia accepted the letter with a murmured word of thanks and turned it over, expecting that her brother had finally got around to communicating with her. But the hand was not George's. For a moment she did not recognise it, but then, with a sinking heart, she recollected the rather mannered italic script. Last time she had seen it, it had addressed the note that Henry had sent her containing the detailed plans of their elopement.

She began to slip it surreptitiously under her napkin but, finding Hal's eyes on her, she realised how suspicious that looked and broke the seal with her butter knife. Before she had time to con the contents of the single sheet, the tranquillity of the breakfast table was broken by a most unchurchmanlike oath from Mr Wyatt. 'Good God!' he exclaimed.

'Mr Wyatt!' his good lady reproved in scandalised tones. 'Please, your language! And in front of Sophia and Elizabeth too!'

'I do apologise, my dear, but I am in receipt of most distressing and scandalous news and must go to the Archdeacon's at once.' He had dropped his napkin and was gone before any of them had a chance to question him further.

Mrs Wyatt looked at his retreating back with astonishment. 'Well, whatever can that be about? I do hope none of our acquaintances have suffered some calamity. Still, we must not speculate. Elizabeth, Sophia, my dears, this invitation is to Lady Cussons's At Home tomorrow. It seems she is now settled in rooms here to be near her sister for the remainder of the Season, for her sister is in indifferent health. However, she is eager to renew her acquaintance with you, Sophia. Sophia?'

Sophia was gazing at Henry's note, which suggested, in a tone which was more a command than an invitation, that they meet where he had first encountered her in York. 'At eleven of the clock, my dear Sophia. And do not think of telling anyone else, that really would *not* be wise.'

Sophia pulled herself together and answered Emma, but her mind was on the note. After last night's revelations that Hal knew Henry was her would-be seducer she had no fears on that score, but she remained deeply uneasy about Henry's intentions towards Elizabeth and the harm he could do the girl if he embroiled her in some intrigue. Last time they had managed to extricate her from the coils of her foolishness: but Henry was more devious than Justin Fanshaw.

She folded the letter away, conscious of Hal's eyes following her movements. She could still not look at him with any composure, all she could think about was the depths of his passion for her last night, the thrilling, shocking strength of his arousal—and her own amazement at the strength of her response. All night she had felt the brand of his kisses on her skin and all night she had longed for the weight of him on her again. Now, this morning, she felt as though some mark of her wantonness was indelibly branded on her face.

There was an interminable amount of time to pass before her rendezvous with Henry. How was she going to spend it without her companions suspecting something was amiss?

Fortunately Hal excused himself immediately once breakfast was over and Sophia retired to her room with the excuse of a headache. The clock moved incredibly slowly that morning, but at twenty minutes of eleven she donned her bonnet and pelisse and slipped out of the front door without being observed.

She arrived at the meeting place as the clocks in the city struck eleven, but Henry kept her waiting for nearly ten minutes more, by which time her nerves were jangling and she was on the point of leaving.

When he did saunter to her side she snapped at him, unnerved, 'You are ten minutes late, I was about to leave.'

'That would have been unwise,' he answered coolly, taking her arm. 'Come along.'

'Where?' she demanded, shaking her arm to free it, then stopping when a passing couple gave her a very curious glance.

'My lodging. It is close by here and we can talk uninterrupted.'

'Very well,' Sophia conceded, assuming that his landlady would provide chaperonage. The lodgings were respectable, but very quiet and there was no sign of any servants other than the young maid who appeared in the hall and then vanished at a word from Mr Winstanley.

In the front parlour Sophia sat stiff-backed in a chair, watching while Henry went through the motions of removing his gloves with agonising slowness. If he wanted her to demand an explanation of his summons she was determined not to satisfy him. Her dislike grew with every second she was in his company. How could she ever, ever have been so deceived? Imagine being tied to him, married to him! The only thing that was keeping her there was her concern for Elizabeth.

Finally he strolled across to a set of decanters and poured himself a glass of pale liquid. 'A glass of canary for you, Sophia?'

'No, I thank you.'

'Very well.' He sat down and crossed his legs elegantly, smoothing an imaginary wrinkle in his immaculate trousers. 'You are probably wondering why I asked to meet you. You may have observed that little Miss Wyatt is developing quite a *tendresse* for me.' He glanced at his well-tended nails, then continued. 'Quite understandable, of course, I have invested quite some effort in attracting her and, you must admit, she is a good catch.'

Sophia controlled the temptation to upend the contents of the decanter on his head. 'My dear Mr Winstanley, one word from me to either of Miss Wyatt's brothers and you will be horsewhipped.'

Henry tutted. 'Now that shows a nasty, resentful spirit, Sophia! Our past is in the past, and I have every intention of leaving it there—provided...' he paused and his tone was as hard as his eyes '...provided you help me.'

'You have no hold over me, Mr Winstanley,' Sophia retorted, two spots of angry colour burning in her cheeks. There was a noise in the hall, but both of them were too intent on their verbal duel to notice. 'Lord Wyatt is fully appraised of my...connection with you. Do not seek to blackmail me, sir, it will not work!'

'No doubt you have spun him some tale,' Henry said dismissively. 'But I wonder what his reaction would be if I were to describe your body to him?'

A voice behind him said, 'There is no need to wonder.' Hal strode into the room, seized Henry by the shoulder, spun him round and landed him a crashing blow to the jaw. The young curate landed with a splintering of wood on the small side table.

'You hit me,' he wailed plaintively as he sprawled there. 'I will have the ecclesiastical authorities on you!'

'Well?' said the Reverend Mr Wyatt, entering behind his brother. 'I think I can be said to be representing the Archdeacon. I have just had a very interesting conversation with him about you, Mr Winstanley.' The amiable cleric that was John appeared to Sophia to have changed into someone else entirely, so cold and hard was his voice.

Hal, who had been absently massaging his bruised

fist in the other palm, strode across and hauled Henry to his feet. 'You will apologise to Miss Haydon.'

'I…I am sorry…I did not mean…' Henry stuttered, then stopped in the face of Sophia's expression of contempt.

'You meant blackmail, seduction and mischief, sir, and I look forward to seeing you suffer for it,' she said coldly.

'There is more than that, Miss Wyatt, it is so bad that I must request that you leave the room, for what I have to say is not fit for the ears of a lady,' John said.

Sophia's chin came up in defiance. Hal recognised the gesture if his brother did not. 'Let Sophia stay, John. After all, this man has attempted to blacken her character in your hearing: it is only just that she knows what he has done.'

'Very well. Mr Winstanley, I have to tell you that Maria Jones is with child.'

'Maria Jones?' Henry said with an attempt at nonchalance, his brow furrowing as if he could not quite place the name. 'Maria Jones… Oh, yes, her. What, is the little slut pointing the finger at me? She was any man's for the having.

John took an impetuous step forward, but Hal's hand on his sleeve checked him. 'No slut, sir. She was a fourteen-year-old virgin. An uneducated, innocent servant in the vicarage where you were curate, in a position of trust. You seduced her with promises, then discarded her as soon as you had taken what you wanted. She may be a simple child, but she is from a good family of local craftsmen. And she is not the only one you have despoiled, is she?'

'Oh, poor girl,' said Sophia impetuously. 'Is there

anything we can do? What has become of her? Have her family cast her out?'

'Fortunately not,' John said grimly. 'They recognise that she has been wronged and is not the wrongdoer.' Here he broke off and looked with deep contempt at Henry Winstanley. 'And the Vicar's wife is continuing to employ her and will do so, even when the child is born. And then there is the little matter of the Squire's daughter,' John said with quiet menace.

Henry went pale. 'I...I never laid a finger on her,' he said swiftly, but his guilt was written all over his face.

'That is not how the Squire sees it. He writes to the Archdeacon that should you ever show your face in Wrexham again he will take a shotgun to you. You may not have seduced her in body, but you most certainly seduced her from her duty to her family. I am sure it was only a matter of time before you made an assault on her virtue as you did on poor Maria's. No, sir, you are a scoundrel and an offence to the cloth.'

Sophia looked at John's set and angry face, his mouth hard in a line of disgust. She scarcely recognised him from the affable host and loving husband: instead he seemed like an Old Testament prophet, casting out a sinner. She found her voice. 'What are you going to do with him?'

John, who had obviously forgotten her presence, threw her a quick look. 'It is out of my hands now, Miss Haydon. I am going to take him to the Archdeacon, who will decide how this should be handled. Come, Mr Winstanley, I am not prepared to discuss this in front of a lady any longer.'

Silently Henry picked up his hat and followed John. Looking at him, Sophia saw how diminished he was.

All the spirit had gone from him, taking his good looks with it. Now he seemed merely weak and insignificant with his bruised face and trembling lower lip.

As they left the room Hal saw her looking at Henry and asked, 'Are you sorry for him?'

'No, I am not sorry for him,' she declared firmly, turning to face Hal. 'I am sorry for those poor women he deceived and the hurt this will give Elizabeth. I am also sorry that I am such a bad judge of character that I could have been so deceived in him. And even sorrier that I hesitated in warning Elizabeth about his true character. I thought perhaps he had reformed: after all, it has been four years.'

Surprisingly Hal did not agree with her. He took a step towards her as though to take her in his arms and then checked himself, opening the door for her and escorting her out of the parlour. 'You are too harsh on yourself. From what you had told me, I understand that you were much put upon by your brother and his wife.' He closed the front door behind them and tucked her hand under his arm as they went down the steps. 'It would have taken a wiser woman than the sheltered young girl you were then to have seen through Winstanley's wiles.'

Sophia glanced up at his face and thought how much she loved him. After all, it was she who had embroiled the Wyatt family in this unsavoury situation: if it had not been for her, Elizabeth would never have encountered Henry Winstanley. She scarcely dared hope that his feelings for her were warming into love.

'Thank you for being so understanding, Hal. I still blame myself, but it helps that you do not.'

'It is not a matter of blame,' he said repressively.

'It just struck me that your shared past with Mr Winstanley might be what was holding you back from agreeing to do the sensible thing and marry me. Well, that impediment is out of the way.'

They had reached the Wyatts' front door as he spoke. Sophia felt the breath leave her lungs at the calculating way he dismissed Henry and her relationship with him. She had hoped to hear some words of affection at least, not this.

'You are very misguided indeed if you believe that Henry was the reason that held me back from marriage to you,' she snapped. 'It would be wrong to marry you, I do not *want* to marry you, and I am not going to marry you!' She swept through the door just as Grayling opened it.

As she ran up the stairs she heard Hal say soothingly, 'I am sorry, Grayling. Pre-wedding nerves, you know.'

'Quite natural I am sure, my lord,' Grayling agreed imperturbably.

Furious, Sophia stormed into her bedchamber and wrenched off her pelisse, throwing it angrily at the foot of the bed, heedless when it slid off and landed on the floor. She stamped her foot in anger. 'Men! They are all the same! Even the butler feels free to comment on my "nerves". I would not have nerves if it was not for Hal.'

She splashed her face with cold water from the ewer, tidied her hair and was suddenly conscious of feeling very hungry. It seemed a long time since breakfast, when she had eaten very little and a lot had happened in the intervening period. Surely the luncheon gong would go at any moment?

Determined to put on a calm face before she met

the Wyatt brothers again, Sophia trod downstairs slowly, consciously practising her deportment lessons of long ago. Head up, chin in, back straight, deep breaths, calm thoughts…she recited to herself.

But as she reached the bottom of the stairs it became apparent that two people at least were not experiencing calm thoughts. From John's study the sound of men's raised voices penetrated to the hall.

'All I am trying to say, Hal, is that it is not as though this man is simply an old friend or acquaintance of Miss Haydon,' John was saying in an agitated tone. 'Goodness knows, we heard enough as we entered his rooms to know he could still do her—and, by association, this family—great damage.'

Sophia tiptoed up to the door, appalled by John's words.

'She was misguided enough to elope with him, it is true, John. I will not try and deny it and nor will she. She has always been totally honest with me on the matter. But she only went with him believing he meant marriage and her brother found her before any further harm could be done.' Sophia could hear Hal pacing, his boots sounding on the bare boards.

There was a short silence, then John said, apparently with some constraint, 'Are you certain you have been told the truth? After all, you only have Miss Haydon's word that nothing improper occurred between them, and for a gently bred young woman to admit the truth would be hard indeed. But damn it all, man, he made reference to her…body. To speak in such terms implies an intimacy—'

He was not allowed to finish. Hal's voice was harsh and angry. 'If you were not my brother I would call you out for that remark. You are speaking of the lady

I am about to marry. If you do not choose to accept her, then I will take her to London to be married and our association is at an end. You must choose.'

John's voice as he replied was alarmed. 'Now, steady on, Hal, I was only trying to point out the difficulties that may lie ahead. If there is a scandal, it will taint the whole family, including Elizabeth's prospects.'

'There will be no scandal. I will see to that, and I expect your full support, John.'

Sophia, standing so close to the door she almost touched it, heard John say, 'But of course, Hal, you have my support, but I have the gravest misgivings and I cannot wish them away.'

The door opened suddenly, revealing Sophia, obviously listening on the threshold. Hal's angry eyes raked her from head to foot. 'Eavesdroppers rarely hear well of themselves, Sophia, as you have just discovered. You see, I am prepared to split my family in order to do the right thing by you.'

Hal stalked off down the corridor, his boots ringing on the stone-flagged floor, leaving Sophia and John in an appalled silence. John produced a large pocket handkerchief and mopped his agitated brow. 'I...Miss Haydon...I must apologise for...'

Sophia spoke hastily to save him further embarrassment. She liked John, he was a good man and she could well understand and sympathise with his scruples. 'Mr Wyatt, I fully understand your concerns. Let me assure you that nothing improper occurred between myself and Mr Winstanley, beyond my youthful indiscretion in agreeing to elope with him. I would not permit so much as a kiss between us. I would never lie to you in this matter, sir, believe me. I have too much respect for you and for your calling to do such a thing.'

For the first time for a long time John smiled. 'I know that, my dear Sophia.'

Chapter Twenty-One

George and Lavinia and their party arrived at Aller-thorpe Hall on the second of May on an unseasonably hot day. Lord Sydney, true to his promise to Hal, had turned over his house to the wedding party and the Wyatts drove Sophia over there to join her family.

James Sydney greeted them from his vantage point on the sweeping terrace set before the classical portico of his fine Palladian house. The Hall was situated four miles from the City centre in the midst of rolling park-land. The estate sat in a shallow valley, cut in two by a winding river. The prospect was charming and So-phia managed to keep her mind off the coming re-union with her family by admiring the landscape.

'The grounds are very fine,' she commented to John. 'That would appear to be quite a new temple on that rise over there.' She pointed a gloved hand at a distant Grecian temple.

'Yes, James Sydney has spent a considerable for-tune on improving the house since he inherited it from his uncle,' Hal cut in. 'Ah, there he is, waving to us.'

On seeing how close the house was, Sophia's dread at facing her family again increased. She suddenly felt a little queasy and found it a struggle to greet her host with her usual warmth.

James Sydney, whom she had last glimpsed from beneath her veil at Lady Newnham's philosophical symposium, proved to be an affable, plump, blond young man. He and Hal seemed chalk and cheese, yet she gathered they had been schoolboy companions and had remained fast friends. She was only thankful that Lord Sydney showed no signs of recognising in her the veiled lady at Dr Eustace's lecture. It was only just over four weeks since she had encountered Hal for the first time there, yet it seemed like a lifetime— and she could hardly imagine life without him now.

'My dear chap,' Lord Sydney exclaimed, clapping Hal on the shoulder. 'Please introduce me this instant to Miss Haydon. I had wondered if you would ever find the right lady, now I see exactly why you have chosen to end your bachelorhood!'

He bowed low over Sophia's gloved hand, greeted Mr and Mrs Wyatt and Elizabeth with a smile, and, tucking Sophia's hand firmly under his arm, escorted her into the house. He was scarcely taller than her, but his pleasant face and air of expecting to be pleased at all he encountered made him seem a much larger personality than his stature suggested.

'Now your brother and his family should be here in the garden room,' he explained. 'It is such an unseasonably lovely day I have ordered the tea table to be set out on the terrace outside it.'

John was fanning his heated face with his broad clerical hat. 'Unseasonable is the word, Lord Sydney. I cannot recollect such a hot day so early in the year.'

'We can only hope it is as lovely as this in eight days' time for your wedding day.' Emma smiled warmly at Sophia. Mrs Wyatt had completely thrown herself into the wedding preparations, apparently believing that Sophia's plan to escape had been merely nerves.

Sir George Haydon got to his feet with alacrity at the sight of his half-sister, striding forward to greet her with an enthusiasm he had never shown before. 'My dear Sophia!' he cried, crushing her to his portly figure. 'Such happiness! My dear, I had never hoped to see you make such a connection.' He released her, somewhat abruptly, and turned to the Wyatts. 'My lord!' He bowed. 'Such a pleasure to meet you. Such an honour! Why, I was only saying to Lady Haydon the other day that we could not imagine our little Sophia receiving such a declaration.'

Hal smiled thinly and shook hands with his future brother-in-law, following Sir George across to be introduced to Lavinia and the two girls. Lady Haydon, her sallow looks and thin chest emphasised by a gown of vivid pink silk stripes, her faded blonde curls topped by an over-elaborate cap, simpered up at him. 'Oh, I am so overcome, my lord. Dear Sophia.' She sent her a look of cloying affection. 'Such a dear, good girl. So deserving of her good fortune. How I will manage without her—such a support, such a good influence on my girls—I cannot imagine, but how can I argue with such good fortune?'

To Sophia's incredulity her sister-in-law produced a scrap of lace and dabbed at her eyes, which appeared to be perfectly dry.

Hal bowed with impeccable correctness over her bony hand. 'A sacrifice indeed, ma'am, and I can only thank you for making it.' Sophia shot him a warning glance, for she knew perfectly well that his tongue was very firmly in his cheek. Ignoring her frown, he continued, 'And you must introduce me to these charming young ladies. But surely they cannot be your daughters? Why, they are quite grown up.'

Charlotte and Grace simpered and giggled and clutched one another's arms in delight at being so addressed, while their mother looked fit to burst with pride and pleasure. As Charlotte declared afterwards to her sister in their chamber, 'I do declare him to be the most handsome man in England! Oh, lucky, lucky Sophia.'

'She will find us equally eligible husbands,' Grace pointed out. 'Dear Sophia will take care that we attend all the most glittering events! Oh, I cannot wait!'

The sight of Hal making himself pleasant to his future in-laws would have been amusing but for the fact that it reminded Sophia that her wedding day was getting dangerously close. Not only had she failed to think of any way to escape, but the closer it came, the more people were involved and the more scandalous any disruption would be.

But despite her sinking heart she could not help smiling at the sight of Hal as he handed Lavinia a cup of tea. He was dressed with great care in a tail coat of dark blue superfine and his legs showed that the fashion for tight trousers could be most flattering on the right figure. On George, on the other hand, the effect was ludicrous, especially when it was teamed with a bilious yellow waistcoat.

Sophia, while watching Hal from under her lashes, reflected that both George and Lavinia had spent lavishly to reflect the elegant society they could now expect to move in. Not only was Lavinia's gown expensively made and trimmed, but her shawl, her shoes and her reticule were all new, all expensive purchases.

After tea Lavinia swept Sophia upstairs ostensibly to rest, but in reality to grill her thoroughly. Much of the caressing sweetness with which she had greeted her errant sister-in-law vanished as the chamber door closed behind them.

'Well, Sophia! What a very lucky girl you are to fall on your feet like this,' Lavinia observed tartly. 'Now sit down here and tell me exactly what has transpired and where you have been for the last four weeks!'

Sophia, who had been braced for this, sat as directed and fixed her gaze modestly on her clasped hands. Lavinia's manner might be objectionable, but she had every right to demand to know where her errant sister-in-law had vanished to. 'I found myself in a position to assist Miss Wyatt when she found herself at the mercy of an unscrupulous young gentleman.'

'Indeed?' Lavinia asked suspiciously. 'And how did you come to be acquainted with Miss Wyatt? She is not part of our circle.'

'I had not met her before, but I had met Lord Wyatt.'

'Where, pray?'

'At his cousin's. You remember you gave me permission to attend Mrs Lovell's Literary Circle? She is a cousin to Lord Wyatt, and he arrived later in the evening.'

'I gave you permission to attend a Literary Circle, not to go off flirting with gentlemen and disappearing without trace. We know where that leads, do we not?'

Sophia had had enough. 'In this case,' she retorted

equally tartly, raising her eyes to challenge her sister-in-law, 'it has led to a somewhat eligible marriage, has it not, Lavinia?' Not for anything would she have admitted that she deserved Lavinia's reprimand, but in her heart of hearts she knew she had behaved shockingly.

Lavinia was taken aback by this show of defiance and the absolute truth of Sophia's riposte. Neither she nor George could have dreamed of such an alliance for Sophia, tainted as she was by her history.

'Well, yes, indeed, on this occasion there has been a happy outcome,' Lavinia conceded huffily. Then her eyes sharpened again at the new hint of scandal. 'But what is this you say about Miss Wyatt?'

'She was totally innocent and much deceived in the young man concerned, and Lord Wyatt and his family brought her off safe at the end,' Sophia said firmly. 'Lord Wyatt will not tolerate any mention of the matter. I am sure you would not want to displease him, Lavinia, by so much as hinting to any of your acquaintance that there has been anything untoward.'

Lavinia might be insensitive, but she knew when enough was enough. 'Very well, just so long as you know what a very fortunate young woman you are.'

'Oh, yes, I do know,' Sophia said dreamily, achieving a modest blush which was quite suggestive enough to elicit an answering, deep flush of embarrassment from the older woman.

Lavinia got to her feet with a show of busyness. 'We will meet again at dinner. I will send Fanny to you and she can unpack your wardrobe. Your brother has been most generous. In addition to the bank draft he sent to Lord Wyatt on your behalf for your trousseau he also asked me to purchase replenishments for your wardrobe. There is a fine gown for this evening: make sure Fanny dresses your hair fetchingly, this is a big moment.' She looked at her sister-in-law as if for the first time. 'By the by, Sophia, what has happened to your hair?'

'I cut it,' Sophia said maddeningly.

'I can see that! Why?'

Sophia smiled enigmatically. 'You really do not want to know, Lavinia,' she said calmly.

Lavinia flushed at the snub and marched out, closing the door with emphasis.

Sophia laughed out loud and was still giggling when Fanny Meadows came in. 'Oh, Miss Sophia! How lovely to see you, I was so worried about you. And so happy, too! Not that I am surprised at that— what a fine gentleman your lord is!'

Sophia hugged her maid tightly, tears suddenly flooding her eyes. 'Oh, Fanny, it is all such a mess!'

An hour later as the clock chimed six Fanny stared back at her mistress with a puzzled frown. 'But I don't understand, Miss Sophia. Why are you unhappy? It was all very shocking, I can see that, but so romantic! And he wants to marry you, otherwise he wouldn't have asked you.'

'He is only marrying me because he has compromised me and his honour demands it. But it is not enough, I want more than that, Fanny, and he deserves more. I suppose I would be considered just about eligible if this were a love match, but as it is not he could do so much better. And I am so afraid that in a few months he will come to regret his gallantry and tire of me.' Sophia got to her feet and went to the window to gaze out over the tranquil park to the lake.

It was idyllic and peaceful, a complete contrast to her turbulent emotions. 'His family are very kind, but they know of my past, and they cannot approve of the match.'

The maidservant joined her mistress at the window, and touched her arm in comfort, her eyes shrewd. 'You say this is not a love match, but, Miss Sophia, *you* love *him,* do you not?'

Sophia turned to her, aghast. 'Oh, no, Fanny, I am not so transparent, am I? Surely it is not evident to everyone that I love him with all my heart?'

'I know you so well, miss, of course I can tell. Others, not knowing you better, will not see it. After all, you would be expected to look happy…'

'But I am not happy,' Sophia burst out. 'Oh, Fanny, you have got to help me escape! I cannot go through with this and have him come to resent me.'

Fanny gazed at Sophia with her mouth open in frank horror. 'Run away before your wedding day, Miss Sophia? Beg your pardon, miss, but have you taken leave of your senses? You would never have a place in Society again, you could never marry. The scandal!'

'It would be less scandalous than a divorce,' Sophia replied grimly.

Fanny plumped down on the end of the bed and burst into tears. 'Oh, Miss Sophia,' she wailed. 'You can't do this! *We* can't do this!'

Sophia knelt down beside the distraught maid and took her plump hands between her own. 'Do not cry, Fanny, it will all come right in the end, you'll see. George will be furious, of course, and quite cast me off—but he will have to give me my fortune, or at least enough of it to be an independence. He will not want me in his household, so I can find a house of my own, and you will come and live with me.'

Fanny mopped her brimming eyes and sniffed. 'Oh, miss, if you say so, of course I'll help you. But I'm not happy, and I think you're doing the wrong thing—he seems a lovely gentleman. Don't cast away this opportunity to be happy!'

Sophia got to her feet suddenly. Now that Fanny was here to assist her, it all became very clear. 'Tomorrow you will go into York. I am sure Lord Sydney will place one of his grooms and a gig at my disposal if I tell him my maid needs to do some shopping for me. In York you will go to a livery stables and enquire about hiring a chaise and four and postillions. Tell them that you will need the carriage at very short notice as your mistress may be summoned at any time to return to Hertfordshire.' She paced about the room, waving her hand in the air as she sought for inspiration. 'Oh…say I have a sick relative and I will need to be there with all dispatch.'

Fanny blew her nose and got to her feet, a look of disapproval still evident on her homely features. 'That's as may be, miss, and I can do that, but how are we going to pay for it? It'll be more than a shilling a mile for each horse!'

Sophia was momentarily taken aback, thinking of the amount Emma had lent her for the Mail—and what she had left after buying that abortive ticket. It was nowhere near enough. The money George had given her was all in bank drafts and she could hardly ask Hal or her brother to change such a large amount for her in advance of the bills she would incur for her bride clothes.

She paced restlessly. 'I have it! I have enough to

start the journey and they will not expect to be paid off until we reach my final destination. When we get to Hertfordshire George's steward, Mr Gold, will pay. That is settled then, Fanny. I will speak to Lord Sydney about the gig for you in the morning.'

Fanny, far from reconciled to the scheme, began to lay out Sophia's evening clothes, muttering darkly under her breath as she did so.

Lord Sydney placed Sophia on his right hand at dinner that night, reflecting that his old friend had really come up trumps on this occasion. Many were the débutantes who had set their caps at him—with the full approval of their mamas—and many were the married ladies who had shown no reluctance to encourage his more discreet attentions, but none had engaged his heart. Looking at his friend now, Sydney reflected that he was always difficult to read, but Hal seemed relaxed, comfortable with this young woman.

And, he thought, as they exchanged views on the relative landscapes of Yorkshire and Hertfordshire, she was not only a very lovely young woman, but had the sort of intelligence and humour that would suit Hal. Not the most brilliant of matches, of course. He looked down the length of the table and shuddered inwardly at the florid features of Sir George and the face of Lady Haydon, shrewish under her exotic toque. Still, everyone had a few queer fish in the family and Miss Haydon had a certain sort of style all her own, which more than compensated for her friends.

'May I ask a favour of you, Lord Sydney?' Sophia asked, her green eyes turning to him in a way that set his pulses racing.

'Of course. In what way may I serve you?'

'I do hope it is not an imposition, but now that I have been joined by my own maid I would like to send her into York on a number of errands for me.'

He understood at once. 'And you would like me to furnish her with a gig and one of the grooms to drive her? But of course, that will be no trouble at all. I will instruct the stables that she should have whatever she needs, whenever she needs it.' His amiable face crinkled into a smile. 'I am certain you will have many commissions for her over the next few days!'

When the ladies rose to leave the gentlemen to their port Hal touched her hand as she passed him. 'Are you flirting with my friend Sydney?' he whispered huskily. 'I warn you, I can be very jealous.' She met his eyes and they were warm with promise and desire and she shivered with an answering desire: the sooner she escaped the better, while her resolve was firm.

At half past two that morning she was still lying awake, tossing and turning, making lists in her head of every detail of her escape. What should she pack? How much luggage must she take to convince landlords along the road that she was a respectable traveller? How could she put Hal off the scent? Surely he would not guess that she had the means to hire a chaise? Restlessly Sophia threw back the bedclothes and padded barefoot to the window, pulling back the drapes to look out over the moonlit park.

It was still warm and the scent of the wisteria hugging the wall below her window drifted in soothingly. But all this planning would be to no avail if she could not get out of the house. An owl drifting across the lawn made her start. This would never do, she would need more steadiness of nerve than this to carry off her escape.

Now, there would surely be a night porter…would the front door be locked and bolted, or simply bolted from within? And if she pulled the bolts, would it be noticed and the alarm given? She could not leave this until the night of her escape, she must reconnoitre.

Sophia pulled on her peignoir, leaving her feet bare, and opened her door gently. All was quiet, except for the rattle of George's snores from further along the corridor. Lamps were burning, turned low, at intervals, and she was able to creep down the main stairs and into the hall without difficulty.

The night porter's hooded chair by the front door was empty, but a plate with the heel of a loaf and a tankard stood beside it, so he would doubtless be doing his rounds. The door itself was massive with heavy bars, which would be noticed immediately were they to be drawn back: there was no escape that way. But the long windows in the Salon faced the back of the house and she could open and then close one of those from the outside.

Sophia was congratulating herself on this thought as she made her way silently along the corridor towards the Salon when the runner in front of her was suddenly illuminated by a shaft of light as the library door opened wide.

She stopped, casting round wildly for a hiding place, but it was too late for Hal stepped out and saw her immediately. He was wearing his dressing gown, his feet bare, his hair tousled. In one hand he held a leather-bound book, in the other, a candlestick.

'What the hell do you think you are doing, Sophy?' he demanded, his eyes sharp.

'I…' Sophia's heart was racing. 'I could not sleep, I thought it might help if I came for a book.'

'Indeed.' He did not seem convinced. 'I too could not sleep, but I doubt if reading is going to help.' He put both book and candle down on a side table and took a step towards her. 'You really should not be wandering around strange houses by yourself at this hour, Sophy.'

Her throat was tight, but she managed to say, 'Why not?'

'You might encounter all sorts of dangers,' he said, taking her in his arms and kissing her with a hard desire that left her in no doubt of his need for her.

His chin was slightly rough with stubble, she was aware of his body close to hers through the thin silk of her nightclothes and as she raised her hands to run her fingers through his hair it felt alive under her touch. He seemed very hot: her hand trailed down from his nape to his chest, bare where the neck of his nightshirt was open. Sophia, all thoughts of escape banished, flattened her palm and let it move over the hard muscle of his chest and he groaned.

Hal released her mouth and dropped his lips to the angle where her neck sloped into her shoulders. His tongue tasted its way down the swell of her breast until it met the filmy edge of the muslin peignoir. He nuzzled impatiently at the barrier and Sophia arched against him, gasping with the sensation as he reached her aroused nipple.

What might have happened next she had no idea, for the sound of footsteps on the marble hall floor brought them both back to their senses. Hal seized her wrist, snatched up the candle and bundled her into the library, closing the door behind him.

They stood, their breath loud in the silence, as the night porter paced by outside. When Hal spoke his voice was very unsteady. 'Well, Sophy, are you going to tell me the real reason you were creeping around down here in the small hours?'

His blue eyes were very dark in the flickering candlelight and Sophia realised that, however aroused he was, his mind was still sharp and his suspicions alerted.

'I told you, I could not sleep. It is very warm, and I am very...er, excited.'

'So I noticed,' Hal said, his voice like cream, smiling slightly at the blush that swept over her cheeks. 'But forgive me, Sophy, I somehow do not trust your protestations. Go back to your chamber—but before you get into bed, take a look out of your window. Goodnight.'

Sophia fled out of the door and up the stairs. Once inside she dashed across to the window, but instead of looking across the lawns she stepped out on to the balcony. There was nothing to be seen until she leaned over the edge and looked directly down. Below her a flame flickered, and a small gust of smoke barely rose in the still night air. She heard someone shift, heard the pull of a man smoking a clay pipe, heard him cough softly as the tobacco hit his lungs. She had no doubt why he had been stationed there, and no doubt on whose orders he was acting. Hal had meant it when he said he was not going to give her an opportunity to escape.

Chapter Twenty-Two

The stone floor of the Minster struck cold through the thin soles of Sophia's kid slippers as she walked down the long aisle on George's arm. The interior seemed to shimmer before her gaze as the strong sunlight cast a myriad of colours and patterns from the great windows across the floor in front of her. The gauze of her veil blurred the scene, but even without it she would still have been dizzied by the shock of finding herself at last on the point of marriage.

The days since she had realised that Hal had blocked all her chances of escape had rushed by. Obediently, like a puppet, she had surrendered herself to the rituals of visits and arrangements, of fittings and plans. To everything she had submitted: agreeing without demure to whatever George or Lavinia suggested. She had been so meek that Lavinia had been moved to remark that her good fortune had improved her character out of all recognition.

Lord Sydney had invited Hal to remain at Allerthorpe, but Lavinia felt it was unsuitable for a bridegroom to remain under the same roof as his intended, so he had moved back to York. Sophia had hardly seen him, which had made the whole sensation of being in a dream even more acute. The more she was apart from him the more she longed for him, and the more she longed for him, the more she knew she could not trap him into this marriage.

Lavinia scolded her to eat more, complaining that her gowns had already been taken in twice. But Sophia had no appetite, no energy or will, only a growing panic at what was to come.

The faces of the guests turned to watch her as she passed, but she could make none of them out. Nor did she hear their whispered appreciation at the sight of the slender figure in the elegant primrose silk gown, her heavy lace veil covering the fashionable poke bonnet and carefully arranged russet curls.

At the sight of Hal, waiting at the altar with Lord Sydney at his side, her eyes filled with tears and the Archbishop in all his magnificent vestments remained a blurred figure throughout the ceremony.

Sophia pulled herself together as the Archbishop began to intone the wedding vows and forced herself to concentrate on the solemn words. His Grace spoke the first sentence and there was a silence which seemed to stretch for ever before Hal responded and began to repeat the wedding vow. Sophia felt as though she had been stabbed through the heart as she realised what an effort it must be for him to take this final, irrevocable step. His sense of honour had won, but his voice—and his heart—were obviously lagging behind.

'I now pronounce you man and wife,' his Grace said firmly and Hal turned to lift the veil from her face. She hardly knew how she managed to lift her eyes to his face and when she did it was to find him looking down at her, his face set and pale, his eyes devoid of all their usual laughter. He bent to kiss her and his lips on hers were cold: she felt as though she had been kissed by a statue. And inside her heart was breaking. What had she done? Not only had she ruined her own life, but she had blighted Hal's as well.

As she walked with her husband to the vestry to sign the marriage register, Sophia did not know how she managed to put one foot in front of the other. Her hand shook as she took up the pen and signed *Sophia Wyatt* for the first time. Hal's cold hand closed over hers as she laid down the pen and he asked in an undertone, 'Well, Lady Wyatt, shall we go out and face our friends?'

It was enough to stiffen her resolve. However she felt, from now on—for the rest of her life—she was going to have to pretend that she was a contented wife with a husband who loved her. As she walked down the aisle, smiling and nodding to acknowledge the good wishes of the guests in the pews, she knew that a divorce was out of the question. No one, except in the desperate cases of cruelty or flagrant infidelity, would plunge themselves into the public disgrace and ignominy of having their private affairs dragged through the newsheets and of having to secure a private Act of Parliament to achieve their freedom. No, she was locked into this marriage, condemned to loving Hal, but not being loved in return. To being a good wife, bringing up their children and knowing full well, that however discreet and considerate he was, he would have to set up a mistress to satisfy his other needs.

As the open barouche bowled along the green country lanes from York to Allerthorpe she was afraid Hal would try and talk to her, but he seemed oddly constrained. It must be the presence of the liveried grooms standing up behind, gripping firmly on to the straps, she thought. As the cavalcade passed through the hamlets along the way children ran out and people stopped about their business to wave and cheer at the sight of the bride and groom and the procession of carriages bedecked with ribbons that followed in their wake.

This should be the happiest day of my life, she thought. The sun was shining, she was surrounded by people wishing her well, and she had just married the man she loved. Sophia stole a glance sideways under her lashes and thought she had never seen Hal looking so handsome. His saturnine expression only added to his good looks, but she had never seen him so still, so restrained. It must be the reaction to what he had just committed himself to, Sophia thought miserably.

As the barouche turned on the gravelled sweep before the Hall, Sophia saw that all the servants had come out and were lined up in their Sunday best uniforms in order of precedence. From the most junior tweeny and the boot boy, his face scrubbed scarlet, to the majesty of the housekeeper in her rustling black satin and the butler in his tails, they beamed on the happy couple.

The grooms jumped down and unfolded the steps. Hal got down first and turned, offering her his gloved hand. Sophia ventured a small smile and received a fleeting smile in return, then he placed her hand on the crook of his arm and was turning to receive the butler's respectful good wishes.

Sophia swallowed down the tears and straightened her shoulders. She was Lady Wyatt now and she could not let Hal down. They walked slowly up the line of

servants, receiving their bows and curtsies and entered
Allerthorpe Hall.

Lavinia was hard on their heels and whisked Sophia
away as soon as she decently could to remove her
bonnet, tidy her hair and generally prepare the bride
for the wedding feast.

Sophia stood obediently while her sister-in-law
fussed around her, unpinning the veil, taking off her
bonnet, then ordering Fanny around.

'Take all the pins out of your mistress's hair, girl,
do not stand there like a great nodcock!'

Sophia thought that at any moment she would
scream, but she forced herself to sit down at the dressing table and gradually, under Fanny's practised fingers and calm disregard of Lady Haydon's shrewish
comments, she relaxed a little.

Eventually even Lady Haydon was satisfied, although still grumbling about the bride's lack of colour.
'There, you look more the thing,' she pronounced.
'But just drape this spangled scarf over your elbows…'

Sophia saw a chance to escape from Lavinia's presence. 'Oh, no, not that one at this time of day. I think
the Indian silk would be better. Now where…oh, yes,
I left it in Grace's room. No…no, it is all right, I will
fetch it.' And before Lavinia could open her mouth
she was almost running from the chamber and along
the landing.

The swell of voices from the reception rooms below
rose to meet her as she reached the stair head. No, she
could not face that great company of people yet! Hastily she opened the first door she came to and found
herself in the small dressing antechamber of one of
the guest bedrooms. The door into the chamber be-

yond was ajar and a babble of female voices came from within.

Sophia sat down on an ottoman and concentrated on calming her breathing. It was several moments before what was being said entered her consciousness. But when it did it had all her attention.

'God knows what darling Hal sees in that little church mouse!' a well-bred voice drawled.

'Hariette darling, you are so right!' another answered her. 'Such a whey-faced little nothing. And her relatives—beyond the pale, darling.'

Hariette? She had heard that name before. It must be Lady Hariette Miller, who she had heard spoken of as the most likely candidate for Hal's hand. Sophia got to her feet and crept nearer, drawn by a horrid fascination. This conversation was bound to hurt, but she could not have left to save her life.

Another chimed in. 'And her sister-in-law! Well, did you ever see anything quite so frightful as that hat? She smells of the shop, I think: doubtless Sir George married her for the money.'

Well, that was accurate enough!

'So why has Lord Wyatt married the chit?'

Lady Hariette laughed. 'God knows, one cannot think of a single reason why—other than…' her voice dropped, and Sophia was aware that the other ladies were hanging on her words '…other than that he has got her in the family way.'

There was a gasp of delighted horror, then one of the girls said, 'No, you cannot be serious! But perhaps he has compromised her and finds himself unable to escape the alliance.'

Lady Hariette's voice was flinty. 'Well, if he has been so foolish, he certainly knows what he has done—and judging by his face in the Minster, he is ruing it now.'

'And did you hear him hesitate before he made his vows?' another offered breathlessly. 'You could have heard a pin drop in that moment! I thought he was going to refuse her.'

Sophia stuffed her clenched fist into her mouth to stop her agitated breathing becoming audible.

Lady Hariette said, with the authority of someone who claimed to be very close to the bridegroom indeed, 'Dear Hal would not make a scandal in the Minster. But there is still a way out and, judging by that look on his face, it has already occurred to him.'

'You cannot be suggesting that he…divorces her?' There were gasps of horror all round.

'No need to. If he simply does not go to her bed tonight, then it can all be annulled. It will make a stir, of course, but no one will be surprised: he has obviously been trapped into this.'

'Lady Hariette! You go too far,' one of her cronies gasped. 'Surely no gentleman would ever risk such a slur on his manhood?'

Lady Hariette's laugh was as brittle as glass and as cutting. 'Catherine darling! Those who know Hal as well as I will be in no doubt as to where the fault lay. No, I can assure you there is nothing wrong with Lord Wyatt's manliness.'

Sophia fled, not caring if anyone heard her go. Outside on the landing she nearly knocked poor Fanny flying. 'Quick, Fanny, in here.' She bundled the startled maid into an empty chamber and shut the door. 'I know what I have got to do. I cannot make Hal miserable, I love him too much. That wretched Lady Hariette Miller has shown me the way out. If I run away now, before the wedding night, he will have no difficulty in having our union dissolved.'

'Oh, Miss…I mean, my lady! Please don't say such things!' Fanny wailed, appalled. 'Lady Haydon sent me to find you, she says it is time we went down for the wedding breakfast.'

'In a moment. Now, sit down, Fanny, and listen. After the wedding breakfast—which will go on for at least four hours—I will plead fatigue, or a headache, and say I am going to lie down before the ball this evening. You must go to York now and secure a chaise and four with outriders—take all the money from my dressing case—and arrange to have them pick us up outside that old disused lodge at the back of the mews at six o'clock.'

Fanny tried to interject, but was silenced by a gesture. 'No, listen. Then come back and pack enough things for two nights on the road, and your own of course. Wait for me in the chaise. Fanny—I mean this, do not fail me!' She took the distressed girl by the shoulders and looked pleadingly into her face. 'Please, Fanny, if you love me, do not desert me now when I need you!'

The girl gave her one anguished look, then nodded her head in agreement. 'Very well, my lady. I don't like it, but if I don't help you, goodness knows what you'll end up doing. But, please, you must go down now or people will start to talk.'

It took all her composure, but Sophia took a deep calming breath and went downstairs, her head high. She faltered only momentarily when she saw Hal waiting on the half-landing for her, his eyes on her as she moved towards him. He took her hand and raised it to her lips, brushing a warm caress across her knuckles. 'There you are, Lady Wyatt. Come, our friends are waiting.'

Sophia looked up into his face, seeking reassurance, but she could not read his expression, or the meaning in his eyes. He looked more like the old Hal, but with that edge of constraint she had felt in the barouche on their journey from the Minster. He seemed very formal, almost as though he was working from a book of etiquette and all his natural charm and insouciance was repressed. But then, how else could he force himself to go through this endless charade of wedding breakfast, dinner and the formal ball which would mark the end of this endless day?

Entering the dining room on her husband's arm Sophia gasped at the magnificence of the table. Lord Sydney, ably supported by his staff, had set a meal fit for royalty and every piece of the Sydney family silver was on display. Doubtless this was a great satisfaction to George and Lavinia, but Sophia found it completely overwhelming.

At least she did not have to meet the eyes of her bridegroom for they were seated side by side in the middle of the long top table. It was amazing what training in deportment and social etiquette could do for one, Sophia thought, masking her feelings as she made conversation with the Archbishop in the seat of honour on her left.

His Grace seemed well pleased with her and the interminable meal passed more quickly than she had expected. At last she noticed Lavinia's expression and realised the grimaces she was directing in Sophia's direction meant that it was time that she rose and gave the signal for the ladies to retire.

As soon as she could, Sophia sought out her sister-in-law and pulled her to one side. 'Lavinia, I do feel quite faint and I have a shocking headache. I fear I might be developing a migraine.'

Lavinia was alarmed. 'Nothing could be worse! You have the ball this evening: you must go to your room at once, ring for Fanny, lie down and have her fetch lavender oil for your temples and a tisane. I will stay here and just let the other ladies know why you are not present. They will all understand.'

In her chamber it needed only a quick glance to see that Fanny had packed what she had been told to. The dressing case stood ready and a travelling gown and bonnet were on the bed. Sophia wrenched off her wedding dress, heedless of tearing the buttonholes, and was soon tiptoeing out down the backstairs. As she had surmised, all the staff were fully employed clearing the dining room and setting up the ballroom for the dance. The kitchens were heaving with activity, but she was able to slip past the open door while all was frantic within and was soon hurrying across the stableyard, the heavy dressing case making her arm ache.

Fanny had followed all instructions to the letter and was looking anxiously out of the window of a smart-looking chaise. One of the postillions relieved Sophia of her burden and helped her into the carriage, then they were away.

It was a surprisingly smooth journey south. Nothing could have been further from the excitement, alarms and rigours of her journey north. They were fortunate in both horses and postillions at every change and the two inns where they broke their journey were clean and welcoming with a private parlour available at each.

But Fanny was far from the ideal travelling companion. She was agitated, given to weeping at odd intervals and curiously unable to meet her mistress's eyes. Sophia, even in her distracted state, was concerned as she watched Fanny's fingers twist and untwist her handkerchief in her lap.

Eventually she asked gently, 'Fanny, what is this? You are normally so sensible.'

To Sophia's amazement the maid wailed, 'Oh, do not ask me, my lady! I should not have done it!' She buried her face in the handkerchief and wept.

Sophia felt like joining her in despair. She was so sure she had done the right thing: so why was she so unhappy? Was it possible that a breaking heart was not just a figure of speech? She felt a physical pain, deep in her breast and her longing for Hal threatened to overwhelm her.

For the hundredth time she asked herself what would he be doing now? He could not be pursuing her, for he did not know where she had gone. Was he even now discussing with his brother and the Archbishop the dissolution of his short-lived marriage? Was he even now explaining to their friends that it had all been a terrible mistake, and was Lady Hariette already at his side consoling him?

The church clock was chiming three as the chaise finally turned through the gates of Bright's Hill. George always left a skeleton staff at his Hertfordshire country seat, and the old manor house looked well kept and welcoming in the hot afternoon sun. Sophia felt her spirits lift: she had always been happy here, even when she had been exiled here in disgrace after her failed elopement with Henry Winstanley.

The house seemed curiously still, despite the presence of the footman who was in charge and the housekeeper who bustled out to greet her and shower her with congratulations. It had not occurred to Sophia that she would need to explain the absence of her husband, but faced with the staff she was too weary and heartsore to even attempt it.

To her surprise Mrs Drage did not ask questions, merely saying, 'Your room is made up as always, my lady. Why do you not go upstairs and rest now?'

Sophia turned and began to climb the familiar shallow treads of the old oak staircase, Fanny at her heels, when the housekeeper called, 'Oh, Meadows, just one word, if you please.'

So she was alone when she pushed open the door of her old room and walked wearily in. It was in heavy shadow, the curtains drawn and billowing across the open casements. The curtains were drawn at the end of the Tudor four-poster bed with its familiar ornate carvings of foliage and flowers, which she had traced with her fingers when she was a small girl.

Sophia sighed with relief at reaching this sanctuary at last, for sanctuary it was after barely more than a month where her life had been turned upside down. She tossed her bonnet on to a chair, pulled off her gloves and began to unbutton her dress, wondering vaguely why Fanny had not appeared to help her. She stepped out of her gown, rolled off her stockings and stood undecided whether to ring for hot water or simply to fall on to the bed and sleep.

It was then that she realised she was not alone. In the silence of the room she heard a soft sound, unmistakably the sound of a sleeper's breathing. Her heart in her mouth she tiptoed around the bed to the side and there, deep in sleep, lay Hal.

He was lying face down, naked under the sheet which covered him from the waist down. One hand was on the pillow beside him, the other thrust underneath and he was deeply, profoundly, asleep.

His dark hair contrasted with the whiteness of the bed linen, his long lashes fanned his cheekbone. His face was turned towards her and although one cheek was pressed against the pillow she could see the dark shadow of fatigue under his eyes and the shading of stubble above his sensuous lips.

'Hal,' Sophia whispered, too overwhelmed by love for him to wonder how he could be here in her bed. She reached out a hand and touched the hard muscled plane of his back, tracing his spine to where the sheet began.

'Mmm?' His eyes did not open, but his free hand reached out and before she knew it Sophia was being pulled down beside him. His eyes were still closed when he kissed her, at first gently, then, as she recovered from her shock and responded, with more urgency.

Breathlessly she emerged from the embrace and found him looking at her, his blue eyes burning with passion and an expression that made her catch her breath and swallow hard.

'Hal?' she asked tentatively.

'You should never have run away from me, my love,' he said softly, touching her cheekbone with gentle fingers.

'What...what did you just call me?' she breathed, her eyes widening, hardly daring to hope.

'My love, because you are. Surely you never believed I would let you go?'

'But you never told me!' she protested, struggling to sit up so she could look at him properly. 'And in the Minster, you hesitated as though you could not bring yourself to make that final vow. You looked so pale, so cold: I knew I had trapped you. Oh, Hal, I love you, how could I live with you knowing you had married me for honour only?'

'Sophy, that moment in the Minster when I saw you coming up the aisle to me I realised, for the first time, that what I was feeling for you was love. Complete, overwhelming, absolute love. When I had to speak I could hardly find the words, the feeling was so intense, so beyond my experience. I could scarcely believe I had the opportunity to make you love me as much as I then knew I loved you.'

For a long moment they looked into one another's face, saying nothing. Then Sophia whispered, 'I have loved you for weeks, darling Hal. I knew I was not a brilliant match, that my reputation was already sullied. I could not bear the thought that, because you believed you had ruined me, you had to marry me.'

'My foolish love, why did you not tell me any of this?' He cupped her face in his warm, sure hand.

'You did not love me—I was sure of it. And I thought if you guessed, you would pity me, be even nicer to me because of it, and I could not bear that, loving you as I do.'

Hal pulled her close to him and kissed her softly before burying his face in her hair and murmuring, 'Well, it is a good thing that your maid is more perceptive than either of us.'

'Fanny?' Sophia shot upright again, staring down

at Hal's amused face. 'What has Fanny got to do with anything?'

'How do you think I got here—and ahead of you?'

'*She told you?*' Sophia was stunned. 'But when?'

'She came to me when you sent her to get the chaise. She told me she had seen us together on the stairs and knew that I loved you. You had already told her how you felt, and she, loyal as she is to you, took the decision to tell me all.'

'But what did you tell your guests?'

'Left Sydney to tell them we had run off together because we could not bear not to be alone. Very eccentric, but, you have to admit, it was a lot easier than telling them that my rebellious bride had left me four hours after the ceremony! I took my curricle, overtook you as dusk fell and I have been a few miles ahead of you all the way down.'

'But, Hal, can you ever forgive me? I thought if I ran away you would get the marriage annulled.'

'And that would be less scandalous than getting a divorce, I gather?' He was laughing at her, his eyes very bright. But his ragged breathing betrayed his slipping control. 'I will never divorce you, wife, and let me make it quite plain you are never going to have any grounds for an annulment!'

His lips traced kisses down the curve of her throat as his hands pushed down the chemise, leaving her naked to his touch, to the loving caress of his eyes. 'You are beautiful, my Sophy, and I love you very much.'

'Show me, Hal,' she breathed. 'Show me how much you love me.' And she stretched out her arms, pulling his head down to her breast.

It was a new pleasure to map his body with her

questing fingers, to explore further than she had ever gone before. At first she was shy, shocked by the power of him, but he was careful with her, took her at first gently until her startled response swept them both into a fire of urgency and desire that culminated in pleasure beyond her wildest imaginings, far beyond the burgeoning desires that his earlier caresses had promised.

Afterwards they lay in one another's arms in the cool shadowed room and slept. The church clock striking six woke them together and Sophia began to rise.

'Where are you going, Lady Wyatt?' Hal murmured, pulling her down beside him again.

'It is six o'clock! I must order dinner and…and…'

'You would neglect me already, would you? I am prepared to tolerate a rebellious bride, but a rebellious wife is quite another matter,' he teased, his teeth white in the gloom.

'But Hal!' Sophia struggled against his restraining arm, thrilling at the sensation of his strength. 'What will the servants say?'

'I do not give a damn what the servants say, or indeed anyone else for that matter. I intend staying here in bed with you until I have quite definitely, comprehensively, pleasurably, ruined you all over again.'

'Twice ruined?' she asked him with mock innocence before yielding to the pressure of his arm.

'Oh, at least, Sophy my love, at least. Now come here and kiss me again.'

* * * * *

The Duke's Mistress
by
Ann Elizabeth Cree

Ann Elizabeth Cree is married and lives in Boise, Idaho, with her family. She has worked as a nutritionist and an accountant. Her favourite form of day-dreaming has always been weaving romantic stories in her head. With the encouragement of a friend, she started putting those stories on to paper. In addition to writing and caring for two lively boys, two cats and two dogs, she enjoys gardening, playing the piano, and, of course, reading.

Prologue

Sussex, July 1813

He never would have anticipated that the means for his
revenge would come through his wife. But when he saw
how Justin Everard, the young Marquis of Wroth, looked
at Isabelle, the sudden admiration in his eye, the way his
gaze frequently fell on her during the interminable din-
ners, he knew he had found his tool. He would destroy
Wroth, and with that destruction bring about the destruction of Wroth's father, the Duke of Westmore. And then
his own father's death would be avenged at last.

He had made his plans carefully. The two-week house
party had proved perfect. He had thrown Isabelle in
Wroth's way as frequently as possible, appealing to her
disgustingly sweet nature to befriend him. With satisfaction, he had watched Wroth become more enamoured
with his wife each day. But, despite Wroth's reputation,
he made no move to actually seduce Isabelle, instead
treating her with a protective chivalry which set his teeth
on edge. For he needed an excuse to call Wroth out. To
his fury, he realised his wife was succumbing to Wroth's

charm. There was nothing overt in her behaviour, for after two years of marriage she was still too prudish, too rigidly moral to ever display an illicit passion. If anything, she was undoubtedly horrified at her lapse.

He did not love Isabelle. He had married her because, as Baron Allingham's only child, she had brought to the marriage a generous portion. And in two years, on her twenty-fourth birthday, she would inherit a sizeable fortune from her grandmother.

He had married her as well because he desperately wanted an heir but, despite her lovely body with its supple curves and his persistent efforts, she had failed him. Her barrenness only made him despise her more. But she belonged to him and he could not let her go unpunished.

So the plan he had devised would destroy not only Wroth, but humiliate and chastise Isabelle as well.

The knock on the door startled Belle. She had crept upstairs early as she had every night since arriving at Greystone nearly a fortnight ago. The other female guests of Sir Farley Greystone were too busy with their cards and gossip and lovers to notice or care if she left.

She rose from the edge of the bed, her heart thudding. She unlocked the door and opened it. Eliza Pomeroy, her husband's current mistress, stood on the other side. 'Your husband wants you below,' Eliza said without preamble.

Belle stared at her, her stomach taking a sickening turn. 'But why? Is he still not at play?' She could not imagine what he could possibly want.

Eliza looked at her, and her expression was not unkind. 'Yes, and he wants you there. I think you had best go straight away. He is not in a pleasant mood.'

But then Lucien rarely was, except when it served a purpose. And since she had served her purpose when he married her, she rarely saw the charm he could turn on at will. She followed Eliza down the hallway and down the winding staircase to the floor below. To her bewilderment, Eliza led her to the small saloon where there always seemed to be a card game in progress. She stepped inside the dimly lit room, its stale, rancid scent of smoke, sweat and alcohol assailing her senses. Confused, she saw several men still sitting around one of the small tables. She looked away, embarrassed to be there.

Lucien rose in a fluid motion that was rarely impaired by drink. He had removed his coat and his elegant waistcoat was rumpled. He came to her side, smelling of brandy. 'Ah, my lovely wife.' His eyes glittered down at her with an odd sort of excitement.

She suppressed the shiver that darted through her and forced herself to look at him and speak calmly. 'Mrs Pomeroy said that you wished to see me.'

'Yes. I do.' His mouth curved in a cruel smile. He caught her wrist in a hard grip and pulled her around so she was forced to face the others. 'My wife, gentlemen. And my next stake.'

She froze. She heard Sir Farley say, 'Damn it, Milborne. It's one thing to wager your doxy, but your wife. Not at all the thing.'

Lucien's grip tightened on her wrist. He laughed. 'Why not? I've nothing else left. She is my possession, even more so than any man's doxy. So, who will cover?'

'You are mad.' Lord Wroth spoke. Belle's head jerked up. She had not known he was there. For an instant his eyes met hers, but there was none of the warmth and laughter that had lurked there since she had arrived at this hellish house party.

She looked away, humiliated and ashamed beyond belief. 'Lucien, please do not do this,' she said softly.

He didn't glance at her, his fingers only dug into her arm more, his gaze fixed on Wroth. 'So, what do you wish to wager for a week with my wife?'

'What do you want?' Wroth asked.

Her stomach turned even more sickeningly. He couldn't possibly be considering Lucien's offer.

'Five hundred pounds,' Lucien said.

'One thousand,' Lord Banbury said. His gaze went to her face and fear shot through her. He was thin and had a pallor that seemed unnatural and the whispers she had heard of his sexual proclivities had sickened her.

'Two thousand,' Wroth said. His voice was so cold she hardly recognised it.

'Very well. Two thousand.' Lucien laughed again. He released her so abruptly, she nearly stumbled. With a numb horror she watched him take his seat.

Her eyes never wavered from the game but she hardly knew what took place. Her mind and body no longer seemed connected and when the last of the cards were played, it hardly registered. Not until Lucien stood. 'She is yours, Wroth.'

Shock coursed through her. 'No,' she whispered.

Wroth rose and came towards her. 'Come with me, Belle.'

She backed away. 'No. I cannot.'

'You must come with me. You cannot stay here.'

She stared at him. 'I will not do this.'

Lucien was at her side. 'You have no choice, Belle.' He glanced at Wroth. 'Leave us for a moment.' He took her arm and dragged her from the room to the hallway.

His eyes glinted. 'Do not worry, my dear. It will not be a permanent arrangement. Just a week.' He cupped her chin, his fingers hard against her flesh. She kept perfectly still. 'Although I've no idea why you find the idea so repugnant. I have seen how he looks at you, and how you look at him. I only trust you will show more willingness in his bed than you do in mine, or I doubt he will feel you are worth two thousand pounds. On the other hand, he may enjoy tutoring you. I will own, I've not much patience for blushing virgins. I had thought at your age you might prove a more adept student, but I was wrong. At least you've no fear of his getting you with child.'

His cruelty still managed to pierce her like a sword. She resisted the urge to beg for she knew it would only inflame him more.

He dropped his hand away. 'Go upstairs and pack.'

She watched him walk away, then forced herself up the stairs and to her room. Once inside she shut the door and sat down on the bed, a cold numbness seeping through her. How could Justin betray her in such a way? She had thought that, of all the people at this nightmarish house party, he had been the one person she could call a friend. Older than her by a mere four months, at two and twenty, he possessed a boyish charm with his slightly rakish smile. She had been wary when she found him frequently at her side and thought he had chosen her for a flirtation.

Gradually it dawned upon her that he was at her side because he meant to protect her from the others. She was shocked when one of the other women told her he had mowed down Lord Amberly for insulting her. And although she suspected he had developed a *tendre* for her, the advances she was certain he would make had not come. Instead he had teased her and talked to her, and told her of his own family: his strict but just father, and the generous, warm woman who was his mother and who was not very well. She had envied him, for her own parents had died of diphtheria when she was twelve. As loving as her grandmother, Lady Townsend, had been, she still missed her parents and the family life they had shared.

And for the first time since entering the prison that was her marriage, she had started to feel a little of her own self again.

She had thought they were friends. But he was no different from her husband. In fact, he was worse. She had trusted him. She had never trusted Lucien.

She forced herself to rise and found the portmanteau. She started to pack, hardly caring what she put into it. She hesitated over the jewels Lucien had given her. She hated most of them. They were heavy and ornate and reminded her she was nothing more than a prisoner. She picked up one of the necklaces, a circlet of rubies and diamonds that felt like a collar around her neck. She stuffed it into her reticule. She could sell it if she needed money. With more than a little surprise she realised she did not intend to return to Lucien.

Nor would she allow Justin to touch her. She would die first.

She left the rest of her jewellery except for the pearls her grandmother had given her for her first Season. Her fingers brushed over the smooth strand and she fought back the tears that sprang to her eyes. 'Oh, Grandmama,' she whispered. 'You were right about him.' Lady Townsend had considered Lucien cold and calculating. But after Lady Townsend's death, when Belle was just nineteen, he had been so charming and solicitous to Belle that she thought Grandmama had been wrong.

She sat back down and put on her stockings and a pair of half-boots. The knock on the door startled her. She looked up, expecting to see Lucien, which made no sense because he never knocked. But it was Justin. Stunned, she could only stare at him.

He stepped into the room and shut the door behind him. 'Are you ready?' There was no boyish smile on his face. Instead, his dark eyes were hard and cold, his expression impossible to read. He looked almost a stranger to her.

'Yes,' she said coolly. She stood and draped her travelling cloak over one arm and then picked up her portmanteau.

He looked at her. For a moment she sensed he did not know quite what to do, but the impression quickly vanished. He stepped towards her. 'I will take that. We are leaving now.'

'I can carry it myself.' She started to walk by him.

He blocked her way. His brow crashed down. 'Give it to me, Belle.'

'I prefer to carry it.' She forced herself to meet his gaze.

'This is not the time to argue. You can do that as much as you please in my coach.'

'Can I? You did not buy my tongue as well as my body?'

He flinched. 'The portmanteau.' His hand closed around her wrist and he easily removed it from her grasp. His touch sent a shiver through her.

Justin took her hand, his fingers strong and warm around hers. She realised she had not put on gloves, and for the first time her bare flesh contacted his. She had a sudden vision of those hands on her and she felt almost shaky.

He did not seem to notice her reaction as he led her down the dimly lit hall. To her astonishment, he did not head for the main but the back staircase.

'Why are we going down here?'

'Do you want the rest of the company to see you are leaving with me?' He did not look down at her.

'If you must know, it really does not matter.'

His mouth tightened but he said nothing. He kept her hand tightly in his as he led her down the staircase to the small hall below. He paused and glanced at her.

'Damn it, Belle, don't look like that. I will not hurt you,' he said roughly. He touched her face, his hand gentle.

She flinched. She thought then that she hated him. 'You already have.'

He looked as if she had slapped him. His hand dropped from her face, his eyes cold and hooded. 'My carriage is outside.'

She went with him, careful not to touch him. The cold night air whipped around her and she drew her cloak tighter around her. She would rather die than let him touch her. And she would die a thousand deaths before she returned to Lucien.

He helped her into the carriage. 'I will ride,' he said. His voice was expressionless before he turned away and then the door was shut.

As the coach started to move, the thought crossed her mind she should jump. But where would she go? She could not return to Greystone and Lucien. But surely they would need to stop somewhere and then she could escape.

But if she did manage to escape, what would she do

next? Lord Ralston was her only relation, but he was Lucien's stepfather and what explanation could she possibly give them? And Maria adored her only son and could never see any fault in him. She had never been happier than on the day Belle had wed Lucien. She had clasped Belle to her breast with tears in her eyes. 'Now you are truly my daughter!'

Belle had pushed away her doubts. She had gone to live with Lucien's stepfather, the Earl of Ralston, who had been a distant cousin of Lady Townsend's as well as her closest neighbour. Lucien's mother, Maria, had done everything she could to encourage a match and, after a while, Belle had started to believe herself in love with Lucien. Maria had been so kind to Belle, treating her as a second daughter, and their own daughter, Chloe, six years younger than Belle, had been the sister Belle had always wanted. When Lucien had offered her marriage a year after Lady Townsend's death, it seemed ungrateful to refuse. So she had married him, despite the fact he sometimes scared her with his temper and that he frequently seemed to drink to excess. But then, she knew so little of fashionable gentlemen that perhaps being frequently in one's cups was normal. And his temper had never been turned directly on her. That is, until after they were wed, and she failed to produce an heir.

By the time the carriage halted, she was no closer to a solution. She saw they were in an inn yard and that faint fingers of light were creeping across the sky. The coach doors opened and Justin waited for her. He helped her down and then released her. 'We will stop here and rest.' He made no move to touch her as they walked across the silent yard and into the inn. The proprietor came out and Justin bespoke two rooms. If the proprietor doubted that they were brother and sister, he did not reveal it. He showed them to a private parlour where they were to wait until their rooms were ready. He shut the door behind him.

'What are you going to do with me?' she asked. She was beginning to feel an odd calmness.

'I have a lodge in Scotland. You will be safe there.' He looked down at her.

'Will I?' she said bitterly.

'Yes.' He took a step towards hers. 'I love you, Belle,' he said hoarsely.

'And so you buy me for two thousand pounds. I fear, my lord, that is not enough to induce me to share your bed. I will never let you touch me.' She was angry and scared and confused. Her eyes searched his face. Lucien had said those words to her when he was courting her, but she soon learned they meant nothing. But he had never looked at her with the sort of despairing longing she saw on Justin's face.

'Is that why you think I wagered for you? So I might force you to my bed? I love you,' he said again.

Something painful and raw twisted inside of her at his words. 'No, do not say that to me! I do not want your love. I cannot bear it!' The door opened and she turned, a terrible shock coursing through her. Lucien stood there, a pistol in his hand. His gaze went from her face to Justin's. 'Very touching, but alas, I fear I must put an end to your impassioned declaration.' He motioned with his pistol. 'Come here, Belle. I must applaud you on your performance, but it is time for the farce to end.'

She stared at him. 'What are you talking about?'

Lucien smiled, a cold cruel smile that sent a sliver of fear through her. 'You are coming home with me, just as we planned.' He looked at Justin. 'As for you, I fear

I must call you out for abducting my wife. She is a splendid actress, do you not think? She played the role of innocent, betrayed wife to perfection and, as we had planned, you walked neatly into her trap.'

Justin's face turned to stone but not before she caught a flash of anguish that tore at her being. 'Is this true, Belle?' His cold gaze bore into hers.

'No!'

Lucien caught her arm and pulled her to him. 'My love, there is no need to continue the act.' His mouth crashed down on hers in a hard, possessive kiss that reminded her of exactly who was master. He lifted his head a little. 'If you continue to deny this, I will shoot Wroth on the spot. Do you understand?' he said against her mouth.

She nodded, sick with fear. He released her. 'Tell him the truth, Belle.'

She forced herself to look at Justin. 'Very well. It…it was a trap.'

His eyes remained on her face, the coldness in them chilling her soul. 'Why?' he asked.

'I…' With sickening clarity she knew what Lucien meant to do. How could she have been so blind, so stupid to not suspect his motives for telling her to pay attention to Justin? When Lucien was only ten, his father had lost most of his fortune to Justin's father, the Duke of Westmore, in a London gaming hell. That night he had shut himself up in his study and put a bullet through his head. Lucien made no attempt to hide the fact he considered Justin's father a murderer.

Lucien's grip tightened on her arm. 'Can you not guess? I am going to avenge my father's death.'

Justin's gaze did not waver. 'My father was not responsible for your father's death.'

Lucien laughed. 'Oh, but he was. Westmore took everything from him without mercy. Your father did everything but put the gun to his head. And so I plan to take everything from your father. Without mercy.'

'So you will murder me. Then you will hang. I fail to see how that will give you satisfaction.'

'But I do not plan to murder you. There will be a duel. And alas, you will be the loser.'

There must be a way to stop him. Lucien was a deadly shot; he spent hours practising—it had of late become an obsession and now she knew why. No matter why Justin had wagered for her—she could not let him be killed.

'Because I abducted your wife? I won your wife, if you recall. There were witnesses.' Justin had folded his arms. His voice was deadly calm, almost conversational as if he were merely curious about what Lucien planned.

'There were witnesses to the fact you cheated.' Lucien smiled gently. He pulled two sheets of paper from his pocket. 'After you left, we discovered some of the cards were marked. I have signed statements from both Farley and Banbury, who by the way, was not pleased you stole the prize. So it will be an affair of honour. You may examine them if you wish.'

Justin ignored his offer. 'I assume there will be the usual witnesses to this affair of honour.' His voice held more than a trace of a sneer.

'Banbury will be my second and...' Lucien paused deliberately '...your cousin will be yours.'

'My cousin! Damn you!' He started to move forward, then checked himself. 'Why the hell did you involve Brandt?'

'So there would be no questions about the fairness of the duel.' He glanced towards the window. 'It is nearly

dawn. It is time to proceed. There is a field across the
road which will serve our purpose.' He looked down at
Belle. 'You will come as well.' He motioned with his
pistol. 'Go, Wroth. I trust you will not attempt to escape
or I will shoot Isabelle.'

Justin finally looked at her, his eyes so full of contempt, she nearly quailed. 'That is a matter of supreme
indifference to me.'

But he made no move to run and merely went with
them across the inn yard, now coming to life. With the
sensation of a nightmare she saw Eliza Pomeroy was
there as well as Lord Banbury and Justin's cousin, Lord
Salcombe. Banbury's expression was indifferent but Salcombe's was grim. He was a year older than Justin, and
tall and broad-shouldered, with the same handsome dark
looks.

Still in a dream, she crossed the road to the field with
the others. She watched as a short balding man arrived.
From his manner, and the bag he carried, she presumed
he was the local surgeon. Lucien had released her and
seemed to have forgotten her presence. She closed her
eyes for a brief moment. If only she could stop this. But
Lucien was beyond reason.

Justin stood with his cousin. He had removed his coat
and stood in breeches, waistcoat and linen shirt. Belle
started towards him. He looked up, his eyes boring into
her. 'What do you want?'

'You must not do this! He never misses and he means
to kill you.' Justin merely looked at her. She turned to
Salcombe. 'Can you not stop this?'

Salcombe met her eyes, his own hard. 'It is too late
for an attack of conscience, Lady Milborne. It is a pity
it did not happen two weeks ago before you ensnared
my cousin.' He turned to Justin. 'It is time.'

She felt as if she had been slapped. Salcombe walked towards Banbury, who held the pistol case. Justin started after him and then paused. He turned and looked down at Belle, his dark eyes remote. 'Why did you do this?'

'I had no idea…I did not know what Lucien meant to do.' She looked at him, willing him to understand.

A cold smile touched his mouth. 'There is no need to continue the act. We are not on stage.' He stepped towards her and she made herself remain still. 'By the way, I was acting as well. I intended to bed you using any means possible. But for now, I will have to be content with this.' Before she could protest he had pulled her against his hard unyielding chest. He tilted her chin and then his lips found hers. His kiss was bruising and punishing, and when he released her she stumbled. But he was already striding across the field.

She watched as they took their pistols and paced off. It all happened in such slow motion. The handkerchief dropping and the shots and then Justin falling to the ground. She started to run forward and then in a sort of shock realised Salcombe had helped Justin to a sitting position. She heard shouts and saw the surgeon was at Lucien's side. Eliza caught her arm. 'You must go to your husband. Salcombe will see to Justin.' Confused, she allowed Eliza to lead her across the grass. Lucien lay there, a dark red stain spreading across his shirt. The surgeon had pressed a pad to his shoulder. Belle fell to her knees on the other side of him. As if sensing her presence he opened his eyes and his eyes glittered. 'I will still win. Even if I die, Wroth will hang for my death. And you, Isabelle, will learn that allowing your affections to stray is fatal.' Then his eyes closed.

* * *

Justin kept his gaze on his father. 'So when do I leave England?'

'You will leave for Dover with Giles tonight,' the Duke said coolly.

A sob escaped the Duchess's throat. Justin was consumed with guilt and anger that he had brought her such anguish. He forced his own voice to remain expressionless. 'And if Milborne lives, when can I return?'

'When the affair has died down. Unfortunately duelling is illegal and despite the fact you had no choice, you could be tried for his murder.' His father's expression was grim. The Duke's immense position and power had not been enough to quell the rumours that Justin had cheated at cards and when Milborne had called him out, Justin had callously shot him. At least there had been no mention of Belle. For some reason Milborne had not seen fit to spread that tale. 'You may be in even more trouble if he lives. He will do everything in his power to harm me through you. You will have some measure of protection away from England.'

'I would rather take my chances in England.' He could not bear to leave when his mother was so ill.

'No, my dearest, you must go.' The Duchess rose from the sofa and came to his side. 'You will be safe with Lord Haversham, and I will not worry that Milborne will seek to have you arrested.' She caught his hands. 'How I wish you were not going so far away, but I cannot see what else is to be done!'

The tears in her eyes tore at his heart. She was so thin and fragile and her hand so delicate in his that he felt he held a small bird in his palm. 'I will return as soon as possible. I promise you that,' he said roughly.

'I will not let you forget.' She reached up and brushed her lips over his cheek. She smelled softly of roses, a scent he always associated with her. He brought her hand to his lips and then released it, fighting down the premonition that he would not see her again.

If it were possible to damn Belle Milborne to hell at that moment, he would have. He cursed himself for his gullibility. From the first moment he saw her on Milborne's arm, her face as lovely and pure as a Madonna's, her expression apprehensive as she surveyed the company, he had wanted to protect her. Milborne's evident neglect and her unhappiness had aroused chivalrous instincts he'd never suspected he possessed and within a week he had tumbled head over heels in love for the first time. He could talk to her and she listened as if she truly cared about him, rather than the fact he was heir to a dukedom.

But it had all been the performance of a consummate actress. She must have laughed when he made his impassioned declaration of love. Laughed to think he was so infatuated with her that he paid two thousand pounds to save her from her husband's schemes. He shoved aside the image of her anguished face when she pleaded with him not to accept Milborne's challenge. He had no idea whether she had actually felt a twinge of guilt or whether she was merely acting. It made no difference. He hated her more than he had hated anyone in his life.

Three years later, he stood at the rail of the ship that carried him towards England. He had not seen his mother again. Or his father. He had spent the last three years in the army under Lord Haversham. When his mother had finally succumbed to the wasting illness, three months after he left England, he had been on the Peninsula. His father had died a year and a half later from pneumonia, but by then Justin was in Brussels. The ews of his father's death had been delayed so by the time it reached him his father had been laid to rest in the cool marble tomb next to the woman he had loved since childhood.

He watched the seabirds circle and dive as the cliffs of Dover slowly appeared on the horizon. He was returning home. Home to England. And to Isabelle Milborne. The hot, passionate anger he had felt over her treachery had cooled to a cold desire for revenge.

Milborne was dead; he had finally died months after the duel from a lingering infection. He despised Milborne, but in some sense he could understand the man's obsession for revenge. But Belle's complicity was beyond his comprehension. That she had participated in a plot that was to result in his death was despicable enough, but that she had hastened his mother's death was unforgivable. He had no doubt his mother's distress had only served to weaken her already fragile health. And because of Belle Milborne, his father had died without the comfort of wife or son at his side.

So, Belle Milborne would pay in hell for her treachery. Even if he went there with her.

Chapter One

London, 1816

Belle took one last glance at herself in the looking glass. Her soft grey silk ball gown was elegant but severe. As was the rest of her appearance. Which was exactly what she wanted. She knew certain males of the *ton* considered her cold and had unkindly dubbed her 'the unassailable' but she had no desire to be viewed as anything but unapproachable.

She picked up her gloves and tried to quell the nervous flutter in her stomach. She had been in London ten days and had accompanied her mother-in-law, Lady Ralston, and her sister-in-law, Chloe, to half a dozen affairs already, including a ball, without such apprehension. But tonight was different. The Duke of Westmore was in London.

She very much dreaded he would be at the Hartford ball. She had not seen Justin since he returned to England nine months ago. Lord Ralston had died six months before that and they had still been in mourning and had not gone out into society until now. But she had heard enough about him. About how, despite a broken arm, he had returned to the battlefield at Waterloo and braved the enemy lines to rescue his wounded superior, Lord Haversham, from certain death. He had left England in disgrace but had returned to it a hero. And a duke, for his father had died on the eve of the battle.

The thought of possibly meeting him nearly threw her into a panic. Only last night at a rout, she had heard two women discussing him. Usually, she did not eavesdrop but the mention of his name had drawn her attention like a magnet. By the time the women had moved away, she had learned he had just arrived in town and that his aunt, the Dowager Countess of Knowles intended to find him a wife and every mama in London was nearly in a swoon over the idea.

Perhaps he would be so preoccupied with swooning mamas and daughters he would hardly notice her. Belle was not hopeful. Lucien had not destroyed him physically, but had managed to ruin his life in every way possible. She doubted he had forgotten that.

Or that Belle had confessed to taking part in Lucien's plan.

If it weren't for her mother-in-law and Chloe, she would be tempted to flee London. But Maria, who suffered from a nervous constitution, insisted she badly needed Belle's support during the ordeal of a London Season. And Belle loved Chloe as dearly as if she was her own sister, and had wanted to be in London with her.

The scratch on her door jerked her from her thoughts and reminded her she had a ball to attend. Her housekeeper, Mrs Bates, entered. 'Lord Ralston is below. Impatient as usual.' She sniffed. 'I don't know why since you are always prompt.'

'Tell him I will be with him shortly.'

She sighed. Arthur was another ordeal. He was the reason she had insisted on staying in the comfortable townhouse in Gower Street her grandmother had left her. Maria and Chloe were staying with Arthur, now the Earl of Ralston. Arthur was also Chloe's guardian, and although Belle tried to like him, she could not like someone who so thoroughly disapproved of her. The idea of living under the same roof as Arthur had been unthinkable and so, over Maria's protests that Belle could not possibly manage on her own, she had opened the house for the Season. Once a year, from the time she had been thirteen until Lady Townsend had become ill, they had come to London. Maria had not been able to understand that Belle wanted to surround herself with something of her family and had exclaimed that she and Chloe were her family. Belle had not even bothered to explain that she looked forward to the silence as well. A place where she could be left to her own thoughts and do as she wished.

She left her bedchamber and went to the drawing room. Arthur was standing in front of the mantelpiece, hands clasped behind his back. He turned when he saw her and moved towards her. He was dressed as usual in black, a colour that only served to make his bony features even more severe. Only four years older than her five and twenty, he seemed a decade older than that. 'Good evening, Belle,' he said, without smiling. He ran his eyes over her dress and frowned. 'Must you persist in dressing as if you were a governess or a poor relation? It will hardly help Chloe's chances at making a good match if her sister-in-law is considered an eccentric.'

'We will hope that any man who truly cares for her would be willing to overlook her eccentric relations.'

His thin lips tightened. 'And if you truly cared for her you would see to it that you do nothing to call attention to yourself.'

What did he think she would do? Run about in her shift in the middle of a ballroom? She bit back a sharp retort. 'I intend to behave with the utmost decorum.' As she always did.

Maria and Chloe waited for them in Arthur's carriage. Belle seated herself next to the younger woman. Chloe leaned towards her. 'Did he lecture you very much?' she whispered to Belle.

'I fear I dress like a poor relation,' she whispered back.

Chloe made a face. At nineteen she was very pretty with a pair of sparkling brown eyes and a smile that often held a hint of mischief. She tended to laugh off much of Arthur's admonitions although she always gave the air of listening intently. And then she did as she pleased.

Nearly three-quarters of an hour later they finally stepped into the Hartfords' small ballroom. The room was already crowded with fashionable members of society—the women in silks and muslin and jewels, the men in elegantly cut evening clothes. Chloe was soon engaged for the first dance and, after giving his approval, Arthur wandered off towards the card room. Maria and Belle started towards the wall where the chaperons congregated.

They were just about to join two of Maria's friends, when Maria gave a sharp gasp. She stared towards the double doors that led from the ballroom to the hall, her face white.

'Maria, what is it?' Belle said, alarmed.

'Oh, dear God! He is here! Whatever shall we do?'

Belle looked towards the doors. A dark-haired man was just bowing over Lady Hartford's hand. Then he straightened and her heart nearly stopped. Even after three years, she could not fail to recognise him. Her worst fear had just come true. The Duke of Westmore had arrived.

'I do not think we must do anything.' She put a re-assuring hand on Maria's arm. 'The best thing would be for you to pretend as if nothing is amiss.'

'But what if he should approach us? I daresay he blames Lucien for exiling him to the continent although it was completely his fault.'

'I doubt if he will even notice us.'

But a half-hour later, despite her best efforts to remain hidden behind a potted plant, Belle knew she was wrong. She glanced across the room and found herself staring into his dark cool face. She yanked her gaze away, but not before she saw the slight inclination of his head. He had not forgotten her and she had no doubt he had not forgotten the past at all.

Justin finally managed to extricate himself from his aunt's side. Since his arrival in London, Lady Georgina had been determined that he meet every young lady she considered eligible for the next Duchess of Westmore. He had already met half a dozen girls under the age of twenty who either stammered and blushed or coyly dropped their gazes upon his being presented to him. However, none of them interested him in the least. The only woman who did had just left the ballroom.

And he did not intend to allow her to leave the ball without confronting her.

He stalked to the hall. At first he did not see her

among the guests who had also decided to escape the hot, crowded ballroom. Then he spotted her. She stood near a long window, partially hidden by a statue, her back to him. She was alone. Despite his desire to remain detached, his pulse quickened as he approached her.

She seemed to be staring out the window and did not turn until he was right behind her. She spun around, almost running into him, then she took a step back and paled, her eyes widened with shock.

'Hello, Belle,' he said softly.

'I...' She stared at him as if he were a ghost.

He allowed his gaze to wander over her face. 'I had heard you were in London, and had hoped I might see you this evening. And here you are, nearly throwing yourself into my arms. Dare I hope that means you are pleased to see me?'

She might have flinched, but he could not be certain. Her eyes were fixed on his face. 'I cannot imagine why you would want to see me.'

'Can't you? You are still the most beautiful woman I know. And you owe me a debt.'

She flushed, something that surprised him, but then she was a consummate actress. This time he insolently ran his eyes over her, allowing his gaze to linger on the creamy flesh above her modest bodice. Desire, hard and swift, shot through him. Hell. After all this time, he should feel nothing for her but contempt.

Worse, he did not lie. Despite the unbecoming grey gown she wore, she was even more beautiful at five and twenty than she had been at two and twenty. Her oval face with its slightly patrician nose, and her rosebud mouth and expressive hazel eyes had only improved with maturity. She still reminded him of a Madonna, a lovely, untouchable virgin, but now he knew what lay beneath that lovely façade.

'A debt? Do you mean the two thousand pounds?' The flush on her face made her look vulnerable. 'I want to repay it but I cannot do so all at once.'

He shrugged. 'Two thousand pounds is mere pin money to me. No, I want something else.'

'What is it? I have only the money my grandmother left me. And her townhouse, which is not very grand. That is all I can give you.'

'Not quite all.' He kept his gaze on her face. 'If you recall, I bought your company for two thousand pounds. That is what you owe me.'

She paled so much he thought she was about to swoon. She backed away as if she feared he planned to ravish her on the spot. 'But I thought… You cannot possibly want my company! I would give you anything but that.'

'I do not want anything else.'

She stared at him, a flash of anger in her eyes. 'I would rather die than consider such a thing! I did not make that wager, my husband did. I went with you because I had no alternative.'

'Didn't you? If I recall, your choice was to deliberately participate in a scheme to bring about my demise. Do you deny that you told me that it was a trap?'

'No, but Lucien left me no choice. He would have shot you on the spot if I did not,' she said quietly.

For an insane moment, he almost believed her. But then he recalled how she had repulsed him when he said he loved her. Nor had she once, in the aftermath of the duel, made any attempt to deny the lies her husband had spread about his cheating at the card game. All the bitterness and anger rose up again.

He smiled coldly. 'Very convenient of you to cast the blame on your husband, particularly since he is dead. The debts may have been his, but they now are yours. I want to collect what you owe me. I would prefer to continue this conversation in private, however.'

'And I do not want to continue the conversation at all.' She lifted her chin. 'I will not deny we...I did you a great wrong. You do not know how many times I wished it had all been different. But I will not do this!'

'No? I have no doubt I can change your mind.'

'You never will.' She started to move past him. 'If you will please allow me to pass. I must return to the ballroom. I have been gone far too long. They will notice.'

'Perhaps you will honour me with a dance.'

'I never dance with anyone. There would be talk.'

'That matters little to me. I have no doubt I would survive a dance with you.'

She bit her lip. 'But I will not. My sister-in-law is here. This is her first Season and I cannot do anything that will ruin her chances. She is an innocent child and does not deserve to be caught up in this. None of this is her doing.'

'No? It is a pity you did not think of these things three years ago.' He stepped aside. 'But I will have my payment.' He did not give her a chance to reply but turned and walked away. But not before he saw the stricken look on her face. He shoved down the twinge of conscience that smote him and cursed himself for still wanting to think her innocent. He had no intention of allowing anything to get in the way of his revenge.

Belle returned to the ballroom, and paused inside the double doors, her breathing hard almost as if she had been running. Which she had been for all purposes.

She forced herself to take a breath. She could not let anyone see how agitated she was. It would not be at all in keeping with the cool, remote persona she had cultivated since Lucien's death.

But one encounter had managed to strip that coolness away and she had felt as exposed as she had that horrible night. Why ever had she left the ballroom? She should have suspected he would follow her. Despite her best efforts to remain invisible, he had spotted her within a half-hour of his arrival. More than once she had found his cold gaze on her and she knew that a confrontation was inevitable. Perhaps by leaving the ballroom she had hoped it would force his hand and she would know what he wanted.

And now she did.

He wanted her.

She felt almost sick at the thought. He had a ruthlessness about him that had not been there before and she knew he would grant her no mercy. There had been nothing of the charming young man she had known in his hard, handsome face. But then she had watched that young man disappear three years ago. If he had ever existed.

Belle realised the music had stopped and the dancers were dispersing. She looked around and saw Chloe, standing near the side of the ballroom with her friend, Serena, and Serena's mother, Mrs Hurst. She looked so normal that Belle thought that perhaps the whole scene had merely been a bad dream. She made her way to Chloe's side and the young girl looked over, her lovely oval face lit with a smile. 'Where were you? Arthur was looking for you. He seemed quite out of sorts that you had left the ballroom.' She lowered her voice. 'I suggested that perhaps you had an assignation and he looked quite apoplectic. Mama was looking for you also. She also seemed somewhat distressed.' Chloe peered more closely at Belle. 'Are you well? You look rather peculiar.'

'It is the heat.' She managed a smile. 'I merely left the ballroom for a few moments in hopes it would be cooler in the hall.'

'If that is all,' Chloe said. Her attention was caught by Serena who wanted to point out a particularly amazing headdress worn by one of the dowagers.

Mrs Hurst moved to Belle's side and began to talk about the shocking expense of living in London. Belle half-listened to her light chatter, but she felt distracted, waiting for Westmore to appear. Had he entered the ballroom or was he still in the hall or perhaps the card room? But surely there was nothing he could do in the middle of a ball.

Serena's hand was solicited for the next dance and Mrs Hurst moved off. Maria bustled up to them a few minutes later. 'Here you are my love, thank goodness.' Her voice was quite agitated. 'I saw you leave and then he left just after you and I feared he had followed you. Oh, how can he be here, so haughty and proud, as if he had never done such a despicable thing! And everyone thinks he is a hero!'

Guilt shot through Belle as it always did when Maria spoke of Justin in such terms. No matter what she felt about Justin, Lucien had cruelly used him.

'But he did save his superior officer's life at Waterloo and if the tales are to be believed, in a most heroic fashion,' she said lightly. 'Would you like a lemonade? I would be happy to fetch one for you.'

As Belle had hoped, Maria was distracted. 'How kind you are. A lemonade would be just the thing but I do hope it is not too strong. Perhaps you could add a little water if it appears to be so.'

'Of course.' She started to move away and then she saw Lady Hartford coming towards them. To her horror, she saw Justin was with her.

She froze. At the same time she heard Maria gasp. Dear lord. Surely he could not be planning to speak to them!

But he was. Lady Hartford stopped in front of them, the smile on her face a trifle strained. Maria's face was rigid with shock and disapproval. Belle prayed she would not do or say anything to create a scene.

Lady Hartford cleared her throat. 'Maria, his Grace wishes to be presented to you and Lady Chloe.' She cast Belle a nervous glance. 'I believe you have made his acquaintance, Lady Milborne.'

'Yes, we are acquainted,' Belle said. 'Good evening, your Grace.' She kept her voice as even as possible despite the knot in her stomach.

'Good evening, Lady Milborne.' His voice was polite, but the sardonic gleam in his eye filled her with apprehension. She had done him a terrible wrong and she could not fault him for being angry, but why must he throw down the gauntlet so publicly?

For he would have to be supremely insensitive not to realise they were the centre of attention as Lady Hartford performed the introductions. Maria barely held out her hand, her lips set in tight lines as he bowed over it. She snatched it away as soon as he released her as if she had just touched something nasty. Chloe greeted him properly, her expression hard to read.

At least no one had said anything amiss. If only Westmore would go away. But he still held Chloe's hand. 'Will you do me the honour of standing up with me for the next dance, Lady Chloe?'

Chloe stared at him. Belle felt almost light-headed and even Lady Hartford appeared stunned. Maria gasped. 'Most certainly n—'

Chloe recovered first. 'I would like to, Mama.' She gave Belle an imploring look.

'I am certain it would be a great honour.' Belle hardly knew what she said. She had never expected him to ask Chloe for a dance, but to refuse him would only cause gossip, something Chloe seemed to recognise. She attempted a reassuring smile. 'Shall I fetch the lemonade you wanted, Maria?'

'I…' Maria's face had taken on a most alarming colour and, for a moment, Belle feared she was about to swoon. She caught Maria's arm. 'Perhaps you should sit.'

'An excellent notion,' Lady Hartford said. Her colour was almost as high as Maria's.

Belle glared at Justin, angry he was causing so much distress. He met her eyes, an expression crossing his face she could not fathom and then he yanked his gaze back to Chloe. 'Lady Chloe, should we join the next set?' He held out his arm.

'If you please.' Chloe laid her gloved hand on his arm, her face still worried, but she went with him.

Belle watched them for a moment, Chloe looking young and vulnerable next to his dark, forceful figure. If only she could march up to him and demand he release Chloe instantly, but that would only cause the sort of scene she wanted to avoid. Maria's soft moan forced her attention back to her mother-in-law.

She and Lady Hartford helped Maria to a place near

the wall and a footman quickly procured a chair before he was sent off for a glass of watery lemonade. Belle pulled out the smelling salts Maria kept in her reticule but Maria waved them away. Her normal colour was starting to return and she sat more stiffly upright. Several of her friends had by this time gathered to offer their assistance and she managed a weak smile. 'I am quite recovered. It was only the shock of… My love—' she looked at Belle '—you will see to Chloe, if you please.'

'Yes.' Belle hastened away, glad to leave the circle of chattering women.

Arthur joined Belle just as she reached the side of the ballroom. 'Is it true Westmore has asked Chloe to stand up with him?' he demanded.

'Yes, unfortunately.'

'Unfortunately? Not at all, my dear, not at all.' His eyes gleamed. 'Having Westmore's attentions will only serve to secure her place in society. It is quite fortunate.'

'He has distressed Maria no end by doing so. She nearly swooned and I could clearly see Chloe was equally distressed. I cannot imagine how you consider it a good thing!'

He looked down his thin nose at her. 'I had hoped that, after all this time, you would have forgotten the affair. Apparently Westmore has. And may I remind you, he is a duke and very powerful, so I trust you will do nothing to provoke him.'

It was all she could do to hold her tongue. She turned towards the dancers and looked for Chloe and Justin. They were not hard to find. Justin could not be considered exceptionally tall, but his dark head and arrogant grace stood out. She watched as he and Chloe came together. He said something to Chloe and she shook her head, a slight smile on her face. At least he was not doing anything to distress her, thank goodness, but even that did not provide much reassurance. She had no idea why he had sought out her sister-in-law and none of the suspicions whirling in her head gave her the least comfort. Had he meant to punish her for refusing him by approaching Chloe? A shiver darted through her. She knew without a doubt he was not about to let things rest.

She felt overwhelming relief when the music finally stopped. She waited while Justin tucked Chloe's hand beneath his and brought her to their side. Arthur pasted a smile to his face. 'Good evening, Westmore. We are most honoured by the compliment you paid my ward by asking her to stand up with you.'

Justin released Chloe's hand and glanced at Belle. 'And is Lady Milborne honoured as well?'

Arthur looked at her, his expression daring her to disagree. 'Most certainly Lady Milborne is honoured. Quite honoured, in fact.'

'Is she?' A slight smile touched Justin's mouth. 'I am delighted to know that.' He turned back to Chloe. The smile at his lips was full of charm. 'Good evening, Lady Chloe. I hope you will stand up with me again.' He inclined his head towards Arthur and Belle. 'Ralston, Lady Milborne.' He walked off.

Belle was too furious to speak. Chloe's face was anxious. 'Is Mama well?'

'I think so. When I left her, she was drinking lemonade. She refused her smelling salts.'

Chloe sighed. 'Then it wasn't so bad.'

'You should be grateful Westmore stood up with you. As should Maria,' Arthur said. 'I will talk to her and make certain she understands that.' He stalked off before she could say a thing and Belle hoped he was not planning to accost Maria just now.

She linked her arm through Chloe's. 'I must bring you back to your mama. She will want to know you are unharmed. He did not say anything untoward to you, did he?'

'Oh, not! He was really quite…quite nice,' she said awkwardly. 'Oh, Belle I did not mean to overset her but I feared if I did not stand up with him, it would result in a horrid scene. I pray you will not think too badly of me.'

She looked at Chloe's sweet face and felt the surge of love she always did for her. 'I would never think badly of you for anything you did. You were quite right to avoid a scene. It is exactly what I would have advised.'

'I hope so.' Chloe's smile was relieved.

Belle returned her smile, not wanting Chloe to sense her distress.

But later that night, in the quiet of her bedchamber, she could not suppress the growing fear that Justin meant to use any means possible to extract payment from her. Including Chloe. Because of Lucien and because of her, he had been banished from England. And from his family. He may have acted despicably in wagering for her, but she had no doubt he had cared deeply for his family.

She sat down on her bed. Tonight's encounter had brought up memories she had thought buried. The warmth she had found in his presence. The way his eyes lit with laughter when he had teased her. Sitting with him in the secluded garden at Greystone and watching his face as he described the house that his father had just granted him for his twenty-second birthday. It was perched on a cliff in Devon, overlooking the sea, and at various times in its history had been used by smugglers.

She couldn't think of anything more romantic and for a moment, as he told her of his plans for the house, she had allowed herself to imagine being there with him.

How naïve she had been. Perhaps he had believed himself in love with her. Or confused the emotion with lust. She had almost believed his declaration of love before Lucien had burst in.

Lucien had entertained no doubts Justin had a *tendre* for her. During the time between the duel and his death he had taunted her with it often. 'How foolish of Wroth to fall in love with you. I would not have thought him capable of such weakness. But then it provided me with the perfect weapon to use against him. He would have gone to any lengths to save you.'

She set down the basin she carried on the table next to his bed. She had come to change the dressings on his arm. The wound in his shoulder had never properly healed and the physician had been forced to drain it more than once. Despite his increasing weakness, Lucien was not so ill he was unable to torment her. He insisted that only she should nurse him and refused to allow anyone else to attend him, including Maria. 'He was not in love with me,' she said.

Lucien laughed softly. 'Certainly not when he realised the woman he adored had planned to kill him. I've no doubt he quite hates you.'

She kept her gaze on the wash basin, not wanting him to see how his words hurt her. Had Justin cared for her at all, or had it merely been an act, as he had claimed? A means to bed her in any way he could? Or had her betrayal prompted his cruel words?

She forced her thoughts back to the present. It did not matter now whether he had ever cared for her, for after tonight she had no doubt he detested her. She could not

imagine that he could possibly want her, but she had not
mistaken the blatant desire in his eyes.

What if he decided to use Chloe as a weapon against
her? She had never thought him capable of such an act.
But then, the dark, cold man she saw tonight was a
stranger to her, and she had no idea what he was capable
of. Marriage to Lucien had taught her the capacity for
anger and revenge was bottomless.

And she very much feared that, this time, Justin truly
intended to use any weapon at hand to get what he
wanted.

Chapter Two

When Belle called in at Grosvenor Square the next morning, she was stunned to find Maria in hysterics. Chloe knelt by her side, the relief on her face apparent when Belle was shown in. 'Thank goodness you are here!' Chloe exclaimed, rising. 'I did not want her to see the card, but she insisted.'

'What card?' Belle asked. She sat down next to Maria and took her soft, plump hand.

Maria sat up, sniffed loudly and gripped Belle's hand. 'The card on the flowers. He...he sent my innocent child flowers!'

Belle's stomach churned. 'Westmore?'

'Yes!' A militant light appeared in Maria's eye. 'I have already disposed of them. I wish I might tell him exactly what I feel to his face! If he thinks to work his wicked wiles on Chloe, he will be very sorry.'

Belle glanced up at Chloe. 'Was there something in the note to give offence?' she asked.

Chloe shook her head. 'He merely thanked me for the dance and signed his name.'

'That does not sound so dreadful.'

Maria glared at her. 'It is dreadful enough that he even

noticed her. I have no doubt that he means to cause mischief. I have no idea why when he was at fault for the whole affair. If only I could tell the entire world what really happened! Then we would see how welcome he would be!'

Oh, dear! The last thing they needed was for Maria to decide to stir up the old rumours. 'You must not say anything. Westmore was not completely at fault. Lucien wished to provoke him,' Belle said quietly.

'How can you possibly defend him?' Maria's mouth tightened. 'He cheated and then, when Lucien challenged him, instead of behaving like a gentleman and allowing himself to be shot, he killed my son. Sometimes I think you did not care for Lucien at all!'

Belle looked at her helplessly and knew she should have said nothing. She had no doubt Lucien had induced Banbury and Farley to sign the statements. Her instincts told her that Justin would not cheat. He did not need to, for one thing. She had watched him play enough during that fortnight to know his skills far exceeded those of any of the others at the house party. But trying to tell Maria that was hopeless. She would not hear anything against her beloved first-born. Any of Belle's efforts to suggest that Justin was not completely at fault was met with recriminations and palpitations.

'Of course I cared for Lucien,' she told Maria. The lie fell easily from her tongue, adding one more sin to her long list. She had cared for Lucien at first, had wanted to love the handsome man with his fair hair and charming smiles, but his charm faded almost as soon as the vows had been said. Under his continuous mockery and derision, her fragile love had withered away. She had not let on to Maria, however, not wanting to hurt the woman who had been so kind to her, almost a second mother. After her parents had died and Belle had gone to live with her grandmother, Maria had often invited Belle to her home on the rambling estate that bordered her grandmother's more modest property. Maria had welcomed Belle as a second daughter and mothered her in her rather fussy, warm way. Lord Ralston, although more reserved, had been kind as well. And after Lady Townsend had died, and Belle had nowhere else to go, Maria had insisted she must live with them.

Maria was finally calmed. By the time they had set out for Bond Street, she had been distracted by thoughts of ribbons, gloves and stockings and a visit to Gunther's for ices. She chatted happily about the soirée they were to attend the following night and the small dinner at the Sherwoods' that night. The Duke of Westmore was not mentioned at all.

Belle only wished it were possible for her to be so easily distracted. She could think of nothing but Westmore and it took all of her willpower to concentrate on the matching of ribbons to a new gown and later, to force a few bites of lemon ice down her throat.

For she very much feared that for once Maria was right, he meant mischief. He meant to force her to do his bidding.

And if he intended to use Chloe to achieve his ends, Belle would have no choice but to do what he wanted.

Justin rose from behind his desk as his aunt was shown into his study. From the bright colour in her plump cheeks he surmised she was in high dudgeon over something. She sailed towards his desk and stopped in front of it. 'What do you mean by standing up with Lady

Chloe Daventry last night?' she demanded. 'Have you gone mad?'

His brow rose. 'Not at all. Why would you think that?'

'Why?' She fixed him with her sharp blue eyes. 'Because she is Isabelle Milborne's sister-in-law, not to mention the sister of the man who nearly ruined you.'

'Perhaps so, but Lady Chloe is also very lovely. And very eligible.'

She gasped. 'You do not mean…really, Westmore, you could not possibly consider her!'

'Why not? She is the daughter of an earl and has a significant portion. Her family is old and respectable. I see no reason why she should not be considered in the running.'

'You would have Lady Milborne as your sister-in-law! I could never countenance that!'

'Indeed.' He smiled a little. 'However, your worries are premature, for I've not made up my mind at all.'

She did not look particularly mollified but, after spending a few more minutes attempting to dissuade him from the notion, finally gave up. She left shortly after that and said she hoped he would come to his senses.

He watched her go and then sat back down. He did not intend to marry Lady Chloe, but he was not above using her for his own purposes. That Belle was fond of her sister-in-law, he had no doubt. He wondered how far she would be willing to go to stop him if she thought he did intend to wed her.

He had very little else to use. None of his discreet inquiries had revealed the slightest hint of scandal attached to her. After her husband's death, she had gone to live with her in-laws. This Season was her first venture into society since then. Milborne's stepfather had died a year after Milborne and she, Lady Ralston and

Lady Chloe had remained in mourning until a few months ago. She had inherited a sizeable sum from her grandmother as well as a townhouse, but continued to live in a modest fashion. Since coming to London she never stood up with anyone and had made it clear she was not interested in either an affair or marriage. She had been nicknamed 'the unassailable'.

He could understand why. She had a remoteness about her that had not been there three years ago. The plain clothing she now wore gave her the appearance of a nun and only added to her air of aloofness.

He intended to change all of that.

Belle forced her attention to remain on the voluptuous soprano who stood in front of the assembled guests in Mrs Beaufort's drawing room. Her voice was lovely, pure and sweet, and quite in tune, but Belle had scarcely heard the performance. Her thoughts were preoccupied—this time by Justin's latest move.

Thank goodness he was not here tonight or Maria would probably have hysterics on the spot. Belle had no idea whether she wanted to kill Justin for his despicable behaviour or Arthur for gleefully telling Maria every detail, sending her into hysterics and distressing Chloe. Chloe had been driving with Serena and her brother, Roland, in the park. And as Arthur told them, Justin rode by their carriage for a full five minutes.

Belle was about to depart for her house so she might have a light dinner and then prepare for tonight's musical, when Arthur had arrived.

'He has made it quite clear he has an interest in Chloe.' He clasped his hands behind his back and smiled in a superior fashion at the women seated in the drawing room. 'What would you say to having your daughter a duchess?' he asked Maria.

'I would rather see her in a convent than marry him! Have you no conscience, no sensibility! He murdered my son!'

'Hardly, madam. If you recall, Lucien did not die for months after the duel. A healthy man would have recovered instead of developing such a putrid infection, which was no doubt due to his excessive fondness for drink.'

'His infection was due to the fatal wound he sustained from the duel! The only reason that…that creature is not hanging from the gallows is because he is a duke!'

'You are ridiculous,' Arthur snapped.

'And you are unfeeling and callous and disrespectful! My daughter will never marry him!'

All this time Chloe had sat on the sofa, her expression increasingly stricken with each word. Belle had finally got up. 'This entire conversation is ridiculous. Arthur, I pray you will restrain yourself from speculating on Westmore's intentions. I doubt very much he wishes to marry Chloe.'

As she had hoped, her words managed to turn Arthur's attention away from Maria. 'And how would you know Westmore's intentions? Are you in his confidence?'

'Of course not. But one dance and a brief meeting in the park hardly constitutes a proposal of marriage. I've no doubt he has paid such attentions to dozens of young ladies. Besides, you are distressing both Chloe and Maria. Until there is an actual proposal, I would suggest you not say a word on this topic again.'

His lips tightened. 'May I remind you that none of this is your concern? I could forbid you to see Chloe, if I wish.'

Maria promptly burst into noisy tears and Arthur, who could not tolerate one of her outbursts, finally took his leave. It took nearly three-quarters of an hour for Belle and Chloe, with the assistance of Maria's maid, to calm her. After that she had to be coaxed to eat a few bites of a light repast. Belle barely had time to return home and change her muslin for a silk lavender gown that was more suitable for a musical soirée before she turned around again and headed back to Grosvenor Square.

By the time they had arrived at Mrs Beaufort's elegant townhouse, vexation was her overriding emotion and she thought if she saw Justin, she could cheerfully strangle him.

But there was no sign of his dark-haired figure when they first arrived. His paternal aunt, Lady Georgina, was there. As they took their places in the second row of chairs, she turned and fixed Chloe with a pair of sharp blue eyes. She was an intimidating figure: thin and upright, her features patrician and she held herself with regal bearing.

There was nothing in the look she bestowed upon Chloe to indicate approval. Chloe, thank goodness, was not aware of her perusal, but Belle was. She stared at Lady Georgina until the lady allowed her gaze to fall on her. Her stare was so icy Belle nearly quailed, but she would not let her gaze drop. Lady Georgina finally looked away, but not before Belle knew she had made an enemy.

Oh, dear. She turned and sighed. Why could she not let things alone? Now she would worry Lady Georgina would take her wrath out on Chloe. Arthur might welcome a match between Justin and Chloe, but it was more than apparent Lady Georgina would not. From what little she knew of Lady Georgina, she was not a woman to cross.

Belle had met her once, over a decade ago, when she had come to London with her grandmother for her first and only Season. Belle and Lady Townsend had been about to leave a rout when they came face to face with Lady Georgina. Grandmama had greeted Lady Georgina politely, but Belle had never forgotten the hostile stare Lady Georgina had bestowed upon the other woman before saying, 'Good evening, Sarah.' She had turned equally cold eyes upon Belle. 'I suppose this is your granddaughter. She resembles you.' Belle had known her words were not a compliment. She had been glad to escape the cold, aristocratic Countess who so intently disliked her grandmother. Grandmama had said nothing about Lady Georgina and had instead gone on to talk about the people they had met at the rout.

Belle's hand tightened around her fan. She could not allow him or his family to hurt Chloe, which made it even more imperative for her to deal with Justin.

The soprano had just begun her last aria when someone entered the room. There was a slight stir among the guests. Belle glanced towards the door almost without thinking. Her heart pounded and her hand trembled around her fan when he strode through the double door. He glanced around. She dropped her gaze and hoped he would not see her. If only she could crawl under the chair, but it would not do.

She forced herself to look towards the door again. He stood near the wall, arms folded. He looked every bit as male and elegant as he had two nights ago. And every bit as dangerous.

She yanked her gaze away. How could she ever confront him? But she must before he caused any more trouble. She would do it for Chloe's sake. And for Maria's.

She belatedly realised the soprano had finished and she had forgotten to applaud altogether. Chloe was already standing, as were many of the other guests. The first half of the performance had ended and the guests were milling towards a smaller room next to the drawing room where refreshments had been laid out. Belle forced herself to not look in Justin's direction. She smiled at Maria. 'I think we should find some refreshment. Shall I escort you there?' If only she could move Maria from the room before she spotted Justin.

'I do not know.' Maria looked around. Belle moved in front of her, hoping she could block Maria's view. 'Perhaps a small cake and some punch. I believe I would prefer to stay here, however. I am feeling rather fatigued as I always do after such a disagreeable scene. Thank goodness, Arthur cannot abide music. But you and Chloe must go and if you wish you may bring me back a little refreshment.'

'Would you like me to stay with you?' Chloe asked.

'Oh, no.' She smiled wanly.

Belle glanced around. To her horror, she saw Justin stood a few feet away with a tall, dark-haired man she recognised as his cousin, Lord Salcombe. Justin suddenly glanced up and met her eyes. The mocking look that crossed his expression did not bode well. She turned away and touched Chloe's arm. 'Shall we get refreshment, then? I see Serena near the door.' She moved down the short row of chairs away from Justin. Chloe, who appeared rather bewildered, followed.

They were just about to leave the refreshment room when she saw that Westmore and Salcombe now stood directly near the doors between the rooms. Unless she and Chloe were to turn around, making it quite obvious they wanted to avoid the men, they had no choice but to pass them.

'Good evening, Lady Milborne, Lady Chloe,' Justin said. His gaze lingered on Chloe in a way that made Belle want to hit him.

'Good evening, your Grace,' she said coolly. 'Lord Salcombe.'

Salcombe inclined his head but his expression was icy. Chloe looked confused. Belle would have just walked past them, but Justin spoke. 'I hope you enjoyed your drive in the park, Lady Chloe.'

'Very much,' Chloe said politely. Slight colour stained her cheek.

A slight smile touched his mouth. A smile Belle considered predatory. 'I am glad,' he said. 'Perhaps you will do me the honour of driving with me some time.'

Chloe raised startled eyes to his face. 'I—'

'No, she most certainly will not,' Belle snapped. She had the satisfaction of seeing Justin start.

Then his brow rose. 'No? But you are not her guardian, are you?' His smile was lazy. And dangerous.

'No. But I am her friend.' She turned to Chloe. 'Can you manage the refreshments? I will join you in a moment, but I have something I wish to say to the Duke.'

Chloe's eyes widened. 'Belle, I do not think—'

'I will be fine. Just tell your mama that I was feeling rather warm and I wished to sit in the hall for a moment where it is cooler.'

Chloe nodded. After casting a worried look at Justin, she left. Belle looked at him. 'I would like a word with you, your Grace. In private.'

By now many of the guests had taken their places. He

glanced around. 'I am your servant, of course. However, this does not seem the place for a tête-à-tête.'

'We can step into the hall, then.'

Salcombe spoke. 'Anything you wish to say to my cousin, you may say in front of me.' He looked down at her, his dislike for her evident.

'This does not concern you, my lord.' She turned back to Justin. His expression was unreadable but she sensed he was enjoying her discomfort. Well, she could not stand here and argue with him in full view of the rest of the guests. She could see Lady Georgina staring at her and feared any moment she would come forward to forbid her to talk to him. And if Maria should happen to notice…she did not want to think of that. 'I am going to the hall. I would like to talk to you.' She turned and walked away.

By the time she reached the hallway, her knees were shaking. What had she done? It was just that Justin had made her so angry that she felt if she did not say something she would explode. She doubted that he would follow her. He probably enjoyed tormenting her too much.

An even worse thought occurred. What if he really did intend to pursue Chloe? That he wasn't merely trying to bend her to his will but actually had an interest in Chloe? The idea was too awful to contemplate.

'I believe you wished to talk to me.'

She whirled around and gasped and his brow rose at her expression. 'Or was I mistaken?'

'I…I did not think you would come.'

'After such a forceful demand, I had no choice. Come into Beaufort's study. We can be more private there.'

She nodded. She did not want anyone to know what she said. She stepped past him into the small room and he shut the door. He leaned against it and fixed his gaze on her. 'What is it you wish to say to me?'

For some reason the cool indifference in his voice steadied her. 'I have no doubt you know very well. But rather than play games with you, I will tell you. I want you to cease your pursuit of Lady Chloe.'

'Am I pursuing her?'

'I pray you will not fence with me. You are, and I cannot think what you hope to accomplish by doing so. I can understand your desire for revenge, but I pray you will not use Chloe to accomplish it.'

'And how do you know my purpose is for revenge? She is a lovely girl and I am in need of a wife. There is no reason why she would not make a suitable duchess.'

Her blood ran cold. 'No. You cannot possibly consider such a thing. You would make her miserable. If your purpose is to punish me then I wish you would do so directly.'

She took a deep breath. 'When I met you, two nights ago, you said I owed you a debt and you told me what you considered payment. I will give you what you ask if you will promise to leave Chloe alone.'

'You do understand what I want, do you not?' He had moved closer to her and she resisted the urge to back up.

'I believe you wish me to…to spend a night with you,' she said calmly.

'A night? Not precisely. If you recall, I was to have you for a week. But of course, there is interest which by now is quite considerable.'

'What is it you want?' She could barely speak.

'I want you to be my mistress until the end of the Season.'

The world seemed to spin for a moment. She felt as

unfocused as if she had sustained a blow. Her vision cleared. 'Until the end of the Season? I...I cannot do that.'

'Then I will continue my pursuit of your sister-in-law. You might consider that although you object, Lord Ralston does not. And he is her guardian, not you.'

Dear God. She could perhaps bear one night, but how could she stand to come to him night after night? But if she did not, Chloe would pay for her debts, just as Lucien had made Justin pay for the wrong done his father. Another innocent would suffer. And that she could not bear at all.

She looked into his cool, haughty face and took a breath. 'Very well, your Grace. I will be your mistress until the end of the Season. But I want a contract outlining the terms.'

He frowned. 'A contract? Do you want my solicitor to draw it up?'

'No! I...I don't want any one to know about this. I will prepare the papers myself.'

'Will you? If no one knows, then how do you know I won't cheat you? Once you come to me, the advantage will all be on my side.'

'I will trust that you won't.' Her gaze did not waver from his face.

'Will you?' An odd expression appeared in his eyes. 'I will call on you tomorrow. We will discuss the terms then. And you must hope I will prove to be more trustworthy than you.'

She bit her lip. 'I must return to the drawing room before my in-laws worry.'

'Yes.' He looked at her, his eyes darkening and her breath caught. For a moment, she thought he was about to kiss her and then he pulled away. 'You are right, you had best go.' His voice was cold.

She left him without looking back.

Belle stared at the paper in front of her. She usually spent Tuesday mornings in her study, answering her correspondence and going over her accounts. She supposed she was over-cautious but Lucien had never paid attention to such things. He had left behind a mound of debts after his death. The dowry she had brought to her marriage was gone; spent on gaming and horses and jewels. Even after she had sold everything she could, there had been more bills. If the former Lord Ralston had not stepped in, she had no doubt she would have ended up in debtors' prison, for until she turned four and twenty, she had had no money of her own.

But today she had not even glanced at the business that awaited her. She had spent the morning on something else entirely. Even after wasting several sheets of paper, she still was not certain she was pleased with the results. She rubbed her neck and then nearly jumped when the footman appeared in the door of the small room. She looked up. 'Yes?'

She did not even need to look at the calling card he carried to know who it was. 'The Duke of Westmore is below.'

She stared at him, her heart starting to pound, and then realised he still waited expectantly. 'Please, show him up.'

She shoved the paper aside she had been working on since she had risen far too early and, after a moment of hesitation, placed a dictionary on top of it. The last thing she wanted was to have him catch a glimpse of the contract before she presented it to him. She rose, feeling as if she waited for her executioner. Surely he didn't plan to seduce her in the middle of the morning. Not that she knew a thing about how these affairs were arranged.

His footsteps sounded outside the door and then he stood in the doorway. Her mind suddenly went blank.

He spoke. 'Good day, Belle.'

She started. 'Your Grace. Please, come in.'

He stepped into the room and she knew it was a mistake to have him here. For some reason the thought of discussing such business in the drawing room seemed inappropriate, but the study seemed to shrink with his presence.

He came towards her. He was dressed in a dark coat and buff breeches, his cravat starched and tied in an elaborate knot. She backed up against the desk, her eyes on his face. He stopped in front of her and his brow shot up. 'There is no need to look so frightened. I have no intention of ravishing you at this moment. In general, I prefer more comfortable surroundings.'

'Oh. Of course.' She felt a flush steal to her cheeks in spite of her efforts to remain composed. 'Will you not be seated? Would you care for refreshment?'

'No, refreshments are not necessary.' He remained standing and she hastily seated herself in the chair behind her desk. He moved around the side of it to the window at her back and although he appeared to be merely observing the view, he had neatly blocked her in. And he was still standing, which gave him an unfair advantage. He looked down at her. 'Have you changed your mind since last night?'

She stood again, hoping to feel less intimidated. 'No. Have you?'

'No.'

'Very well. I have drawn up the contract. If you would

care to look at it.' She reached for the dictionary and moved it, then picked up the paper.

She held it out to him and he looked at her face for a moment before taking it. He moved away from the window and she folded her arms, her eyes on him as she waited in silence for him to finish. He had changed. His shoulders were broader and tapered to narrow hips. The youthful handsomeness of his face had matured into an arresting maleness. She felt a peculiar tremble go through her. Since Lucien's death she had never thought about lying in a man's arms again. She had wanted to forget that part of her marriage along with the rest of it.

All last night, as she'd tossed and turned, and again this morning when she had sat and written the contract, she had tried to put the physical intimacy aside. But now, with Justin standing in front of her, the full implication of what she had agreed to hit her.

She tore her gaze away. Oh, lord. Could she really do this? But what choice did she have? None if she wished to protect Chloe. Just as Lucien had wanted payment for the wrong done his father, Justin wanted payment for the wrong done to him. She was the one to pay.

'I must compliment you.' His voice broke into her thoughts. 'This would put my solicitor's contracts to shame. However, there are one or two points I would like to discuss.'

She eyed him with more than a little apprehension. 'What are those?'

'You stated you would spend no more than three occasions a week in my company. I want to increase that.'

Her cheeks coloured. 'I would think that would be enough time to…to conduct our business. I cannot spend all of my time doing that and I am certain you have other things to do as well.'

For the first time, a hint of amusement crossed his face. 'But none as pleasurable.'

'Perhaps for you!' Her cheeks must be on fire.

He stared at her and a rather wicked smile touched his mouth. 'I intend to see our meetings are pleasurable for you as well.'

'I...' She swallowed and wished she had held her tongue. She did not want him to flirt with her. She wanted him to be cool and controlled. And passionless. Just as she intended to be. 'Three times a week is enough for me,' she managed to say.

'But I will want your company for other things.'

'What other things?'

He shrugged. 'To attend the opera or the theatre. Perhaps Vauxhall. Or to drive with me.'

'But why? I cannot imagine why you would wish to spend any more time with me than you must.' She had not expected this. She had thought they would meet clandestinely and then pretend they hardly knew one another in public.

His expression cooled. 'I wish to make it very clear you are mine.'

'I see.' She moved away from him. 'You wish to publicly shame me. But I fear you will hurt my mother-in-law and my sister-in-law as well. And perhaps your own family. Surely they will not be pleased that I am in your company.'

'No, but it will tell society that you do not hold me responsible for your husband's death.'

'Will it? And will I have paid my debt—Lucien's debt—at the end of the Season? Because I do not want to pay forever. Nor do I want my sister-in-law or any one other person to pay as well.'

'It will be paid.'

She took a deep breath. 'Very well. How often do you want my company?'

'Three nights a week and for other occasions as I demand.'

'I will not be at your beck and call, your Grace.' She lifted her chin and met his eyes squarely. 'If I am available I will consider your request, but I certainly have no intention of ordering my life around your convenience.'

His eyes never left hers. 'Then three nights a week and two other occasions at my request. Any more than that will be at your convenience.' His voice held a note of mockery.

She had not realised she was holding her breath. 'That will be acceptable. Do you wish to add the amendments or should I? Then I suggest we sign the contract. I have made two copies.'

He gave a short surprised laugh. 'I had no idea your mind ran along such damnably methodical lines. How many of these contracts have you drawn up?'

She gave him a cold look. 'None. But I have read enough contracts to know what they should contain. If it were possible, I have often thought I would like to study law.'

'I've no doubt you would do admirably. I have always thought you were one of the most intelligent women of my acquaintance.'

The words seemed to surprise him as much as they did her. For a moment, they stared at one another and then she looked away, oddly unsettled. He took a pace towards the mantelpiece before looking at her. 'You may add the amendments. We will sign them tonight when you come to dine with me.'

She faltered. 'Dine with you? Tonight?'

'Yes. I see no reason to delay.'

'But…' Her stomach had started to knot again. 'I have promised Chloe and my mother-in-law that I would accompany them to Lady Fairfield's rout and then there is some other affair after that.'

'Lady Montgomery's soirée. I assure you both affairs will be dead bores. You will be much better off dining with me.'

A little smile had touched his mouth and for a moment she was swept back into the time before he had come to hate her. Regret and a bittersweet longing shot through her. 'Will I?'

His smile faded. 'Yes. Can you cry off? The sooner you fulfil your terms the sooner I will fulfil mine.'

She understood his meaning perfectly. She took a deep breath. 'Very well. I will dine with you tonight.'

'I will send a carriage for you at eight.'

She frowned. 'I can take my own.'

'It will be less obvious if I send one of mine.'

She raised her brow. 'I hardly think a carriage with a ducal crest would be less obvious.'

He scowled. 'I have a plain, unmarked carriage.'

'The one you always use for your mistresses?'

'No.' His voice had lost all trace of warmth and he moved towards her. 'I will see you tonight, Belle.' His gaze went to her face and then strayed to her lips. For a moment, just as she had last night, she thought he would kiss her. Instead, he backed away. 'Goodbye.'

She watched him leave the room and heard his footsteps echoing down the hall. She had no idea what to think. None of it made sense at all.

Chapter Three

Belle followed the housekeeper into the drawing room. The lamps had been lit and cast a warm glow around the elegant room. The housekeeper, a stocky woman with greying hair and a brisk manner, regarded her with a not unkind expression. 'His Grace will be with you soon. Please be seated, my lady.'

Belle managed a thank-you and took the nearest chair. She pulled her cloak more tightly around her and watched the stout woman bustle away. She took a deep breath and tried to force herself to be calm, but her heart was beating as fast and loudly as the clock on the mantelpiece.

She had told Chloe and Maria that she feared she was developing the headache…which was not exactly untrue, for an acute attack of nerves was doing just that. A particular spot at the back of her neck had started to ache, a sure sign of an impending headache. She had not even considered using that as an excuse to avoid Justin tonight for she doubted he would believe her and for the most part her headaches were infrequent and usually not very bad. So, promptly at eight, she had climbed into the comfortable coach and after an all-too-brief ride through the streets of London, had arrived at his townhouse.

She rubbed her neck and closed her eyes for a moment. What was she doing here? No, she knew exactly what she was doing. She was paying off the enormous wrong Lucien had done Justin. And she was protecting Chloe. She had tried to tell herself that surely she could endure his touch. She could endure anything after marriage to Lucien where she had learned to shut her mind far away from what happened to her body. She opened her eyes. It would not do to think of such things now.

The ticking of the clock only increased her apprehension. She finally rose and went to look at the landscape over the mantelpiece.

'Good evening.'

Her heart slammed to her throat. She whirled around to find Justin behind her. 'I did not hear you!'

Slight amusement showed in his face. 'You seemed to be engrossed in the painting.'

Her mouth suddenly went dry. 'It is fascinating. Is it of the Yorkshire moors?'

He looked a little surprised. 'Yes. Have you been there?'

'Once. With my parents when I was twelve. They wanted to tour some of the more remote parts of the kingdom and so we went to Yorkshire and even to Northumberland. I especially remember the moors. They looked so wild and I instantly thought of *Udolpho*.' It was the last trip she had taken with her parents before they died and she went to live with her grandmother.

'You were allowed to read such a work then?'

'Well, no. Mama was very strict about such things. A young lady on the neighbouring estate loaned me her copy and I read it in great secrecy whenever I could manage. As well as several other romances.'

His mouth curved in a smile. 'I had no idea you were a secret romantic.'

'I was. Once.' The smile made her catch her breath. Oh, lord. The last thing she wanted was to feel some sort of attraction towards him.

'But no longer.'

'No.'

The smile faded. 'We can dine in my apartments.' His voice was impersonal. She nodded. The coolness had returned to his face, thank goodness. He made no move to touch her as they left the drawing room and passed through the hallway. They went up the tall winding staircase to the floor above. The house was quiet and their footsteps were a soft pad on the rugs. He pushed open a door to a room and allowed her to precede him. She stepped in and saw it was a large sitting room. In one corner was a long table covered with papers. A sofa flanked one side of the fireplace.

She stood in the room, having no idea what to do. He came up behind her and his hands were on her shoulders. Belle jumped and then froze.

'I am only intending to take your cloak,' he said. 'Don't run.'

She stood perfectly still as he removed the garment from her shoulders. His fingers brushed her nape and she shivered. But she had no idea whether it was from fear or something else.

He draped her cloak over a chair. Despite the modest cut of her gown she felt exposed. But his expression was still polite when he looked at her.

'Would you like something to drink?' he asked. 'Wine?'

She almost refused and then decided that perhaps it was exactly what she needed. She watched as he strode across the room to the wine, which sat on a table. He poured two glasses then came back and gave one to her. Her hand was not quite steady as she took it.

'I wasn't certain if you would come tonight,' he said.

'Why? I told you I would be here.'

'You must be very fond of Lady Chloe.'

'She is like a sister to me. I would not see her hurt for the world.' She looked at him. 'Or Lady Ralston.'

He was silent for a moment and then his gaze moved to the papers she still held in one hand. His brow rose slightly. 'The contract?'

'Yes. I would like you to sign it before we…we…'

'Dine?'

'Yes.' Colour tinged her cheeks.

'Come and sit down, then.' He held out one chair at the table. She sat down and he took the chair across from her. She gave him the paper then took a nervous sip from her wine, watching him as he perused the document. He finally looked up. 'It seems to be in order.'

'Should we sign the contracts, your Grace?' She attempted to keep her voice detached as if the papers merely contained the terms for the sale of a piece of property.

'Yes. Although I am beginning to think we need to clarify that you are to call me by my given name. Under the circumstances, ''your Grace'' does not seem appropriate.'

'We are entering into a business arrangement. It does not mean we must be on…on intimate terms with each other.'

A sardonic light leapt to his eye. 'You don't think coming to my bed constitutes intimate terms?'

'No, not necessarily. I think true intimacy can only be based on mutual affection and trust. Since we do not have those between us then we cannot truly be on intimate terms. I do not think a mere physical relationship can be defined as an intimate one.'

'So you consider our relationship to be a form of prostitution?' His eyes narrowed.

She flinched but forced herself to meet his eyes. 'Yes, of course.'

'You are remarkably matter of fact about this affair. I would almost suspect you have entered into such a relationship before.' His words were deliberate and cruel.

Anger shot through her. 'Perhaps I have. Although I was young and naïve and thought physical intimacy was equivalent to love. I know better now.'

She was unprepared for the blaze of fury in his eyes. 'Who was he?'

'That is not your concern.' She had undoubtedly had too much wine or she would not have provoked him in such a way.

He stared at her for a moment longer. 'We will sign the documents and then eat.' His voice was indifferent again.

He crossed to the small desk to find an inkpot and pen.

His shoulders were broad beneath his coat and his thick hair, slightly longer than the fashion, brushed against his collar. A peculiar pit began to form in her stomach. She should not have made him so angry but his words had pierced her. And why should he be so angry? In another man she would have thought he was jealous, but of course that could not be it. She picked up her wine again and took another sip and realised she had just finished the entire glass.

She watched him with the pen in his strong, lean fingers. He signed both copies and then pushed them towards her. 'Your signature.' He gave her the pen, his fingers brushing hers. A dart of awareness shot through her and she took it with a shaky hand. She had no idea whether it was from the wine or his touch.

She wrote her name beneath his bold, impatient signature and then gave him one copy. He took it and put it on the desk behind him.

She nearly jumped when the door opened. She turned and saw two footmen enter, carrying trays. She moved away from the table and watched while they deftly laid the covers then they departed as quietly as they had come. 'Sit down, Belle,' Justin said.

She took the chair he held out for her and sat. He again took his place across from her. Her appetite had fled, but at least if she made some pretence of eating she could put off the inevitable.

She glanced across the table at him. The candle flickered over his strong features and she could tell herself and him that there was no intimacy between them, but the setting itself conspired against her. Her gaze fell to his lips and she swallowed. She took another sip of wine. The smell of the food drifted up and to her surprise she felt a pang of hunger. At least eating would be something to do besides staring at him and anticipating what was certain to come after dinner so she picked up her fork.

The food was good. She had eaten several mouthfuls before she looked up to find Justin had stopped eating and was watching her instead. 'Must you stare at me?'

His eyes drifted over her face. 'You are very beautiful.'

Her face heated. 'I wish you would not pay me compliments.'

'I am merely stating a fact.' His eyes remained on her.

She put her fork down, feeling self-conscious. 'I would prefer it if you would not make such personal remarks.'

'Ah, yes. The business relationship we are embarking on. Very well, then talk to me.'

'Talk to you?' She started. Her hand hit the empty wine glass and it fell to the floor and rolled under the table. Mortified, she pushed her chair back with some idea of retrieving it. And then froze when his hand closed around her wrist. Her eyes flew to his face. His mouth twitched and he released her hand. 'Sit down. There's no need to panic yet. I was merely suggesting conversation.'

'Oh.' She took her seat, feeling foolish.

'More wine?' he asked.

She glanced swiftly at him. 'Yes, if you please.' She rarely drank wine, but perhaps if she had a bit more she would not be so...so nervous. It seemed to have dulled her emotions and thankfully her headache as well.

He poured her another glass and brought it to her. She sipped it and watched him take his place across from her. She was suddenly aware of the broadness of his shoulders and the lock of hair that had fallen across his forehead. With a sort of detached fascination she stared as he picked up his own wine glass and brought it to his lips. Lips that would soon be on hers. As would those strong lean hands that were now wrapped around the stem of his glass.

Heat coursed through her and she felt almost dizzy. She set her glass down and nearly set it on her plate. She stared down and realised she was having a difficult time focusing. Oh, lord. She was not just relaxed but on her way to becoming inebriated. Only once before had it happened, when she was only eighteen, and it had not been an unpleasant experience. Except for the dull headache and horrid taste in her mouth the next day.

Perhaps becoming foxed was not a bad idea. When he started to…to…seduce her she might not mind so much. Or maybe she would not mind at all.

'You are not hungry?' he asked.

His voice jerked her from her contemplation of the plate. 'No, not very.' She glanced at him and forced herself to focus. 'Are you?'

'No.' His eyes met hers. Despite the amount of wine she'd drunk, she could not mistake the desire in his eyes. He pushed back his chair and stood. 'Come here, Belle,' he said roughly.

Her heart leapt to her throat. She started to rise and knocked her chair over.

Her cheeks burned as she stared at the downed chair. 'You must think I intend to destroy your house.'

He came around the table and set the chair upright then he turned to look at her. 'Not at all. I do think, however, you have had too much wine.'

'Do you? I am not certain I've had enough,' she blurted out.

'It won't be that bad,' he said almost gently.

'Won't it?' Her eyes searched his face and what she saw there made her tremble. She stepped back and stumbled into the chair.

He caught her against his chest. 'You are foxed.' He sounded bemused.

'No, I am not. Perhaps if I sat down.' His chest felt hard and strong and warm. He smelled nice, she thought with vague surprise. Unlike Lucien, whose odour had been harsh and unpleasant.

'I think that is a good idea,' he said.

He took her arm and led her to the sofa. To her dismay, her gait was unsteady and it took all her willpower to keep from swaying. She sank down on the sofa and closed her eyes. Everything spun for a brief moment. Then he was beside her, his thigh pressed against hers. The sensation was not unpleasant. She opened her eyes. 'I never drink wine,' she told him.

'I thought not.' His eyes were on her face. 'As soon as you have er…sobered a bit, I will take you home. First you need some tea.' He started to rise.

'No!' She grabbed his coat sleeve. 'I…I think we should start the contract.'

He sat down and stared at her. 'As tempting as the offer is, I think it best if we wait until we are both sober.'

'No. I really prefer we start now.' She must be mad or perhaps he was. 'Otherwise I…I will be afraid.' She undoubtedly made no sense at all.

'Of me?'

'Of…of any man.'

Something flickered in his eyes. 'Then come here.' He held out his arm.

She scooted next to him and he pulled her to his side. He bent his head towards her, and she felt a bolt of panic as she always had with Lucien. He stilled for a moment. 'You can kiss me first,' he said.

She stared at his mouth, firm and sensuous, with a hint of dark beard around the edges. His eyes were dark and still and waiting. She closed her eyes and forced herself to lean towards him.

Her mouth found his. His lips were warm and firm. He made no move to possess her and merely waited. She tentatively nibbled at him and then kissed him more firmly. Her hands caught his arms so she might brace herself and she realised with a sense of wonder she had never explored a man's mouth before. She lightly ran her tongue over his lips, tasting him. A low sound escaped from his throat, almost a groan, and his muscles tensed under her hands.

She lifted her head and opened her eyes. 'Is something wrong?' she whispered. 'I have not done this before.'

'No.' His eyes shot open.

She touched his face. His cheek was rough under her palm. 'Should I kiss you again?'

'No!' He looked as if she'd offered to shoot him. 'That is…' He ran a hand through his hair. 'If you continue kissing me like that you will end up in my bed.'

Perhaps she was more drunk than she thought. She blinked, trying to clear her vision. And her hearing. 'Isn't that what you wanted?'

'No. At least not tonight. Hell.' He stood. 'I thought—' He stopped and turned to look at her. 'I'd best take you home.'

'Why?' She seemed to be rapidly sobering. 'Why not tonight?'

'Because I have no intention of taking advantage of you. I would prefer that you are sober and fully conscious of what you are doing.'

'I see.' She rose, feeling a little dizzy. She supposed she should be relieved, but she only felt confused. To make matters worse, her headache was returning in full force and she rubbed the back of her neck.

'What is wrong?'

''Tis nothing. I have had a slight headache most of the day.' She was beginning to feel a little sick as well.

His brow shot up. 'And you drank three glasses of wine? My dear, you will have the devil of a head tomorrow.'

'Was it three? I thought it was only two.' She sat back down as another wave of light-headedness overcame her. Why must this happen now?

'Most definitely three.' He looked down at her for a moment. 'I will take you home,' he said abruptly.

Although he draped the cloak over her shoulders and helped her into his carriage, his touch was as impersonal as her maid's. Once in the carriage, he sat in the corner opposite her, his legs stretched in front of him and said nothing. Belle tried to look anywhere but at him as they made the short journey to Gower Street.

Once they arrived, he stepped down and then held out his hand to assist her. Despite his hand, she stumbled. His arms closed around her. 'Please 'lease me,' she said as coolly as she could but, to her chagrin, her words were slightly slurred.

'You cannot go in by yourself.'

'Yes, I c...can.' She swayed again.

'No.' Before she could protest, he had swung her up in his arms. She hardly registered the bewilderment on the face of James, her footman, before Justin was carrying her up the stairs. They met Mrs Bates at the top.

'My lady?' Mrs Bates said, her face alarmed.

'Your mistress has the headache,' Justin said. 'If you show me her bedchamber, I will take her there.'

'It is this way.'

He did not put her down until Mrs Bates had pulled back the covers and then he gently laid her on the bed. Belle thought she would die of humiliation. She closed her eyes and hoped it was all a bad dream brought about by too much wine.

'Belle.'

She was not dreaming. She opened her eyes to find Justin bent over her. 'Will you be all right?'

No, she was dreaming after all. He sounded almost concerned, which was impossible. 'Yes, of course.'

He straightened. 'Then I will leave you. Goodnight, Belle.'

'Goodnight,' she whispered. But he had already left the room. To her chagrin, she felt tears prick her lids. Why did he have to behave in such a gentlemanly fashion? She wanted to think him cold and callous. Otherwise, she could never keep her emotions uninvolved.

Justin asked himself the same question the next day. He threw a punch that nearly sent Brandt reeling. Brandt held up his hand. 'Wait! What are you trying to do, bloody my nose? Might I remind you we are relations? Damn, Westmore, what's the occasion?'

Justin scowled at his cousin, still breathing hard. 'None,' he finally said. They were at Gentleman Jackson's. He'd hoped a good sparring match would at least temporarily distract his thoughts from Belle. However, it seemed to have the opposite effect and he could think of nothing but when he would see her again.

What the hell was wrong with him? He had had her exactly where he wanted her last night, in his arms and kissing him, her body soft and pliant against his. The contract aside, taking her would have been easy—he had only to scoop her into his arms and carry her to his bed.

Except she had been three sheets to the wind and her pliability had little to do with wanting him. And she had said she was afraid. Perhaps he had been a fool to believe her, but something in her voice told him she did not lie. Had it been the lover she claimed had hurt her? Or her wretch of a husband?

'Let me guess. Isabelle Milborne.'

Justin yanked his thoughts back to his cousin. 'What?'

'Lady Milborne. She was not seen at all last night although her relations were. Nor were you.' He picked up a cloth and threw it to Justin.

'So?'

'Completely unremarkable except you were seen calling on her yesterday morning.'

'Who the devil saw that?' He wiped the sweat from his brow and frowned at Brandt.

'Percy Ormund. He was calling on an acquaintance in Gower Street.' He cocked a brow at Justin. 'Taken together with your absences, I would almost suspect you were with her last night.'

It was on the tip of his tongue to deny it, but why, since he wanted it known he had an interest in her? 'You would not be incorrect.'

Brandt stared. 'I've no desire of interfering in your business, but what the devil are you about?'

Justin shrugged. 'Payment for my two thousand pounds. With interest.'

Brandt choked. 'The hell you are!' He stared at Justin, a peculiar light coming into his eye. 'And what role does Lady Chloe play in this?'

'Lady Chloe is my trump card.'

Brandt's eyes narrowed. 'She may be the late Lord Milborne's half-sister but she's an innocent. I would hope you have the decency to leave her out of this business.'

'Precisely Belle Milborne's sentiments. Which is why she is willing to co-operate with me.'

Brandt continued to stare at him. 'Are you certain it is payment you want? Or is it revenge? Because as much as I appreciate your desire for the latter, I fear you will pay part of the price yourself.'

Justin thought of how pale and vulnerable she had looked in her bed last night then shoved the thought aside and gave a short laugh. 'That is something I do not intend to let happen.'

Chapter Four

Belle pulled on her glove and picked up her fan. She was in no mood to go to another ball but after crying off last night, she could hardly do so again. So she would go despite a heavy head and a dry mouth. Reminders of last night—a night she would have preferred to forget. Not only had she disgraced herself by drinking too much wine, she had thrown herself at Justin in a way that made her blanch just thinking about it.

Worse, was his own behaviour. He had been nothing but a gentleman even after she made it patently obvious she was willing to do whatever he wanted. Instead of taking full advantage of her, he had taken her home.

She had no idea why. She would have thought it would have suited his purposes perfectly to have seduced her last night. But he had not attempted to at all and had only insisted she kiss him after she practically begged him. Never in her life had she behaved in such a wanton and despicable way.

And, she thought bitterly, her behaviour had no doubt confirmed she was exactly what he thought her. She would not let such a thing happen again. If she saw him tonight, she would be cool and composed and completely in control. The unassailable Lady Milborne.

Justin finally spotted Belle near the faux Grecian pillars at the far end of the ballroom. She stood with her mother-in-law and Ralston. He started across the room. It was time to make his intentions public.

She stiffened at his approach and then she quickly looked away. To his annoyance, she kept her gaze on Ralston, apparently so absorbed in what he was saying that she did not notice him until he stood directly in front of them. 'Good evening, Lady Ralston, Ralston. Good evening, Lady Milborne.'

'Good evening, your Grace.' Despite the flash of apprehension in her face, her voice was polite as was her expression, as if they were nothing but mere acquaintances. He fully intended to shake that composure.

He turned to Lady Ralston, who looked as if he had come to escort her to the gallows. 'Lady Ralston, I trust you are well.'

Her eyes widened. 'I...' She swayed a little and Belle caught her arm.

She cast Justin an angry look before turning to her mother-in-law. 'Do you need to sit down, Maria?' she asked.

'Oh, no. I will be fine,' Lady Ralston said with a wan smile.

'Then perhaps you will not object if I solicit your daughter-in-law for the next dance?' Justin said.

Lady Ralston gaped at him. 'Belle? You wish to dance with Belle?'

'I fear Lady Milborne does not dance,' Ralston said icily. The ingratiating smile on his face had disappeared.

He shifted, just barely towards Belle, but the movement signalled possession.

Unaccountably annoyed, Justin's brow rose. 'I was not aware you were Lady Milborne's guardian.'

Ralston's face reddened. 'I am not, naturally, but since she never dances she should not make herself a source of gossip by doing so now unless, of course, she dances with a relation.'

'Such as yourself?'

Ralston frowned. 'I would consider that more acceptable, yes.'

'Do you wish to stand up with Lord Ralston?' Justin asked Belle who still held Lady Ralston's arm.

'No, I do not!' she snapped. 'I do not want to stand up with anyone, if you must know!'

Lady Ralston gasped and Ralston's mouth opened and closed like a landed trout. Belle coloured fiercely when she seemed to realise how much she had shocked her family. 'That is, I do not dance, your Grace.'

A cool smile curved his mouth. 'There is the contract.' He spoke softly enough that he doubted Ralston could hear him over the music and chatter.

She frowned and then her gaze went to something over his shoulder. He half-turned and saw young Roland Hurst escorting Lady Chloe towards them. Belle looked back at him. 'Very well, your Grace, I will stand up with you.'

Lady Ralston gasped. 'You cannot!'

'Belle!' Ralston exclaimed. 'I forbid you to make a spectacle of yourself.'

Justin was rapidly developing a desire to mow Ralston down. He eyed the man with a look that made him pale. 'I assure you she will not.' He turned to Belle and held out his arm. 'Shall we, Lady Milborne?'

She nodded and, after a brief hesitation, took his arm. He led her to one of the sets that was forming and released her. 'Does Ralston always attempt to dictate to you like that?' he demanded.

'He always dictates to everyone.'

He scowled. 'But why the devil do you allow him to ride roughshod over you like that?'

'Because if I do not, he will forbid me to see Chloe.'

'The devil take him,' he said softly. She merely looked at him without speaking but she did not need to. He was using her affection for Chloe to dictate to her in an even more despicable fashion than Ralston.

He looked down at her lovely face and reminded himself that she deserved no sympathy. She had used him in a way that had nearly killed him, but even worse had destroyed his parents. Her actions were every bit as despicable as his.

The music started. It did not take him long to realise that if his intentions were to shake her composure by dancing with her, he had sadly miscalculated. She was polite but she had put up that impenetrable barrier that made him want to grit his teeth. Or kiss her until she surrendered to him.

Then he wanted to curse because he did not want her to affect him in any way. He wanted no emotion involved where she was concerned because he intended to use her as heartlessly as she had used him.

By the time the dance had finished, he was in a foul mood. He led Belle from the set and to the side of the ballroom and there he looked down at her. 'I would like your company tomorrow night. You will attend the theatre with me and after that you will come to my house.'

'Tomorrow night is not convenient for me.'

'You had best make it convenient then. May I remind

you that until you start to fulfil your terms of the contract, my side is not enforceable.'

She lifted her chin. 'If you recall, you said you would require my company on two other occasions each week. I would consider last night one occasion and tonight another unless you wanted last night to count towards the other part of my terms.'

The fact she could continue to look so composed and sound so damn reasonable annoyed him even more. 'Hardly, my dear. Since very little happened.'

'That was not my doing. I was willing but you were not.'

He stepped towards her. 'Oh, I was very willing, but I was not about to take advantage of you.'

'How odd since that was what I thought our entire contract was about.' A little smile touched her mouth.

Which had the unfortunate effect of drawing his attention there. He could almost taste her lips. The urge to take her into his arms and kiss her until she was breathless was nearly overwhelming. He took another step towards her and her eyes widened.

'Westmore!'

His aunt's sharp voice suddenly recalled him to his senses. He was in the middle of a ballroom. He spun around to find Lady Georgina behind him. With her was her latest protégée, Lady Clarissa Blackwood, an icy beauty of eighteen, whose conversations seemed to consist solely of monosyllables. Lady Georgina's sharp gaze went from his face to Belle's. Without acknowledging Belle, she turned back to him. 'I have promised Lady Clarissa that you would stand up with her for the next dance.'

Hell. He wanted to strangle his aunt, first for cutting Belle and then for putting him in a position where he was obligated to dance with the girl. He could hardly refuse with Lady Clarissa standing in front of him. ''Very well,' he said coolly.

He turned to find Belle. But she had vanished. Had his aunt's snub distressed her so much that she had left? But why should he care if it had if he wanted to punish her in any way possible?

He had no answer.

Chapter Five

Belle stared down at the note she held in her hand with a great deal of dismay. It had arrived just as she sat down for breakfast and had had the immediate effect of ruining her appetite. The note was very curt and to the point.

—As one of your contractual obligations you will do me the honour of accompanying me to the Theatre Royal tonight. We will return to my house after the performance.

Westmore.

She crumpled it and resisted the urge to tear the page into small pieces and forget she had ever made such a bargain. But that would never do. Then he would distress Chloe with his attentions and poor Maria would probably go into a severe decline. Arthur would do everything in his power to make certain Chloe became a Duchess while Lady Georgina would do everything in her power to make certain Chloe did not. She shuddered just thinking about it.

Oh, dear. She took a sip from her coffee, which was now cold, and then shoved the cup aside. Agitated, she rose and went to stand near the window. Everything was about to become very complicated. She must cry off from attending the theatre with Maria, Chloe and Arthur and then they would see her there with Justin. She could hardly keep it a secret from them.

She really had no choice but to tell Maria the truth. She was going to the theatre with Justin.

Her mother-in-law stared at her, her face incredulous. Two spots of red colour appeared in her cheeks and then she fell back against the sofa with a little shriek. 'No! It was bad enough you stood up with him last night. But to attend the theatre with him?' Her voice rose. 'How can you? Are you so unfeeling that you would consort with the man who…who killed my son? You have always been a daughter to me and now you are betraying me!'

Belle tried to take Maria's hand but the older woman snatched it away. 'Please do not touch me! I do not know why you are doing this? Is it possible you are in love with him?'

Belle flinched and a wave of anger hit her with stunning force. She spoke before she could think. 'No! How can you say such a thing? How can you even think such a thing? The only reason I am doing this is to protect Chloe. He will leave Chloe alone in exchange for my company. Otherwise he will continue to pursue her.'

Maria's mouth fell open. 'You are protecting Chloe from his attentions?' She stared at Belle, her eyes growing wider. 'Oh, how can he be so wicked as to pursue her when he must know we revile him? But if you go to the theatre with him he will stop? Why?'

Belle suddenly regretted she had spoken. She said tiredly, 'I do not know. It is what he has agreed to.'

She had no idea what Maria would say but she was hardly prepared for Maria's next words. 'Oh, my dear! I quite see how it is. You are sacrificing yourself for Chloe. How could I doubt you! You must be the best of daughters-in-law!' She enfolded Belle in a swooping embrace that smelled of cloying perfume. She released her then sat back and sniffed. 'How brave you are! I do not care what anyone will think or say when they see you with him.'

'I pray you will not say a thing to anyone about this. Particularly not to Chloe.'

'Of course I will not,' she said indignantly. A little frown creased her brow. 'So you are only going to the theatre with him?'

'No, he wishes me to spend more time in his company.'

Maria stared at her. 'More time? Does he wish you to…to become his *mistress*?'

'I…' She looked at Maria, feeling helpless. Her cheeks heated. 'No, of course not.'

Maria's eyes widened. 'I am certain he does. I see everything now! He was in love with you and wished to provoke a quarrel with Lucien so he might have you. But you refused him and now he means to have you any way he can!'

'No, it is not that at all.'

Maria paid no heed. 'Oh, my love, you must be careful. You will have no reputation and then Chloe's will be quite ruined! The Duke of Westmore's mistress! I quite see, he means to ruin all of us!' She closed her eyes and emitted a wail.

'No, he will not. I will see to it he does not.'

Maria's eyes opened. 'No, I know you will not let anything happen to us. Or to harm Chloe. Which is why

I must ask that you do not see Chloe for the rest of the Season.'

Belle stared at her. 'Not see Chloe?'

'You do understand why, do you not?' Maria asked. Her eyes were fixed on Belle. 'I perfectly understand the sacrifice you are making, but others will not and if it appears we condone your association…my dear, you must see that it will not do Chloe any good at all!'

'No, it would not,' she said slowly. She rose, her legs unsteady. 'I must go. Please give Chloe my love and tell her…tell her…' but she could not finish. She picked up her reticule and bonnet and nearly ran from the room. She heard Maria's surprised protest but she had no desire to burst into tears in front of her. She climbed into her carriage and sat down, clutching her reticule and praying she would not weep. But she could not so easily stop the wretchedness in her heart that made her feel as if she had just cut herself off from all that was good.

Justin glanced at his companion who was seated next to him in the box. She had been quiet and obviously distracted ever since he had called for her three-quarters of an hour ago. She had politely answered his questions, but she might as well be on another continent as far as he was concerned.

She suddenly stiffened, her attention caught by something. He looked over and saw Lady Ralston and Lady Chloe being escorted into a box by Lord Ralston. 'Do not worry, I have given you my promise that I will not pursue your sister-in-law,' he told her.

She turned and looked at him. Her fine eyes were full of such misery that he was taken aback. Then her expression veiled. 'I am not worried,' she said politely.

'Then what is it?'

'Nothing at all.' She folded her hands back in her lap. 'I have not been in the Theatre Royal before.'

'Your husband did not bring you here?'

'No, he did not.' She made an obvious effort to look at him. 'I have heard this is an excellent play.'

'Yes. There is no need to force yourself to make conversation,' he said drily.

'I beg your pardon. I fear I cannot think of much to say tonight.'

'Apparently not. You might, however, look as if you take some pleasure in my company.'

For the first time her eyes flashed anger. 'Why? Is that part of our contract? That I must enjoy this?'

At least she showed him something besides indifference. He folded his arms. 'I would like that, yes.'

'Very well.' She gave him a tight smile. But then her gaze went in the direction of Ralston's box. She looked quickly away. Her cheeks heated with colour. The curtain went up, but not before Justin caught a glimpse of Ralston's outraged face.

Brandt was the first person to join them at the interval. With him was Henry Aubrey. Justin stood, and Belle did as well. He glanced at her. 'You know my cousin. Have you met Aubrey?'

'Yes,' Belle said. Her smile was strained. 'Good evening, Lord Salcombe, Mr Aubrey.'

Brandt inclined his head. 'Lady Milborne.' His expression was cool. 'You are enjoying the performance?'

'Very much.' She was still polite, nothing in her expression revealing how she felt at Brandt's icy manner.

For some reason Justin wanted to box his cousin's ears.

Aubrey's face held curiosity, but his manner was more

open. 'Are you? Will own I could not understand the actress who played Perdita or Prudence or whatever the d…she was called.'

Belle's face relaxed a little. 'Her diction was not the best.'

Brandt had turned to Justin. 'So you purchased Chiswick's colt today.'

His preoccupation with Belle had almost made him forget about the animal. 'I signed the papers this morning. I'll leave for Surrey tomorrow to fetch him.'

'Chiswick's bay devil?' Aubrey said. 'Good God! His bloodlines are impeccable, but he's a nasty temper from what I've been told. Bit a groom. Bolted with Chiswick and dumped him in a heap of…' he glanced at Belle '…er mud.'

'Which is precisely what I'd do if someone as heavy-handed as Chiswick was on my back,' Brandt said.

By this time Lord Henly had joined them. He was stout with a face that resembled a pig's and a roving eye. He ran his gaze over Belle in a brazen fashion that made Justin want to hit him and then positioned himself far too close to her. When he launched into a discussion of the various attributes of the actresses, Justin decided it was time to leave.

He turned to Belle, who stood quietly listening. 'Come and take a turn around the lobby with me.'

She hesitated and then followed him from the box. 'Do you not wish to stay with your friends?'

'No. Henly will undoubtedly regale us with his comments on certain parts of the female anatomy. They are not fit for your ears.'

'I can assure you that after marriage to Lucien I am not easily shocked. Besides, Lord Henly visited Lucien more than once.' She spoke calmly but colour touched her cheek.

'Of course. I had nearly forgotten you were married to one of the most notorious rakes in England.' As well as that beneath her quiet façade was an adventuress, and the slight flush staining her cheeks had nothing to do with modesty.

She looked at him. 'Had you? I fear that is something I have never been allowed to forget.' She glanced over his shoulder. 'Good evening, Lady Burlington.'

He started, having nearly forgotten where they were. In the middle of a London theatre where he had intended to parade to the *ton* that she was his. Certainly he had accomplished his objective if the number of curious stares they received were any indication. Only Belle did not seem to notice. She stood a little aloof and he wanted more and more to shake her out of it. He did not want to return to their box. He wanted to be alone with her. To feel her mouth beneath his and her soft curves pressed against him. He scowled. 'We are leaving,' he said abruptly.

Surprise showed in her face. 'But the next act is about to begin.'

'The prospect of missing it hardly pains me. I came to be seen with you, not because I wished to watch the play.'

'Indeed. I do not suppose it might occur to you that I might actually want to watch the play?'

'No.' He frowned at her, wanting to tell her that it did not matter what she wished, but her expression gave him pause. 'Do you?'

She lifted her chin and looked at him. 'No, for it is really not a very good play, but I might have wanted to.'

His brow shot up. 'I fail to see the point of this conversation. I wish to leave and you wish to leave.'

'The point is that I am not your lap dog. I will not allow you to dictate to me.'

He bit back his impatience. 'I was not attempting to dictate to you. I've no idea why you decided to disagree with me when there was no need to. Shall we go since we are both in agreement?'

Belle opened her mouth as if she wished to say something else and then closed it. She turned and started towards the steps. He felt his temper rise but, before he caught up with her, she stopped.

Her mother-in-law was coming towards her with Lady Chloe and he watched as Lady Ralston drifted past Belle without the least acknowledgement that she was there. Lady Chloe sent her a brief stricken glance before continuing on. Belle lifted her head and then continued walking as if nothing had happened.

He reached her side and caught her arm. 'What the devil was that all about?'

She barely looked at him. 'I have no idea what you are talking about.'

'Lady Ralston just gave you the cut direct. As did your sister-in-law.'

'Did she?' She looked straight ahead.

He realised several people watched them. His desire to be on display had been abating rapidly and now it died. 'We will discuss this later. We are leaving now.' He took her to the entrance hall and then sent for her shawl, and his hat and gloves. He did not speak again until they were in his carriage and it had started to move through the London streets.

'Do you know why your in-laws just cut you?' he demanded.

She tore her gaze from the window. 'I rather expec
it was because I was with you. I would rather not discus
it, if you please.'

She sniffed as if she were fighting back tears. If she
had actually cried or raged at him or raged at her in
laws, he might have remained unmoved or perhaps beer
even contemptuous, but that little sound took him aback
The next thing he knew he was sitting next to her. His
arms went around her and he pulled her against him
'Don't,' he said roughly.

'Don't what?'

'Cry.' Her scent filled his nostrils. A soft blend of rose
and femininity. He suddenly thought of his mother, fo
she too had smelled of roses. But Belle's warm fram
was hardly maternal. His arms tightened.

'I am not crying.' She lifted her head and looked a
him. She sniffed again.

'You are.' Her lips were too invitingly close. With a
groan he covered them with his. A little gasp escaped
her and her hands clutched at his coat as the carriage hi
a bump. His arms tightened, pulling her closer and his
mouth moved roughly over hers, demanding her re
sponse.

Her lips parted slightly and he deepened the kiss. He
taste and smell intoxicated him and it wasn't until he
felt her stiffen under him and heard her little sound al
most of pain that he realised he was half on her in the
darkened carriage.

He lifted his head and dropped his arms. 'I beg your
pardon.' He moved away from her, trying to regain his
senses.

'There is no need to under the circumstances. It was
just my reticule was under me. I think I sat on a pin.'

'Are you hurt?'

'No. It was the merest of pin-pricks.'

Her voice was calm, too calm, whereas he felt as if he was on fire. He moved back to his seat across from her. What the devil was wrong with him? He'd nearly lost control of himself, attacking her with the loss of restraint of a callow youth with his first love.

That was not part of his plan. He had no intention of relinquishing control. He might desire her, but he intended to keep it firmly in check with no other complicating emotions.

Justin realised the carriage had halted in front of his house. He stepped down first and then helped her out.

He kept his voice and expression as cool as hers as he escorted her up the steps of his townhouse and into the entry hall. But he did not feel nearly as cool inside when he said, 'We can go to my apartments.' His voice came out rougher than he'd intended as he held out his hand.

She nodded and that was when he saw the apprehension in her eyes. It was gone quickly, but there was no mistaking it or the tremor of her hand as his closed around it. He realised then that she was not nearly as calm as she appeared to be. In fact, just the opposite. She was frightened. Which, whether he liked it or not, would complicate everything.

Her mouth dry, Belle glanced at Justin as they climbed the winding staircase. His expression was brooding. He had said little since he had kissed her in the carriage and then apologised, which had completely confused her. His manner had been polite almost as if she was a stranger he found himself entertaining, certainly not that of a potential lover.

He pushed open a door and she found herself in a

darkened bedchamber. Only the light of the full moon provided any illumination. Her legs had quit trembling and she found she was detached, the way she had been when with Lucien. With a calm indifference she noted the bed was simple and old-fashioned with brocade hangings and there was a small table next to the bed and that the wardrobe was plain. A portrait hung over the mantelpiece. He put the candle down on the small stand and then turned to look at her. 'Do you want more light?'

'No. This will be adequate.' She moved towards him. 'What would you like me to do? Should I undress?'

'No.' His eyes swept over her face and then narrowed. 'Are you always this aloof when you are with your lovers?'

'I have never had any lovers.'

'No? Then what of the man you mentioned before? The man who taught you that physical intimacy and love are not the same?' His voice had a hardness to it.

She looked at him, surprised, and then remembered what she had said to him in her anger. 'I was referring to Lucien.'

'Lucien?'

'Yes. My husband. I have never been with anyone but him.'

'Were you in love with him?' he asked harshly.

She looked away. 'I do not wish to discuss Lucien.'

'No.' He moved away from her. 'I have changed my mind. You may undress now.'

She looked up and realised he had come to lean against the bed post. His arms were folded, but the shadows prevented her from seeing his face. But she knew one thing, he was going to watch her.

Having no clue how to proceed, she finally sat down on the bed and pulled off her gloves. She placed them n the table near the bed and then bent down to remove er slippers. Her hand trembled as she untied the laces nd then slipped them off. She pulled up her skirt as far s she could without baring her entire leg and started to nroll her silk stockings. She kept her eyes on the task, er face heating with unwelcome colour. She managed o get both stockings off and then rose.

Did he expect her to unlace her own dress? She had nly attempted to do so a few times in her entire life. She forced herself to look at him. 'I do not think I can ndo the laces of my dress myself.' Her voice did not ound at all like her own.

'I'll do it. Come here.'

She came to stand in front of him and felt his fingers t her back, cool as they brushed her bare skin. She losed her eyes as he undid the fastenings of her dress, rying to quell the disturbing sensations his touch wrought in her. And then her silk gown was falling from er shoulders and his hands were at her hips sliding the naterial so that it pooled at her feet.

She heard him catch his breath. 'Turn around, Belle.' His voice was husky with desire.

She did and resisted the urge to close her eyes as he ooked at her. She felt vulnerable and stripped of every-hing as his darkening gaze rested on the mounds of her reasts pushed high by the stays. His eyes travelled to he curve of her hips and she felt almost faint with ap-prehension.

'You are so damnably beautiful.' He sounded almost eluctant to admit it. 'Take the pins from your hair. I want to see it around your shoulders.'

She hesitated and then lifted her hands to her hair. Her fingers shook as she removed them and she felt her hair falling to brush her bare shoulders. She put the pins

on the table with her gloves and then turned. He still
watched her. 'What do you want me to do now?' she
asked. At least this time her voice was more contained
and normal. She would get through this. Nothing he did
could be any worse than being with Lucien.

He stared at her and blinked almost as if he had
awoken from a trance. 'Do next? My dear Belle, does
nothing shake your composure? You are standing in
front of me half-dressed and you still sound as if you
are inquiring whether I would like a cup of tea. Does it
not fluster you in the least that I want to take you to my
bed and ravish you until dawn?'

She started. 'Until dawn? I rather thought we would
be finished within an hour. Perhaps two at the most.'

His smile was dangerous. 'An hour or two? That is
not nearly enough time.'

'But whatever does one do for so long?'

He stepped towards her and she found herself backed
up against the bed. 'That, my sweet Belle, is what I
intend to show you.'

She forced herself to remain still, her eyes on his face.
He looked rather angry and his eyes had a wild glitter.
Her heart was beating so quickly she felt almost dizzy
and her legs trembled. Justin's hand cupped the back of
her head and he brought his mouth down on hers in a
hard, possessive kiss. She gasped and then stilled as his
mouth moved over hers, demanding her surrender. His
arms locked her to his hard chest and she fought to force
the panic down, forced her mind to go elsewhere as she
had done with Lucien. So when his arms fell away, she
felt completely disorientated. 'Damn it, Belle,' he said
harshly. 'This is not what I want.'

Her eyes opened and she stared at him. 'What is
wrong?'

He took a pace away from her and ran a hand through his hair. 'This. I feel as if I'm about to commit a rape. I cannot force you to my bed.'

'But you are not. I am willing.'

He gave a short laugh. 'Are you? Then why did I have the sense you were terrified when I held you? I thought you were about to swoon in my arms.'

She looked away, mortified and ashamed. 'I do not like to be held so tightly. I feel as if I cannot breathe.' Which was not exactly a lie.

'Is that all?' he demanded.

'Yes.' She forced herself to look at him. 'So, if you wish to proceed, I am more than willing.'

'Not with you so terrified. What the hell did Milborne do to you?'

'Nothing.' She rubbed her arms where his hands had grasped her. 'I did not like the marriage bed at all. He left me in no doubt that he found me quite inadequate, although he assured me that his mistresses made up for my lack. I fear, however, you will find me a poor mistress, which is why I think it best if we proceed to the point quickly and then I can go home.'

'No.'

She glanced up at him. The anger in his face stunned her. She backed up a pace and stared at him.

His face was dark. 'I've no intention of taking you while you lie there forcing yourself to submit. I am not that base. When you come to my bed it will pleasure you as much as it pleasures me.'

'It is really not necessary.' Oh, lord. She did not want to find out what he meant by pleasure. She wanted to stay as uninvolved as possible and then, after she paid her debts, return to her quiet life.

'Oh, but it is.' The menace in his voice coupled with

the look in his eye told her he had no intention of letting this go.

With growing trepidation she watched as he sat down on the edge of the bed and removed his shoes. Then he deliberately removed his stockings. He stood and started to shrug out of his evening coat.

'Wh…what are you doing?' Surely he wasn't planning to strip in front of her? Not even Lucien had done that.

'Merely levelling the field.' He removed his coat and then his waistcoat followed. He picked them up and draped them over a chair and then picked up her gown from the floor and dropped it carelessly on top of his clothing. She swallowed as he came towards her and took a step back. Her knees hit the bed and she sat down abruptly. With a smooth movement he joined her.

'Good. This is where we start.' His thigh pressed into hers as he squarely met her eyes. 'I'll wager that by the end of this lesson you will not be so eager to quit my bed.'

'What lesson?'

'The lesson we are about to start. The lesson where I teach you what a man wants in a mistress.' A peculiar little smile touched his mouth.

She swallowed again. 'I don't really want any such lessons. I do not plan to do this again.'

'That does not matter,' he said softly. His hand lightly brushed her cheek and then he tilted her chin up. 'I am going to kiss you. We'll start there.'

'No—' Her protest was silenced by his mouth. She braced herself, expecting the same harsh assault as before, but instead his lips moved over hers in gentle exploration. One hand cupped the back of her neck, tangling in her hair. With some surprise, she realised the sensation of his mouth on hers was not at all unpleasant. Her lips parted under the light pressure and then he pulled her more firmly against him.

His tongue slipped inside. Instead of the revulsion she had felt with Lucien, she found the sensation pleasurable. She tentatively touched his tongue with her own. Justin made a sound almost like a groan in his throat and his kiss deepened. Instead of pulling away, she pressed against him.

Then his mouth left her neck and was placing a fiery trail of kisses down it to the soft exposed skin of her breasts.

He lifted his head and she opened her eyes to find him watching her with a dazed expression. 'I think you are ready for the next lesson,' he whispered. 'But first this must come off.' His hand brushed her stays. 'Turn around.'

She obeyed, wondering what she was doing. Her lips felt swollen and her body curiously languid. The touch of his fingers as he undid the laces made her feel peculiar. Her stays fell away. One arm came around her and pulled her against him and through the thin linen of her shift she could feel the hard muscles of his chest against her back. He began to kiss her neck again, but when his free hand cupped her breast, she stiffened.

His hand fell away. 'What is it?' he asked. His breath was warm on her cheek. 'Do you not like that?'

'I do not mind. Please go on.' Her face was suffused with colour and she was glad he could not see her. She supposed it was something women liked or at least were expected to tolerate but she had always felt violated.

His hand left her breast. 'Not if you do not like it. But do you like this?' He caressed her stomach through her shift in gentle, languorous circles. A slow heat began to

grow in her and she pressed back against him. When his
hand circled closer to the juncture of her thighs, she
grabbed it. But then remembered she was supposed to
let him do these things to her so her hand fell away.

He did not seem to notice. 'We can lie down now.'
And then she was on her back and he was over her. She
closed her eyes and waited for him to lift her shift but
instead he stroked her face. And then he was kissing her
again in that slow exploratory way as if he had all the
time in the world.

Belle's arms came around his shoulders and she felt
the hard muscles of his back through his shirt. Her hand
moved up and entangled in his thick hair. Her head
seemed to spin and she was kissing him back. She was
vaguely aware that his hand was again caressing her
stomach and hips, creating exquisite sensation. His hand
moved lower and she forced herself to relax. But she
could not quite help her little start of surprise when he
began to caress her most private parts. 'Shh…' he said
against her mouth. His fingers were stroking her and
despite the barrier of her shift, she could feel a warm
growing heaviness between her thighs. His tongue was
teasing hers and his hand kept its steady slow rhythmic
caress. She fought the urge to part her legs but the spiral
of sensation seemed to be growing smaller and smaller
and focused on where his hand was. She pressed against
him and then cried out as the heaviness shattered into
an exquisite pleasure.

He withdrew his hand and lifted his head. She kept
her eyes closed, not wanting to see the triumph he must
feel over her surrender. Worse, he had not even had to
remove all of her clothes. Or his.

'Belle.' She felt his weight shift away from her.

She opened her eyes. Justin sat on the edge of the

bed. 'I believe that is enough of a lesson for tonight. I will help you dress and then take you home.' His voice was polite.

'Very well.' She sat up, trying to tell herself she should be grateful for his manner, that he was not rubbing in his victory, but instead she felt confused.

He helped her dress, his movements so efficient she thought he must do this often, hardly a pleasing notion.

'Damn,' he muttered.

'Is something wrong?'

'I've managed to miss a fastening. I'll have to start again.'

'No!' She turned around, not wanting to have him touch her any more than necessary. 'It does not matter.'

He scowled. 'But there's a gap in the back.'

'Since I am only going home and not out in public it hardly matters. I will be taking it off again anyway.' Although her maid would probably wonder what she had done. But it was too late for any of those considerations now.

'Always so practical.'

She had no idea whether it was a compliment or not. She followed him down the stairs and then he fetched her shawl. He had fallen into another brooding silence and she had no idea what he was thinking. He said nothing until he had helped her from the carriage. 'I will leave for Surrey tomorrow.'

'To get your horse?'

'Yes. I will return the day after. I will call on you then.'

'As it pleases you. Good night, your Grace.' She had started to leave when he caught her hand and pulled her around to face him.

'It does please me. As you did tonight. We'll finish

the rest of the lessons when I return.' He cupped her chin and brushed her mouth quickly with his. 'Goodnight, Belle.'

'Goodnight,' she whispered and turned and ran up the steps without looking back.

Chapter Six

Belle had thought that with him gone some sort of normality might return despite the loss of Maria and Chloe.

But that her life had been irrevocably altered became quite apparent the very next day when she went to find a new pair of gloves. She had made her purchase and was about to step out of the shop door when Lady Blanchard and Mrs Cunningham entered. There were no smiles on their faces when they saw her and Mrs Cunningham, who was usually quite pleasant, had a distinctly frosty look in her eye. Their acknowledgement was so brief that they might as well have cut her.

She thought it must be her imagination, however, when she was at William's Lane Library and Mrs Barry greeted her politely enough. But was there a speculation in the other woman's eye that she had not noticed before? Particularly when she asked if Belle had enjoyed last night's performance. In fact, as the conversation progressed, Mrs Barry's comments seemed to border on the impertinent. Belle finally made her escape by claiming she had another appointment.

Once in her carriage, she tried to tell herself that Mrs Barry was a notorious gossip and that she always asked questions that were a trifle presumptuous. But she could not shake off the sense that something was very wrong.

With a start, she realised her carriage had stopped in front of her house. She took her parcels and stepped down. Mrs Bates opened the door. 'Lord Ralston is waiting for you. In the drawing room.' Her mouth was puckered with disapproval.

Belle handed Mrs Bates her parcels and went directly to the drawing room. She might as well see Arthur straight away instead of putting off the unpleasant task. He sat in one of the wing chairs near the window. He looked up when she entered and stood. 'Good day, Belle.'

'Hello, Arthur. Mrs Bates said you were here.' She came into the room and removed her bonnet.

'Yes.' He clasped his hands behind his back and frowned at her. 'I have come to speak to you about last night. You cannot imagine how shocked I was to see you in Westmore's box.'

'Were you?'

'Most certainly. I would like to know why you would do such a rash and ill-advised thing. I have no doubt he has designs on your virtue.' He paced away from her and then looked back. 'I will own I was mistaken. I thought he wished to contract a proper alliance with Chloe. Instead I see he wishes an improper alliance with you.' His face showed distaste. 'You are foolish beyond belief if you think he intends to offer you marriage.'

'I do not think he intends to offer me marriage,' Belle said. She suddenly felt weary. 'Is there anything else you wanted to say to me?'

'I can think of no explanation for your behaviour other than you have developed a most unwise *tendre* for him. Why else would you risk the censure of society by ap-

earing alone with him for all to see? Do you wish to
uin Chloe's chances?'

'No, I do not and that is why I have agreed not to see
Chloe. Did Maria not tell you that?'

'Yes. Along with some ridiculous nonsense about
your sacrificing yourself for Chloe.'

'You are right, that is most ridiculous.' She sighed. 'I
am very tired, Arthur, and if all you want to do is scold
me then I pray you will leave.'

He stared at her. A tinge of colour appeared on his
cheekbones. 'I suppose you will be with him tonight,'
he said tightly.

'Why would you think that? I rather thought I would
remain at home.'

'You will not attend Lady Perth's rout?'

She had forgotten about Lady Perth's rout. Her first
instinct was to say no, but the dowager Countess had
been a close friend of her mother's and, the last time
Belle had met her, had expressed the greatest desire that
Belle would attend. 'I have not made up my mind.'

'Because Westmore will not escort you?'

'Westmore has nothing to do with this,' she said quietly, although she was seething with anger. 'Nor can I
see what any of this has to do with you.' She started to
walk towards the door. 'I am going to my bedchamber.
Mrs Bates can show you out. Please give my love to
Chloe and Maria.'

His mouth fell open but she was too furious with him
to care. How dare he involve himself in her business?
She was not related to him nor did he have any control
over her affairs. None the less, he had always attempted
to dictate to her just as he did to Chloe and Maria.

The whole conversation had been odd. As odd as her

encounters earlier today. Is that what the *ton* already
thought? She was Justin's mistress?

Which she was in every sense of the word except for
the actual consummation. Every time she thought of last
night, she shuddered. She had not wanted to feel anything with him; she had only wanted to lie with him
while he did what he wanted. But he had not let her
remain aloof. He had brought her to an ecstasy she had
had no idea she was capable of and for the first time in
her life she had experienced a desire so overwhelming
she had no choice but to surrender to him. Her coupling
with Lucien had been humiliating and sometimes painful, but always mercifully brief. His only purpose in
coming to her had been to procure an heir and he had
never cared if she took pleasure in the proceedings. Her
duty had been to submit. She had learned to disengage
herself, to bury any emotion she might feel, and to force
her mind elsewhere.

She had no idea why Justin would not allow her to
remain detached. Did he, or any man, really care if the
woman was pleasured as well? Or was it another way to
gain power over her, make her desire him so that when
they parted she would feel his rejection as strongly as
he had felt hers?

Whatever his reason, she would do everything in her
power to resist him.

She knew almost as soon as she set foot in Lady
Perth's crowded drawing room she had made a grave
error in attending. She had not wanted to come, but Bell
had not wanted to disappoint Lady Perth. Lady Perth, as
always, was welcoming, her kindly face wreathed in
smiles when she saw Belle, but others were not so kind.
More than one lady moved away at her approach and

he wished more than anything she could turn tail and
un, but she would not give them the satisfaction of leav-
ng right away. She forced herself to move further into
he room.

'Lady Milborne.' She turned to find Mr Aubrey be-
ind her. 'Quite a crush. Hot as well.'

She managed a smile. 'Indeed it is.'

He looked a little uncomfortable, but before he could
ay more they were joined by Lord Henly and Sir Reg-
nald Malven, a middle-aged fop with a dissipated air.
ord Henly leered at her. 'My dear Lady Milborne I am
urprised Westmore did not take you with him. I would
ot have thought him to be so careless.'

'Indeed.' She did not seem able to move but she must,
or she could not stand in the middle of a drawing room
vith two of London's most jaded rakes.

Someone touched her arm. 'Belle.'

For once in her life, she was relieved to see Arthur.
ven his disapproving frown was welcome. He glanced
t her companions, his distaste evident. 'I would like to
peak to Lady Milborne. If you will excuse us.'

Lord Henly smirked. 'Taking advantage of West-
nore's absence, are you?'

'Your comments are most unwelcome,' Arthur said
tiffly. 'Come, Belle.'

Belle's face flamed for Henly's voice was loud. Her
tomach took a sickening churn when she saw that Lady
Jeorgina stood near them. From the malicious gleam in
he older lady's eye, Belle suspected she had heard.

She followed Arthur out of the room to the hall where
e stopped and looked down at her. She spoke before
e could. 'Thank you for rescuing me.'

He actually looked nonplussed. 'I trust that in the fu-
ure you will avoid such company. I will refrain from

pointing out that to be seen with such persons will onl
do further harm to your reputation.' He cleared hi
throat. 'I fear, however, there are some most unfortunat
rumours circulating. For your own sake, I would sugges
that you should return home. I will be most glad to offe
my escort. I have informed Maria that I intended to d
so.'

'You are most kind.' She really must be in a ba
dream if she was actually thinking of Arthur as kinc
But in his own odd, stiff way she realised he actuall
meant to protect her.

He went off to call for his carriage while she waite
near the table in the downstairs hallway. She heard fe
male voices and realised other guests were coming dow
the stairs. The last thing she wanted to do was to fac
more cold looks, so she moved into the small room of
the hall.

'I could not believe that she would actually show he
face tonight! And to think that she has always put o
such a display of virtue!'

The second voice was softer but no less censorious
'Perhaps she thought that would erase her past.'

'Then she should not have flaunted her relationshi
with the Duke of Westmore so publicly. I pity her re
lations. To be connected with a woman who actuall
attended such…such orgies!' The last word was uttere
in a shocked whisper, but it still carried to Belle's burn
ing ears.

She wanted to die on the spot. Whoever had said suc
things about her? Humiliation seared through her an
she wondered that Lady Perth had even received he
Except her elderly friend was nearly deaf and perhap
had not yet heard the rumours. How could she possibl
face her or anyone, for that matter, again?

She did not want to think that Justin had spread such rumours. But if he had wanted to punish her, he had succeeded. She was, for all purposes, ruined.

Two mornings after he left, Justin returned to London. He stepped into the cool hallway of his townhouse and handed his butler his hat and gloves. 'Lady Georgina has called and is in the drawing room. She would like you to wait on her at your convenience,' Hastings said.

'How long has she been here?'

'Nearly two hours. She said she would remain all day if necessary.'

He bit back a groan. His aunt would not spend the day lying in wait for him unless she wanted something from him.

'I trust your journey was successful,' Hastings said.

'Yes. The colt is in London.' Justin saw the gleam in the butler's eye and grinned. 'As soon as he has settled down I will bring him around for your approval.' Hastings, he knew, would have preferred to be in the stables, but his father and grandfather had both been butlers, and he had not wanted to break the family tradition.

'Very good, your Grace.'

Justin's smile faded as he mounted the stairs. The colt was in excellent health, but he was high-strung and skittish. After the horse had thrown him, Chiswick had neglected the animal and the colt was more than a little wild. Justin had planned to send the colt to his estate in Devon with his head groom. But after travelling with the animal from Surrey to London he had made up his mind he must see that it reached Falconcliff himself.

Ordinarily leaving London was a matter of indifference to him but not this time. Belle was here. He did not intend to leave without her.

He entered the drawing room. 'Good day, Aunt Georgina.'

Lady Georgina glanced up. She held a teacup and saucer on her lap and the *Morning Post* lay open on the sofa beside her. She regarded him with stony grey eyes. 'I had no idea until last night that you had left London. It was very remiss of you not to inform me. I trust you have not forgotten we are expected to dine with the Blackwoods tonight.'

He frowned. 'Are we?' He'd completely forgotten. The last thing he wanted was to spend an evening in the company he was expecting would be present. Nor did he want to find Lady Clarissa under his nose at every opportunity. She currently led the pack as Lady Georgina's favourite candidate for the next Duchess.

'Yes.' Her sharp eyes were on him. 'I trust you intend to give some serious consideration to choosing a wife. I take it you have abandoned the ill-judged notion of considering Lady Chloe as a candidate.'

He folded his arms and leaned against the side table. 'Why do you think that?'

'It is quite obvious.'

He merely waited. She paused for a moment and then spoke. 'It would be extremely unseemly of you to offer for Lady Chloe after taking her sister-in-law for a mistress.'

'What do you know of that?'

'I pray you will not play ignorant. You were with her at the theatre and I doubt if there was not a soul there who did not notice that you failed to return to your box. That in itself is enough to cause a few raised brows, but coupled with the report that you were seen escorting Lady Milborne home not only once but twice late at night…it is all too obvious.'

'Is it?'

'Yes. She is lovely in a rather cool way and has a reputation for being untouchable so I can see the challenge. And she was Milborne's wife, so perhaps you cannot be blamed for wanting her although it would perhaps give you more satisfaction if he were still alive. But you can take some pleasure from the knowledge that she scarcely has a good reputation.'

He'd been listening in growing anger. 'What the devil do you mean by that?'

'Even her in-laws will not acknowledge her.' She placed her teacup and saucer on the table near her. 'I have no idea why Serena Perth admitted her...although she is rather senile, so perhaps she can be excused. One could almost feel sorry for Lady Milborne except she undoubtedly deserves it. No one spoke to her except for Aubrey, who I dare say did feel sorry for her, and Lord Henly and Sir Reginald Malven. Oh, yes and that ninny, Lord Ralston! Lord Henly was quite put out when Ralston marched her away from him. She left with Ralston, I believe.' A peculiar little smile touched her mouth. 'You no longer need to bother yourself with her. Your plot to avenge yourself was quite successful.' She rose. 'I trust I will see you at dinner tonight.'

'What plot are you referring to?'

She arched a brow. 'You know very well. I cannot think of any other reason why you would go out of your way to be seen in her company. I am surprised you can bear to look at her, much less touch her. You would be wise to extricate yourself from her before you are tainted with the same tales.'

He would not give her the satisfaction of asking what tales she was talking about. He would find out soon enough. He said coldly, 'You are wrong if you think I intended to ruin Lady Milborne's reputation. Whatever business might be between us is private.'

'You are quite wrong.' Her eyes glinted with anger. 'You are a duke and the head of one of England's oldest families. Your business is very public, which is why you cannot afford the least hint of scandal attached to your name. Your duty is to make an alliance with a woman whose breeding is equal to yours and whose chastity is unquestionable. You have a duty to produce an heir as soon as possible. You have accomplished what you wanted with Isabelle Milborne so there is no need to distract yourself any more with her.'

'No?' He met her gaze squarely. 'Perhaps I am not finished distracting myself with Lady Milborne. Nor do I intend to marry merely because you have decided it is time I do so. I will wed when I please and whom I please.' He moved away from her towards the door. 'I have not changed from my journey so I must leave you.' At the door he paused and looked back. She stared at him, her mouth tight, two spots of red on her cheeks. 'I will also send Lord Blackwood my regrets that I will be unable to dine with him after all.' He did not wait to see her reaction. He feared if he stayed a moment longer he would lose his tenuous hold on his temper altogether.

Justin stalked to his bedchamber. Hell. He had wanted to punish Belle but he realised that, despite his fury at her, he had not wanted to destroy her. He had no idea what had happened in the short time he had been away from London. Certainly the fact that she had attended the theatre with him had signalled to society they were more than mere acquaintances, but even if she was thought to be his mistress, she should not be so completely ruined.

Not to the point where her relations would not acknowledge her. Except for Ralston, whom she had left with, according to his aunt. The thought of Ralston with Belle made his blood boil and he thought if the man had touched her he would take great pleasure in putting a bullet through him.

He ran a hand through his hair and paced to the window. He scowled, angry with himself. Whatever had happened to his vow to remain indifferent? The possessive jealousy he felt had no place in his scheme to punish her. He had intended to heartlessly seduce Belle, and certainly in his most fantastic desires for revenge he had envisioned having her completely in his power. He had wanted to flaunt her relationship with him in public, both to prove she did not hold him responsible for Lucien's death and to force her to publicly acknowledge him.

His aunt was correct in one regard—her ruin would serve as the perfect revenge.

Unfortunately, he had also discovered he did not hate her as much as he thought he did.

And that he had a conscience after all.

Belle was not home when he called later that day. He called again, just before he left for a soirée, but she was still not in, according to her housekeeper. He could not tell from the woman's closed expression whether Belle was truly not at home or whether she was not receiving. Nor would the housekeeper give him any information regarding her whereabouts. He vowed if he did not see her at the soirée, he would track her down at home even if it meant he cooled his heels on her doorstep.

She was not at the soirée. Lady Ralston and Lady Chloe were present, but he suspected that approaching them would only cause further harm. Ralston was there as well, which afforded him the grim satisfaction that at least he was not with Belle.

He decided he would go to the card room and find Brandt. He had just reached the door when someone called his name. He turned and to his astonishment saw Lady Chloe behind him. He opened his mouth to say something but the white fury on her face stopped him and he found himself backed against the wall.

'I do not know what vile rumours you have spread about my...my sister-in-law, but I just want you to know that if you do anything further to hurt her I will...will...'

Good God! 'Run me through?' He almost expected her to pull out a dagger this very moment.

'Yes! And more than once! You will be very sorry.'

'This is not the time to discuss this. Unless you want even more rumours.' Her lip trembled and he knew she either planned to hit him or burst into tears.

He pulled out a handkerchief. 'Here.' To his surprise she took it. Justin scowled. 'Go sit down by the window before any of your family sees you with me. Unless you want a scene.' Sending Lady Ralston into hysterics was not something he wanted to do. 'I will join you.'

She nodded and walked towards the window seat. He waited to make certain no one was watching and then followed her. He looked down at her. 'I assure you I have not spread any rumours about your sister-in-law.'

'Someone has. And since you wish to ruin her I would think it was you.'

'I do not wish to—' He stopped. She was the last person he wanted to discuss this with. 'Where is Belle?'

'I do not know. I am forbidden to see her or even speak to her and it is entirely your doing. And she has never done a thing to you!'

'Has she told you that?' he said coldly.

'No, but she always takes your side and says you are not to blame for anything!' She glared at him. 'Even when Mama says it is entirely your fault that my brother is dead.'

He was taken aback. Belle stood up for him? He had hardly expected that.

Lady Chloe rose. She sniffed and then handed him his handkerchief. 'I am sorry I could not have it cleaned for you but I would not want anyone to know I had borrowed it. I hope you do not mind.'

'Not at all.'

Apparently her spirit was not completely crushed, however. She lifted her chin. 'I vow I will find a way to make you very sorry if you do a thing to hurt her.'

'I would watch my back if I were you, cousin,' Brandt said from behind them.

Justin bit back a curse. He turned and resisted the urge to wipe the half-amused smile from Brandt's face. 'Eavesdropping?'

'I merely wished to speak to you but since you were occupied, I decided to wait my turn.'

Lady Chloe gave him a look of cold dislike. 'It is very rude to listen to the private conversations of others. And I quite mean what I say. I will make anyone who hurts Belle very sorry, even if I must spend the rest of my life doing so! That includes you, Lord Salcombe.'

She turned and walked away, her head held high.

'I suggest you watch your back as well,' Justin said.

Brandt watched her, a bemused expression on his face. 'I would have thought her a complete mouse. I can see I was quite wrong.'

'Before you arrived on the scene she accused me of spreading vile rumours about Belle. There was some suggestion of running me through as well.'

'Good God! One would never guess she was tha
blood-thirsty from her demure appearance. It is a good
thing, then, that she doesn't know what you have
planned for Lady Milborne or I would very much fea
for your demise.'

'What rumours is she talking about?'

'You have not heard?' Brandt asked carefully.

'No. I've only been in town a few hours.' He did no
like the look on his cousin's face. 'What are they?' he
asked softly.

'Only that Belle Milborne was a very willing partic
ipant in the orgies her husband was fond of attending.'

Justin stared at him. He gave a short, harsh laugh
'You do not think I started them, do you?'

'She is completely ruined. It would be a very complete
revenge.'

'I've no desire to destroy her reputation. Nor would
ever stoop to telling such vicious lies.'

'I did not think so, but I wonder who did. I canno
think of anyone else who would profit by doing so.'
Brandt eyed him. 'But aside from the threat of death by
Lady Chloe's hand, are you really concerned what be
comes of Lady Milborne?'

Justin met his cousin's eyes. 'I do not want her ruin
laid at my door.'

'Then I suggest you be careful. For I fear you are stil
very much in her thrall.'

He left shortly after that and went to Belle's house
Several lights still burned and so he trusted she had no
yet retired.

He signalled the coachman to stop and jumped down
He mounted the steps to her house and rapped on the
door. Belle's housekeeper opened it and regarded him

with a frown. 'Lady Milborne is not receiving visitors, your Grace.'

'If she is still up, I would like to speak with her,' he said impatiently. 'It will not take long.'

She looked at him for a moment and he decided to take advantage of her hesitation, stepping past her into the dim, narrow hallway. 'You may tell Lady Milborne that I am here.'

She opened her mouth to speak, but was stopped by the sound of footsteps. He looked up to see Belle above him. She held a candle and looked at him for a moment before coming down the stairs. She paused halfway down. 'Were we to meet tonight?'

'No.' He started up towards her. 'I wanted to talk to you. It will not take long.'

She bit her lip. 'It is past midnight.'

'I know. I will not stay long.'

'Very well.' She turned and he followed her up the stairs and into a small drawing room. She set the candle down on a table.

'Do you wish to sit?' she asked politely.

'No.' He stopped in front of her. 'Are you all right?'

'Why wouldn't I be?' She looked up at him and he saw the shadows under her eyes and knew she wasn't at all.

'Brandt told me of the rumours,' he said bluntly.

'Yes. I imagine everyone knows of them.' She looked away.

'I did not start them.'

She glanced back at him and said nothing.

He took a step towards her and swore. 'I had no idea I appeared so completely despicable. First your sister-in-law and then Brandt and now you. But I vow I would not hurt you in this way.'

'My sister-in-law? Chloe? What does she have to do with this?'

'She accosted me tonight and accused me of spreading rumours about you. She also plans to make me very sorry if I hurt you.'

'Oh, dear.' Her face clouded with worry. 'I do not want her involved in this. I cannot bear for her to be hurt. I have no choice but to leave London.' She spoke almost to herself.

'Come to Devon with me.'

'To Devon?'

'I have my colt. I need to take him there but I do not want to send him with only my grooms. I swear I won't touch you if you don't want me to. At least you'll be away from here and protected.'

She stared at him. 'But our contract?'

He gave a short laugh. 'Consider it paid in full.'

'But—'

'Where else are you to go? You cannot stay with your in-laws.' He paced away from her. 'You have your house here, but I agree—staying in London is impossible. I would offer to buy you a house anywhere you wished but I've no doubt you would throw it back in my face.' He watched her. 'I have one other thing to offer you, however.' He hardly knew what he was saying. 'My name.'

She turned so white he thought she might faint. 'Your what?'

'My name. I am asking you to become my wife.'

She took a step backwards. 'No. Never!' The horror on her face suggested he had asked her to be guillotined.

Something wrenched in his stomach. 'What choice do you have? You are ruined,' he said harshly.

She caught the back of the sofa for support. 'No.

would rather be your mistress a thousand times over than be married. I would rather die than be a wife again.'

The pain of her rejection and betrayal he thought he'd buried spilled out and enveloped him. 'Very well. I will withdraw my offer and accept yours. You will be my mistress. We will leave for Devon the day after tomorrow.' He started towards the door and then paused. 'And two nights from now you will lie with me.'

He left the room without looking at her.

Belle heard his footsteps recede and then sank down on the sofa. Had she imagined the pain she had glimpsed in his face when she refused his offer? As if she had hurt him. Surely she did not have that sort of power over him. He did not even like her so how could anything she said possibly affect him?

Then why had he cancelled their contract and then asked her to marry him in order to save her reputation? She had thought that ruining her was what he wanted.

None of it made the least sense.

She had spoken unthinkingly, for she could never marry again. Even if she was not barren, she never again wanted to turn her life, her very destiny, over to a man. But she had never dreamed that her words might wound Justin.

Belle doubted he would ever forgive her. How could she possibly go with him?

She slowly rose and knew she could no longer deny the truth to herself.

She would go with him because she still cared for him.

Chapter Seven

Two mornings later, Belle sat at her desk and finished the last of her correspondence. She had been up since dawn in an effort to finish all that must be done before she left London. She sighed and resisted the urge to drop her head into her hands. She had a slight headache and her stomach was unsettled. She only hoped it was from nerves and lack of sleep.

She shoved the last letter aside and looked up in time to see Arthur entering the study. She rose, having no idea why he should call on her. He surely must have heard the rumours by now and she could not imagine a man with his fastidious morals even deigning to look at her. 'Good day, Arthur,' she said politely.

He stepped into the room and to her surprise, he closed the door behind him. He looked at her and tugged at his stock in a nervous gesture. 'Good day, Belle. I trust you are well.'

'I am.' Puzzled, she stared at him. 'Did you have a purpose for calling?'

'Yes.' He cleared his throat. 'First allow me to express my regret for the unfortunate rumours that are circulating. Unlike many of those in Society, I believe in your innocence.'

'Thank you.' She had no idea why he wanted to tell her that.

'However, it does not mitigate the fact that you are now beyond the pale of society. I fear your rash and ill-judged liaison with the Duke of Westmore has only contributed to both the rumours and the unfortunate position you now find yourself in.' He folded his hands behind his back. 'I have heard that Westmore is leaving London today, which is no more than I would have expected from a man who is reputed to be a rake. Unfortunately, when he is gone you will have no protection. Which brings me to the reason for my visit.'

'And that is?'

'I wish to offer you my protection.'

'Your protection?' She stared at him, not certain she had understood him. 'What do you mean?'

He tugged again at his stock. 'I am asking you to become my mistress.' His face was now suffused with high colour.

'Your mistress?' She undoubtedly sounded like a parrot, but she was shocked beyond belief.

'Yes.' To her horror he suddenly advanced upon her. She backed up and found her desk inconveniently behind her. 'It cannot have escaped your notice these past years that I hold you in the highest regard. The fortitude with which you endured what must have been a situation of the most repugnant to you in your marriage to my cousin. The bravery in which you have faced widow-hood. And although you have erred very gravely I cannot hold you to blame for I have no doubt Westmore seduced you. Which is why I cannot abandon you now.'

'So you wish me to become your mistress because you hold me in regard?'

'Yes. I will see to it that you are comfortably situated, perhaps in a town such as Cheltenham, which is conveniently near Braddon Hall. I would, of course, demand the utmost discretion, but there is no reason why I cannot visit you often. Of course, I would see to it that your allowance is increased and that you are provided with the little luxuries a woman wants.'

Surely she was in a bad dream? But no, Arthur was in front of her, the scent of his cologne nearly choking her. The blemishes on his skin were even more pronounced. 'I fear I must decline your offer,' she said.

He gaped at her. 'Decline?' Then he gave a startled laugh. 'My dear Belle, you have no choice.'

Everyone seemed to be telling her she had no choice. 'Yes, I do. I am turning down your offer. I have no desire to be your mistress.'

'Westmore is leaving town. You will have no protector, no one to defend your honour. You will be prey of every rake in London. At least under my protection you will be safe from their advances.'

He planned to defend her honour by making her his mistress? She bit back the inappropriate desire to burst into hysterical laughter. 'You are most kind, but I cannot accept. I—'

'She cannot accept because she is still under my protection.'

They both slowly turned. Justin stood behind them. His face held almost no expression, which was more frightening than if she had seen fury.

'Move away from her,' he told Arthur.

Arthur stared at him and then took a few steps. 'I will

own I am surprised to see you here, Westmore. I thought
you had left town.'

'As you can see you are wrong.'

'But you will be leaving.'

'You are correct.' Justin folded his arms. 'And Lady
Milborne is leaving with me.'

Arthur stared at him and then swung around to look
at Belle for a long moment. He finally spoke. 'I see. You
did not tell me that. However, I will be at your service
if you should need me.'

He started towards the door only to find Justin in his
way. 'She will never need your assistance. I will warn
you that if I discover you have had a damn thing to do
with the rumours I will ruin you. And if you come near
Lady Milborne again, I will put a bullet through you.'
Justin spoke with a deadly calm.

Arthur's eyes bulged, but he stood his ground. 'And
if you fail to protect her I will do the same.' He picked
up his hat and cane and left without looking back.

Justin crossed the room to stand in front of her. 'Did
he hurt you?'

'No. He…he made me an improper offer. I am becoming quite used to them so it was nothing to signify.'
She gave a strangled laugh. 'Can you imagine what Maria would say if she knew? I wonder if Arthur thought
it through. How would he explain it if I actually did
accept?'

She found Justin in front of her, a black look on his
face. 'Don't even consider it.'

Surprised, she met his gaze. 'I assure you I have no
intention of doing so. And I pray you will give up your
ridiculous notion of shooting him.'

'I don't want him near you.'

The day was growing more and more peculiar. 'He

did not mean me any harm. In his own way I suppose he wished to protect me.'

'You are amazingly naïve if that is what you think. He wants you, my dear, in his bed, and in his power, and that is the whole of it. I suspect he has wanted you for some time and finally saw his opportunity. For all I know he started the rumours in order to force you into his arms.'

Stung, she said, 'I hardly think Arthur is capable of that!'

'You are defending him? Is it possible you actually have a *tendre* for that pompous idiot?' he demanded.

'Of course I do not! I am beginning to think you are as mad as he is! I do not have a *tendre* for anyone and if I was so foolish as to have one it would not be for Arthur!'

His gaze locked with hers, his expression still dark. 'I would hope you had better sense,' he said shortly. 'You said you were becoming used to such offers. Has anyone else approached you?'

She was still miffed at him. 'No, only you.'

'It is hardly the same thing. I did not…' His scowl deepened. 'I trust you will be ready to leave today?'

'Yes. I have packed what I need. Mrs Bates will stay a few days to close up the house. I am sending her to stay with her daughter-in-law, who is approaching her confinement.'

'If you need anything else you can tell me and I will see to it.'

'Thank you.'

'Will you bring a maid with you?'

'No, but I have managed before without a maid.' She had considered taking Hetty, Mrs Bates's niece, but the girl had suffered such bouts of homesickness since com-

ng to London, even with her aunt present, that Belle
had not the heart to insist she accompany her to Devon.

'Once we reach Falconcliff my housekeeper will procure a suitable girl for you.' He hesitated. 'I will send
my carriage for you shortly after noon. You will travel
with my secretary, Jackson. I plan to be with the colt
and will most likely not see you until we stop for the
night.'

'Very well.' She clasped her hands, a knot starting to
form again in her stomach.

'Then I will see you later.'

She watched him go and wondered if she was doing
the right thing. But she really had no choice at all now.

Shortly after noon, Belle stood by the window and
watched as a carriage came to a halt in the street below
her house. She was about to turn away from the window
when the occupant of the carriage stepped down. Instead
of the man she had been expecting, she was stunned to
see Lady Georgina alight. She stifled a groan. It was too
much to hope for that Lady Georgina did not intend to
call here. The rap on the door told her otherwise.

She went out to the small hallway and heard Mrs
Bates's soft voice and then Lady Georgina's more forceful one. 'I insist on seeing her. I do not care if she is
about to depart. If you do not show me in, I will show
myself.'

Oh, dear. She could not allow her to bully poor Mrs
Bates. She went to the head of the staircase just in time
to see Lady Georgina brush past her startled housekeeper. Then Lady Georgina spotted Belle. 'There you
are. I will see you now, if you please.' She continued
up the stairs. The militant look in her eye was not promising.

She followed Belle into the drawing room. Withou preamble she said, 'Is it true you are travelling to Devor with my nephew?'

'Why do you wish to know?'

'Because, my dear Lady Milborne, I do not intend to allow you to go with him.'

'I see.' She had no idea whether she was angry, o curious or merely numb.

'He has certain duties that are associated with a duke-dom. One of those is marriage and ensuring that the line continues. If he has no heir, the title will pass to a lesser branch of the family.'

'How very interesting.'

Lady Georgina eyed her sharply. 'You are imperti-nent.'

'Only because I fail to see what this has to do with me.'

'It has to do with you because as long as he is ob-sessed with you he will not look for a wife. I do not intend to allow this to go on. Anything can happen, ac-cidents, an illness. He has a duty to secure the succession as quickly as possible.'

'Then perhaps you should discuss this with him.' Her temper was starting to fray.

She did not appear to hear Belle. 'Which is why I am prepared to offer you a substantial sum to disappear for an extensive amount of time. You will no longer present a distraction and he will see he must marry. When it is accomplished and his wife increasing, then you may re-turn if you wish.'

'And where am I to go?'

'Perhaps Italy. It is very pleasant, warm and sunny My husband's mother was Italian and I still have a villa there. I've no doubt you would be very comfortable.'

'Thank you, but I do not wish to go to Italy. If you will excuse me, I still have some business to attend to before I leave.'

Lady Georgina caught her arm. 'Do you know why he even wants you? For revenge! For the harm you and that knave of a husband did him!'

'I know that.' Belle attempted to pull her arm from the old lady's grasp but Lady Georgina's hand only tightened.

'Then why do you go with him? Do you think he will marry you? You are a fool! You would bring nothing but disgrace upon him and upon this family! You would never make him happy and he would hate you once he discovered you were barren!'

Belle felt as if she had been slapped. She stared at Lady Georgina, feeling ill. 'You do not know that.'

Lady Georgina released her arm. 'You were married for three years and there was no child. I have heard that your husband has sired more than one bastard.'

'I knew nothing of them.' She vaguely heard a rap and realised that Justin's carriage must have arrived. 'I must leave.'

'You will regret this. I will not allow you to ruin him.'

Belle did not reply or look at Lady Georgina as she walked past her. A sandy-haired young man stood in the hall. He looked at her, his gaze impersonal. 'Lady Milborne?'

'Yes.'

'I am Matthew Jackson, the Duke of Westmore's secretary. I am to accompany you today.'

She nodded. Mrs Bates had tears in her eyes when she said goodbye and a lump rose in Belle's throat as she impulsively squeezed her housekeeper's hand.

She followed Mr Jackson outside to the street where

her trunk and valise had already been strapped on to the chaise. Lady Georgina followed her. She looked at Belle for a moment and then stepped into her waiting carriage.

'Lady Milborne.'

Mr Jackson waited for her. She turned and slowly climbed into Justin's chaise and Mr Jackson joined her. The door was shut and the horses set into motion. A wave of loneliness washed over her and she fought it down. She could not allow herself to give into such feelings or she would be truly lost.

Chapter Eight

They reached the inn before nightfall. Belle had fallen into a fitful sleep and she awoke when the motion of the carriage stopped. She opened her eyes, disorientated for a moment, and then realised they had halted.

'We have reached the White Dove. We will stop here for the night,' Jackson said from the other corner.

She nodded. Her travelling companion had proved to be a remarkably efficient young man who had the amazing ability to read in a moving chaise. He had spent most of the journey with a stack of papers on his lap. He was polite but no more and she had no doubt he disapproved of her. Undoubtedly, he wondered why his employer wished to involve himself with a woman of her reputation. Or perhaps he merely disapproved of such relationships on principle. At any rate, his disinclination towards conversation suited her as she was still not feeling particularly well. She peered out and saw they were in the yard of an inn. Another coach was there and a cat sat on a bench outside the door.

Her stomach was starting to hurt again. The coachman opened the door, and Jackson stepped down first and then assisted her down. The cool afternoon air was wel-

come on her overheated cheeks. She blinked, not certain
what to do next.

'Belle.'

She turned and saw Justin approaching them. He
looked completely familiar and until she saw him she
did not realise how much she needed to see him. He
nodded to Jackson. 'I've bespoken two rooms and a private parlour. I would like a word with Lady Milborne
and then I will escort her to the parlour.'

'Very well,' Jackson said.

Justin waited for a moment and then took her elbow.
'Was your journey comfortable?' he asked politely.

'Yes, although I will own I slept most of the way.'

'Wise of you. I've requested an early dinner. I will
see you to the inn and then I must look after the colt.'
He was guiding her towards the building, his touch impersonal.

She suddenly did not want to be left with only the
taciturn, disapproving Jackson. For a moment longer, she
wanted to be with someone who would at least talk to
her. 'May I see your horse?'

He glanced down at her, slight surprise in his eyes.
'If you wish.'

'I would like to.'

'He is in the stable.' With his hand still on her elbow
he guided her towards the stables at the back of the inn.
He released her arm and she followed him inside, lifting
up her skirt a little as she walked. The colt was in the
very last stall. Justin spoke softly to the horse. In the
dim light of the stable, she could see the animal was in
the far corner but at the sound of Justin's voice the horse
moved forward.

'He is beautiful,' she said softly. He was a bay with
a dish-shaped face and dark, intelligent eyes. He tossed

his head but calmed under Justin's hand. 'Have you named him?'

'Not yet.' He stroked the animal's neck. 'You could probably pet him if you wanted to.'

'If he will let me.' The colt stayed still while she touched his soft, sleek neck and then he snorted and moved away. She smiled. 'I think that is as much as he wishes to know me.'

'At least for now.' His thoughts seemed to be elsewhere, but he brought his attention back to Belle. 'I had best escort you to the inn.'

The parlour was small and dark but clean. Jackson was not yet there. She removed her cloak and bonnet and shivered a little. Justin saw her. 'I will have them build a fire for you. Is there anything else you require?'

'Not now.' He was so politely formal. She would prefer his anger over this but the façade around him was impenetrable.

He moved away then. 'I will see to the colt and then join you for dinner.'

'Yes.'

He left the room and she sat down on one of the benches. Her back was beginning to ache a little and she was glad to sit. The proprietor's wife bustled in and built a fire.

Jackson came in a quarter of an hour later and a few minutes after that Justin joined them.

But by the time the pink-cheeked maid brought in the dinner, Belle's appetite had fled. Her head was truly starting to ache and she felt rather ill. She forced a few bites down her throat and listened quietly to the conversation between Jackson and Justin. When the last of the meal had been taken away, she rose. 'I would like to retire. If you will excuse me.'

Justin and Jackson stood as well. 'Will you be able to manage without a maid? Or should I send Mrs Hubbard to help you?' Justin asked.

'I can manage.' She had deliberately worn a gown with a minimum of fastenings.

'I will be up shortly,' he said curtly.

Embarrassed, she nodded to Jackson and then fled. Of course Jackson knew why she was with Justin but nonetheless she could not rid herself of her innate modesty.

Her room was small and clean with a low-beamed ceiling. She washed her hands and face as best as she could with the jug of water. After that she pulled the pins from her hair and took out a clean nightshift. But it was when she was finishing the rest of her ablution that she realised why she had felt slightly unwell much of the day. She sank down on the bed and wondered what she should do next. But there was really no choice, she would have to tell him.

When his knock came, she jumped, and then rose and opened the door. With more than a little trepidation, she saw he wore a dressing gown over his breeches. He stood there, dark and forbidding. 'Come in,' she said. He stepped inside and closed the door behind him. He turned the key with a deliberate motion then turned and his eyes locked on her.

'Come here, Belle,' he said softly. He took a step in her direction. His eyes had a determined glitter.

Her face must be turning a thousand shades of red. 'There is something you should know first,' she began.

He stopped. 'What?'

She prayed she would not die of embarrassment. 'I... have begun my courses.' She closed her eyes briefly and then opened them. 'I am sorry.' She had never had to